You Should Have Known

Also by Jean Hanff Korelitz

Admission
The White Rose
The Sabbathday River
A Jury of Her Peers

You Should Have Known

JEAN HANFF KORELITZ

GRAND CENTRAL PUBLISHING

New York Boston

This book is a work of fiction. Names, characters, places, and incidents are the product of the author's imagination or are used fictitiously. Any resemblance to actual events, locales, or persons, living or dead, is coincidental.

Grand Central Publishing
Hachette Book Group
237 Park Avenue
New York, NY 10017

Printed in the United States of America

Grand Central Publishing is a division of Hachette Book Group, Inc.
The Grand Central Publishing name and logo is a trademark of Hachette Book Group, Inc.

ISBN 978-1-4555-9949-3

For Asher

PART I

BEFORE

CHAPTER ONE

You Just Know

Usually people cried when they came here for the first time, and this girl looked as if she'd be no exception. She walked in with a briefcase and a swagger and shook Grace's hand like the cool professional she clearly was, or at least wished to be. Then she sat on the couch and crossed one long twill-encased leg over the other. And *then*, sort of abruptly, she seemed to register where she was, with a wallop.

"Oh wow," said the girl, whose name—Grace had double-checked a few minutes earlier—was Rebecca Wynne. "I haven't been in a therapist's office since college."

Grace sat in her customary chair, crossed her own much shorter legs, and leaned forward. She couldn't help it.

"It's so bizarre! The minute you come in here, you just want to start bawling."

"Plenty of Kleenex." Grace smiled. How many times had she sat in this chair, with her legs crossed just the way they were now, listening to the room fill up with weeping. Weeping happened here so often, she sometimes imagined her office underwater, as in one of the magical Betty MacDonald stories she'd loved as a child, where the crybaby protagonist literally couldn't stop sobbing until the water had risen to her chin. When there was extreme anger, the shouting kind or the silent, venomous kind, she envisioned the walls of her office (in actuality painted a very innocuous off-white) turning dark with rage. When there was happiness or accord, she sometimes imagined she could smell sweet pine, as from late summer at the lake.

"Well, it's just a room," she said cheerily. "With boring furniture."

"Right." Rebecca looked around, as if this needed confirmation. The room—Grace's consulting room—had been constructed with immense care to be many things at once: comfortable but not particularly inviting, warm without troubling individuality, decorated with things so familiar they commonly resonated: that Eliot Porter print of the birches she had up beside the door—hadn't everyone lived with that poster at some point? dorm room? summer rental?—the red kilim rug, the oatmeal-colored couch, and her own swiveling leather chair. There was a glass-topped coffee table with a single box of Kleenex in a leather holder and an old country pine desk in the corner, its drawers stocked with yellow legal pads and lists of psychopharmacologists, child psychologists, smoking-cessation hypnotherapists, real estate agents, travel agents, mediators, estate planners, divorce attorneys. On the desktop, pens protruded from an unlovely ceramic mug her son, Henry, had made in first grade (this was an item that had, over the years, elicited an astonishing number of comments, ushered into speech a remarkable number of impacted memories), and a white ceramic lamp with a burlap shade threw discreet light on the proceedings. The only window overlooked the back alley of the building, and there was never anything out there to see, despite one attempt years earlier to install a planter of some bright no-brainer flora—geraniums, actually, and ivy. The superintendent had signed off on this project, though his enthusiasm stopped well short of helping her maneuver the wooden planter off its truck and down the alley to its resting spot, but the plants had starved for light and the planter itself disappeared soon after, leaving a dark mark on the cement that persisted. She was not a flower person, really.

Today, though, she had actually brought in flowers: dark pink roses, on the specific recommendation of Sarabeth, who—as the Great Day drew ever nearer—was becoming more and more inclined to micromanage. Not only must Grace purchase flowers for this occasion, but they must be roses, and the roses must be pink—*dark* pink.

Dark pink roses. *Why?* Grace had wondered. Sarabeth wasn't expecting a color photograph, was she? Was it not sufficiently incredible that *Vogue* magazine had a black-and-white picture's worth of interest in her? But she'd done as she was told, plunking them in the only vase she had in the office's little galley kitchen, from a forgotten flower delivery (end-of-treatment flowers? thank-you-for-showing-me-I-had-to-leave-him flowers? Jonathan flowers?), awkwardly and not very prettily spreading them out. Now they sat on one of the end tables, in some danger of being overturned by Rebecca's heavy wool coat.

"You know," Grace said, "you're right about the crying. Usually it takes a lot out of people just to get here. Or in the case of my practice, to get their partner here. It's very common to see people just let go when they finally make it through the door for the first time. It's perfectly all right."

"Well, another time, perhaps," the girl said. She was thirty, Grace thought, give or take, and pretty, if a bit severe, and the clothes she wore had been rather cleverly designed to conceal her actual body type, which was plainly curvaceous and buxom, and present in its place the fiction that she was boyish and lean. The white cotton shirt looked as if it had been tailored expressly for this purpose, and the brown twill pants hit at exactly the right spot to suggest a waist that was barely there. Both pieces were triumphs of illusion and had clearly been made by someone who knew exactly what they were doing—but when one worked for *Vogue*, Grace imagined, one had access to such people.

Rebecca rummaged around in the briefcase at her booted feet, then extracted an ancient tape recorder, which she placed on the glass-topped table. "Do you mind?" she asked. "I know, it's like an antique, but I need it as a backup. I once spent four hours with a certain pop star not known for her ability to speak in complete sentences, and I had this little space-age gadget the size of a matchbook. When I tried to play it back later there was absolutely nothing there. Most terrifying moment of my career."

"It must have been." Grace nodded. "Obviously, you managed to handle the setback."

Rebecca shrugged. Her fine blond hair was cut in a sort of highly constructed mess, and she wore a silver necklace that lay along her clavicles. "I made her sound so smart she'd have been crazy not to confirm the quotes when they fact-checked. Not that I wasn't worried. But her publicist actually told my editor it was her favorite interview she'd ever done, so I came out smelling like a rose." She stopped. She looked squarely at Grace. "You know," she said with a half-smile, "it occurs to me that I should not have said that. Another effect of being in a therapist's office. You sit on the couch, you spill the beans."

Grace smiled.

Rebecca, with an audible click, depressed the pertinent buttons on her tape recorder. Then she reached back into her briefcase and extracted an old-fashioned steno pad and a shiny bound galley.

"Oh, you have the book!" said Grace. It was still so new, it amazed her to see it in anyone else's possession. As if the entire endeavor had been to produce a vanity item for herself alone.

"Of course," said the girl coolly. Her professionalism, her control of the meeting, seemed to have been restored to her in the same instant Grace had shown herself to be such a neophyte. But she couldn't help it. It was still so strange to see the book in its actual book-flesh: her book, *her own book*, not quite in the world but very near now, due with the new year—the best time, Sarabeth the agent and Maud the editor and J. Colton the publicist (J. Colton! that was really her name!) had insisted, to publish a book like this. Even after the months of revision, the actual bound galley (so physical, so solidly reassuring), the contract, the *check* (deposited immediately, as if it might evaporate), the catalog listing—all very realistic, all very *This is actually happening to me*. She had given a presentation at the publisher's sales conference last spring, to a gallery of note-taking, road-weary reps, all grinning at her (a few sidling up afterward to ask advice for their own suffering marriages—well, she'd better get used to that, she supposed). Even after the wild day a year earlier when Sarabeth phoned in every hour to report increasingly incredible tidings. Someone wanted it. Someone else wanted it. Someone... no, two others, no, three, and then chattering away in a dialect Grace could not comprehend: a preempt, a floor (*a floor?* Grace wondered), audio and digital, sweeteners for "the List" (she did not discover what "the List" was until she actually read the contract). None of it seemed to compute. Grace had been reading for years about the death of publishing, but here was a pulsing, pushing, manic industry where she had expected a desiccated corpse: yet another outdated form of American manufacture, moldering alongside the steel mills and the gold mines. She mentioned this to Sarabeth once, when the auction in its third day was upended by a late entry, setting off a rash of new bids. Wasn't publishing supposed to be dead? That's what the magazines kept saying, after all. Sarabeth had laughed. Publishing was indeed fairly dead, she assured Grace, sounding very upbeat about this news. Except when you happened to snag the Zeitgeist. Her book, *You Should Have Known*, was apparently about to snag the Zeitgeist.

It had taken her two solid years to write it, sitting there at that desk in the corner, with her laptop open, between clients, and at the table in their bedroom at the lake, heavy oak, water stained, with its view of the dock, and the kitchen counter at home on 81st Street, at night, with Jonathan still at the hospital or gone to bed, exhausted from his day, and Henry asleep with some book unfurled over his chest and the light still on. She had written it with a mug of ginger tea dangerously close to the keyboard and her notes set out along the countertop all the way down to the sink at the other end, the old case files feathered with Post-it notes. As she wrote, her long-held theories became flesh, then more refined flesh, then downright authoritative-sounding flesh, the folksy wisdom she hadn't known she possessed until she read it on the page, the conclusions she seemed to have reached before she even began her practice fifteen years earlier. (Because she had learned nothing? Because she had been right in the first place?) In fact, she couldn't recall ever having learned how to do the work she did as a therapist, despite, naturally, having gone through the classwork and fieldwork, done her reading and written her papers, and collected the necessary degree. She had always known how to do this; she couldn't remember *not* knowing it. She might have walked out of high school straight into this small, tidy office and been as effective a professional as she was today, helped as many couples, prevented as many women from marrying men who would never make them happy. She knew that this did not make her special, or even clever. She viewed her ability not as God-given (God had never been anything to her but a subject of historical, cultural, or artistic interest), but as synthesized from nature and nurture, something along the lines of a naturally gifted ballerina lucky enough to have long legs *and* a parent willing to ferry her to dance classes. For whatever reason—or, more probably, for no reason at all—Grace Reinhart Sachs had been born with a predisposition for social observation and insight and reared in an atmosphere of ideas and conversation. She couldn't sing or dance or fold numbers together and pull them apart. She couldn't play music, like her son, or make dying children live, like her husband—both skills she would have been thrilled and humbled to possess—but she could sit down with people and see, usually very quickly, usually with unnerving clarity, what snares they were setting for themselves and how not to fall into them. Or, if they were already ensnared—and typically, if they were here with her, they were already ensnared—how to free themselves. That writing down these obvious things had brought *Vogue* magazine to her unremarkable little office was fascinating and naturally a little exciting, but it was also slightly bizarre. Why should anyone be awarded a national platform for pointing out that day followed night, or that the economy was subject to reversals, or any other readily observable thing? (Sometimes, when she thought about her book and what it would say to the women who were going to read it, she felt almost ashamed of herself, as if she were about to market some miracle cure that had long been available on the drugstore shelf.) Then again, there were things that could not be said too many times or loudly enough.

A few weeks earlier, she had sat down for a special lunch in the private dining room at Craft, with a table of clearly cynical (but professionally fascinated) bookers for media outlets. Over the sound of gently clicking silver, Grace had talked about her book and fielded boilerplate queries (one from a notably hostile man in a crimson bow tie) about why *You Should Have Known: Why Women Fail to Hear What the Men in Their Lives Are Telling Them* was different from all other books on the subject of relationships. Clearly, Tom Colicchio's food was the draw here. She spent a bit too much time attending to the magazine editor seated beside her (being, in other words, force-fed the woman's own tale of expensive divorce) and found, to her great regret, that the waiter came to take her plate long before she had had her way with the lamb shank. It had felt very unauthorlike to ask for a doggie bag.

After the lunch, though, J. Colton the publicist had indeed begun to call with news of interviews and television appearances, all as a result of the luncheon. The expensively divorced editor assigned a feature in *More*, and the hostile man in the bow tie booked her for an AP feature (making it all so very worth it, even Grace had to admit). The *Vogue* article was scheduled soon after that. The ball, clearly, was rolling.

She had (at Maud the editor's request) drafted an op-ed piece on why January was such a popular time of year to file for divorce (holiday stresses plus new year resolve) and (at J. Colton the publicist's request) endured a bizarre session with a media coach, learning precisely how to cock her head toward a television host, ingratiate herself to a studio audience, slip the title of her book into the most incongruous of verbal constructs without—she hoped—sounding like a robotic narcissist, and make perfectly formed sound bites.

"My editor sent it a few weeks ago," Rebecca said, placing the galley on the tabletop next to the Kleenex box. "Loved it. You know, people don't really ever hear this: *Don't screw up at the beginning and you won't have a lot of these problems down the line*. And it's very in-your-face. The typical book on this subject has a bit more of a kinder, gentler approach."

Grace, aware that the interview had now actually begun, tried to summon that cock of the head and those perfectly formed sound bites. Her voice, when she spoke next, was not the voice of what she considered her real life; it was a situational voice. It was what she thought of as her therapy voice. "I understand what you're saying. But to be frank, I think kinder-and-gentler hasn't served us especially well. I think women are ready to hear what my book says. We don't need to be handled gently. We're grown-ups, and if we've screwed up, we should be able to take a little truth about it, and make our own decisions. I always explain to my clients that if all they want is for someone to tell them everything's going to be all right, or everything happens for a reason, or whatever the pointless jargon of the moment is, then they don't have to come to my office and pay me for my expertise. Or buy my book, I suppose." She smiled. "They can buy one of the other books. Any of them. *How to Love Your Marriage Back to Health. How to Fight for Your Relationship.*"

"Yes, but your title's rather…confrontational, isn't it? *You Should Have Known.* I mean, that's what we always say to ourselves when we're watching the press conference and some politician's just tweeted a photo of his penis to the world, or got caught with a second family, and the wife's standing there next to him looking stunned. You know, *Really? This surprises you?*"

"I don't doubt the wife is surprised." Grace nodded. "The question is, *should* she be surprised? Could she have avoided finding herself in this position?"

"So this is the title you chose?"

"Well, yes and no," Grace told her. "It was actually my second choice. I wanted to call it *Attention Must Be Paid*. But nobody got the reference. They said it was too literary."

"Oh really? We didn't all read Arthur Miller in high school?" Rebecca asked archly, establishing her bona fides.

"Maybe your high school," said Grace diplomatically. In fact she had read *Death of a Salesman* in middle school at Rearden, the proudly intense (and, once upon a time, vaguely socialist) New York private school where her own son was now a seventh grader. "Anyway, we compromised. You know how we always tell ourselves, *You never know,* when someone does something we don't see coming? We're shocked that he turns out to be a womanizer, or an embezzler. He's an addict. He lied about everything. Or he's just garden-variety selfish and the fact that he's married to you and perhaps you have children together—that doesn't seem to stop him from behaving as if he's still a single, unencumbered teenager?"

"*Oh yeah,*" Rebecca said. It sounded, Grace thought, a little personal. Well, that was hardly surprising. That was sort of the point.

"And when it happens we just throw up our hands: We say: *Wow, you never know about people*. And we never hold ourselves accountable for what we bring to the deception. We have to learn to be accountable. If we don't, we can't act in our own best interests. And we can't prevent it next time."

"Uh-oh." Rebecca looked up. She fixed Grace with a plainly disapproving expression. "We're not about to blame the victim, are we?"

"There is no victim," said Grace. "Look, I've been in practice for fifteen years. Over and over I've heard women describe their early interactions with their partner, and their early impressions of their partner. And listening to them, I continually thought: *You knew right at the beginning*. She knows he's never going to stop looking at other women. She knows he can't save money. She knows he's contemptuous of her—the very first time they talk to each other, or the second date, or the first night she introduces him to her friends. But then she somehow lets herself *un*know what she knows. She lets these early impressions, this basic awareness, get overwhelmed by something else. She persuades herself that something she has intuitively seen in a man she barely knows isn't true at all now that she—quote unquote—*has gotten to know him better*. And it's that impulse to negate our own impressions that is so astonishingly powerful. And it can have the most devastating impact on a woman's life. And we'll always let ourselves off the hook for it, in our own lives, even as we're looking at some other deluded woman and thinking: *How could she not have known?* And I feel, just so strongly, that we need to hold ourselves to that same standard. And *before* we're taken in, not after."

"But you know"—Rebecca looked up from her pad, while her pencil, impressively, continued to write—"it's not just men. Women lie, too, right?" She was frowning, and there was, in the middle of her forehead, a pronounced V. Clearly—happily—the magazine she wrote for had not persuaded her to inject herself with botulinum toxin.

"Right. Of course. And I do talk about this in the book. But the fact is, nine times out of ten it's the woman sitting right there on my couch, totally distraught because, in her view, her male partner has hidden something from her. So I decided, right at the start, this book is going to be for women."

"Okay," the girl said, returning to her pad. "I get it."

"I'm being didactic," Grace said with a rueful little laugh.

"You're being passionate."

Right, Grace thought. She would have to remember that.

"In any case," she said deliberately, "I reached a point where I couldn't stand to see so many decent, well-intentioned women suffering through months or years of therapy, ripping their guts out and spending a fortune, just to realize that their partner has not changed at all, possibly has never seriously tried to change, or even expressed a willingness to change. The women are right back where they started when they first came in and sat where you're sitting right now. Those women deserve to hear the truth, which is that their situation isn't going to improve—at least, not nearly as much as they want it to. They need to hear that the error they've made might be irreparable."

She stopped herself, partly to let Rebecca catch up, partly to savor the impact of this, her "bombshell" (as Sarabeth the agent had put it in their very first meeting the previous year). It still felt just slightly seismic. In fact, Grace could remember the moment she had decided to actually write down the thing she really thought, the obvious thing made ever more blindingly obvious with each passing year of her professional life, with every dating guide (which never said it) and marriage manual (which never said it either) she had devoured in preparation for writing her book, and with every International Association of Marriage and Family Counselors conference she'd attended (where it was never uttered). This thing no one talked about, but which she suspected her colleagues understood as well as she. Should she say it in her book and call down the vitriol of her peers? Or just reiterate that ridiculous myth that any "relationship" (whatever that was) could be "saved" (whatever that meant).

"Don't pick the wrong person," she told Rebecca now, emboldened by the presence of *Vogue* in her bland little office, the artificially long and lean woman on her oatmeal-colored couch, wielding her retro steno pad and tape recorder. "Pick the wrong person and it doesn't matter how much you want to fix your marriage. It won't work."

After a moment, Rebecca looked up and said, "That's pretty blunt."

Grace shrugged. It was blunt, she wasn't going to argue with that. It needed to be blunt. If a woman chose the wrong person, he was always going to be the wrong person: that was all. The most capable therapist in the world wouldn't be able to do much more than negotiate the treaty. At best, Grace thought, it was terribly sad, but at worst it was punitive—a lifetime of punitive. That was no way to have a marriage. If these couples were childless, the effort should go into separation. If there were children: mutual respect and co-parenting. And separation.

Not, of course, that she didn't feel for them. She truly did feel for them, her own patients especially, because they had come to her for help and it was too late to offer them anything but the equivalent of garbage bags and Windex after the oil spill. But what she hated most of all was the sheer preventability of all this distress. Her patients were not unintelligent. They were educated, insightful about others. Some, even, were brilliant people. And that they should have met, on the paths of their younger lives, a potential companion who offered sure or at least likely pain, and that they should have said yes to that sure or at least likely pain, and thus received the very sure or at least likely pain that was promised... well, it baffled her. It had always baffled her, and enraged her, too. Sometimes—she couldn't help it—she wanted to shake them all.

"Imagine," she said to Rebecca, "that you are sitting down at a table with someone for the first time. Perhaps on a date. Perhaps at a friend's house—wherever you might cross paths with a man you possibly find attractive. In that first moment there are things you can see about this man, and intuit about this man. They are readily observable. You can sense his openness to other people, his interest in the world, whether or not he's intelligent—whether he makes use of his intelligence. You can tell that he's kind or dismissive or superior or curious or generous. You can see how he treats you. You can learn from what he decides to tell you about himself: the role of family and friends in his life, the women he's been involved with previously. You can see how he cares for himself—his own health and well-being, his financial well-being. This is all available information, and we do avail ourselves. But then..."

She waited. Rebecca was scribbling, her blond head down.

"Then?"

"Then comes the story. He has a story. He has many stories. And I'm not suggesting that he's making things up or lying outright. He might be—but even if he doesn't do that, we do it for him, because as human beings we have such a deep, ingrained need for narrative, especially if we're going to play an important role in the narrative; you know, *I'm already the heroine and here comes my hero*. And even as we're absorbing facts or forming impressions, we have this persistent impulse to set them in some sort of context. So we form a story about how he grew up, how women have treated him, how employers have treated him. How he appears before us right now becomes a part of that story. How he wants to live tomorrow becomes part of that story. Then we get to enter the story: *No one has ever loved him enough until me. None of his other girlfriends have been his intellectual equal. I'm not pretty enough for him. He admires my independence*. None of this is fact. It's all some combination of what he's told us and what we've told ourselves. This person has become a made-up character in a made-up story."

"You mean, like a fictional character."

"Yes. It's not a good idea to marry a fictional character."

"But... you make it sound as if it's inevitable."

"It's not. If we were to bring to this situation a *fraction* of the care we brought to, for example, our consumer decisions, problems would arise far less than they do. I mean, what is it about us? We'll try on twenty pairs of shoes before we make a purchase. We'll read reviews by total strangers before we choose someone to install our carpeting. But we turn off our bullshit detector and toss out our own natural impressions because we find someone attractive, or because he seems interested in us. He could be holding up a placard that says, *I will take your money, make passes at your girlfriends, and leave you consistently bereft of love and support*, and we'll find a way to forget that we ever knew that. We'll find a way to *unknow* that."

"But . . . ," Rebecca said. "People do have doubts. Maybe they just don't act on them."

Grace nodded. Doubts emerged often in her practice: very old, desiccated doubts, saved and preserved and brought forth by very wounded, very sad women. They were a theme with countless variations: *I knew he drank too much. I knew he couldn't keep his mouth shut. I knew he didn't love me, not as much as I loved him.*

"Many people have doubts," she agreed. "The problem is, few of us recognize doubt for what it is. Doubt is a gift from our deepest selves, that's how I think of it. Like fear. You'd be amazed how many people experience fear just before something bad happens to them, and when they go back to that moment later, they understand that they missed an opportunity to avert what was about to take place. You know: *Don't walk down that street. Don't let that guy give you a ride home.* We seem to have a highly developed ability to ignore what we know, or suspect. From an evolutionary standpoint alone, that's fascinating, but my interests are more practical. I think doubt can be an extraordinary gift. I think we need to learn to listen to our doubt, not just dismiss it, even if that means putting a stop to an engagement. You know, it's much easier to cancel a wedding than it is to cancel a marriage."

"Oh, I don't know about that," Rebecca said with heavy sarcasm.

"Some of the weddings I've been to lately. I think it might be easier to cancel the Olympics."

This—without knowing anything about Rebecca's recently married friends—had to be true. Grace's own wedding had been small because her family consisted of her father and herself, and Jonathan's family had chosen to absent themselves. But she, too, had attended her share of insane nuptials.

"Last month," Rebecca said, "my roommate from college had this complete blowout, five hundred people at the Puck Building. The flowers—oh, my God. At least fifty thousand dollars, I kid you not. And they had all the wedding presents out on a long table in another room, like they used to do, remember?"

Grace remembered. It was an old rite that, like so many other old wedding rites, had somehow returned in all of its materialistic glory, because apparently the modern wedding wasn't busy or flashy enough. Her own parents' wedding at the St. Regis had featured such a display of gifts in a foyer off the ballroom: Audubon silver, Haviland china, and a full set of Waterford Crystal, every bit of which was now in the clutches of Eva, her father's second wife.

"Half of Tiffany's. Plus every gadget Williams-Sonoma ever came up with. Which is a scream"—Rebecca laughed—"because she can't cook and I don't think he'll ever be civilized enough to eat with silver."

Grace nodded. She had heard this before, these details, and so many others, from the oatmeal-colored couch in her office. She had heard about the massive search for the pastel-colored mints served at the bride's parents' wedding (apparently still produced only at one tiny storefront on Rivington), and the engraved lockets for the bridesmaids, and the precise make of vintage car to drive them to their wedding night at the Gansevoort, and then, at the end of it all, those ten days at the same resort in the Seychelles where some celebrity couple had honeymooned, in a hut on stilts in the vivid blue Indian Ocean.

Which was where they had had the argument that cast a pall over the entire nuptials and still reverberated here, years later, in front of the therapist who already knew that these two people brought out the worst in each other, and probably always had, and certainly always would.

Sometimes Grace wished she could take a poison-tipped lance to the entire wedding industry. Downgrade your average twenty-first-century nuptial extravaganza to quiet vows, taken in the presence of dear friends and family, and half the engaged couples—the right half—would drop the entire notion of marriage on the spot. Persuade couples to save the party for their twenty-fifth anniversary, when his hairline had evaporated and her waist was thick from childbearing, and a whole lot of them would retract in horror. But by the time they came to her, the barn door was bolted and the horse long gone.

"*Doubt can be a gift.*" Rebecca spoke the phrase aloud, as if testing its weight and repeatability. "That's good."

Grace felt the weight of Rebecca's cynicism. Then she felt the weight of her own.

"It's not that I don't believe in human transformation," she said, trying not to sound as defensive as she felt. "Human transformation is possible. It requires immense courage and selflessness, but it does happen. It's just that we spend so much effort on that slim possibility of correction and none at all on the side of prevention. That's a serious disconnect, don't you think?"

Rebecca nodded vaguely, but now she was busy. She was scribbling, her left hand all knuckles, the pen jerking and sputtering along the wide-ruled lines. After a moment, she came to the end of whatever she was trying to get down. Then she looked up and said with perfect therapeutic intonation: "Can you say more about that?"

Grace took a breath and went on. It was one of the more pointed ironies of her profession, she explained, that when you asked people what they wanted in a mate, they tended to offer you sobering, mature, insightful truths: Protection and companionship, they said, nurturing and stimulation, a snug harbor from which to be outward bound. But when you looked at their actual partnerships, where were those things? These same insightful and eloquent people were alone or in combat, perpetually diminished. There was abandonment and friction, competition and hindrance, and all because, at some point, they had said yes to the wrong person. So they came to her with this broken thing that needed fixing, but there was nothing to be gained by explaining it all now. You had to explain it all *before* they said yes to the wrong person.

"I'm getting married," Rebecca said, quite suddenly, when she had finished writing all or some of this down.

"Congratulations," Grace told her. "That's wonderful news."

The girl burst out laughing. "*Really.*"

"Yes. Really. I hope you will have a beautiful wedding and, more importantly, a wonderful marriage."

"So wonderful marriages are possible?" she said, enjoying herself.

"Of course. If I didn't believe that, I wouldn't be here."

"And you wouldn't be married, I suppose."

Grace smiled evenly. It had been a struggle to give up even the limited amount of information her publisher insisted on. Therapists did not advertise their personal lives. Authors, apparently, did. She had promised Jonathan that their lives as a couple, as a family, would stay as private as they possibly could. Actually, he hadn't seemed as bothered by it all as she was herself.

"Tell me about your husband," said Rebecca now, as Grace had known she would.

"His name is Jonathan Sachs. We met in college. Well, I was in college. He was in medical school."

"So he's a doctor?"

He was a pediatrician, Grace said. She didn't want to say the name of the hospital. It changed things. All of this was readily available on any Internet search of her name, because she was mentioned in the short piece *New York* magazine had done a few years earlier, in the annual Best Doctors issue. The photograph showed Jonathan in his scrubs, his curly dark hair well past the point at which she usually urged him to get it cut. He wore the ubiquitous stethoscope, and there was a large pinwheel lollipop sticking out of his breast pocket. He looked as if he were trying to smile through exhaustion. A bald and grinning boy sat in his lap.

"Kids?"

"One son. Henry is twelve."

She nodded, as if this confirmed something. The buzzer on Grace's desk sounded.

"Oh good," said Rebecca. "That's Ron, probably."

Ron must be the photographer. She got up to let him in.

He stood out in the lobby, surrounded by heavy metal cases. He was on his phone, texting, when she opened the door.

"Hello," she said, mostly to get his attention.

"Hey," he said mildly, looking up. "Ron? They told you I was coming?"

"Hi." She shook his hand. "What, no hair and makeup?"

He looked at her oddly. He couldn't tell she was joking.

"I'm joking." She laughed, secretly disappointed that there was no hair and makeup. She had allowed herself to fantasize about the hair and makeup. "Come on in."

He stepped heavily inside, carrying two of the cases, then went back for the others. He was about Jonathan's height and might be Jonathan's build, Grace thought, were her husband not so conscientious about holding off this very protuberance of gut.

"Hey, Ron," said Rebecca, who had come to the threshold of the office. The three of them now stood in the vestibule, which was even smaller than her consulting room. Ron looked aggrieved at what he saw: a couple of mission chairs, a Navajo rug, back copies of the *New Yorker* in a woven basket on the floor.

"I was thinking inside?" Rebecca said.

"Let's see inside."

Inside, apparently, was better. He brought in a light, a curved white screen, and one of the cases, from which he began to extract cameras. Grace stood nervously beside the couch, a stranger in this, her own land, watching them banish her leather chair to the vestibule. He pulled back her desk to set up his light, a hot bright box atop a chrome stalk, and wedged the screen against the opposite wall. "I usually have an assistant," he told her without further explanation.

Cheap job, she automatically thought. *Low priority.*

"Nice flowers. They'll look good against that wall. I'm going to move them into the frame."

Grace nodded. That Sarabeth. Amazing, really.

"You want to..." He stopped and looked at Rebecca, who now stood with her arms crossed over her protruding bust.

"Fix up a bit?" Rebecca finished for him. She had morphed into the photo editor.

"Oh. Right."

Grace left them and went into her bathroom, which was very small—so small that it had once elicited a tearful outburst from an obese client—and not terrifically well lit. She regretted this just now, because even if she'd known how to magically transform her current self into a self that would appear, to her own *Vogue*-reader eyes, *Vogue*-worthy, she doubted she'd be able to pull that off in such a cramped, dim space. For want of a better idea, she washed her face with the available hand soap and dried it with one of the paper towels she kept in a dispenser. This produced no discernible effect, and she stared into her clean, familiar face with a sinking heart. From her purse she took out a tube of concealer and attempted two swipes under the eyes, but there wasn't much improvement: Now she looked like a vaguely tired woman with concealer under the eyes. Who was she to treat *Vogue* so cavalierly?

Was this important enough to call Sarabeth about? Grace had found, over the past few months, that she was reluctant to interrupt what she thought of as her agent's real work—that is, her work with *real* writers. It would be wrong, in other words, to interrupt what might be a session of intense literary exchange with a winner of the National Book Critics Circle Award to ask if she—Grace—ought to be sneaking out to Zitomer pharmacy and begging one of the ladies to buff her up. And what about her hair? Should it be in its usual configuration of tight coil and clean lines, pinned with the heavy bobby pins (these were made for old-fashioned plastic rollers and getting harder and harder to find)? Or should she brush it loose, which made her feel untidy, and look like a kid?

I should be so lucky, she thought ruefully, *as to look like a kid.*

Of course, she was not a kid. She was a woman of a certain seasoning, a self-reliant woman of some refinement, with myriad responsibilities and attachments, who had long ago set certain parameters for her appearance and then remained consciously within them, relieved at not having to reinvent herself constantly or even aspire to greater heights of beauty. She was aware of the fact that most people viewed her as formal and contained, but that didn't bother her, because the Grace who wore jeans at the lake house and brushed out her hair as soon as she got home from work was not a Grace she wished to make available to the world.

She was young *enough*. She was attractive *enough*. She seemed competent *enough*. That wasn't it.

The fame part...well, perhaps that was getting a bit closer. If she could have hired an actress (taller and prettier!) to play the role of her book's author, she would have been tempted. An actress with an earpiece, into which Grace could feed the correct lines (*In the vast majority of cases, your potential spouse will tell you everything you need to know very quickly...*) as Matt Lauer or Ellen DeGeneres nodded soberly. *But I'm a big girl*, Grace thought, absently brushing dust against the surface of the mirror with the backs of her fingers. She went back to the others.

Now Rebecca was sitting in Grace's chair, staring deeply into the screen of her phone, and the coffee table had been angled away from the couch, with the pitcher of roses and the bound galley of her book pushed aside and forward, into the frame. No one had to tell her where to sit.

"Your husband's adorable," Rebecca said.

"Oh. Yes," she said. She didn't appreciate being put on the spot. "Thank you."

"How can he do that?" she said.

Ron, who was already looking through the lens of one of his cameras, said, "Do what?"

"He's a doctor for kids with cancer."

"He's a pediatric oncologist," Grace said evenly. "At Memorial."

At Memorial Sloan-Kettering, in other words. She really hoped they'd drop it.

"I could never do that. He must be a saint."

"He's a good doctor," Grace said. "It's a difficult field."

"Jesus," said Ron. "No way could I do that."

It's a good thing no one's asking, she thought irritably. "I was trying to decide what to do with my hair," she said, hoping to distract them both. "What do you think?" She touched the tight coil at the nape of her neck. "I can take it down. I have a hairbrush."

"No, it's good. I can see your face. Okay?" he asked. But he was asking Rebecca, not her.

"Let's try," she confirmed.

"Okay," he said.

He picked up the camera again, looked through it, and said, "So this is just a practice, all right? No sweat." And before she could respond, he produced a heavy metallic click.

Instantly, Grace went stiff as a board.

"Oh no." Ron laughed. "I said it would be painless. Aren't you comfortable?"

"Actually, no," she said, trying to smile. "I've never done this. I mean, had my picture taken for a magazine."

Thus completing my public infantilization, she thought as the last of her courage fled.

"Well, what better magazine to start with!" Ron said merrily. "And I'm going to make you look so stunning, you'll think some supermodel came in and pretended to be you."

Grace produced a highly disingenuous laugh and rearranged herself on the couch.

"Very nice!" Rebecca said brightly. "But cross your legs the other way, all right? Better angle."

Grace did.

"And we're off!" said Ron, sounding chipper. He began to take pictures in a rat-tat-tat of clicks. "So," he said as he dipped and leaned, producing—as far as she could tell—tiny variations on the same angle, "what's your novel called?"

"Novel? Oh, I didn't write a novel. I couldn't write a novel."

It occurred to her that she probably shouldn't be talking. What would talking do to her mouth in the pictures?

"You don't have a new book?" he said without looking up. "I thought you were a writer."

"No. I mean yes, I wrote a book, but I'm not a writer. I mean..." Grace frowned. "It's a book about marriage. I specialize in work with couples."

"She's a therapist," Rebecca said helpfully.

But wasn't she a writer, too? Grace thought, suddenly perturbed. Didn't writing a book make her a writer? Then something else occurred to her. "I didn't hire anyone else to write it," she insisted, as if he'd accused her. "I wrote it."

Ron had stopped shooting and was looking down into the digital monitor.

"Actually," he said without looking up, "I need you a bit to the left. Sorry, my left. And could you lean back a little?... Okay," he said, considering. "I think we might have been wrong about the hair."

"Fine," Rebecca said.

Grace reached back and deftly removed the three heavy pins, and down came one shoulder-length coil of highly conditioned dark brown hair. She reached for it, to fan it out, but he stopped her. "No, don't," he said. "This is better. It's sort of sculptural. You can't see it, but there's a nice contrast with the dark hair and the color of your blouse."

She didn't correct him. It wasn't a "blouse," of course. It was a soft, thin sweater of parchment-colored cashmere—one of about five she owned. But she didn't really want to talk blouses with Ron, even if he shot for *Vogue*.

Then came a small adjustment of the vase. Another small adjustment of the book on the table. "Good," he announced. "Right. Let's go."

He began again. Rebecca looked on, saying nothing. Grace tried to breathe.

She almost never sat here, on the couch, and the perspective was odd. The Eliot Porter poster, she noted, was askew, and there was a grimy mark over the light switch by the door. *I must get that*, she thought. And maybe it was finally time to replace the Eliot Porter. She was tired of the Eliot Porter. Wasn't everyone tired of that Eliot Porter?

"Marriage," he said suddenly. "That's a biggie. You'd think there wasn't much left to say."

"Always more to say," said Rebecca. "It's the kind of thing you don't want to get wrong."

He went down on one knee and shot up at an angle. Grace tried to remember if that was supposed to make your neck look shorter or longer. "I guess I never thought too much about it. I thought, you meet somebody, if it's the right person, you just *know*. I mean, I knew when I met my wife. I went home and told my friend I was living with, 'This is the girl.' Love at first sight kind of thing."

Grace closed her eyes. Then she remembered where she was,

and she opened them. Ron put down his camera and picked up another one, which he proceeded to fiddle with. It seemed safe to speak.

"The difficulty is when people count on that 'you just know,' and they dismiss people they don't respond to right away. I actually think there are lots of good matches for each person, and they cross our paths all the time, but we're so wedded to the idea of love at first sight that we can miss the really great people who don't come with a thunderbolt attached."

"Can you look over this way?" Rebecca said.

Can you shut up, in other words? Grace thought. She looked at Rebecca, who was seated in Grace's own chair, at Grace's own desk. To compensate for this unpleasant fact, she felt herself smile broadly. That was even more unpleasant.

But there was another thing, too, and as she sat, uncomfortably angled, uncomfortably twisted, that other thing began to move up through the situational distraction of being photographed for *Vogue* (in whose pages, she was quite sure, not a single reader would mistake her for a supermodel) and the displacement of being on her own couch, until it had set itself indisputably before her. That thing was the unalterable fact that she—like Ron the photographer, like any number of patients in this very room, like an unknowable portion of the future readers of her book—had absolutely *just known*, the first time she had laid eyes on Jonathan Sachs, that she would marry and love him for the rest of her life. It was a truth she had hidden from Sarabeth the agent and Maud the editor and J. Colton the publicist, just as she was now hiding it from Rebecca the about-to-be-married writer and Ron, who, like her, had *just known* that he had met the woman he was supposed to marry. That night she had crossed the Charles River in the first trill of autumn, with her friend Vita and Vita's boyfriend, to go to a Halloween party in some ghoulish cavern in the medical school. The others had gone in first, but she had wanted the bathroom and gotten herself lost in the basement, turning like a mouse through underground corridors, losing herself, growing increasingly irritated, increasingly afraid. And then, very suddenly, she was not only not alone, but in the presence of—the company of—a man she recognized instantly, though she was quite sure she had never seen him before. He was a scrawny guy with neglected hair and several days' growth of inelegant beard. He wore a Johns Hopkins T-shirt and carried a plastic tub of dirty clothes with a book about the Klondike wobbling on top, and when he saw her, he smiled: an earth-on-its-axis-halting smile that had lit up the grimy hallway, making her stop on a dime, changing her life. Before Grace had taken her next breath, this still-unnamed man had become the most trusted, valued, and desired person in her life. *She just knew.* So she had chosen him, and now, as a result, she was having the right life, with the right husband, the right child, the right home, the right work. For her, it really had happened that way. But she couldn't say that. Especially not now.

"Hey, can we do a few close-ups? You mind?" said Ron.

Should she mind? Grace thought. Did she get a vote?

"All right," said Rebecca, confirming that the question was not for her.

Grace leaned forward. The lens seemed so close, only inches away. She wondered if she could look through it and see his eye on the other side; she peered deep into it, but there was only the glassy dark surface and the thunderous clicking noise: no one was in there. Then she wondered if she would feel the same if it were Jonathan holding the camera, but she actually couldn't remember a single time when Jonathan had held a camera, *Click*, let alone a camera this close to her face. She was the default photographer in her family, though with none of the bells and whistles currently on display in her little office, and with none of Ron's evident skill, and with no passion at all for the form. She was the one who took the birthday pictures and the camp visiting-weekend pictures, *Click*, the photo of Henry asleep in his Beethoven costume, and *Click*, the photo of him playing chess with his grandfather, *Click*, her own favorite picture of Jonathan, minutes after finishing a Memorial Day road race up at the lake, with a cup of water thrown over his face and an expression of unmistakable pride and just distinguishable lust. *Or was it only in retrospect*, Grace thought, *Click*, that she had always seen lust in that picture, because later, running the numbers, she had realized that Henry was about to be conceived, just hours after it was taken. After Jonathan had eaten a bit and stood for a long time under a hot shower, after he had taken her to her own childhood bed and, *Click*, rocked over her, saying her name again and again, and she remembered feeling so happy, and, *Click*, so utterly lucky, and not because they were actually in the act of making the child she wanted so badly, but because at that specific moment even the possibility of that did not matter to her, nothing but him and, *Click*, them and this, and now the memory of this, rushing up to the surface: the eye and the other eye through the lens that must be looking back.

"That's nice," Ron said, lowering the camera. Now she could see his eye again: brown, after all, and utterly unremarkable. Grace nearly laughed in embarrassment. "No, it was good," he said, misunderstanding. "And you're done."

CHAPTER TWO

What's Better Than Raising Children?

The highly intentional neglect of Sally Morrison-Golden's East 74th Street town house began with its exterior, which featured window boxes of nondescript greenery, both dying and dead, and a drooping red balloon tied to the iron grille over the door. The house sat on its leafy side street between two elegant and immaculate brownstones of the same vintage (made, more than likely, by the same architect and builder), whose dignified and doubtless expensive plantings and bright polished windows seemed to bear their slumming neighbor with a certain long-suffering forbearance. Inside, when the stout German au pair opened the door to Grace, that theme of defiant disarray was taken up by immediate and relentless mess, which began just inside the door (indeed, the door could not open completely because of the bulging shopping bags behind it) and continued along trails of child-related debris down the hall to the kitchen and up the stairs (where it undoubtedly led to messy spaces unseen). This was all thoroughly deliberate, Grace thought, as the au pair (Hilda? Helga?) pulled back the door and she stepped carefully inside. In a city of wealth, Sally was perhaps the richest person Grace personally knew, and with a staff that certainly included at least one person whose job was to keep order, if not cleanliness, even in the wake of the four children who lived here (and the two from Simon Golden's first marriage, who visited on weekends with their own accompaniments of homework, sports equipment, and electronics). Yet this assertive accumulation of stuff had to be Sally's preference. The stacks of discarded shoes, the teetering pile of *Observer*s and *Times*, the bulging shopping bags from the Children's Place and Sam Flax blocking the bottom of the staircase—Grace looked at these with an involuntary calculation: five minutes to move them, unpack them, fold the shopping bags into order, and store them in the place one kept shopping bags for some future use; two minutes to put the receipts into the box or file where they lived (or ought to live), remove the tags from the new clothes and take them to the laundry room; another two to place the paints and papers wherever art got made; and a final two to gather up the papers and dump them outside in the recycling bin. Eleven minutes at most, and really, how hard could it be? The elegant Greek Revival house was shouting for release, its dentiled moldings and fine plaster walls nearly obscured by children's finger paintings and macaroni assemblages, tacked or taped up at random, as if the entryway were the hallway outside a kindergarten classroom. Even the Morrison-Goldens' ketubah, richly colored and solemnly Hebrew, like a page from a Semitic Book of Kells, had been framed in a Popsicle-stick contraption with bits of dusty fuzz and dried glue protruding from between the shards. (This was oddly fitting, Grace had to admit, since Sally had converted to Judaism at the request of her then fiancé and after the marriage had effortlessly drifted into her husband's neglect of all other things Jewish.)

She followed the noises of a meeting in progress to the back of the house, where new construction had extended the kitchen into a small garden. There Sally sat, between the sycophantic Amanda Emery and Sylvia Steinmetz, single mother of the brilliant Daisy

Steinmetz, adopted from China as a one-year-old and—after leapfrogging third grade—the youngest student by far in Rearden's middle school.

"Thank God..." Sally laughed, looking up. "Now we can actually accomplish something."

"Am I that late?" said Grace, who knew she wasn't.

"No, no, but we can't seem to settle down without your calming influence." She adjusted the wiggling toddler on her lap: her youngest, named Djuna (Sally had informed them) after her late mother-in-law, Doris.

"Should I make more coffee?" asked Hilda or Helga, who had followed Grace into the kitchen. She stood barefoot, her feet looking none too clean, Grace thought. She also had a dark metal nose ring that communicated a certain lack of cleanliness.

"Yeah, maybe. And would you mind taking the ba? We'll get done a lot quicker without her contributions," said Sally, as if she had to apologize.

Silently, the au pair reached out for the squirmy Djuna, whom Sally extended over the table. Djuna, sensing her departure from center stage, let out a diva's cry of protest.

"Bye, sweetie," said Sylvia. "God, is she cute."

"She'd better be," Sally said. "She's my last."

"Ooh, are you sure?" Amanda said. "Neil and I keep saying we wish we'd kept our options open."

Grace, who did not know Amanda very well, was unsure of what this might refer to. Vasectomy? Egg freezing? Amanda had ten-year-old twins and despite some recent "facial rejuvenation" was easily forty-five.

"Done and done. To tell you the truth, Djuna was a bit of a surprise, but we figured, what the hell? I mean, why not?"

Why not, indeed? thought Grace, as thoroughly aware as the other women in the room of what four children (or, indeed, six children) signified in New York City. Two children meant that you had reproduced yourself, numbers-wise, which was expensive enough. Three meant that a third round of private school and summer camp and ice hockey lessons at Chelsea Piers and college counseling at IvyWise was inconsequential. But four children... well, not many families in Manhattan had four children. Four children meant an extra nanny, for one thing, and a town house. You couldn't ask kids to share a room, after all. Children needed their private space, to express their uniqueness.

"And I mean," she went on, "what's better than raising children? I had this big career, seriously I haven't missed it for one second since Ella was born. Even at my reunion last year, when all these women I'd gone to college with gave me crap about giving it up, like I have some big responsibility to Yale that's supposed to dictate how I live my life. I just looked at them, like, *You're so wrong*. Don't let anyone tell you it's not the most important thing you can do," she insisted to Amanda, as if this were the issue at hand.

"Oh, I know, I know," Amanda said weakly. "But I mean, the twins, they're so much work. God forbid they should want to do anything together. If one wants Broadway Kids, the other wants gymnastics. Celia won't even go to the same camp as her sister, so thanks very much, two visiting weekends in Maine."

Hilda/Helga brought coffee and set it down on the long farmhouse table. Grace produced the box of butter cookies she'd stopped for at Greenberg's, and these were greeted with mild enthusiasm.

"My thighs hate you," Sally said, taking two.

"Your thighs have no right to hate anyone," Amanda told her. "I've seen your thighs. Your thighs are the envy of the entire Upper East Side."

"Well," Sally said, looking pleased, "you know, I'm sort of in training. Simon said if I finished the half marathon out at the beach, he'd take me to Paris."

"My mother used to bring these home," said Sylvia, tasting her cookie. "You know those little cinnamon buns they make? They had a German name."

"*Schnecken*," Grace said. "Delicious."

"Should we start?" Sally asked. She had not grown up in the city and, having nothing to contribute to the shared nostalgia, sounded almost irritated.

Pads were produced and pens uncapped. Everyone looked deferentially at Sally, who was chairing the committee as well as hosting the meeting. "Right. Two days to go. And we are..." She trailed off with a girlish shrug. "But I'm not worried."

"I'm a little worried," said Sylvia.

"No, it's fine. Look..." Sally turned her yellow pad to display a neat column of items in blue Sharpie. "People want to come and they want to spend money. That's what's important. The rest is just details. And we've got two hundred confirmed. Almost two hundred. It's already a success."

Grace looked over at Sylvia. Of the three of them, she knew Sylvia the best, or at least had known her the longest. Not that they were particularly close. Sylvia, she knew, was holding her tongue.

"So I was over at the Spensers' yesterday morning. I did a walk-through with Suki's assistant and the house manager."

"Suki wasn't there?" said Sylvia.

"No, but I went over everything with the staff."

Grace nodded. To be granted admission to the Spenser abode—that alone had been a serious coup and certainly a big motivator for those two hundred RSVPs, at $300 a pop. Suki Spenser, third wife of Jonas Marshall Spenser and the mother of Rearden preschoolers, presided over one of the most storied apartments in the city (it was actually three apartments, combined into two floors the width of their Fifth Avenue building). She had called out of the blue the previous month—well, her assistant had called—and said that while Mrs. Spenser wasn't able to serve on the committee, she'd be pleased to host the event. Her staff would serve whatever food was brought in, and they could also offer the wine. The Spenser family had their own vineyard in Sonoma.

"Do you know her?" Grace asked Sally.

"No, not really. I've nodded to her in the halls at school, that's all. And of course I e-mailed inviting her to work on the committee, but I didn't expect to hear from her, let alone all this." The RSVPs had had to go through security checks, which had been a hassle. But it was worth it.

"Oh, my God, I am so excited," Amanda chirped. "Did you see the Jackson Pollocks?"

There were two of them, on facing walls of the dining room. Grace had seen them in *Architectural Digest*.

"I think so," said Sally, honestly enough. "Sylvia, your friend's all set? It's so great he's doing this for us."

Sylvia nodded. She knew someone at Sotheby's who had agreed to handle the auction. "He told me it's payback for getting him through trigonometry at Horace Mann. Actually I barely got him through trigonometry."

"And the auction itself?" Grace asked. She was visualizing Sally's list, trying to push things forward.

"Right. I have a proof of the catalog. Amanda, what did I do with it?"

Amanda pointed out the ragged-edged booklet amid the scattered papers on the table.

"Okay," Sally said. "This isn't final, we can still add till tomorrow morning, but he's printing tomorrow afternoon, and... Sylvia?"

"Picking them up Saturday at one," she said efficiently.

"Good." She put on her glasses, opened the cover, and started down the printed page.

Flowers from L'Olivier and Wild Poppy. Stays in no fewer than six Hamptons houses, one on Fire Island ("But the family part," Sally said reassuringly), a pair each in Vail and Aspen and one in Carmel, New York (this particular offering relayed with less than effusive gratitude). There was a design consult with an A-list decorator (daughter in twelfth grade), a cooking lesson for eight in an excessively popular Tribeca restaurant (son of chef's publicist in seventh), a chance to shadow the mayor of New York for a day (policy analyst's twins applying for two of the extremely valuable spots in next year's pre-K), and something called a "stem-cell face lift" with a doctor at NYU, which sounded so appalling (yet so intriguingly bizarre!) that Grace made a mental note to ask Jonathan what it was.

"And—I think I sent out an e-mail about this," Sally said. "Or maybe not. But Nathan Friedberg offered us a place in his camp."

"Sally, that's fabulous!" Amanda said.

"What camp?" Grace asked.

Amanda turned to her. "You know, his camp? That he's starting?"

"It was in *Avenue*," said Sally. "He's starting this camp?"

"It's going to cost twenty-five thousand dollars for the summer," said Sylvia.

"That's . . . a lot of waterskiing," Grace observed.

"No waterskiing. No knot tying. No campfires," said Sylvia, sounding suitably bemused. "Children of mere mortals need not apply."

"But . . . I'm sorry, I'm not understanding. This is a summer camp?" Grace said slowly.

"I think it's a little bit brilliant, actually," said Amanda. "I mean, let's face it, these are the kids who are going to be running things. They need to know how business works, and they need to know how to be philanthropists. Nathan called me about it. He was wondering if the twins might want to enroll. I said I'd love it, but they'd kill me if I took them out of their camps in Maine. They have these whole posses up there."

Grace still couldn't grasp it. "Where exactly do they go for this camp? What do they do?"

"Oh, they'll all live at home. A bus picks them up in the morning. And all these great people are going to come talk to the kids," Sally said. "People from business and the arts. They learn about business plans, and investments. They take trips to visit companies downtown and outside the city. I know they're going out to Greenwich at least once. And they get the weekends off so they can do whatever they'd usually do then. I signed Ella up. Bronwen just wants to stay out at the beach all summer. She has her horse out there. But then I thought, *I wonder if he'd donate a place*. I mean, a twenty-five-thousand-dollar value! If we could get that for the school, it would be great."

"Bravo, Sally!" Amanda smiled. "That is completely brilliant."

"Yes," Grace managed, but she was still mystified. And now slightly appalled, as well.

They went back to the list. A college admissions counselor. A preschool admissions counselor. A genealogist who came to your house with her computer, so you didn't have to do all that online stuff, and made a gorgeous family tree for you, which she painted like a Shaker dream design. (Grace wondered briefly if she ought to buy that one herself—she would probably have to buy something, and wouldn't that be a good thing to give Henry?—but the thought of Jonathan's terrible family stopped her. To have such hateful people on her son's Shaker family tree made her angry, then guilty, then just sad for him. Bad enough that he was down to a single grandparent. Knowing that those people were still out there, and only a few hours' drive away, in spite of their showing not the slightest inclination to see their grandson, somehow made it worse.) And then the doctors: dermatologists, plastic surgeons. And someone Amanda referred to as "the toe guy."

"He has a daughter in third grade and one in Daphne's class," she explained to Sylvia.

Sylvia frowned. "He's called the toe guy?"

"He's famous for making the second toe shorter than the big toe. So I waited till I saw his wife at pickup and I asked if he'd donate a toe shortening."

Just one? Grace thought. *What about the other foot?*

"I mean, I'll ask anybody anything. Why not? What can they say except yes or no? But they almost never say no. Why should they, this is their kid's school! They should be happy to donate their services. And what's the difference if it's a plumber or a doctor, right?"

"Well, but...," Grace couldn't stop herself interjecting, "you're talking about elective things. Most doctors aren't dealing with—" She nearly said *human vanity* but caught herself. "With...things people actually want to be seeing a doctor about."

Amanda sat back in her chair and looked frankly at Grace. She did not seem angry, just perplexed.

"That's not true," she said. "I mean, we all want to safeguard our health. Even if it's...I don't know...a tummy doctor or a heart doctor, it's all about taking care of ourselves, and you always want to go to the best person, whether it's a financial adviser or a doctor. How many wives would buy a consultation with a famous heart doctor for their husbands?"

"Grace's husband is a doctor," Sylvia said. She said it matter-of-factly, and Grace knew exactly why she'd done it. Now they both watched its inevitable effect.

"Oh right, I forgot that," Amanda said. "What kind of doctor is he again?"

"Jonathan's a pediatric oncologist."

Amanda frowned for a baffled moment, then sighed. She had concluded, appropriately, that no one wanted the services of a pediatric oncologist, no matter how famous.

Sally was shaking her head. "I keep forgetting. He's always so upbeat when I see him. I mean, how does he do that?"

Grace turned to her. "Do what?"

"Work with those sick kids, and their parents. I could never do it."

"Me neither," said Amanda. "I can barely deal with it when one of my kids has a headache."

"It's different when it's your kid," Grace said. She was sympathetic to this, because she had always found it unbearable when Henry got sick, which he hadn't even done very much. He had been a very healthy child. "When it's a patient, and you're bringing your expertise to their illness, it's just a whole different thing. You're there to help. You're trying to make their lives better."

"Yeah," Amanda said disagreeably. "But then they die."

"You still tried," Grace insisted. "No matter what doctors do, people still get sick and die, and some of them are kids. That's never not going to be true. But I'd much rather have a kid with cancer now than twenty years ago. And I'd much rather have a kid with cancer in New York than anyplace else."

Amanda, impervious to this argument, only shook her head. "I couldn't deal with it. I hate hospitals. I hate the way they smell." She shuddered, as if assailed—there, amid the expensive squalor of Sally Morrison-Golden's town house—by a puddle of Lysol.

"I just wish we had more, you know, artists and writers," said Sylvia, who—having raised this particular topic, was now obviously attempting to move on. "Lunch with an opera singer or a visit to the painter's studio. Why don't we have more artists?"

Because they don't send their children to Rearden, Grace thought irritably. In the topography of New York private schools, Rearden was located in a mountain pass between the Wall Street Range and the Peaks of Corporate Law. Other schools—Fieldston, Dalton, Saint Ann's—got the children of creative parents, theater people, and novelists. It hadn't been delineated quite so clearly when Grace had been a student there. One of her friends had been the daughter of a poet who taught at Columbia, another was the unmusical son of two members of the New York Philharmonic. But Henry's classmates were growing up in the homes of personal wealth managers and hedge fund warriors. It wasn't particularly pleasant, but it couldn't be helped.

"Well, I think we're in pretty good shape," Sally announced.

"Forty lots—something for everyone, right? Unless I've missed something. There's still time to get it in if anyone has something?"

"I was thinking...," Grace said, alarmed by a wave of shyness. "I mean, if you want. I have my book. Just galleys at the moment, but you know I could promise one. I mean, a signed copy."

All three of them looked at her.

"Oh, that's right," Amanda said. "I forgot you wrote a book. What kind of book is it? Is it a mystery? I'm always looking for a good book for the beach."

Grace felt herself frown. It was the best way she knew of not laughing.

"No, no. I'm not that kind of writer. I'm a therapist, you know. This is a book about marriages. It's my first book," she said, noting—and disapproving—the distinct whiff of pride in her voice. "It's called *You Should Have Known*."

"What?" Amanda said.

"You Should Have Known," she repeated, louder this time.

"No, I heard you. I mean, I should have known what?"

"Oh. It's...you always know people better at the beginning of a relationship."

In the very long and very silent moment that ensued, Grace had ample time to reevaluate her title, her thesis, and pretty much everything she held dear. Professionally, at least.

"Could you maybe do a therapy session?" Sally said eagerly. "You know, 'Authority on marriage will do couples therapy for you'?"

Shocked, Grace could barely keep it together enough to shake her head. "I don't think it would be appropriate."

"Yeah, but people might really go for that."

"I'm sorry. No."

Amanda gave the tersest, tiniest frown of disapproval. Then, from the front of the house, they all heard the doorbell sound, a low and lazy chime. Grace, with immense gratitude, felt the tension drain from their little group. "Hilda?" Sally called. "Will you get that?"

There was movement in the kitchen.

"Was someone else supposed to come?" Amanda asked.

"Well, no," Sally said. "Not really."

"Not really?" Sylvia said, laughing a bit.

"No. I mean, someone said they might, but they didn't follow up with me, so I thought..."

There were voices now, muffled and indistinguishable. And something else: a squeaking sound, like something on springs. Then Hilda reappeared. "She's leaving the carriage in the hallway. Okay?" she asked Sally.

"Oh." Sally looked mildly stunned. "Okay." She shook her head. "Okay." When she looked up again, she had affixed a bright and toothy smile to her face. "Hello!" she said, getting to her feet.

A woman had arrived, stepping around from behind Hilda. She was a person of medium height with dark hair curling to her shoulders and skin the color of caramel. She had very black eyes and above them very dark and full eyebrows that arched in a manner that made her look vaguely flirtatious. She was wearing a tan skirt and a white shirt open far enough to reveal two items of note: a gold crucifix and a substantial cleavage. She seemed somewhat cowed by her surroundings, the large but messy home, the baffled women, the evidence of a meeting already in progress, if not—as indicated by the note pages and printouts on the table—nearing its end. She gave them all a furtive sort of nod and stood awkwardly in the doorway.

"Please. Sit." Sally pointed to the chair beside Grace. "Everyone, this is Mrs. Alves. She's the mother of Miguel Alves in fourth grade. I'm so sorry, you're going to have to help me pronounce your first name."

"Malaga," the woman said. Her voice was light, nearly musical. "Malaga," she said again, more slowly and with the emphasis clear on the first syllable.

"Malaga," Grace repeated. She extended her hand. "Hello. I'm Grace."

Sylvia and Amanda followed suit. "Hi, hi," the woman said. "I sorry. I late. The baby, she fussy."

"Oh, that's okay," Sally said. "But you know, we've gotten a great deal done. Please," she said again. "Sit."

The woman sat in a chair next to Grace and angled herself away from the heavy wooden table, crossing one leg over the other, and Grace couldn't help noticing her legs, which were fleshy but rather graceful. She leaned slightly forward, nearly touching the wood of the table: more flesh, visible through the silk of her shirt, but somehow, again, not unattractive. She had mentioned a baby? Grace thought. She looked like someone who might have given birth in the not too distant past. Still convex, still producing. Her hands were folded together on the tabletop. On the left hand, fourth finger, was a thin gold band.

"We've been talking about auction items," said Sally, speaking—Grace could not help but feel—inordinately slowly. "Things to auction off at our benefit, to raise money for the school. For scholarships," she added, now looking pointedly down at her notes. "Generally, we ask the parents to come up with ideas. If someone can offer something related to their work. Like an artist or a doctor. If you have any ideas, please let me know."

The woman—Malaga—nodded. She looked thoroughly sober, as if she had just been given terrible news.

"So... let's move on," said Sally, and she did. The newcomer's arrival had the effect of a starting pistol, and suddenly everyone sped up. They barreled through everyone's schedule for the next few days, and who would be manning the table downstairs in the lobby (not a desirable position), and who would be greeting guests upstairs in the Spensers' grand marble foyer, and whether Sylvia had the software she needed in order to cash everyone out at the end of the evening. There was to be a pre-party— "Cocktails with the Headmaster"—technically not their responsibility but necessitating some coordination, and an after-party in the Boom Boom Room at the Standard, which Amanda was more or less in charge of (her friends being the core group of attendees, in other words). But they tore through it all.

Malaga said nothing, nor did her expression seem to change, though she turned her head with the others as conversation moved among the other three. But then, just as they were raising the thorny issue of how to leave the benefit en masse when it was time for the after-party, but without creating an air of exclusivity (because, after all, the final numbers had now been given to the Standard and there could really be no tagalongs), the talk was cut by a sharp, gulping infant cry, and the silent woman jolted to her feet and left the room. She returned a moment later with a tiny, dusky infant wrapped in a green striped cloth. Nodding in acknowledgment of the women's cooing, Malaga took her seat again, shrugged her arm out of her long-sleeved silk shirt, and roughly pulled down a white bra, exposing the entire side of her body. This was done so quickly that Grace barely had time to be uncomfortable, but looking furtively across the table, she saw that Amanda seemed scandalized. With eyes widened, she gave a minuscule shake of her little head, sufficient only to convey this to herself and anyone else who might have chosen that nanosecond to glance in her direction.

The issue, of course, was not the breast-feeding, which Grace assumed they had all (with the exception of Sylvia) happily done, and out of a combination of principle, pride, convenience, and concern for the health of their babies. The issue was the blunt and thoroughly nonchalant nakedness on display: one breast descending freely into the sucking mouth of the baby, the thick flesh of the belly, even the full upper arm warmly positioning the infant's head. There was no designated nursing garment like the one Grace had worn, with its discreet slit for the nipple and artful drape to shield her from, for example, prurient teenage eyes incapable of differentiating between the sexual and the maternal. Malaga Alves, having seen to the baby, continued to look around the table, waiting for the conversation to continue; so, in an act of collaborative theater, with a set of cooperative stage directions, the other four women proceeded to pretend she wasn't there. The baby sucked loudly and made little sounds of frustration. After a few minutes, just as Grace had reached a state of relative imperviousness about the situation, Malaga extracted the nipple, which flopped wetly against the infant's cheek, after which, instead of covering it up, the woman beside Grace simply exposed the other breast by the same method and positioned the baby anew.

By now, the level of anxiety in the room was palpable. The women spoke in rapid, frill-free sentences, barreling as quickly as possible toward the end of the meeting's agenda. Absolutely no one looked at Malaga, except—Grace saw—for Hilda, who had arrived in the doorway and was staring balefully at the half-naked woman. Malaga herself sat imperviously, her silk shirt flung back over her shoulders like a cape, her bra wedged below her unfurled breasts. It occurred to Grace that if this woman were of an even remotely venal disposition, her behavior could be seen as exquisitely hostile, but on balance she thought this was probably not the case. For all the resentments a New Yorker named Malaga Alves might hold toward a New Yorker named Sally Morrison-Golden, she had emitted not even a whiff of anything like ill temper. There was, to the contrary, an absence of reaction, a retreat into negative energy; her actions were those of a woman who did not consider herself visible, let alone inflammatory. Glancing furtively at her, Grace suddenly found herself remembering a person she had once seen in the locker room of her gym on Third Avenue. She had been changing after an aerobics class when she noticed a woman standing in front of the mirror near the entrance to the showers, quite naked, without even the usual gym-issued towel knotted around the hips or over the breasts. She was in her thirties or forties—in that ill-defined middle place where how old you look depends so much more on how well you're taking care of yourself than how many years you've been alive—and in that equally ill-defined terrain between heavy and thin. As Grace went through the usual motions of extracting herself from her sweaty leotard, stepping into and out of the shower, drying her hair, and opening her locker, she had gradually noted that the woman was still standing in precisely the same place and that same position: before the full-length mirror, combing her hair. Her stance and behavior added up to far more than the sum of their parts, a fact equally obvious to everyone else in the locker room, fifteen or twenty other women who studiously avoided this person, stepping carefully around her, averting their eyes. Nakedness in a locker room, of course, is far from unusual, and hair combing and looking into mirrors are also quite common. But the woman had emanated a visceral wrongness as she stood, so still, a little too close to the mirror, staring with a little too much concentration at herself, her legs a little too far apart, her left arm motionless at the hip while her right hand dragged the comb carefully, rhythmically, through her wet brown hair. That woman had had just this expression on her face, thought Grace, testing the insight by looking briefly back at Malaga Alves, then turning again to Sally in an effort to seem nonplussed. They were racing now, crossing t's and dotting i's, removing any possible impediment to finishing the meeting and getting the hell out. Sally, perhaps recalling the days of her "big career," ran what remained of the session like a merciless managing partner, thoroughly indifferent to the private lives of her subordinates. Tasks were assigned and a pre-event rendezvous scheduled for Saturday afternoon at the Spensers'. ("Does that work for you, Malaga?" Sally paused to ask. "Oh, good.") The baby continued to suck throughout, and it seemed to Grace almost bizarre that such a tiny thing could sustain hunger for such a long time. Then, without warning or comment, she turned her head away from her mother's heavy breast and looked avidly around the room.

"I think," Sally said firmly, "that may be it. I don't have anything else. Sylvia? Do you have anything else?"

"Nope," Sylvia said, shutting her leather-encased folder with a smack.

Amanda was already getting to her feet, gathering the papers before her as she did. She wasn't wasting time. Malaga, having jostled the infant into a more or less vertical position, had still not shown the smallest inclination to cover herself.

"It was nice to meet you. I think your little boy is in my daughter Piper's class. Miss Levin? Fourth grade?"

The woman nodded.

"I haven't gotten to meet any of the new parents this year," Amanda said, shoving the papers into her pale green Birkin. "We ought to have a get-together, just Miss Levin's class."

"How is Miguel doing?" Sally asked. "He's a sweet little boy."

Malaga, in response, showed the slightest animation, offering a brief smile as she patted her infant on the back. "Yes. He doing well. The teacher, she working with him."

"Piper said she played a game with him on the roof," said Amanda.

The roof was where the elementary students went for recess. It was covered in safe, rubbery flooring and full of primary-colored playground equipment and a net, to prevent the children from flying away.

"Okay," Malaga said. The baby emitted a deep, unladylike burp. Suddenly, Grace wanted desperately to leave.

"Well, bye, all," she said cheerily. "Sally, if you think of anything else, please call. But obviously we're in great shape. I can't believe you've pulled this all together in such a short time."

"Well, with a little help from Suki Spenser." Sally laughed. "It doesn't take a village if you have a multizillionaire with a ballroom and a winery."

"So that's what I'm missing," Grace said with practiced goodwill. "Good-bye, Malaga," she said, noting that the woman was finally putting her heavy breasts back into the bra. Grace lifted her leather briefcase by its shoulder strap and placed it squarely on her shoulder.

"You going back to work?" Sylvia said.

"No. Taking Henry to his violin lesson."

"Oh, of course. Is he doing Suzuki still?" Sylvia asked.

"No, not really. After Book Eight or Book Nine, somewhere around there, they sort of head away from all that."

"You still take him to his lessons?" said Sally, with the faintest whiff of disapproval. "God, if I took my kids everywhere myself, I'd never do anything else. Two of them do gymnastics, and there's piano and ballet and fencing. Plus Djuna, of course. She only does Music Together and Gymboree, but you know, the fourth go-round with Gymboree? I couldn't take it anymore, so Hilda goes. The moms were like, 'Oh, my baby's so special because she slid down the slide!' I keep wanting to say, 'This is my fourth kid, and I hate to tell you, but gravity makes them *all* slide down the slide.' And I almost lost it so many times in Music Together, I finally told Hilda she had to do that one, too. I feel like I've been shaking the same egg maraca for a decade."

"I'm sure if I had more than just Henry, I'd have stopped a long time ago," Grace assured her. "It's not that hard when it's just one."

"I've been thinking of starting Celia on the violin," said Amanda. Celia was Daphne's twin, a sturdy girl, at least a head taller than her sister, with an overbite that was going to be very expensive. "Where is his teacher?"

Grace wanted very much to say that it didn't matter where Henry's teacher was, since Henry's teacher would not possibly consider taking an eleven-year-old beginning violin student, no matter who his parents were or how much money they had. Henry's teacher, an acerbic and depressive Hungarian in his seventies, had become Henry's teacher only after a hair-raising audition and an exhaustive assessment of his musicality. And though it was clear to all involved that Henry was headed for university, not conservatory (a state of affairs that suited Grace and Jonathan, and certainly Henry, just fine), it was also true that his talent was sufficient to keep Henry's place on his teacher's very small and very precisely maintained roster of students. She might have answered Amanda's question by saying that Vitaly Rosenbaum taught at "Juilliard" (which had until recently been true) or even "Columbia" (which was also somewhat true, since a few of his students, who had similarly departed the conservatory track, were now undergraduates and graduate students there, and everyone came to his Morningside Heights apartment for instruction), but it was necessary only to answer with a third truth to make the entire conversation evaporate, so she opted for that.

"He's on West 114th Street," she said.

"Oh," said Amanda. "Well, never mind."

"I love Henry," said Sally. "So polite, every single time I see him. And oh, my God, is he good-looking. I'd kill for his eyelashes. Have you noticed his eyelashes?" she said to Sylvia.

"I... don't think so." Sylvia smiled.

"It's so unfair, boys get the best eyelashes. I mean, I'm spending a fortune on that eyelash-growing stuff, and Henry Sachs walks down the corridor and blinks and you practically feel a breeze."

"Well...," Grace said. She was fairly sure that Sally meant to compliment Henry, or more probably Grace herself, but she found the observation of her son's beauty distasteful. "I guess they are a little on the long side," she managed finally. "I haven't thought about them in a while. When he was a baby, I remember noticing they were long."

"She have long lashes," Malaga Alves said suddenly. She nodded at the baby in her lap, who was sleeping now and whose eyelashes were indeed quite long.

"She's beautiful," Grace said, grateful for the shift in focus. It wasn't difficult to endorse the beauty of an infant. "What is her name?"

"Her name Elena," said Malaga. "My mother name."

"Beautiful," Grace said again. "Oh dear, I'd better leave. My kid with the long eyelashes gets upset when I make him late for violin. Good-bye, everyone," she said, already turning. "I'll see you at school, or...on Saturday! It's going to be great."

With her bag slung over her shoulder, she made for the kitchen.

"Hang on a sec, I'll walk out with you," Sylvia said. Grace, who at least preferred Sylvia to anyone else in the room, paused unenthusiastically in the front hall. After the door shut behind them, they stood for a moment on the town house steps and looked at each other. "Wow," said Sylvia.

Grace, who didn't want to agree until she knew exactly what she was wowing, said nothing. "You going to school now?" she asked.

"Yeah. I have another meeting with Robert. One in my long, long series of meetings with Robert. I'm surprised they're not gossiping about us."

Grace smiled. Robert was Rearden's headmaster. His marriage to his long-term partner, the artistic director of a major off-Broadway theater company, had been one of the first gay weddings featured in the *Times* "Vows" column. "About Daisy?" she asked.

"Yes, always Daisy. Do we move her ahead or do we keep her back? Is it better for her to do trigonometry with the tenth graders or hygiene with the fifth graders? Can she skip introductory biology and go ahead to advanced chemistry, or is it more important for her to keep taking seventh-grade social studies with her class? It's exhausting. I know I shouldn't complain. I understand I'm supposed to support her academically, but at the same time, I want her to be a seventh grader, you know? I don't want her to go tearing through her childhood. She only gets one, like the rest of us," Sylvia said. Together, the two walked east to Lexington and turned uptown.

This little truth, offered so nonchalantly, gave Grace an unexpected sting. Henry, like Daisy, was an only child, and she had also sighted the far shore of his childhood. He was still recognizable as the child-Henry (even, to his mother, at least, as the toddler-Henry), but it was all going too fast, and she knew it. The fact that there had been no other children made this looming transition more fraught still. When he left her embrace she would become, in a real sense, childless again.

Of course, it had not been their plan to have only one child, and now she understood that she had squandered precious time when Henry was little worrying over when (*if*) the next one would come (Jonathan, who had seen too much cancer to let her go very far down the infertility treatment road, put a stop to it after a half dozen rounds of Clomid, which had not been successful). In time she had settled into this Henry-centric configuration of her family, but like any other family configuration in New York City, this one came with baggage. If families with two children were modestly procreating and families with three and more were displaying entitlement, parents of single offspring possessed an inverse arrogance all their own. A single, perfect child, they seemed to suggest, was worthy of their full attention, effort, and nurturing. A single child, so remarkable in himself or herself, negated the need to reproduce repeatedly, since he or she was obviously capable of contributing more to the world than any number of lesser children. The parents of only children had an annoying way of offering their children to the world as if they were doing the world a big favor. It was a phenomenon Grace had long been familiar with. She and her closest friend, her childhood friend Vita, had once made up a song about this type of parent, to the tune of a song from *Bye Bye Birdie*:

One child, one special child,
One child to mother forever and ever
One child, not two or three . . .

One child, one perfect child,
One child who'll love me forever and ever
One child, that's the way it should be...

Grace, of course, had been an only child herself. She hadn't exactly been inflated to world-saving stature by her mother and father, and she had often been lonely. Or—she corrected herself now—not exactly lonely, but alone. Alone at home or at the lake in the summer. Alone with Mom. Alone with Dad. The power and messy intricacies of sibling relationships fascinated her. Sometimes, at Vita's labyrinthine apartment on East 96th Street, she had stood out in the hallway and just let the sounds of movement and argument (usually argument) among Vita's three brothers wash over her. That, in a complete negation of her own family, had become what family was supposed to be. She had wanted it for Henry and had not been able to give it to him.

Vita was gone. Of course, not *gone*. Not *dead*. But gone nonetheless. Vita had hung in there—confidante, companion, roommate in a dilapidated (actually slanting) house in Central Square when they were seniors in college, Grace at Harvard and Vita at Tufts, and climactically maid of honor—until Grace married. And then she had just...evaporated, removed herself from Grace's life, leaving her with only facsimiles of friends. And precious few of those. Grace, even all these years later, was too bereft about it to be angry, and too angry to be sad.

"Did you know she was coming?" Sylvia asked after a moment.

"Who?" said Grace. "That woman who came late?"

"Yeah. Did Sally say anything to you?"

Grace shook her head. "I don't know Sally very well. Just at school."

Then again, the same could almost as easily be said of Sylvia, despite the fact that Grace and Sylvia had actually been students at Rearden at the same time (Grace two years behind) and that she did sort of like Sylvia, now as well as back then. Certainly, she admired Sylvia. It couldn't be easy to raise a daughter alone, work full-time (Sylvia was an attorney specializing in labor disputes), and care for first one parent and then the other as they had taken ill and died over the past couple of years. She supposed what she respected most about Sylvia was the fact that she had not married herself off to a man who wouldn't make her happy, solely for the purpose of having the child she'd obviously wanted. In fact, when Grace explained to her clients—her female clients—that forgoing marriage to the wrong man did not mean they couldn't have children, it was sometimes Sylvia who passed through her thoughts. Sylvia and her brilliant daughter from China.

Once, at morning drop-off, another mother had praised Daisy Steinmetz's obvious and astounding intelligence, and Sylvia had shrugged it off. "I know," Grace had heard her say. "But it has nothing to do with me. These are not my genes. Daisy never heard English until she was nearly a year old, but she was chattering away a month or two after I brought her home to New York, and she read before she was three. Of course, I'm delighted for her, that she's smart. I think it will make her life easier. And I'm a good mom, but I'm not responsible for that."

This, to say the least, had been a highly unusual thing to hear in the marble entry foyer of the Rearden School.

"She's very odd," said Sylvia.

"Sally?"

"No." Sylvia allowed herself the briefest laugh. "That woman, Malaga. She sits across the street on one of those benches in the park, you know? After she drops the son off. She just stays."

"With the baby?" Grace frowned.

"Now with the baby. Before she came when she was pregnant. She doesn't even read a book. Doesn't she have anything to do all day?"

"I guess not," said Grace. For her, as for Sylvia and probably for every person they knew on the island of Manhattan, not having anything to do—indeed, not being frantically busy at all times—was an unfathomable state of being. It was also, for women like themselves, the most supreme New York put-down possible. "Maybe she was worried about her kid. Miguel?" Grace asked.

"Miguel, yeah."

"You know, and wanted to stay nearby in case he needed her."

"Hm."

They walked a block or so in mutual silence.

"It was just bizarre," said Sylvia, finally. "I mean, sitting there like that."

Grace said nothing. It wasn't that she didn't agree. Just that she didn't want to go on record agreeing. "Could be cultural," she offered finally.

"Please," said the woman whose Chinese daughter was now preparing for her bat mitzvah.

"Who's the husband?" said Grace. They were nearing the school now, converging with mothers and nannies.

"Never seen him," Sylvia said. "Look, for the record, I was just as shocked as you were when Sally suggested you auction off a couples therapy session."

Grace laughed. "Okay. Thanks."

"I know it's supposed to take a village to raise our children, but why does ours have so many village idiots? I mean, did I really just hear about toe shortening?"

"I fear so. Then again, I once had a client, this was years ago, whose husband left her because he said her feet were ugly."

"God." Sylvia stopped. After another step, Grace stopped, too. "What an asshole. What was he, like, a fetishist?"

Grace shrugged. "Maybe. It's irrelevant. The point is, he made himself very clear about what mattered to him. He was a guy who had always told her she had ugly feet. From day one. And when they split up, her feet were right at the top of his list for why he couldn't live with her anymore. He was an asshole, of course, but he was a straightforward asshole. And she married him anyway, even though it was blindingly obvious that he was at least capable of contempt for her. What was he going to do? Change?"

Sylvia sighed. She was reaching into her back pocket and removing her phone, which was apparently vibrating. "They say people do."

"Well, they're wrong," said Grace.

CHAPTER THREE

NOT MY CITY

Rearden had not always been the demesne of hedge funders and other assorted Masters of the Universe. Founded in the nineteenth century to educate the sons *and* daughters of workingmen, the school had once been identified with atheist Jewish intellectuals and their red diaper babies and attended by the offspring of journalists and artists, once-blacklisted actors, and socially conscious folksingers. Students of Grace's generation had taken perverse pride in their school's having been disparaged as "Bohemian" (by *The Official Preppy Handbook*, no less), but over the following decades Rearden, like nearly every other private school on the island of Manhattan (and a few in Brooklyn to boot), had shifted substantially—not so much politically, but in the general direction of money. Today, the typical Rearden dad made money out of other money, that was all, and he was intense, distracted, extraordinarily rich, and nearly always absent. The typical mom was a former attorney or analyst, now consumed with the work of running multiple houses and overseeing the development of multiple children. She was very thin and very blond and usually rushing to SoulCycle with her entire life mashed into a white-stitched Barenia Birkin. The school was preponderantly white (if no longer preponderantly

Jewish), though there was now a sizable contingent of students from Asia and India. These students, and the even smaller number of black and Hispanic students, were featured prominently in Rearden's admissions literature, but the truly—if far more covertly—advantaged students were hiding in plain sight: These were the offspring of Rearden graduates, alumni men and women who were not, in actual fact, titans of modern industry or its money-spinning equivalents, but simply men and women who toiled as their predecessors had, in the arts, academia, or—like Grace—the so-called healing professions. They had attended the school before the deluge of money, when it had been not nearly so consumed by a sense of its own importance.

Her era (the 1980s) had been the last of the school's innocence, before all those Masters of the Universe had swarmed the city's independent schools and hurled the old guard over the parapets. Back in those Elysian days, Grace and her classmates knew they were not poor, but they did not exactly think of themselves as *rich*, either. (Even then there had been some quite rich children at Rearden, who were driven to school in long cars by men who wore caps—and appropriately ridiculed as a result.) Most lived in basic "classic six" apartments on the Upper East and Upper West Sides (back then, such apartments were within reach of most families with a single professional parent—a doctor, an accountant), though a few iconoclasts were in the Village or even SoHo. On the weekends and during the summers, they decamped to small (and not very well-kept) houses in Westchester or Putnam County, or in Grace's case to the modest lakeside house in northwest Connecticut mysteriously purchased by Grace's grandmother (and namesake) at the height of the Depression for the bizarre sum of $4,000.

Today, the parents Grace met at Back to School Night visibly glazed over when they learned that she was a therapist, her husband a doctor. They would not have understood how it was possible to live in such cramped quarters as Grace's three-bedroom apartment, or what was the point of driving all the way to Connecticut if not to a gated estate with its own horse barn, tennis court, and guest cottage. The world these parents inhabited was one of titans and the people they hired to do things for them. They dwelt on Fifth or Park Avenue, in homes fashioned from multiple apartments, purchased and merged and overflowing to two or three floors, configured for (and dependent upon) live-in staff and suited to lavish entertaining. When these new Rearden families went away for the weekend it was to private islands, soaring mountain estates, or Hamptons palaces where horses waited in their stalls and boats in their slips.

She tried not to mind. She tried to remind herself that this was Henry's school experience, not her own, and why should the inequity of rich versus disgustingly rich bother her so much when Henry himself was such an amiable, noncovetous type anyway? Henry's classmates might be growing up in opulent apartments tended by resident couples (he the butler, she the cook) and shepherded by tag teams of nannies, then tag teams of tutors and private coaches. They might get iPhones in kindergarten and credit cards in third grade, but it didn't seem to affect Henry. So she struggled mightily not to let it affect her.

Then, one Saturday, had come the snub so artlessly dealt that it landed like a door in the face, and shattered her attempts at sanguinity once and for all. Grace had been dropping Henry off at a birthday party in a Park Avenue penthouse where the windows framed breathtaking views on all four sides. From where she stood on the mosaic floor of the entranceway, just off the private elevator, the children could be observed beyond a marble archway, tearing around the massive living room in pursuit of a magician in a bowler hat. Grace had just handed over a gift-wrapped science kit to an employee of some kind (secretary? party facilitator?) when the hostess gaily passed by.

This hostess, this birthday party mother—Grace did not know very much about her, except that her first name was Linsey and she hailed from somewhere in the South. She was willowy and tall, with breasts disproportionately high and suspiciously spherical, and she made good use of the catchall pronoun substitute *y'all* when navigating morning drop-off at the third-grade classroom doorway. (*Y'all* was admirably useful when you couldn't recall someone's name, Grace had to admit. She was not at all sure that Linsey, three years after their sons had been assigned to the same class, knew her name.) In addition to Henry's classmate, Linsey's husband had older children at Rearden, from his first marriage. He was something at Bear Stearns. It had to be said that Linsey had never been anything but pleasant, but past the veneer of good manners there seemed to lurk nothing at all.

One other important fact that Grace had gleaned about Linsey was that she had a mind-boggling collection of Hermès Birkins, a veritable color wheel of them in ostrich, crocodile, and occasional leather. Grace noticed Birkins, and she possessed exactly one, in basic brown-pebbled Togo, a gift from Jonathan on her thirtieth birthday. (Poor Jonathan had been made to jump through many hoops down at the Hermès store on Madison, where, in his charming naïveté, he had assumed he could just walk in and purchase a Birkin bag. It was adorable, really.) She took care of this beautiful object with great devotion, and it lived on a cloth-lined shelf in her closet with its dowager aunts, the two Hermès Kellys she had inherited from her mother. Grace secretly itched to see Linsey's bags, especially in situ, wherever in the great apartment they might reside (possibly in their own closet or, indeed, vault!), and was hoping to be offered a tour.

"Hello!" Linsey had said when she saw Henry and Grace arrive. Henry, without prompting, took off to join the kids in the living room, and Grace stood before her hostess, wondering if some kind of actual intimacy was about to be launched. She could see, through yet another archway, and down past a very long dining room, and through an open door, a few other mothers positioned around a kitchen island, drinking coffee. She could do coffee, actually, Grace thought. It being Saturday morning. And though she had made a special arrangement to see a couple in crisis that afternoon, she had no obligations until then. "So glad y'all could make it!" the hostess said with her customary warmth. The party would be over at four. Then she let Grace know that one of the doormen would be glad to hail a taxi for her, if she needed one.

The doorman would be glad to hail a taxi for her.

Grace had moved numbly to the door and stepped numbly into the elevator for the long ride down. In her own building, where she had grown up and still lived, the doormen were mainly Irish or Bulgarian or Albanian, friendly guys who volunteered for their local fire squad in Queens and showed you pictures of their kids. They also held the door and took your bag unless you waved them off. And they hailed taxis, of course. Of course they did. She did not need to be told that they did.

Stepping out onto Park that morning, she had had a queasy feeling, like a twister-tossed girl from Kansas emerging into unreal Technicolor. This particular apartment building, Linsey's building, was famous and had been the home of many a robber baron in its time. Her own father's law partner had lived here for years, and Grace had attended many New Year's Day open houses on a floor a few stories below Linsey's, in a dress specially selected by her mother, wearing patent leather shoes from Tru-Tred and carrying a little purse. The building's lobby had been redecorated since then, of course—probably many times—and she found that she could no longer recall the specifics of Jazz Age opulence that she had always associated with the building; today, all was granite and marble and sleek technology, with the uniformed concierges and guards just conspicuous enough to get their point across. And it was from this cold vision of forbidding wealth that she had emerged onto the street. It was springtime, and the bulbs planted abundantly along the Park Avenue medians were crowding up out of the expensive dirt: hot pink and hot yellow, jostling for the thin sunlight. How many years of how many bulbs had she seen grow up out of the Park Avenue medians? How many years of Christmas trees and Botero statues and the steel Louise Nevelson on 92nd Street that was supposed to represent Manhattan itself? She even remembered the long-ago holiday cross, made by office lights left on at night, back when the MetLife Building had been the Pan Am Building, back when the sight of a cross illuminating the lower end of Park Avenue might have passed without comment, let alone outrage—that's how far back she could remember this thoroughfare.

The doorman would be glad to hail a taxi for her.

Not my city, she had thought then, turning north along the avenue. Once, but not any longer. She had never, with the exception of college, lived anywhere else, had never, in fact, *considered* living anywhere else. But then again, New York gave little weight to longevity. The city was funny that way; it took you in, straight off the bus or plane or however else you managed to arrive, with no long-enforced period of audition in which you might be considered a foreigner or a flatlander or a Yankee until your great-grandchildren finally showed up to inherit the privilege of being a local. Here, you belonged on arrival, or just as soon as you looked as though you had somewhere to go and wanted to get there fast. New York didn't care about your accent or whether someone had come over on the *Mayflower*; it was enough that you had chosen to be here when you might have gone somewhere else (though why anyone would choose to go somewhere else was, in itself, mystifying). Grace, who had been born on 77th Street and reared on 81st, who now lived, indeed, in the apartment of her childhood and sent her son to the school she herself had attended, who used the dry cleaner her mother had used and still ate in some of the restaurants once favored by her parents, and bought Henry shoes at Tru-Tred, the very store she had been taken to as a little girl (where he might have been seated in the same little chair Grace had once sat in and had his foot measured by the selfsame measuring tool that had once measured his mother's foot)...was a New Yorker. Jonathan had grown up on Long Island, but he, too, had transmogrified into a New Yorker the minute he turned the key on their first unlovely New York apartment, in a white-brick tower on East 65th, near Memorial. And Linsey, lately arrived on the arm of a new husband and ushered directly into one of the great apartments at one of the city's legendary addresses, whose Manhattan life had been presented to her in a kind of Big Apple welcome wagon (this store, this school, this facialist, this domestics agency), whose companions were the similarly arrived and espoused and attired, who conceived of the city not as a story that had begun long before her entrance and would endure (one hoped) long after her exit, but as a place she happened to be living, instead of, say, Atlanta or Orange County or one of the nicer suburbs of Chicago—she, too, was a New Yorker. God!

Sally had been right, of course, that Henry did not need delivery to his violin lesson, let alone picking up. New York kids generally ran loose in the city after the age of ten or so, and many other twelve-year-old boys would not have been pleased at the sight of their mothers in the marble foyer of the Rearden School at three fifteen. Henry, though, still searched for her with his long-lashed eyes as he descended the stone steps from the classroom floors above, still showed that briefest flash of relief at finding that she was here, that she had come for him after all. It was her favorite moment of the day.

He came now, carrying his violin in its backpack configuration, a sight that always gave Grace pause (such an expensive instrument, such a casual mode of conveyance, etc.). To his mother he gave the briefest embrace, more *Let's get out of here* than *Happy to see you*, and Grace followed him out, repressing the usual admonition to zip up his parka.

When they were about a block away from the school, he took her hand. He still did that, and she tried not to clutch back. "How was today?" she asked him instead. "How was Jonah?"

Jonah Hartman was Henry's former best friend. One day the previous year, he had coldly announced that their long partnership was now severed and had barely acknowledged him in all the months since. Now Jonah had two new friends he seemed never to be without.

Henry shrugged.

"You're allowed to find other friends, too," she told him.

"I know," Henry said. "You told me before."

But he wanted Jonah. Of course he did. They had been together since kindergarten and had had what amounted to a standing playdate every Sunday. Jonah had come to the lake house in Connecticut for a few weeks every August, and the boys had attended a local day camp. But Jonah's family had imploded the year before, his father moving out and his mother taking the kids to an apartment on the West Side. Privately, Grace was not at all surprised that Jonah was acting out, exerting control over one of the few things in his life he felt he could control. She had tried to discuss the situation with Jennifer, his mother, but without success.

Henry's violin teacher lived in a shabby building on Morningside Drive, with a wide, dark lobby and a population of aging European refugees and Columbia professors. There was supposedly a doorman on duty at all times, but he seemed to be on break whenever they arrived, no matter what time of day that was. Grace pressed the intercom button just inside the outer doors and waited the usual minute or two for Mr. Rosenbaum to make his deliberate way from the lesson room to the kitchen phone, where he buzzed them in. In the creaking elevator, Henry removed his violin from its backpack configuration and gripped it properly by the handle. He seemed to use these last moments to prepare himself for the exacting Mr. Rosenbaum, who, over the years, had often reminded his students that others—more talented others, the implication was—were always in the wings, hoping to replace any who proved less gifted than originally thought or were not sufficiently devoted to practice. Henry was aware, because Grace had made him aware, that he had been granted his place on Vitaly Rosenbaum's roster because of his ability and promise, and paradoxically this seemed to mean more to him as the years passed. He did not want to lose his slot, Grace understood. He did not want the decision made for him.

"Good afternoon." The violin teacher was waiting for them in his open doorway, the dim corridor of his apartment extending behind him. From the kitchen wafted an unmistakable smell of cabbage, part of Malka Rosenbaum's highly limited repertoire of straight-from-the-shtetl food.

"Good afternoon," said Grace.

"Hi," said Henry.

"You practice?" Vitaly Rosenbaum said immediately.

Henry nodded. "But I had a math test this morning I had to study for. So not last night."

"Life is constant test," he scolded predictably. "You can't stop practice for math. Music is good for math."

Henry nodded. Over the years, he had also been told that music was good for history, literature, physical health, mental health, and, of course, math. But he also knew he had to study.

Grace didn't go with them into the lesson room. She took her customary seat in the hallway outside, a low and ornate wooden chair from an earlier era, when comfort in furniture was not highly prized, and took out her cell phone to check messages. There were two: one from Jonathan, to say he'd admitted two patients to the hospital that day and would not be home until late, and the other from one of her own patients, canceling an appointment for the following day without explanation or any mention of rescheduling. Grace frowned. She was wondering how worried to be about this woman, whose husband had chosen the previous session to admit that his self-termed "college experimentation" with other men had not ended in college but was in fact ongoing and not—to Grace's mind—experimental at all. The couple had been married for eight years and had five-year-old twin girls. After a moment, Grace found the woman's number and left a message to call her back.

From down the hall, she heard the music: Bach's Violin Sonata no. 1 in G Minor, the Siciliana movement. She listened for a moment, until Mr. Rosenbaum's voice broke into both her son's melodic line and her own distracted lull, then returned to her appointment book and drew a line through the canceled session. She had been working with the couple for about eight months, and her initial wariness about the husband had quickly focused on his sexual orientation. She had chosen not to challenge him about this, giving them a little time to see if it arose on its own, and indeed it had. There followed weeks and weeks of circular talk about his distance, his lack of connection, and his failure to nurture that had caused the wife to wilt in sadness on the oatmeal-colored sofa. And then, suddenly, she alluded to some moment in their first date or their second date, when he had mentioned a relationship with someone in his fraternity. "Well, I mean," he had said, "I told you about that. I don't know why you're bringing it up now. I'd always been curious."

Ping. It was like a little chime going off in the room.

But it had been only one person. One *serious* person. The others…

Ping.

Oh please, she thought now, doodling a nautilus around the crossed-out appointment. And here again, right now, on the less than comfortable chair in Vitaly Rosenbaum's cabbage-infused hallway on Morningside Heights, came the pounding frustration she had experienced that afternoon in her office. That so very familiar frustration.

To him, she might have said: *A few things to do and not to do if you're a gay man? Do: Be a gay man. Don't: Lie about being a gay man. Don't: Pretend not to be a gay man. Don't: Marry a woman and have children with her, unless she knows damn well that you're a gay man, and it's her own decision.*

And to her: *When a man tells you he's gay, don't marry him. And yes, he told you. In his half-assed, dishonest, utterly irresponsible way, he told you. So don't say you didn't know. You should have known!*

Grace closed her eyes. She had now been coming to this apartment for eight years, and every time she rounded the corner from 114th, she thought of her old adviser from graduate school, who had also lived on Morningside Drive, only two blocks north. Dr. Emily Rose—Mama Rose, as everyone called her, as she actually *encouraged* everyone to call her, something that still amazed Grace—had been a therapist from an earlier era: a time of long hugs when you arrived and longer ones when you departed, and (literal, physical) hand-holding, and more than a few of the accoutrements of the human potential movement, in which she had done what passed for her academic work on "transpersonal psychology." Mama Rose had met with her students in the very room where she saw patients, a light-filled chamber overlooking Morningside Park, full of hanging spider plants and unframed abstract paintings and oversize kilim floor pillows on which everyone was expected to sit cross-legged, and whose every class, advisory meeting, and undoubtedly therapeutic session began with that soul-crunching (at least to Grace) embrace. So appallingly intrusive. For the longest time, she had pined for another adviser, but in the end she stayed, and for the worst of all reasons. Mama Rose had never, to her knowledge, given a single one of her students a grade lower than an A.

Padded footfalls in another part of the apartment. Malka Rosenbaum, seldom seen and generally silent when she did appear. Her husband had made it over first, after the war, but she had been netted by some iron curtain bureaucracy and stuck for years. They had missed their chance to have children, Grace supposed, but for some reason she felt less sympathy for them than for the many clients she had worked with who had struggled, or were struggling, with infertility. Vitaly had skill and passion for the violin, if not for his actual students, but he was a joyless person, and Malka was not a person at all. It wasn't their fault. They had been robbed and deeply harmed and seen terrible things, and while some people might still find a wellspring of life and joy for the world after that, most could not. The Rosenbaums, clearly, could not. When she thought of them caring for an infant, a toddler, a little child, she felt the slow pain of a dimming light.

Vitaly's next student, a thin Korean girl in a Barnard sweatshirt, her long hair encased in a pink scrunchie, arrived a few minutes before Henry's lesson ended and ducked past the chair where Grace was sitting, avoiding eye contact. She leaned against the wall in the narrow hallway, grimly looking over her music, and when Henry came out, the three of them did an awkward limbo around one another. Grace and Henry stepped out onto the landing to put on their coats.

"Okay?" said Grace.

"Okay."

They got a cab on Broadway, headed south, and drove through the park to the East Side.

"I heard some very nice playing," Grace said, mainly because she wanted him to speak to her.

Henry shrugged, his bony shoulders pointing through his sweater. "Not according to Mr. Rosenbaum."

"No?" Grace asked.

Another shrug. A patient of Grace's had once joked that the shrug was the most accurate barometer of adolescence. More than one per hour signaled its onset. More than two per hour was a full-blown case. When words reemerged, if they ever did, the kid was coming out of it.

"I think he thinks I'm wasting his time. He just sits there with his eyes closed. It's not that he says I'm doing bad..."

"Badly," Grace said softly. She couldn't help it.

"Badly. But he used to say more good stuff. You think he wants me to quit?"

Grace felt a pulse of distress go through her, like some radioactive dye injected into a vein, then shot out from the heart. She waited for it to subside. Vitaly Rosenbaum, old in years and far from robust in health, might very well wish to divest himself of those students least likely to perform at concert or even conservatory level, but he had said nothing to her.

"No, of course not," she said as cheerily as she could. "Sweetie, you don't play for Mr. Rosenbaum. You owe him your respect and your hard work, but your relationship with music is between you and music."

Though, even as she said it, she thought of the years, and the sweet sounds of his playing, and the pride she and Jonathan had felt, and yes, also the money. God, so much money. He couldn't quit. Didn't he love music? Didn't he love to play the violin? She realized suddenly that she didn't quite know, and didn't quite want to know.

Henry—now predictably—shrugged again. "Dad said I could quit, if I wanted."

Shocked, Grace stared ahead, at the muted taxi TV screen, on which new Zagat reviews were listed. *L'Horloge*, *Casa Home*, *The Grange*. "Oh?" was all she could manage.

"Last summer. We were up at the lake, and I didn't bring my violin up with me. Remember?"

Grace remembered. She'd been annoyed about that. Those three weeks in the Connecticut house were three weeks of lost practice. "He asked me if I still liked it and I said I wasn't sure. He said life was too short to spend so much time on something I didn't like. He said my main responsibility was to myself, and lots of people go through their whole lives without learning that."

Her head was spinning. *"My main responsibility is to myself"*?

What did that mean? Of course he didn't feel that way. No one who did the work he did could feel that way. Jonathan gave everything to his patients and their families. He took their calls at all hours, got up from his bed to rush to the hospital, put in heartbreaking death vigils during which he frantically searched for some unexplored solution to the problem of a dying child, like a death row attorney on execution day. He was the opposite of a hedonist. He declined most pleasures and all luxuries. His life, and her life, was a life of service to terribly unhappy people, carefully balanced by the precious, personal joy of family love and the modest enjoyment of comforts. *My main responsibility is to myself?* Henry must have misunderstood. She felt as if she'd been hurled up out of the taxi and didn't know where to alight first—on her need to correct this notion as soon as possible, on her own guilt, on her sudden, overpowering resentment of Jonathan, or on the unfamiliarity of that. What had possessed him to say such a thing?

"Do you want to quit?" she asked, willing her voice to be steady.

Another shrug, but this one was softer, slower, as if Henry had tired himself out.

"Tell you what," she said as the taxi turned south on Fifth Avenue, "let's talk about this again in a few months. It's a major decision, and you'd need to be really sure. Maybe there are other things we should be thinking about, like a different teacher. Or maybe there's another instrument you'd like to try."

Though even this took a toll on her. The acerbic and depressive but highly sought Vitaly Rosenbaum was no ordinary violin teacher. Each August, he tested dozens and dozens of boys and girls from families who knew enough to find him, and he permitted just a few to become his students. He had taken Henry on as a four-year-old with a missing front tooth and big hands for his age and perfect pitch obtained from some unknown genetic source, certainly not his parents. And as for other instruments, Grace secretly disliked most of them. True, there was an upright piano in their apartment, a relic of her own enforced lessons as a child, but she had never enjoyed piano music and would have had the thing removed if two attempts to donate it had not proved so discouraging. (Shockingly, no one wanted an out-of-tune, circa 1965 piano of undistinguished make, and the cost of getting it out was totally obscene.) She did not enjoy brass music, woodwind music, or most other string instruments. She liked the violin, and she liked violinists, who had always seemed intent and serene to her. And smart. There had been a girl in her own Rearden class who disappeared early most afternoons, skipping sports practice and after-school clubs, apparently undaunted by her lack of school-related social life; she'd exuded a calmness and confidence Grace had admired. Then, one day when Grace was about ten years old, her mother had brought her to a small, music-burnished chamber adjacent to Carnegie Hall, and there she and a number of her classmates and their mothers all sat for an hour listening to this girl perform a concert of astoundingly complex music, accompanied by a very grown-up, very bald, and very fat pianist. The kids were fidgety in general, but the mothers, Grace's own mother in particular, were rapt. Afterward, Grace's mother had gone to speak to the mother of the girl, a regal woman in classic Chanel, and Grace had stayed in her seat, too embarrassed to congratulate her classmate. The girl had left after seventh grade, bound for homeschooling and an even more intense schedule of violin study, and Grace had lost track of her. But when the time came, she had wanted her own child to play the violin.

"Whatever," she heard him say. Or thought she heard.

CHAPTER FOUR

Fatally Softhearted

Taking one for the team, Grace ended up in the Spensers' vast lobby on the night of the Rearden fund-raiser, checking in the guests and handing out auction booklets at a table in front of the private elevator. It was a bit surprising how few of the parents she knew by name. Some of the mothers were familiar, part of the regular three-fifteen crowd at pickup. These women squinted at Grace as they clicked across the marble floor, perhaps rummaging about for her name, perhaps not even sure whether she was one of them or merely someone efficient hired for the occasion; then, opting to err on the side of caution, they greeted her with a noncommittal, "Hi there! Nice to see you!" The men were complete strangers. One or two she had actually attended Rearden with years earlier, though their childhood faces seemed to float behind a scrim of years and prosperity. Most of them, though, she had never laid eyes on; save the occasional parent-teacher conference or disciplinary intervention, they had not crossed the school's threshold since their initial admissions interviews (which they always made time for, of course), and Grace didn't doubt that they were attending a school function on a Saturday night under significant domestic duress.

"We've got an amazing auction," she told a woman whose lips

were so swollen, Grace had to wonder if the mild-looking and distracted man beside her had recently hit her in the face. "The view is unbelievable," she said to one of the moms in Henry's class, who could barely contain her eagerness to get upstairs. "And the Pollocks in the dining room. Don't miss them." And when the rush ebbed after seven thirty, she found herself alone in the immense marble lobby, tapping a fingernail against the surface of the table they had set up for her and wondering how long she was supposed to stay here.

Being on the fund-raiser committee was Grace's one and only volunteer role at Rearden, and she was happy enough to do it, though she was the first to acknowledge how crazy the entire endeavor had become. Once, not so many years before, these events had been distinguished by their specifically unglamorous charm, with distinctly cheesy decorations and the retro glam of the menu: cheese fondue and pigs in blankets, washed down with some highly alcoholic concoction of yesteryear. They had been sort of jolly parties, not too serious, and the auctions lots of fun, with people getting tipsy and bidding for a session with a personal trainer or a walk-on role in *One Life to Live*. Everyone had a good time, and twenty or thirty thousand went into the till, en route to the school's scholarship fund, so that not all of the kids were children of privilege and students like, she supposed, Miguel Alves could make the school a more diverse and interesting place. That wasn't a bad thing, she reminded herself. That was a laudable thing. And this new incarnation of the school fund-raiser, which she—snob that she was—found so distasteful, was only a bigger, better version of that laudable thing, raising more money (way, *way* more money) for its admirable cause. Which ought to make her happy. But did not.

Grace lingered on in the lobby at her little table. She was moving the few remaining name tags around like a three-card monte dealer and fingering her left earlobe, which hurt just a bit more than the right earlobe, which was also hurting. She was wearing a pair of large diamond earrings, clip-ons that had once belonged to her mother (who, like Grace, did not have pierced ears). Grace had decided that they were more than appropriate for a duplex of staggering size, overlooking a front lawn comprising Central Park, and had built her outfit around them: a silk shirt in basic black (her go-to color, like that of so many of her Manhattan sisters), her highest heels (which brought her to Jonathan's exact height), and the shantung silk pants in highly hot pink, a purchase that surprised no one more than herself when she found them at Bergdorf's the previous fall. This was precisely what to wear when cowering before a Jackson Pollock or explaining to some captain of industry, who clearly cared not at all, that she was a therapist in private practice.

The earrings were part of a collection of somewhat ostentatious pieces that had been presented to Marjorie Reinhart, piece by piece, over the years, by Grace's father, Frederich, and which Grace still kept in a mirrored vanity her mother had owned, in the bedroom that had once been her parents' and was now hers and Jonathan's. There were, among many other items, a pin comprising a large pink rock of something grasped by little gold hands against a misshapen gold surface, a fat jade necklace her father had found who knew where, a leopard-print bracelet of black and yellow diamonds, a sapphire necklace, and a necklace of chunky, oddly proportioned gold links. What they all had in common was their very—how, really, could one avoid this word?—vulgarity. Everything seemed larger than it needed to be: big links of gold, big rocks, a certain quality of "look at me" in the designs. How her father could have chosen so poorly for her elegant mother was almost sweet, it occurred to her. Her father was such an oaf in this department that when he walked into a jewelry store to get his wife a present, he must have been easy prey for any bigger-is-better salesman. The jewels were a representation of someone doing his best to say *I love you* and someone else doing her best to say *I know*.

Tap, tap, tap with her fingernail, manicured for the occasion.

Grace removed the clip-on earrings and placed them in her evening bag—she couldn't take it anymore. Then she rubbed her earlobes in relief and scanned the empty lobby, as if that would somehow move things along. Twenty minutes had passed without a single guest's arrival, and only five forlorn name tags remained unclaimed on the table: Jonathan and two missing couples Grace didn't know. Everyone else was upstairs, including the rest of the committee, the headmaster, and the large group he had arrived with (from the pre-event "Cocktails with the Headmaster" party held at the very apartment where Linsey of the Birkins had once told Grace that the doorman could hail her a taxi). She had even seen Malaga Alves come past her table, though she had not stopped. Which was just as well, since there had been no waiting name tag for her. She wasn't surprised, and she wasn't upset, that Jonathan hadn't arrived yet. Jonathan's eight-year-old patient had died two days before, a horrible thing that never got less horrible, despite the fact that it happened over and over again. The parents were Orthodox Jews and the funeral had been held almost immediately, so Jonathan had gone to that, and this afternoon he had gone back to Brooklyn to pay a shiva call at the family's apartment in Williamsburg. He would stay as long as he needed to stay, and then he would come here. That was all.

Grace did not know the child's name. She was not even sure whether it was a boy or a girl. When Jonathan told her about the patient, Grace had thought with appreciation of that barrier they both maintained, or labored to maintain, between the life of their home and family and his life of the hospital. Because of that slender barrier, the dead child was only *the patient*, *the eight-year-old*, which was bad enough. But how much worse, for her, if she'd known more?

"I'm sorry," Grace had said when he told her about the shiva call and that he would probably be late.

And Jonathan had said: "Me too. I hate cancer."

And that had nearly made her smile. He said this very often and had said it for years, just like this: as a matter of fact, a matter of benign opinion. He had first said it to her many years before, in his dorm room at the medical school in Boston, though back then it had sounded like a battle cry. *Jonathan Sachs, about to be an intern, one day to be a pediatric oncologist specializing in solid tumors, hated cancer, so cancer had better watch its back! Cancer's days were numbered! Cancer had been put on notice, and payback was a bitch!* Today, there was no bravado left. He still hated cancer, more than when he was a student, more with every lost patient, more today than yesterday. But cancer didn't give a rat's ass how he felt.

Grace had hated having to remind him about A Night for Rearden, to distract him with that from the pain of children and the dread fear of parents. But she had to. The fund-raiser. The school. The Spensers. The three apartments combined into one: an urban McMansion, she had called it when she'd first described it for him weeks earlier. Jonathan remembered everything, only there was so much on his mind that it wasn't always completely accessible. It needed to be called up, like a book at the New York Public Library. Sometimes it took a little time.

"Grace," he had said, "I hope you haven't had to waste a lot of energy on this. Can't you leave it to the women who don't work? You have far more important things to do than raise money for a private school."

But it was about the participation, she had said tersely. He knew that.

And they didn't have enough money to mitigate her nonparticipation. He knew that, too.

And all of it had come up before, of course. In a long marriage, everything has come up before: circulating currents of familiarity, both warm and cool. Of course they couldn't agree on everything.

He would just...get here when he got here. And if anyone wanted to know why he was not here, she would be glad to enlighten them, because her husband had a little too much on his plate to make time for everyone else's sick fascination with what he did for a living.

It was something no one else seemed to understand about Jonathan, that you had to dig such a small way into his general affability before you hit a man who was perpetually, brutally affected by human suffering. People felt emboldened by Jonathan's matter-of-factness on subjects like cancer and the death of children, but when they broached these dreaded subjects, they did it in a way that was almost accusatory: *How can you do what you do? How can you stand to see children in pain? Isn't it terrible when a patient you have cared for dies of the disease? Why would you go out of your way to choose that specialty?*

Sometimes, Jonathan actually tried to answer these questions, but it never helped, because despite people's obvious scrounging for the details, most of them just couldn't handle the stuff he carried around all day, and they almost always stalked off to find someone with a more upbeat profession to talk to. Over the years, Grace had watched some variation on this script at dinner parties and camp visiting days and previous Rearden fund-raisers, always with a sinking heart, because they reminded her that this pleasant mom from Henry's second-grade class, and the terrific couple who'd rented a house on their lake one summer, and the radio talk show host who lived two floors above them (the closest their building had to a celebrity) were almost certainly not going to become their friends. Once, she had simply assumed their social life would necessarily be populated by oncologists, people living within the same constriction of intense emotions as Jonathan, and their partners, but in fact those relationships never really developed either—probably, Grace decided, because Jonathan's colleagues had the modest goal of leaving cancer behind in the hospital when they departed the building, and perhaps they were better at doing that than her husband was. Years ago, the two of them had socialized a bit with Stu Rosenfeld, the oncologist who still covered Jonathan's practice if he had to be away for some reason, and Stu's wife, and that had been agreeable. The Rosenfelds were passionate theatergoers who always seemed to know, months in advance, which tickets were going to be impossible to secure and ended up sitting in the fourth row next to Elaine Stritch on the first Saturday after the *New York Times* rave. She admired rather than liked Tracy Rosenfeld, who was Korean-American, an attorney, and a fanatical runner, but it felt good to be out with another couple, enjoying the city and its pleasures. The two women dragged their husbands away from the default topics (hospital personalities, hospital politics, children with cancer) and generally pretended to be better friends than they actually were while discussing Sondheim and Wasserstein and the general disgrace of John Simon's hostilities in *New York* magazine. It was all fairly innocuous, and it might still be going on, except that Jonathan had come home one day about five years earlier and reported that Stu had said the most extraordinary thing to him, about a plan for dinner (nothing elaborate, just a Sunday night at a restaurant they all liked on the West Side) that had fallen apart a couple of times. Stu had said that he was sorry, but maybe for now they would just keep things professional. Tracy was up for partner and . . . well . . .

"Well?" Grace had asked, heat streaming into her cheeks. "Well what?"

"Did you and Tracy . . . quarrel about something?" Jonathan had asked her, and she'd had that sudden guilty feeling that came over you when you were sure you had done nothing wrong, or at least nearly sure, because how could you ever be *sure*? People hid their tender places. Sometimes you just couldn't know when you were hitting some nerve.

So they'd stopped seeing the Rosenfelds, except at hospital-related events, but there were precious few of those, or occasionally by chance at the theater, where they always chatted in a friendly way and talked about getting together for dinner sometime, which neither of them ever followed up on, like countless other couples who were crazy-busy with work, whatever the underlying intention.

Jonathan never mentioned this again. He was used to loss, of course, and not just in the sense of loss—to death—because of terrible, grueling, painful, and merciless disease. There had been other losses, not to be slighted because the parties in question might still be among the technically living and no farther distant than, say, Long Island. This, in Grace's personal and indeed professional opinion, had everything to do with the family he had grown up in, the parents who had failed him in almost every way short of violence or physical harm, and the brother who had never understood that he, too, would be harmed by losing that fraternal connection. Jonathan didn't need many people in his life, and he never had, at least as long as Grace had known him, so long as he had his own family: the one he had made with Grace and Henry.

Then, as the years passed, she started to feel that way as well, and she, too, started to let people go. It was harder in the beginning—hardest *at* the beginning when Vita dematerialized—then less and less as the one or two friends from graduate school drifted off, and the Kirkland House friends (now scattered everywhere in any case and convening only for weddings), and the one or two others from nowhere in particular whose company she had enjoyed. She and Jonathan were not reclusive people, obviously. They took an active part in the city's life, their days were full of human beings and their troubles. And if she never thought of herself as, precisely, a sweet person or a soft person—that wasn't a terrible thing. She cared very much about her patients and what they did or experienced when they left her office. Of course she did. And there had been plenty of middle-of-the-night phone calls for her, too, over the years, and she had always taken them and done what she needed to do, even meeting distraught men and women in emergency rooms or getting on the phone with dispatchers and paramedics and intake specialists at hospitals and rehabs all over the country. But her default setting was "off," not "on," and if she did not have to worry about their anxiety or their depression or whether they were going to meetings every day as promised, then she generally did not worry.

Jonathan, though, was a very different animal. Jonathan was just fatally softhearted, a profoundly humane and selfless person, capable of comforting the dying child and the almost bereaved parents with the right words and the right touch, giving hope and removing it deftly, kindly, when it had no place anymore. There had been times when he was so twisted with sadness about what he had left on the wards, or even in the morgue, that he could not speak to them when he got home and would go into his study at the back of the apartment, in the room they had once hoped would belong to a second child, taking himself out of the family equation until he could get free of it.

Once, the autumn they'd met, she had arrived at the hospital where he was doing his internship and watched him hold an elderly woman who physically shook in his arms. The woman's son, a middle-aged man with Down syndrome, had been dying nearby of his congenital heart defect, a death that could not have been unexpected since the moment of his birth, yet the woman had been howling with grief. Grace, who'd arrived a few minutes before Jonathan's thirty-six-hour shift was due to end, had stood at the end of the corridor watching this, feeling the shame of her own observance, the contamination she knew she was bringing to this purest human interaction.

She was already, that year, her last in college, a student of behavior, a dedicated future practitioner of the art of healing human pain, subcategory: psychic. And yet, and yet... the sonic boom of the suffering she saw at the other end of that long hospital corridor very nearly knocked her back. The power of it... no one had mentioned that in her senior seminar on Freud's Dora or the fascinating course she had taken junior year on abnormal psychology. There had been wheels and cogs and mice running through mazes, theories and drug trials and various forms of therapy: aversion, primal, art and music, and dull, inefficient talk. But this . . . she could hardly bear to be so close to it, which wasn't very close at all.

The truth was that Jonathan found suffering everywhere—or, more accurately, it seemed to find him: wherever it might be hiding or lying dormant, waiting for a passing soul to stick to. He collected the random sadness of strangers and the confessions of the guilty. Taxi drivers offered him their bereavements. He could not pass the doormen downstairs without taking on some discouraging report of the paralyzed nephew or the parent sinking into dementia. He couldn't eat at their regular Italian place on Third without asking the owner whether his daughter's cystic fibrosis was responding to the new drug, a conversation that had never once ended with less than utter dejection. When the three of them were alone together, he could be buoyant, which was one reason Grace protected their family time so efficiently, but out there people seemed unable to resist taking advantage of his good nature.

Perhaps what it came down to was that in spite of his personal suffering, he did not seem to fear pain the way others did, but instead dove straight into its whirlwind, determined to keep thrashing away, as if he would ever—*ever*—be capable of dealing it the slightest blow. She loved and admired that about him, she supposed, but it exhausted her, too. And sometimes it worried her. Cancer, obviously, would defeat him in the end. The struggles people endured, and the infinite varieties of sadness they carried—those would never ease, even a tiny bit. And all of that left him so vulnerable. She had tried to express this to Jonathan more than once. She had tried to make him understand that his very decency, amid the less-decency of others in the world, might come to harm him in some way, but he generally declined to see it. He could never seem to think as badly of other people as she could.

CHAPTER FIVE

Access to the Quick of Things

When she stepped off the elevator and into the now packed space of the Spensers' foyer, Grace immediately saw that their hosts' absence had become the topic of the evening. Sally, in particular, was still visibly reeling from the unexpected news that both Spensers not only had failed to meet with them before the party, but were not expected to join their guests at any point in the evening. Jonas, they were told, was in China—this was less egregious—but Suki's whereabouts were unknown. She might have been across town or at her Hamptons compound. She might have been elsewhere in the epic apartment, for all the eager benefit committee knew, but it didn't really matter: she was not where they had all imagined she would be, which was with her fellow parents in the Spenser abode. Sally had been apoplectic, her state rendered almost comical by the difficulty she was having maintaining her veneer of jolly gratitude in front of the Spensers' staff.

At the little table in the lobby, only one arriving guest had asked Grace outright if the Spensers were upstairs at the party. "I think he's in Asia," she had said, keeping it vague, as she assumed Sally would wish. But Sally evidently did not wish. Sally seemed to have decided that everyone must be brought up to speed on the situation. Now, as Grace watched from the foyer with a glass of champagne in her hand—Sylvia had brought her the champagne, and Grace had gratefully accepted it—Sally could be seen in clear spin mode, flitting from group to group, watching, pollinating the party like an unhappy hummingbird, trailing a distinct odor of panic behind her. Grace and Sylvia drank their champagne and watched her make her way. Earlier, the two of them had tried hard to calm Sally down. The apartment was breathtaking, they reminded her. With its oversize rooms and MoMA-worthy art, it had not one thing to apologize for, and if the guests were disappointed to find that its owner, a media titan of global stature, was not in attendance, they would at least revel in the glories of the space. Media titans of global stature might understandably be somewhere more important than a school fund-raiser (most of the guests, when you got right down to it, might understandably be somewhere more important than a school fund-raiser), and the men would not notice, let alone care, that his wife was similarly missing. The women were another story. It was the women who were going to twist the knife when they realized that both Spensers had skipped the party. But that would be later, after the bidding was over and the checks written. Wasn't that the whole point?

In the actual Spensers' place stood a cordon of their attendants: the secretary, who was in charge, and at least ten uniformed guards stationed around the rooms and protecting the doors to more private areas of the apartment, who reported to her. (This, of course, in addition to the maids and servers and two Caribbean women Grace saw emerge from the kitchen, carrying dinner trays and passing through one of the blockaded doorways to parts unknown.) The effect, the inescapable effect, was that of an event thrown in some opulent but ultimately rentable public space—a Newport mansion, say, or the Temple of Dendur—not of a parent's home thrown open to the parents of their children's schoolmates. Grace, who had earlier quelled her own disappointment, knew precisely what Sally had hoped for, if not expected outright: witty, personal anecdotes about the artwork and the trouble taken to find just this damask for the living room curtains, perhaps even a peek inside the famous closets (Suki Spenser was a "Best Dressed" regular). She knew that Sally (like Grace herself, she had to admit) had hoped to see the vast and elaborately detailed larder, which Suki, native to Hokkaido, had apparently stocked with a comprehensive array of Japanese ingredients—in *Vanity Fair*, Grace had read that the Spenser children followed a strictly macrobiotic diet—or that ultimate manifestation of New York real estate porn, the large laundry room photographed in *Architectural Digest*, with three uniformed laundresses ironing the zillion-thread-count sheets. But with access to all but the most ceremonial rooms emphatically blocked, such personal gestures were obviously not to be experienced, and Sally seemed to be experiencing real difficulty in making the adjustment. In the hour before A Night for Rearden formally began, she ricocheted through the public spaces (followed closely by two of the uniformed guards), straightening the auction table and checking the temporary bar (erected in the foyer, beneath its grand staircase), with Sylvia and Grace in her wake. She was perhaps compensating her disappointment by indulging in a fantasy that she herself was the lady of this urban manor. Certainly she had dressed this part, in a scary, tiger-patterned Roberto Cavalli that showed quite enough of her large (but at least natural) breasts, and teetery-tall heels. She dripped, literally, with diamonds, a real-life version, Grace could not help thinking, of a little girl's play set of plastic necklace, earrings, bracelet, and ring.

"Look at Malaga," Sylvia said suddenly, and Grace looked where she was looking. Malaga Alves stood framed by one of the great windows, holding a glass of red wine in one hand, the other wedged uncomfortably behind her back. She looked awkward and very alone, but she was alone for only an instant. As Grace and Sylvia watched, a captivating scene began to unfold, as first one dinner-jacketed man and then a second—this one being Nathan Friedberg, he of the $25,000 summer camp—came to join her. She looked up at them and smiled, and when she did Grace saw the transition—no, the *transformation*—that occurred. At first, she did not quite recognize what she was seeing, as Malaga stood between the two tall men—one handsome, one not—and seemed to open (as Fitzgerald might have said) like a flower, somehow becoming arrestingly sumptuous. Malaga wore a simple rosy dress, cut close but not tight around her postpartum body, ending just above a shapely knee. Around her neck was the gold cross, and she wore no other jewelry. She smiled tentatively at them, inclining a lovely neck first to one and then to the other of the men, and Grace was newly aware of her smooth skin, her undoubtedly natural décolletage (sufficiently displayed to convey its true-life contours), and her just slightly abundant upper arms, so aggressively untoned. So . . . Grace reached for the right word . . . *womanly*.

There was a third man beside her now, a portly guy Grace recognized vaguely as the father of a girl in Henry's class—something at Morgan Stanley. Very, very rich. All three men were talking to Malaga Alves, or to one another over her head, as she looked up at them. She herself didn't seem to be talking or even doing much agreeing with whatever they might be saying. The three of them flapped and dipped, hovering within reach. As she and Sylvia stared, a fourth man came, pretending to greet one of his predecessors before turning his attention fully to Malaga Alves.

To Grace, no neophyte as a student of human social interaction, it was a stunning display of raw attraction. Malaga Alves might have features that were unremarkable in themselves (and she was plump! with extra flesh in her cheeks, neck, and arms!), but somehow the sum of their parts was another animal altogether. Grace, watching the men, felt amused and sort of disgusted, appalled at their hypocrisy. It was more than likely, for example, that these four had employees who resembled Malaga Alves, women with the same flat features and creamy skin and fleshy waists and breasts and thighs beneath their classically understated uniforms. Quite probably, they interacted with women who looked like Malaga Alves many times a day in the course of their work or in their own homes. Women who looked like Malaga Alves might at this exact moment be tending to their children or doing their laundry. But did they behave around those familiar women as they were apparently behaving around this unfamiliar one? Not if they wanted to stay married, she thought.

The magnificent room was full of highly tended women, acknowledged (even celebrated) beauties who were aerobicized and massaged, colored and coiffed, mani-pedied and Brazilled, and clothed in the most editorialized clothing, yet the distinct aroma of attraction in the crowd came from the place occupied by Malaga Alves. It was remarkably pure and powerful, a force plainly capable of toppling titans, yet it seemed undetectable by any of the sparkling sisterhood. This siren song, Grace thought, her gaze sweeping the crowd from gilded walls to glittering windows, was apparently detectable by the Y chromosome alone.

Grace gave her glass to one of the waiters and went to help Sally, who was half herding, half leading the crowd from the foyer into the great living room so that the auction could begin. Sylvia collected her friend, once a struggling trigonometry student, now apparently the head of American furniture at Sotheby's. He was bald and very thin and thoughtfully wore a silk bow tie of green and blue (Rearden's school colors), and Sylvia led him to the podium in the corner of the room. "Hello!" Sally trilled into the microphone, then tapped it with a long fingernail until people stopped talking and covered their ears.

"Is this on?" she asked.

Resoundingly, the crowd gave her to understand that it was.

"Hello!" said Sally. "Before I do anything, I'd like to ask for a round of applause for our hosts, Jonas and Suki Spenser. What a magnificent and gracious offer this was," she said rather disingenuously. "We are so grateful."

The parents applauded. Grace applauded, too.

"I also want to thank our very hardworking committee," Sally was saying. "They strong-armed you all into coming here, and made sure you had good things to eat and lots of great stuff to spend your money on. Amanda Emery? Where are you, Amanda?"

Amanda chirped, "Hello!" from the back of the room, and waved a glittering cuff above her bright blond head.

"Sylvia Steinmetz? Grace Sachs?"

Grace lifted her own hand, suppressing the automatic irritation. She was not "Grace Sachs," ever. Not that she disliked the name or its superficial "Our Crowd" associations (Jonathan's branch, however, had had nothing to do with Warburgs, Loebs, and Schiffs; his people had come from a shtetl in eastern Poland, via Boston), but it wasn't her name. She was Reinhart, at all times: Reinhart at work, Reinhart on the cover of her almost-a-book, and Reinhart on every single document related to the Rearden School, including her listing on the auction program. Strangely enough, the only person who ever referred to her as Grace Sachs was her own father.

"And I'm Sally Morrison-Golden," said Sally, pausing for acknowledgment. "I'm so delighted that we've come together tonight, to celebrate our wonderful school and do what we can to make our children's educational experience the best it can possibly be. Now I know," she went on with a merry grin, "some of you may be thinking, 'Don't I already pay enough tuition?' "

The expected nervous laughter rippled uneasily through the crowd.

"And of course, you do. But it's our responsibility to make sure that Rearden can accept the students it wants to accept, and that those students will be able to attend the school despite their financial circumstances."

Really? thought Grace. *Since when?* The crowd clapped halfheartedly.

"And of course," said Sally, "it's also up to us to see that our wonderful teachers are so well paid that we don't lose them to other schools. We love our teachers!"

"*Right on!*" said someone over by the Jackson Pollocks, causing a surge of laughter, for the archaic expression if not for the sentiment. Of course it was true that Rearden valued its teachers, thought Grace. Just not enough to invite them to tonight's event. But how many could have dropped $300 on a ticket?

"So I hope you've all brought your checkbooks, people, because while we are certainly here to drink beautiful wine, eat fantastic food, and check out the view, the bottom line is the bottom line!" Sally grinned at the crowd, delighted with her own cleverness. "We accept Visa, MasterCard, American Express Black Cards! Stocks and bonds!"

"Artworks!" chimed in Amanda Emery. "Real estate!"

People laughed awkwardly.

"And now," said Sally, "before we roll up our sleeves and get down to the serious business of spending money, our own Mr. Chips, Robert Conover, would like to extend an official welcome. Robert?"

The headmaster waved from a far corner of the long room and began making his way toward Sally.

Grace let her mind wander as he began to say all of the expected things, lingering on the thank-yous (again) and reminding them all (again) why the money was needed, and what a wonderful thing it was to be able to honor the superlative education their kids were receiving, and how much that meant to the teachers. Then Grace let her gaze wander, too. On a small table beside her sat Sylvia, her laptop at the ready to record the bids. The time, plainly visible on the laptop screen, was 8:36, which meant that Jonathan was now more than merely running late, he was seriously late. She looked first at the bodies at the edges of the room, then made a grid of the crowd and worked it, left to right, back to front. He wasn't there. He wasn't in any of the doorways. He wasn't in the little group that, at that moment, erupted into the foyer, comprising the missing couples from the pre-K class, who must have come together following a private celebration of their own and were perhaps already too drunk to have noticed the coatrack in the lobby. They came in a dark bubble of cashmere and fur, laughing at something undoubtedly fully separate from A Night for Rearden, until one of them realized what an entrance they were making and hushed the other three. He wasn't with them, a part of their revelry. He wasn't behind them in the private elevator, which had released them into the apartment and then gone away.

So. The shiva call was taking longer than he'd thought, they had pressed food upon him, or the mother would not let him go away, because when her child's doctor went away her child would have gone away as well, or there was a minyan to say kaddish, and he would have had to stay for that, or at least to nod along with it, since she doubted he knew it by heart—even after all these years of funerals. It astounded her that he could bear another shiva call, another devastated family, another kaddish. The burden he carried, those kids and their terrified parents—it was another world from the imperviousness and entitlement in this room, she thought, looking around at the others, at their faces, a little flushed, nodding happily at whatever surely reassuring thing the headmaster was telling them, perhaps that their healthy, nurtured children had ranked well on some newly commissioned analysis of New York private schools or that they were on track for a higher rate of Ivy League acceptances than Trinity and Riverdale. They were smiling in harmony and laughing as if being conducted from the podium. And why not? All was well in their world, high above the city: these men who spun money out of other money, and the women who lined their nests with it, and even the shared endeavor at hand: to make "charitable donations" to—what an incredible coincidence!—their own children's school. How could it even occupy the same planet with what her husband was doing right now? She imagined him in that little apartment in Crown Heights, toe-to-toe with the others, a square of torn fabric pinned to his coat, shaking hands and bowing his head for the prayers and feeling—she knew this perfectly well—as if he had failed utterly.

Who knew when he might arrive. Who knew *if* he might arrive, she admitted to herself. And for a little moment she allowed the mildest surge of resentment to push at her. But then that went away and was followed by a surge of terrible guilt.

She really hated herself sometimes.

Right out of the gate, the Sotheby's auctioneer went off script.

"Observe," he said. He was holding up a half-full glass of water, an ordinary glass. Grace, who was pretty sure she knew where this was going, didn't dare look at Sally. "My own donation to Rearden School, the reason we're all here. I hereby offer for sale a glass of tap water, from the kitchen sink. Ordinary New York City tap water. Any of you could have gone out to the kitchen and poured it yourself."

No, they couldn't have, thought Grace.

"So let me ask you something—what is the value of this glass of water? What is it really worth to you?" He looked them over. He had done this, or something like this, many times, obviously, but he still relished it, that was equally obvious.

"Is that glass half-full or half-empty?" said a man at the back.

The auctioneer smiled. "What am I bid?" He raised it overhead.

"A thousand," said someone in the center of the room. It was Nathan Friedberg.

"Ah!" said the auctioneer. "Now this glass of water is worth a thousand dollars. Does that mean, sir, that you are willing to donate one thousand dollars to the Parents' Association of Rearden School in exchange for possession of this glass of water?"

Nathan Friedberg laughed. His wife, Grace saw, stood beside him, clutching her equally ordinary wineglass with one rock-encrusted hand and her husband's elbow with the other.

"No," he said, grinning, "but I am willing to donate two thousand dollars."

The crowed seemed to let off tension in a hiss of movement and breath.

"Now this glass of water is worth two thousand dollars." The auctioneer nodded approvingly. "It's that point in the evening when we pause to remind ourselves why we're here. Do we need a free ticket to see a Broadway show? Probably not. Can we make our own arrangements to rent an apartment in Paris? Of course we can. But that isn't the point of our gathering. We are here because giving our money to the school our children attend is *worth* our while. These objects we're about to auction off are *worth* our money. Though I have to say"—he grinned—"I've seen a lot of auctions, and you people really know how to put together a great auction."

"Three thousand," said Simon Golden, lifting his hand.

"Thank you!" the auctioneer said, raising the glass of now highly valuable water in approbation. "I did mention, didn't I, that I fully intend to collect on this item?"

Everyone laughed now. Another husband entered the fray, then another. The number rose, $1,000 per bid. The auctioneer held up the glass again when it reached $11,000. It was as if even he felt it was wrong to go higher. "Any further bids? Fair warning."

There were no more bids.

"Sold! One glass of New York tap water, *aqua Giuliani*, to the gentleman in the very attractive blue tie, for eleven thousand dollars. Sir? Your water."

Amid thunderous applause, Nathan Friedberg made his way to the front of the room, took the glass from the auctioneer's outstretched hand, and drained his prize. "Delicious!" he reported. "Worth every penny."

And with this testosterone throw-down, the auction proper began. Trips and jewelry, a chef's table at Blue Hill, tickets to the Tony Awards, a week at Canyon Ranch... the bids came and came on a cushion of helium, each crisp tap of the auctioneer's gavel on the podium followed by a little collective ecstatic sigh. Sally was beside herself, Grace could see. Only halfway through the roster of lots, they were ahead of their projections for the entire evening.

It was absurd, but it wasn't out of the ordinary—even Grace knew that. At Dalton, someone had auctioned a visit to the Oval Office for the winning bidder's child. At Spence, somebody bought the right to sit next to Anna Wintour at a show during Fashion Week (conversation with the great arbiter of taste, presumably, not included). At Collegiate, there was a rumor about face-to-face interviews with the deans of admission at Yale and Amherst. Access, in other words, and not to something that didn't matter, like backstage at the Garden, though that little item also turned up at private school benefits all over town. Access to information. Access to the quick of things.

She let herself slip out of the room during heated bidding for a week in Montauk and made her way to the bathroom off the foyer, but it was occupied. "Is there another?" she whispered to the inevitable guard, and he inclined his big head to the door those two Caribbean women had disappeared behind an hour earlier. "I can go back there?" she asked.

Back there was a corridor, not very wide, carpeted with some sort of crackly sisal. Miniature chandeliers, all dimmed, hung every ten feet or so, but the old master drawings on the walls had their own illumination, perfect little spotlights that made them glow. Unable to help herself, she stopped before a Rembrandt nude, marveling at the fact that she was not in a museum but in somebody's house, and in a back corridor at that. When she closed the door behind her, the rest of the apartment, and the massive party, seemed to dematerialize completely.

There were rooms along one side of the corridor, like dormitory rooms or rooms in the servants' wing of a great house, which was, Grace supposed, precisely what they were. She thought of those uniformed Caribbean women disappearing through that same door with their dinner plates, relieved—presumably—of their charges, who were either here or not here, in which case they must be with other nannies in other Spenser homes. All the doors were closed. She went along, from drawing to drawing to drawing, as if she were hopping from one lily pad to the next across a river, passing the closed doors as she went. The bathroom finally revealed itself at the end of the hallway, by a light around the edges of the door and a glimpse of blindingly white tile. This door, too, was emphatically shut, and a fan droned inside. And there was water running. And something else. Grace frowned. A sound with which she, like any therapist, was profoundly intimate: the sound of weeping of the most pure, most brokenhearted variety, muffled by hands making an honest attempt to hide the sound. Even after years of watching people weep, of hearing people weep, there was something acute and terrible about this sound. Grace stood a few feet from the door, afraid almost to breathe, unwilling to let the woman add to her suffering the fact that it was being overheard by a stranger.

It wasn't hard to imagine who was in there or what she was crying about. Grace, like any minimally aware New York mother, knew very well that most of the women who cared for the city's children of privilege had children of their own, but those children were usually far away, on other islands, in other countries; how much regret, how much bitterness, must underlie this particular social contract? The subject never came up at the mothers' group or in the lobby at the school—it never crossed that blood-brain barrier between the actual mothers and the caregivers. It was not a secret, of course, but it felt like a secret: brutal and bottomless, a monstrous irony. No wonder she wept, thought Grace, looking at the shut door, still frozen on the sisal runner a few feet away. Perhaps she had left her own children behind in some unlovely home far in every way from this penthouse mansion, to give care and even love to the children of Jonas and Suki Spenser, high above this unfathomably expensive city. Perhaps she had taken this private moment, with the house jammed with strangers and the family away, to indulge the grief of a mother deprived of her children.

Grace took a step back, willing the rushes underfoot not to rustle. They did not. She took another step, and turned, and went out the way she'd come.

Stepping back into the foyer, she felt a vibration in the hand holding her evening purse and removed her cell phone to find a text from Jonathan. He was indeed not at the party—that was no more than she already knew—but the surprising thing was that he had actually been in the Spenser apartment for at least part of the auction. "Got there late bec of shiva," he had typed. "Just got message from hosp about a pt having bad night, will try to make it back later. SORRY."

In Jonathan's life a "pt" was always having a bad night—a little boy or a little girl, just diagnosed, or interrupted by a sudden setback, or abruptly critical. There was always a frantic call from a mom whose bright five-year-old had been felled in an instant, a quivering guillotine materializing overhead like Ezekiel's spinning wheel. There were always parents, enraged by their impotence, liable to explode. Over the years, Jonathan had been hit, wept upon countless times, reasoned with endlessly. He had been summoned to hear confessions: *Had this happened because of the prostitute? Was it because she had been smoking, secretly, for the past four years and even in the pregnancy?* Jonathan's days were a conveyer belt of routine crises, every single one of them life-threatening, life-altering, of all-consuming implications. Even she, who had many times embarked upon an ordinary therapy session that swerved into a brick wall or a black hole to oblivion, could barely imagine the volatility of her husband's daily life.

"Didn't see you," she typed with her thumbs, a skill at which she'd become sadly adept.

"Waved at you like an idiot!" he wrote back.

Grace sighed. There was no point in continuing. At least he had managed to get here.

"See you at home," she typed in. "XX."

"XX," came back. It was their usual electronic parting.

When Jennifer Hartman came out of the bathroom, Grace managed a benign nod at her and went in. Here, another chandelier glittered with enormous, rough shards of glass, dappling the waxed walls. Over the toilet was a Warhol self-portrait, just the thing (Grace couldn't help but feel) to interrupt the flow of male urine. She washed her hands in lavender soap.

They were near the end now. Only the Millionaire Munchkin Camp (as Grace had privately dubbed Nathan Friedberg's entrepreneurial effort) remained, and that went, after a struggle among four, then three, then two, for $30,000—a bargain, Friedberg announced loudly, when you declare it as a nonprofit donation on your taxes. Grace did not recognize the trim European couple who'd made the winning bid.

With that, the auction ended, and in a collective sigh of relief and self-congratulation. Sally, Grace could see, was basking, accepting an embrace from Robert, the headmaster, and from Amanda, who emitted a fairly undignified "Woo-hoo!" as she squeezed her taller friend and made her jump awkwardly up and down, just like Hillary and Tipper at the Democratic convention. Men gave each other vigorous handshakes, sending the ambient congratulatory rush cascading around the room. Then began the exodus. A few couples were already at the door, slipping away discreetly, and there was Malaga Alves, who held up her auction catalog like a blinker or a fan, in front of her face. Apart from their brief greeting downstairs, Grace had not spoken to her and moved quickly, her head down.

A moment later, Robert Conover materialized beside her, one big hand on her shoulder, a rough cheek at her cheek. What a wonderful job she had done, he told Grace. "It's mainly Sally," said Grace. "And the Spensers, of course. We have to give them a lot of the credit."

"Certainly. In absentia."

"Ours is not to reason why." She shrugged. "And personally I would never look this gift view in the mouth. Besides, you have to admit, there's something kind of cool about being here without them. Sort of *Tailor of Gloucester*."

"Perhaps a bit more cats-away-mice-will-play," the headmaster said. "I bet a few of these guys are plotting how to get into the various Spenser sanctums upstairs."

"And the women want to get into the closets!" said Grace.

Robert laughed. "Hell, I want to get into the closets myself."

"Julian couldn't make it?" Grace asked. She had seen the current production at his theater, a dense and decidedly experimental interpretation of Kafka's *Trial* that she would have loved to talk about.

"Sadly," Robert said, "at a conference at the Taper in L.A. Where's yours? I saw him during the auction."

"Oh, he had a call from the hospital. He had to go back."

She watched as the customary spasm crossed Robert's features. This happened often when the word *hospital* was mentioned in relation to her husband.

"God," said Robert, right on cue. "How does he do it?"

She sighed. "It's all about what they can do for the kids. The forward progress."

"There is forward progress, then?"

"Oh, of course," said Grace. "Not as fast as anyone would like. But yes."

"I don't know how he even gets through those doors every day. When Julian's mother was there—she had colon cancer…"

"I'm sorry," Grace said automatically.

"Yes. She was there for a month about four years ago, and then another few weeks at the end. When it was over and we walked out for the last time, I thought, *I hope I never have to be inside this building for the rest of my life*. I mean, everywhere you look: pain, pain, pain."

Yes, yes, she thought, maintaining her most professional compassion. If Jonathan were here, he would be telling Robert Conover that, yes, the work was intense, yes, the emotions were powerful, but he felt privileged to be allowed into people's lives at these very moments of emotion and intensity, when their instinct might understandably be to circle the wagons and ask everybody to please go away, because the worst thing that has ever happened, the worst thing they could imagine ever happening, was happening right now, to their son or daughter. Jonathan would be saying that he might not be able to fix the child who was his patient, but almost always he could make things a little bit better, and that included taking away pain, which meant something to him and meant something to the child's family. He had been asked some variation on "How do you do it?" hundreds of times—hundreds of times in her presence alone—and he would always respond to it without the smallest shred of irritation and with a broad smile.

But he wasn't here. And she did not feel authorized to deliver his lines.

"It's very difficult," she said to Robert.

"Oh, my God. I mean, I could not even stay functional around that." He turned to greet, in a hearty but nonspecific way, a man who slung a heavy arm onto his shoulder as he passed by toward the elevator. Then he turned back. "I'd be no use to anyone. I'd just bawl constantly. I mean, I even lose it when the kids get rejected by their first-choice colleges."

"Well," Grace said dryly, "that is tragedy on a cosmic scale."

"No, seriously," he said. Apparently, he wanted a serious response.

"It's a very hard job, but he gets to help people, so it's worth it."

Robert nodded, though he did not seem satisfied. Grace, belatedly, wondered why this sort of thing didn't fall within the spectrum of rudeness. Would you say to the guy who pumps out the septic tank, *How you can do that?* But she tried to give Robert the benefit of her considerable doubt. She did like Robert.

"I have some excellent news about your little scholar. He's doing very, very well, you know."

Grace smiled awkwardly. It was not a surprise that Henry was excelling, of course. He was so smart—that was not a virtue, just an accident of DNA—but he worked hard enough that you didn't begrudge his winning of the cerebral lottery. He wasn't one of those kids who coasted or, worse, submarined their own potential because they resented it, or resented that it was important to the people around them. Still, it was odd to be discussing this now, as if they were at some big, social parent-teacher conference where people got dressed in their finery to find out how their kids were doing in school.

"He loves his math teacher this year," Grace said truthfully.

At that moment, Sally Morrison-Golden bounded up and gripped Robert around the shoulders, possibly as much to steady herself as to express affection. She was, Grace saw, more than just a mite drunk. She teetered a bit on her very high heels and sported a faint half-moon of pink lipstick on her left cheekbone. Sometime after the evening's take had been tallied—or even just estimated—she must have cut loose. She was now exceptionally loose.

"What a wonderful night," Robert told her.

"Oh, rah," she slurred sarcastically. "Nice of our hosts to show up, wasn't it?"

Still? thought Grace. "Doesn't matter," she told Sally. "We've had a great time and we did really well. Can you believe this apartment, Robert?" she said.

"If I lived here, I'd be home now," Robert said affably. "And I'd own that Francis Bacon over the couch. Which would be nice." He kissed them both on the cheek and left them. Grace was not sorry to see him go.

"Did Malaga find you?" Sally said. "She was looking for you before."

"Find me?" Grace frowned. "What for?"

"God, can you believe all those men she had drooling on her? They were like Pavlov's dogs. Amanda and I were like, 'I'll have what she's having.' Jilly Friedberg just about lost it. She literally went and dragged her husband away."

Grace, who was a bit sorry to have missed this moment, gave a noncommittal smile. "She did look very pretty," she said.

Sally seemed to wobble a bit. She moved her feet as if she were *en pointe*, which, given the height of her heels, she very nearly was. Then she, too, lurched off in the direction of the dining room. Grace, who really wanted to leave, went to find Sylvia.

"Can we leave?" she asked her. "Do you think it's all right?"

"I think it's more than all right. I think it's required," Sylvia said. "Did you see the way those guards are looking at us? They want us o-u-t."

"Okay, then," Grace said, relieved. She had been sure the staff would not want them to linger, but she'd also worried that Sally would want to remain as long as possible, perhaps even calling a postmortem beneath the Jackson Pollocks. "I'm going. I'm really beat."

"Where's Jonathan?" asked Sylvia. "I thought I saw him before."

"Yes, he was here," said Grace. "But he got a call about a patient in the hospital. He had to go back."

"To Sloan-Kettering?" asked Sylvia, as if Jonathan had ever worked anywhere else.

She wondered if she was about to face another round of "How does he do it?" but mercifully Sylvia seemed to contain herself. She said nothing, and Grace managed to get away before anyone else could stop her. She wanted to be home when Jonathan arrived, to be waiting for him in case he needed her. And if experience was her guide, he might very well need her. He had just helped bury an eight-year-old in Brooklyn, and now he had another patient in crisis in the hospital. He was going to be in terrible shape, whenever he made it home. He felt these things so deeply.

PART II

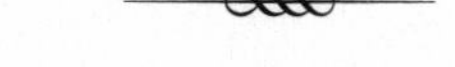

DURING

CHAPTER SIX

Not for Much Longer

The end came not with a bang and not with a whimper, but with the silent blink of the envelope icon on her cell phone. The icon had been programmed, once upon a time, to flash once for a single message, twice for a second message, and so on, until it hit some sort of inner, critical mass of messages, at which point it just blinked in perpetuity, like a fluttering wing of iridescent green at the corner of her cell phone. Later she would remember that blink, so ordinary that she had ignored it through the first patients of the morning (a couple fighting a doomed fight to remain married), and her second appointment (with a long-term patient on the threshold of a manic episode), and even through a lunch break she'd devoted to a pre-interview with a producer from *Today*.

Four days had passed since the fund-raiser, A Night for Rearden.

The *Today* appearance would not take place until after the new year, but with the holiday coming up, the producer explained, they were trying to get ahead of things. "And they gave you the breaking news speech already?"

Grace said no. They hadn't, but wasn't it obvious?

"Yeah, this kind of story can get tossed around a little, if something comes up."

The interviewer's name was Cindy Elder. Grace had jotted the name on a pad, an old habit from years of speaking to potential clients. Ironically, Cindy Elder sounded young, practically collegiate. "What would you say are the most important things you should try to find out about someone you're interested in?"

"I would say," said Grace, "that it's more a question of listening to what someone is trying to tell you than asking questions about specific background information, or the so-called big issues or deal breakers people sometimes concentrate on when they're dating someone, such as money or religion. Those things are important, of course, but I would argue that it's even more important to hear what a person's behavior, or tone, is already communicating when they speak about ideas and people."

Grace could hear the clack of Cindy Elder's keyboard in the background and her encouraging, intermittent, "Mm-hm..."

She had done enough interviews already to see the way the wind was going to blow. Like it or not, *You Should Have Known* was going to be presented to the world as a dating guide, shelved—quite possibly—cheek by jowl with the odious *The Rules* and *Relationships for Dummies*. It couldn't be helped, she supposed, or at least not if she wanted her book to be a bestseller.

"What are some things you might hear in a man's behavior or tone?"

"You might hear disdain for ex-partners, or co-workers, or parents and siblings. We all have negative feelings about some people in our lives, but hostility as a pattern is problematic. And in men, hostility toward women in general is an enormous red flag."

"Good," said Cindy Elder, clacking. "What else?"

"A lack of interest in others. Talking about people as if they only ist in relation to him and not as separate individuals. That's some- ng that may never change, not with marriage or even children. have to remember, this is a person who's reached adulthood his attitudes intact, and he is comfortable enough with them to have them on display with a person he doesn't know very well and is theoretically trying to impress."

"Right," she heard Cindy say.

"So our responsibility, particularly as women, is to really pay attention. We tend to get tunnel vision sometimes, especially with a man we're physically attracted to. If the chemistry of attraction is strong, it can drown out some of our other receptors."

The typing stopped. "You make this sound very clinical. Is that your intention?"

"Well," she said, "yes and no. I think it's possible to be a romantic and still keep your wits about you. Not every attraction has to lead to a long-term partnership. The trouble comes when we're so attracted to a potential partner that we stop hearing what he's actually telling us."

"Such as..."

"Such as...I'm not really that interested in you as a partner. Or I'm not interested in anyone as a partner. Or how about, any *woman* as a partner? That one comes up more often than you'd think. Or, Sure, I'm interested in you as a partner, but only on my terms, and those terms are going to make your life miserable."

"Okay!" said Cindy. "I think I've got enough."

"Fine," Grace said. They thanked each other and Grace hung up. Then she looked at her cell phone again. Earlier, waiting for the office line to ring for her scheduled interview, she had scrolled through the senders and decided to ignore the messages. The first appeared as "M-G," her own abbreviation for Sally Morrison-Golden, whose post-fund-raiser information assault was scarcely lighter than its pre-fund-raiser counterpart. The second sender was Henry's school, but not an actual human at Henry's school, who might be trying to reach her because Henry was ill or some academic or behavioral crisis warranted a meeting with a teacher. It was the generic Do-not-reply automaton at Rearden that sent mass e-mails to the effect that Crazy Hat Day would take place tomorrow, or an early dismissal for teacher training was scheduled for the following Monday, or a case of head lice had been confirmed in the kindergarten. Grace sometimes woke to this same nonperson on winter mornings, announcing snow days or late openings, and in fact it had actually snowed this morning, a little, early for winter but not bizarrely so, and hardly enough to require a response. She scrolled on down. Sylvia Steinmetz. M-G. M-G. M-G.

Ladies, please, she thought irritably.

It would be the last moment of the life she would afterward think of as "before."

Then she retrieved them.

First, from Sally: "Hi, everyone. Still hearing from people how great it was, and a few late donations came in. We do have some stuff to go over, not too much—I think we can get to it all in an hour, ninety minutes tops. Amanda has kindly offered her home. Next Thursday at 9 AM work for all of us? 1195 Park, apartment 10B. Let me know ASAP."

Then the school: "With sadness, we need to inform parents that one of our fourth graders has suffered a family tragedy. Counselors will be visiting all three fourth-grade classrooms tomorrow to talk with the students. We would like to request that everyone in our school community be mindful that sensitivity is required from all of us. Thank you. Robert Conover, Head of School."

Which meant, thought Grace, exactly what? The statement—or e-mail, or announcement, whatever it was—had obviously been so worked over that what emerged was nonsensical. Clearly somebody was dead, but the somebody wasn't the fourth-grade student. That, she thought, would not have been described as "a family tragedy." And "family tragedies" had certainly happened before, at Rearden as anywhere else. Last year alone, two fathers in the middle school had passed away, one from cancer and the other in a private plane crash in Colorado; neither death had given rise to an e-mail like this. *It has to be a suicide*, Grace thought. A parent's suicide, or possibly a sibling's death, but not a sibling who went to Rearden—that, too, would have been phrased differently. The whole thing was, actually, highly frustrating. Why bother sending such an e-mail, which would only ignite speculation and endanger the very sensitivity being requested? If you're not going to communicate anything, why send a communiqué?

Annoyed, she deleted the message.

From Sylvia: "Yes, I can do Thursday. Might be a few minutes late, must drop lovely urine sample at Daisy's doctor that morning."

From Sally: "Re: 4th grade family tragedy. Does anyone know anything?"

And she's off, thought Grace, deleting.

From Sally again: "Grace, call me ASAP."

From Sally again: "Grace, it's Malaga Alves. Did you hear?"

This one, she did not delete. Instead, she read it again, and then again, as if it might change or at least make sense. Malaga Alves was "it"? What was "it"?

When the phone in her hand actually rang, she flinched and gripped it tighter, then held it up with an unsteady hand. Sylvia. She hesitated, but only for a moment.

"Hi, Sylvia."

"Jesus, did you hear about Malaga?"

Grace took a breath. It seemed too much effort to detail what she knew and did not know. "What happened?" she said.

"She's dead. I can't believe it. We all just saw her on Saturday."

Grace nodded. She was aware, briefly, of wanting to say all of the usual things and then just move on. She really didn't want to know more, or care, or be wounded by the thought of the little boy in fourth grade or the baby who had nursed so extravagantly at the planning meeting a few days earlier. "What do you know?"

"The son . . . what's his name?"

"Miguel," Grace said quickly, surprising herself.

"Miguel went home by himself on Monday, after his mother

didn't show up. He found her in the apartment, with the baby. It's so awful."

"Wait—" She was still trying to sort these pieces and still wanting not to know. "Is...was the baby all right?"

Sylvia seemed to give this serious thought. "You know, I don't know about that. I suppose so. I think we'd have heard, otherwise."

Ah, Grace thought. So now she was part of an interested party called "we."

"You got the school's alert?" Sylvia said.

"Yes. I couldn't really understand it. I knew it was something pretty bad, of course."

"Well," Sylvia said with heavy sarcasm, "it did use the word *tragedy*."

"Yes, but...I don't know. It sort of made a fire and then threw fuel on it. Why did they do it? I mean, this is incredibly sad, of course, but why didn't they just come out and say that a fourth-grade parent had passed away? That's what they did last year after Mark Stern died. I don't think they brought in grief counselors."

"That was different," Sylvia said tersely.

"Was it a heart attack? Or an aneurysm? It must have been something sudden. She certainly looked very healthy the other night."

"Grace...," Sylvia said. She seemed to be waiting for something. Later, Grace would decide that she had been indulging her own pleasure at bearing such bad news. "You don't understand. She was murdered."

"She was..." Grace couldn't quite get her brain around this word. It came from paperback mysteries and the *New York Post*—neither of which, naturally, she read. People she knew, even as slightly as she knew Malaga Alves, did not get murdered. Long ago, the son of her family's housekeeper, a Jamaican woman named Louise, had fallen in with a gang and murdered someone else. He'd been sentenced to spend the rest of his life in prison upstate, destroying his mother's health and shortening her life. "That's..." But she couldn't say what *that* was. It was…"Oh, my God, that poor little boy. He found her?"

"The police were in school today, in Robert's office. It was his decision to get the counselors in. I don't know, do you think it's the right thing?"

"Well, I certainly hope they're not going to explain to the fourth grade that their classmate's mother was murdered." She took a moment to imagine this horrific prospect. "And I certainly hope the parents won't be telling their kids."

"Maybe not directly," said Sylvia. "But you know they'll hear about it."

Grace, for her part, wanted very badly to stop hearing about it, but she could think of no way to bring this about.

"How are you going to tell Daisy?" she asked instead, as if Sylvia were the expert in human behavior and she were the one calling for advice, instead of the other way around.

"Daisy told me," she said bluntly. "Rebecca Weiss told her. Rebecca heard from her mother, who heard from our friend Sally Morrison-Golden."

"Crap," Grace said automatically.

"So that's the entire herd of cats out of the bag, basically."

"You'd think…," Grace began, but there was no point in finishing.

"Well, I wouldn't think. I expect very little of Sally, really. But it's beside the point. Sally may have the emotional maturity of a middle schooler, and she may be a bitch, but she didn't murder anyone. This would be devastating no matter who says what to whom. And it's going to be a mess for all of us. Not just the kids. I'm thinking about the press—there's going to be the whole 'Private School Mom Murdered' thing. Even though she wasn't really a 'private school mom,' you know?"

Grace frowned. "You mean…Wait, what do you mean?"

She could hear Sylvia exhale in sharp frustration. "*You* know,

Grace. Full-tuition-paying private school mom. A mom who is paying full tuition to Rearden at the price tag of thirty-eight thousand dollars per year. And yes, I know how bad that sounds, but it's true. They'll come gunning for the school, and then in the last paragraph they'll write that her kid was low-income and on scholarship, but we still get to be the school where one of our parents was murdered."

Grace noted that her irritation—with Sylvia for her selfishness, Robert for his histrionics, and Sally for the clear and unsettling fact that she was baldly disseminating the news—had now apparently elbowed aside her shock. This meant distance, and the relief that came with it.

"I don't think that's going to happen," she told Sylvia. "Whatever caused this, it has nothing to do with Rearden. Really, I think we should wait until there's actual information. We should be focusing on just being available to the kids, if they need us. Not that either of our kids is going to be affected. But the fourth graders..." This was going to be a really profound thing for them, Grace thought, having the parent of a classmate die suddenly, let alone violently, and the effect of that would certainly ripple upward to the older kids, if not downward, where the younger ones would be (presumably, hopefully) shielded from the news. She thought for a moment of Henry, who had not experienced anything like this (Grace's mother had died before he was born, and Jonathan's parents were, while thoroughly absent from his life, at least alive). How to best handle things when he came home from school, today or tomorrow or next week, and said, "Did you hear this kid in fourth grade, his mom got murdered?"

"I'm sure the moms at Dalton are already calling each other up and saying, 'It never would have happened here!'"

"But it didn't happen here," Grace reminded her. "We have no idea what Malaga's life was like. I never heard one thing about her husband. He wasn't there at the benefit, was he?"

"You kidding? The way she flirted with all those guys?"

"They flirted with her," Grace corrected.

"Please."

She sounded so bitter. Why did she sound so bitter? None of those guys had been her husband. She didn't even have a husband!

Instead of saying any of this, she said: "But Malaga was married, right?"

"Yes. Well, according to the parent directory. Guillermo Alves, same address. Nobody ever saw him, though."

How many people, Grace wondered idly, had Sylvia asked in order to produce this "nobody"?

"Did you ever see him?" said Sylvia.

"No." Grace sighed.

"Yeah. It was always just her, taking the son to school every morning and sitting in the park with the baby, and then coming back in the afternoon."

And with that, any distance evaporated, redepositing all of the awfulness—murdered mother, orphaned children, poverty (clearly, relatively), and sorrow—at her feet. This was a terrible, terrible thing. Did Sally, did Sylvia, understand how very terrible it was?

"Oh, I've got to go," Grace said. "I hear my one o'clock patient coming in. Thanks for letting me know, Sylvia," she said somewhat disingenuously. "Let's try to sit tight till we hear from the police about what actually happened."

"Of course," said Sylvia, equally if not more disingenuously. And then, as if to drive the point home: "I'll talk to you tomorrow."

Grace pressed the button to end the call, then set down the phone. Her one o'clock had not, actually, arrived but would soon. Bizarrely, she wasn't sure what to do in the interim. What she wanted, of course, was to talk to Jonathan, but she almost never called Jonathan during the day; his work was too turbulent in itself to be interrupted with trivial matters, and it wasn't fair to make him worry that there was some emergency. But Jonathan wasn't at the hospital today. He was in Cleveland, at an oncology conference, and probably had his phone turned off. Which meant that she could call and leave a message without fear of interruption. But what, really, was there to say?

Henry had programmed her phone with photographs: a violin for himself, a stethoscope for his father, a fireplace for their home line, a boat dock for the house in Connecticut. Grace's father was represented by a pipe (though he hadn't smoked one in years) and Rearden by the school crest. Everyone and everything else was an ordinary number; clearly, the images were the tent poles of Henry's existence, and perhaps her own as well. She pressed the stethoscope and held the phone to her ear.

"This is Jonathan Sachs," her husband said, the voice mail picking up right away. "I can't answer your call right now, but I will get back to you as soon as possible. If this is an urgent matter, please call Dr. Rosenfeld at 212-903-1876. If you are experiencing a true medical emergency, please call 911 or go to the emergency room. Thank you."

After the beep, she said: "Hi, sweetheart. Everything's fine, but something came up at school." She thought quickly. "Not—Henry's fine, don't worry. Just, when you get a chance, give me a call. Hope the conference is going well. You didn't say whether you were getting back tomorrow or Friday. Just let me know so I can tell Dad and Eva if you're there for dinner tomorrow. Love you."

Then she waited, as if he might magically emerge from the other side of the voice mail, out of the cast-iron room into which these disembodied voices were sent to wait until they could be heard—trees falling in the forest, not yet making a sound. She imagined him in a bland but comfortable amphitheater in Cleveland, a bottle of water—provided by some eager drug company in the lobby—uncapped in the cup holder, making notes on a disappointing statistic from the latest trial of a once promising new drug. What was the death of an unknown adult woman—a person neither he nor his son even knew by sight—to someone who routinely tried to comfort children who might or might not know they were dying, and their parents, who always knew? It was like pointing out a smudge of grime to one of those "extreme cleaners" charged with shoveling filth and waste out of foul houses. She pressed the button to end the call and set down her phone.

Now she regretted calling. She regretted the childish impulse to ask him to say some magical thing and make it better. Jonathan, who carried around far more important things, should not be distracted from his own tasks because she needed—and why, again, should she need it?—some sympathy. Like anyone—like Sylvia, obviously—Grace was skilled at the human response of that-would-never-happen-to-me. A woman raped in Central Park? *Of course it's horrendous, but you have to ask, What was she doing going for a run at ten p.m.?* A child blinded by measles? *I'm sorry, what kind of idiot parents don't vaccinate?* Travelers robbed at gunpoint on a Cape Town street? *You're surprised? You were in Cape Town!* But no clear indictment was presenting itself in the death of Malaga Alves. It had not been her fault that she was Hispanic and presumably poor. And it was certainly not a bad thing that she had managed to secure a scholarship for her child at one of the city's best schools. That's what scholarships were for! Where were they—where was Grace—supposed to insert the wall that separated her from this poor woman?

Luck. Plain luck. And money, which in her own case had also been luck.

She lived in the apartment she had grown up in, an apartment she could never have afforded at its current market value, and sent her son—who was probably no more, though certainly no less, bright than any of his classmates—to her own school, which looked kindly on the children of alumnae and which her own father had sometimes helped her to pay for, because the tuition was simply, mind-spinningly, high, and practicing psychotherapy and pediatric oncology were not efficient means of acquiring great wealth in the city of Wall Street. Filthy luck. Not like Sylvia, who might also have benefited from her alumnae status, but who worked like a fiend to send her brilliant daughter to Rearden and keep them both in a one-bedroom on York. *I should be reaching out more to Sylvia,* she heard herself think, as if she were the lady of the manor. Perhaps what she meant was that she ought to have reached out more to Malaga, but then again, maybe it was safe to feel that way now.

And now she really did hear the buzzer from the outer door and pressed the button on her intercom until the door clicked open. There was the sound of talking in the vestibule as the couple settled in the chairs there. She heard the hum of their voices, at ease and subdued, unusually so among her patients, who often came coiled to attack. These two were nice people, open to therapy, earnestly willing and earnestly trying, and she liked them, though they were both so deeply harmed by their early lives that she hoped, in some private way, they would come around to a decision not to have children. Some people should but couldn't; others could but should not—it wasn't fair, really. This couple, having found each other, were luckier than most.

She was not accomplishing anything sitting at her desk, staring at her phone, trying and failing to gain some toehold on what had just happened. Nothing prevented her from giving these extra minutes to the woman and man waiting on the other side of her door—a gift, a gesture on her part. She could get up now, open the door, and greet them early. She could, she ought to, probably, but for some reason she didn't, and the clock ticked forward as if nothing had changed, and Grace just sat there as if nothing had changed, because she wanted to and because she could. But not for much longer.

CHAPTER SEVEN

A Bouquet of Useless Facts

Henry was first violin in the Rearden Middle School orchestra, a secret he and his mother conspired to keep from Vitaly Rosenbaum, who technically forbade the influence of any other teacher over one of his students. Rehearsals were on Wednesday afternoons, after classes had ended for the day, and afterward he walked home alone, or at least alone with his cell phone. She worried, of course, but not terribly, because the city was safe now, and even if it weren't, the Upper East Side was safe. And the phone—that made all the difference.

She made a couple of stops on the way home after her last patient: first to the Duane Reade on Lexington and 77th for gift envelopes (they used them for year-end tips for the doormen and superintendent), then to Gristedes for lamb chops and cauliflower, two items her son could be relied upon to eat. She had been thinking, as she rounded the corner to her building on East 81st, of boiling water and preheating the oven, and then of the name of this new doorman, who stood just outside the door, under the canopy ("The Wakefield," it said), talking to two large men, one of whom was smoking, and then about whether the holiday bonus for a new doorman had to be the same as the bonus you gave to someone who had worked all year. Was that fair? And then, in the instant before the unnamed doorman looked up, and saw her, and pointed in her direction, and the two men also turned, and the one who was smoking tossed his cigarette (or was it a cigar? it looked tan or brown, like a thin cigar a woman might smoke, or might once have smoked) on the ground, and she thought: *Pick that up, you jerk.*

"That's her," she heard the doorman say.

She nearly looked over her own shoulder, to see who was there.

"Mrs. Sachs?"

One of them was wiry and bald, with a gold stud in one ear and a cheap-looking brown jacket. The other, the smoker, was taller and wore a very nice suit. Knockoff Italian, though good fabric. Jonathan had a suit like that, Grace thought. But his was real.

And then it hit her.

Something had happened to Henry. Something…between here and Rearden? How many blocks was that? But it didn't matter how many blocks. It took only one instant. A driver who wasn't looking. A mugger. A crazy person. Most of the crazy people were off the streets, had been since the 1990s, *fucking Giuliani*. But it took only one. She couldn't get the words out.

"What is it?" She didn't want to say Henry's name. How crazy was she? "Did something happen?"

Of course something had happened. Why else would they be here?

"Is it my son?" she asked them, listening to herself. She sounded utterly unlike herself, but calm.

They looked briefly at each other.

"Mrs. Sachs? I'm Detective O'Rourke."

Naturally, she couldn't help thinking. What a cliché.

"It's not about your son," the other one said. "I'm sorry if we frightened you. We do that sometimes. We don't mean to."

She turned to him, but her gaze seemed to follow at its own pace, leaving stop-motion traces behind it, like an acid trip, she supposed. She had never taken acid.

"Joe Mendoza," said the one who wasn't here about Henry. He held out his hand, and she supposed she shook it. "Detective Mendoza. Sorry. Can we talk a minute?"

It wasn't Henry. Was it Jonathan? A plane crash? But he wasn't flying today. He was at the conference today. Was there crime in Cleveland? Of course there was crime in Cleveland. There was crime everywhere. Then she thought: *Is it my father?*

"Please just tell me," she said to both of them. She could see the new doorman staring at her. *Crazy person in 6B*, she thought wildly. *Okay, fine. Now fuck you.*

"You might have heard that a woman whose child attends your child's school was killed," said Mendoza. "I think the school sent out a message? They didn't name the person."

Oh. She felt the relief, like an egg cracking over her head, an endless egg, dripping sweet release through every vein. She could have embraced them both and scolded them: *You had me so worried! Don't do that!*

"Yes, of course. I'm so sorry. It's just... well, any parent would be terrified."

They both nodded, but one more pleasantly than the other.

"Sure. I have two," said the classic Irish cop. He was the one with the earring and the cheap jacket. Not so classic, maybe. "Don't apologize. Do you mind if we talk somewhere? Maybe a little more private?"

She nodded. He was her savior, and she wanted to please him. How could she refuse him now? And yet some new voice was trying to get her attention, holding out against the soaring flow of her relief. It said: *Don't let them upstairs*. And she listened to it.

"There are some seats inside," she told them. Like most lobbies in most New York apartment buildings, there were chairs or couches or both. No one ever seemed to use them. The doormen had their own chairs or desks. Tradespeople waited in the vestibule to be let upstairs and deliverymen waited there, too, to be paid by someone who came down in the elevator. The seating was not so much a vestige of an earlier time as something that had always been out of place, and in all her life—as a child in this building and now a grown-up, a mother raising her own child here—she could not recall a single instance of these armchairs (redone a few years earlier in unsightly hotel-ese floral fabric) being used for actual conversation. She led the two men here, and sat, and set down her purse and plastic bag from Gristedes.

"I just heard about Mrs. Alves," she said as soon as they were settled on the chairs. "I had no idea what the message meant when I read it. The message from the school," she clarified. "I couldn't make any sense of it. Then someone called me and told me she'd died. It's awful."

"Who told you about it?" O'Rourke said. He had removed a small notebook from the breast pocket of his ugly jacket.

"My friend Sylvia," Grace said. Immediately, illogically, she wished she had not volunteered Sylvia's name. Could Sylvia get in trouble for gossiping? Then she remembered that it hadn't been Sylvia, actually. "But...you know, another friend left a message on my cell phone before that. So it wasn't really Sylvia."

"Sylvia who?" said O'Rourke. "What's the last name?"

"Steinmetz," said Grace, feeling guilty. "Though the message was from a woman named Sally Morrison-Golden. She chaired a committee at our school that we were all on. And Mrs. Alves." Though Malaga Alves hadn't really been "on" the committee. That is, she hadn't really done anything, only attended that one meeting. Had her name been listed on the committee in the auction catalog? Grace couldn't remember.

"And that was at what time?"

"I'm sorry?"

"What time did you learn about Mrs. Alves' death?"

That was awfully specific, Grace thought with some irritation. If they were going to go through everyone in the school community and ask them when they'd heard—it seemed more like a sociology project than a police investigation. "Oh . . . ," she considered. "Well, wait, let me just check my phone." She dug it out of her bag and scrolled through the call log. It wasn't difficult to pinpoint. "Twelve forty-six p.m.," she announced, unaccountably relieved, as if this offered some definitive proof of something. "We spoke for a bit over eight minutes. But why is that important? I mean, if I can ask."

The one named Mendoza gave an oddly musical sigh. "I never think about what's important anymore," he said, smiling a little. "Once upon a time I only asked what I thought was important. That's why it took me way too long to make detective. Now I just ask everything, and I sort it out later. You're a shrink, right? You only ask the important stuff?"

Grace looked at him. Then she looked at the other one. They weren't smiling.

"How did you know I was a shrink?" she asked. "I mean, I'm not a shrink, I'm a therapist."

"Is it a secret?" he said. "You got a book out, right?"

"She wasn't my patient," Grace said, jumping to a thoroughly illogical conclusion. "Mrs. Alves? I wasn't her therapist. I was on a school committee with her. I don't think I ever really spoke to her. Just, you know, chitchat."

"Chitchat about what?" said Mendoza.

Grace was suddenly aware of her neighbor, the woman who lived directly upstairs, crossing the lobby. She had her portly Lhasa apso on a leash and carried a Whole Foods shopping bag. She looked amazed to see three people in the lobby chairs, having what looked like an actual conversation. Did she know the men were cops? Grace thought automatically. The woman had lived above her for nearly ten years, alone except for the dog, and another dog before that. Willie, or Josephine—the dog, not the woman. The woman's name was Mrs. Brown, and Grace didn't know her first name. That was a Manhattan co-op for you, she thought.

"I don't... Oh," she said, remembering, "her daughter. Her baby. We admired the baby's eyelashes. I remember that. I told you, nothing important."

"She discussed her baby's eyelashes?" Mendoza said, frowning. "That strike you as odd?"

"We were just admiring the baby. You know." Though perhaps they didn't. Perhaps they had never admired a baby out of politeness. "'What a cute baby. What long eyelashes.' It wasn't a memorable encounter."

O'Rourke nodded, writing this terribly important thing down. "And this was at the committee meeting last Thursday, December fifth."

Had she said December 5? Grace thought vaguely. They seemed to be holding a bouquet of useless facts. "Well, I suppose so. That was the only time I spoke to her."

"Apart from the benefit on Saturday night," Mendoza said.

And then Grace understood. Of course, they had talked to Sally already. Sally had probably called them, she thought irritably. Sally had probably said: *I knew her! I was in charge of the committee! Grace Sachs will confirm it all!* Fuck Sally.

"I saw her on Saturday, at the party," Grace corrected. "But I didn't speak to her."

"Why not?" said Mendoza.

Why not? The question didn't really compute. There wasn't a "Why not," just as, if she had spoken to Malaga Alves at the benefit, there wouldn't really have been a "Why."

She shrugged. "No special reason. I didn't speak to most people at the party. I was downstairs for a lot of it, handing out auction flyers and name tags. By the time I got upstairs there was a huge crowd. And then the auction started. There were a lot of people I didn't talk to."

"Did you happen to notice anyone Mrs. Alves did speak to at the party? Even if you weren't speaking to her yourself. Did you see her with anyone in particular?"

Aha, Grace thought. She looked at them, instantly torn between her feminist and pre-feminist selves, not to mention her wish to be helpful and her disdain for Sally. She was no Sally, full of vitriol at the arrival of a prettier girl—or a girl possessed of some potent pheromone, capable of luring the beaux away. If men like the men at the Rearden fund-raiser wanted to gather around Malaga Alves, forsaking their wives for such a succulent newcomer, she had no opinion about it, especially since her own husband hadn't been one of them. Malaga was not to be blamed for her obvious sensuality, which she seemed—on the contrary—not to flaunt, even in such conducive circumstances. Those men sniffing around her had only their consciences, and of course their wives, to answer to.

Then again, it wasn't her place to point the finger.

"I guess you're asking whether I noticed all the men around her," she said, taking the bait, but on her own terms. "Of course I did. I think it would have been hard to miss. She's…she *was*. An attractive woman. But the little I saw, I thought she was acting very properly."

She waited a moment while Mendoza finished writing this down. She was thinking: *But even if she hadn't been, I hope you're not implying she deserved to be killed. I thought we were past that*, she nearly said. But she stopped herself.

"You said you never spoke to her. On Saturday," Mendoza said, finishing.

"No," Grace agreed. It had occurred to her that Henry would be here any minute. She didn't want him to see this—this tableau in the lobby.

"But you must have greeted her when she came in."

Which one said this? She looked at them both, as if she might read the answer from the muscles of their throats. But one, O'Rourke, had a throat concealed by stubble and the other, Mendoza, by fat. Neck fat was something she'd always been a little repelled by. She had never seriously contemplated plastic surgery, but if her own jaw ever became obscured by neck fat, she knew she would not be able to live with herself. *My personal line in the sand*, it occurred to her now, *is a jawline*.

"Yes?" Grace frowned.

"You said you were downstairs in the lobby. At the party."

"Benefit," the other one, Mendoza, the one without a jawline, corrected.

"Yeah. You must have spoken to her. You said you were giving people the name tag."

"And the catalog," said Mendoza. "Right?"

"Oh. Sure. Maybe. I don't remember. People were arriving all at the same time." She felt so profoundly frustrated. What could it possibly matter if she gave Malaga Alves her stupid auction catalog and name tag? There wasn't even a name tag! Malaga hadn't even RSVP'd!

"So would you like to revisit that earlier statement?" he said, affably enough.

A word had been buzzing at her, for the last . . . how long? Five minutes, at the most. But five minutes was a long time. The word was *lawyer*. Actually, there were more words than that. In addition to *lawyer,* she kept thinking: *Wrong*. As in: *This is wrong*. And also, for some incomprehensible, ridiculous, and incidentally infuriating reason: *You idiots*.

"Mrs. Sachs?" O'Rourke said.

"Look," she said, "I want to help, of course. But I don't see what I can add that might possibly be relevant. I don't know the first thing about this woman. I only spoke to her once, and not about anything important. It's awful what happened to her, whatever happened. I don't even know what happened!" she said, her voice rising. "But whatever it is, I'm sure it has nothing to do with the school. And I know it has nothing to do with me."

They looked at her with an odd satisfaction, as if they had been waiting for her to display some evidence of resentment, and now she had obliged them and made them right about her. Already, she regretted even this mild outburst. But she wanted them to go away. Now—before Henry arrived and saw them. And they were still here.

"Mrs. Sachs," O'Rourke said at last, "we're sorry to have troubled you. I don't want to keep you any longer. I do want to speak to your husband, though, if you don't mind. Is he upstairs?"

She stared at them. Again, without warning, her thoughts flashed to some 1950s universe in which these men—these *men*—had to obtain some Y-chromosome-attached endorsement before leaving her alone, which merely made her crazy. But all she could manage to say was: "Why?"

"Is it a problem?" said the other one.

"Well, it is because he's not here. He's at a medical conference. But even if he weren't, he wouldn't have any idea who you were talking about. He didn't even know this woman."

"Is that right?" said the first one, the Irish one. "Not through the school, like you?"

"No. I take my son to school and pick him up."

They were frowning at her, both of them.

Mendoza said: "Every day? Your husband never takes him?"

She nearly laughed. She was thinking, bizarrely, of a couple she'd once treated, in which the husband and wife had a business they'd created and run together, with great harmony and success. Still, when it came to their home and the care of their two children, the woman found herself entirely on her own, making sure the tuition was paid and the toilet paper didn't run out, keeping track of vaccinations and taxes and up-to-date passports, coming home to make dinner and set up appointments for the kids and wipe down the counters as he decompressed from a hard day at work. The wife's frustration was set to a perpetual simmer. In therapy, the two of them had circled and circled this maddening state of affairs, gently addressing the husband's family-of-origin issues that had given rise to his idea of what married life was supposed to look like, and the wife's traumatic early loss of her father. There had been carefully proposed charts and lists to redress the imbalance of responsibilities. There had been visualization of the family life each wanted for themselves and their children. And then one day, as the wife was explaining to her husband *why* it was not all right to schedule "boys' night" on Back to School Night, he suddenly experienced one of those rare but usually fulfilling jolts of inner illumination for which therapy is so justly lauded. With a rush of the purest outrage, the man sat up on the couch and turned to his wife, business partner, the mother of his children, the only woman he—in his own words—had ever loved, and said: "You're not going to be happy till I do half!"

So maybe she was the tiniest bit of a hypocrite. Or maybe it was just the way she wanted it, walking her son to Rearden, waiting for him, taking him to his violin lesson, not sharing this precious bit of Henry-time with Jonathan, who for the record had never asked to share it. Anyway, what business was it of theirs? And why on earth did it matter?

"Well," she said with a small laugh that sounded forced even to her, "it might be modern times and all that, but I doubt it's any different at your kids' schools. Are the parent-teacher committees and booster clubs full of dads?"

They exchanged a brief look. Then the one who'd said he had two kids gave a shrug. "I don't know. My wife does all that."

Exactly, she thought.

"But still, they might have met, right? Your husband and this lady. Mrs. Alves?"

And then Henry arrived. He slouched into the lobby, wearing his violin on his back, his heavy leather book bag slapping at his hip with every step; then the unfamiliarity of actual people on those chairs made him look up. Grace's heart sank, though she couldn't have said exactly why.

He had been a beautiful boy and was on his way to being a beautiful man, though at the moment he was delayed on an isthmus of preadolescence, the faintest darkening of incipient hair on his upper lip. Like Jonathan, he had curly black hair. Like Grace, he had fine bones and a long neck. Like both of them, he thought more than he spoke.

"Mom?" said Henry.

"Hi, honey," she said automatically.

Henry stood, fingering the key he had taken from his school bag. *Latchkey*, she thought, though he wasn't a latchkey kid, not really. Probably, he had thought she was already upstairs, waiting for him, and if he'd found himself alone would have assumed she was on her way, which she certainly would have been—had been, in fact—before these irritating men had blocked her path. Henry was still waiting.

"Go on up," she said. "I'll be there in a minute."

With another pause, just long enough to convey the message that an explanation would now be required, he turned and left, his violin swinging a little at his back. The two men said nothing until the elevator closed behind him.

"How old's your boy?" one of them said.

"Henry is twelve."

"Fun age. That's when they go into their rooms and don't come out for about a decade."

This comment served as some sort of cue for the two of them. They both chuckled theatrically, and one, O'Rourke, shook his head with a downward gaze, as if recalling his own repellent activities as a twelve-year-old. Grace was torn between wanting to defend her son, who had indeed begun to shut himself in his room a few months before (usually to read or practice his violin) or just walk away from them. She did neither, of course.

"Your son know the Alves kid?" said Mendoza, offhand.

Grace looked at him.

"What's his name?" Mendoza asked O'Rourke.

"Miguel."

"Miguel," he reported to Grace, as if she weren't three feet away.

"No, of course not."

"Why 'of course'?" he asked, frowning at her. "It's a small school, right? I mean, that's what I read on the website. That's why tuition costs the big bucks. All that individual attention? What's it cost, that school?" he asked his partner.

Was she allowed to leave? Grace wondered. Was it ever allowed? Or was it like talking to royalty, where the conversation ended only when they said so?

"Thirty-eight thousand, he said."

Grace thought: *He?*

"Yowza!" said Mendoza.

"Well," O'Rourke said, "you saw that place. Looked like a mansion."

That place, she thought crossly, had been founded in the 1880s to educate the children of laborers and immigrants. That place had also been the first private school in New York to admit black and Hispanic students.

"How do you think she afforded it?" he asked her, serious again. "You got any idea?"

"Do I..." Grace frowned. "You mean, Mrs. Alves? We barely knew each other, as I said. She would hardly have confided in me about financial matters."

"But I mean, she wasn't a rich lady. The husband...what's he do?" This was directed at O'Rourke.

"Printer," said O'Rourke. "Runs a big print shop downtown. Like, Wall Street area."

Despite herself, Grace was surprised, then ashamed of her own surprise. What had she imagined? That Malaga Alves's husband was handing out postcards on Fifth Avenue announcing a going-out-of-business sale at a "famous brand" showroom? Just because their son was on scholarship, did that have to mean that the father was destitute? Wasn't the Alves family entitled to its American Dream?

"I suppose it's possible," she said tactfully, "that Miguel was on scholarship. Our school has a long-standing scholarship program. In fact, I think I'm right in saying this, I believe that Rearden has a higher percentage of scholarship students than any other independent school in Manhattan."

Christ, she thought. *I hope that's true.* Where had she read it? The *New York Times*, probably, but when? Maybe Dalton or Trinity had slipped past them in the meantime. "Anyway, what I meant about my son not knowing Mrs. Alves' son is that a seventh grader probably doesn't have much to do with the fourth grade—not in any school. He might have passed this little boy in the hall or something, but he wouldn't have known him. I'll tell you what," she added, and got to her feet, hoping even this wasn't a transgression, "let me ask him. If I'm wrong, I'll call you and tell you. Do you have a card or something?" She held out her hand.

O'Rourke stared, but Mendoza stood up and removed his wallet. He withdrew a slightly grubby business card and then took a pen and crossed out something on it. "Old cards," he said, handing it to her. "The city of New York has declined to order me new ones. This is my cell," he added, pointing with his blue ballpoint.

"Well, thank you," she said automatically, and extended her hand, also automatically. She was thrilled to be getting away from them, but he held on to her.

"Hey," he said. "I know you want to protect him."

He tipped his head, chin up, eyes flicking to the lobby ceiling. Grace, instinctively, looked up, too, and she understood: He was talking about Henry. But of course she wanted to protect him!

"I know you want to," he said, his expression bizarrely affable. "But don't. It'll only make it worse."

Grace stared at him. He still had her hand in his, in his big hand, and she couldn't leave without it. She thought: *Can I yank it away?* She thought: *What the fuck are you talking about?*

CHAPTER EIGHT

Someone Has Just Sent Your Husband an E-mail

She was so angry. She was so angry that it took every second of the six-floor elevator ride just to calm herself, at least enough to recognize that she was not having some kind of actual, physical, multisystem shutdown requiring actual, physical, medical attention, but was merely very, very angry. The elevator had a mirror in which she declined to look, for fear of seeing this white-hot version of herself, so she focused instead on the faux finished wood of the ceiling, working her jaw as if she were chewing hard on something that refused to be broken down.

Still, it bloomed around her, filling the available, enclosed space. *How dare they?* she thought more than once as the elevator rose. But: How dare they…*what*, exactly? She had not been accused of anything more nefarious than being, perhaps, a less than welcoming fellow parent and fellow committee member to a new, clearly less affluent arrival at her son's school, who would happen, in due course, and in a truly unforeseeable turn of events, to get herself murdered. But why single Grace out for that? Why not go for the fourth-grade parents in general or just parade the class mom down the center of Park Avenue and clap her in the stocks if they wanted to set an example? *What is their problem?*

The worst of it, she thought, rattling her key into the lock of her own front door, was that she had no obvious outlet for all of this fury. She preferred, as infuriating circumstances went, the kind that offered clear avenues of redress. A booted or towed car, for example, might be profoundly annoying, but at least you knew where to go and whom to yell at. Odious parents of odious children at Henry's school could be cold-shouldered, meaning that she no longer had to pretend to like them or mix with them at school events. Rude shopkeepers and inadequate restaurants could be passed over in future—in New York, nobody had a monopoly on anything, which was useful; even the can't-get-into spot of the moment would be replaced, in a week or two, with some other can't-get-into spot. (The only exception to this rule she'd ever encountered was private school admissions, but Henry had been safely ensconced in Rearden's Class of 2019 since the age of three, the Manhattan equivalent of being Set for Life, at least educationally speaking.) This was different—because she, of course, supported the police as any law-abiding citizen ought, more than ever since 9/11, when they and the others had literally gone down in flames. It was maddening.

And even if she somehow identified an appropriate outlet for complaint, what exactly was she supposed to be carping about? That two police detectives, never less than outwardly polite, and trying to comprehend a terrible, dreadfully sad murder that had left two children without a mother, and bring the man responsible (of course it was a man) to justice, had come to her home and asked her some questions? It was nothing she hadn't seen on *Law & Order*. It was nothing.

She wondered, setting down her bag on the hall table and noting the smack of the refrigerator door from the kitchen (Henry, procuring his customary post-school gallon of OJ), whether she ought to be calling Jonathan. It was safe to complain to Jonathan, of course, but perhaps too self-indulgent to interrupt his conference for that purpose. Besides, in his world, the world of dying children, how much sympathy could she expect to extract for a murdered stranger, let alone for herself, the barely inconvenienced acquaintance of a murdered stranger? He would, she knew, be a little annoyed by the thought that two detectives had apparently instructed her not to protect their twelve-year-old son. No—more than annoyed.

Protect him from what? he would say, and she imagined the tracking of his mood on an EKG ticker tape, starting to prick and roil.

Protect him from . . . the news of the death of the mother of a fourth grader Henry had never set eyes on, or at least would not have known by name? *I know you want to protect him.* It would have been laughable if not for the fact that he—the Irish one or the other one—had actually said it.

Maybe she should call Robert Conover and yell at him, but she wasn't really sure what he'd done, apart from send out such an asinine e-mail. *That* was pretty bad. Still, he'd had to do something, say something; it would have been wrong not to try to get ahead of events. And most people were lousy writers, even heads of schools, as likely to say something unhelpful (or idiotic) as what they'd actually set out to say. Or maybe she should be yelling at Sally, because she—as head of the benefit committee—had obviously supplied the police with Grace's name, or just because she was generally objectionable. Maybe she should yell at her father.

In general, Grace did not even yell around, let alone to, her father, who had long ago made clear that he would not engage with any but her most sedate, cerebral self, a self he had reared and paid to educate and whose acerbic and intelligent commentary on most things was more than welcome. She was not flighty or emotional by nature, which was just as well, but even she had had to navigate adolescence as a female, which made necessary certain episodes of hormonal extravagance, certain scenes in restaurants and in view of the old friends of parents. These incidents had had, Grace knew well, an indelible impact on her father's sensibilities. It was just as well she'd been an only child.

Still, he had never wavered in his own brand of paternal devotion. Even after her mother's death (which took place after Grace had—technically—left home), even after his remarriage, he never let slip that garment of paternal authority he had taken on when he became a father, in that far-from-the-delivery-room way that men had once become fathers. They had, she supposed, a good relationship, if that meant they saw each other frequently, and he let her know when she was looking well, and that he approved her choice of husband and the child she had produced, and perhaps was even proud of what she had accomplished professionally. And neither of them was given to heartfelt declarations, so that was all right. And there were certain rituals they both counted on, like the weekly dinners at the apartment he shared with his new wife—the wife of nearly eighteen years Grace still (maliciously?) thought of as "new." (These dinners had at first taken place on Friday nights, in deference to Eva's superior Jewishness, and later on other nights, in deference to Grace and Jonathan's inability to get with the program of the aforementioned Jewishness, and the fact that Eva's daughter and son could no longer manage a baseline courtesy in the face of that inability.)

Now that Grace had thought of her father, she felt an actual need to call him. She had to call him, or call Eva at any rate, to confirm the following night. But she hadn't done it because she hadn't yet heard whether Jonathan would be back in time from Cleveland.

Henry came, bearing a granola bar, the kind marketed as healthy but as fully loaded with sugar as anything in the candy aisle. "Hey, you," said Grace.

Henry nodded. He glanced toward his own bedroom door, and it occurred to Grace that she seemed to be actually blocking his way.

"Walk home okay?" she said.

"Who were those guys?" said Henry, cutting to the chase.

"They were from the police department. It wasn't anything."

He stood, holding his granola bar with a stiff, extended arm, the way the eagle on the American seal holds his olive branch and arrows. He frowned at her from under his too-long hair.

"What do you mean, not anything?"

"You heard about the little boy at your school? Whose mother died?"

"Yeah." He nodded. "But why were they asking you about it?"

Grace shrugged. She hoped she was conveying some distance. She wanted to convey distance. "The mother was on the benefit committee with me, for the fund-raiser last weekend. But I barely knew her. I think we just spoke once, at a meeting. I didn't have anything to help them."

"Who did it?" said Henry, surprising her. Then it occurred to her: *He must think whatever happened to Malaga Alves could happen to his own mother*. He had always been a bit fearful. He'd suffered terrors after scary images, even cartoon images, he'd seen as a little boy. At summer camp, the counselors reported, he waited till other boys were heading to the toilets, out behind the cabin back in the woods, and then went along with them rather than go by himself. And even now he wanted to know where she was. She knew it would change eventually, but it just seemed to be the way he was wired.

"Honey," she told him, "they're going to figure it out. It's awful, what happened, but they'll figure it out. You don't have to worry."

I know you want to protect him, she thought.

Well, of course she did. That was her job. *And* her inclination, thank you very much. Then she pushed back at the thought of those two. Those probing, appalling men.

Henry nodded. He looked thin—thin in his face, Grace thought, or perhaps it was his face that looked, just, different. The head changes shape as the child grows, jaw and cheekbone and eye socket moving into and out of position. Henry's cheekbones seemed to have tipped forward just slightly, making the briefest contact with skin, making shadows on either side. He was going to be handsome, like his father, while actually looking very little like him. He was going to look, she was suddenly aware, like her own father.

"Where's Dad?" Henry said.

"In Cleveland. I'm pretty sure he's coming back tomorrow. Did he tell you when he's coming back?"

Then it struck her as noteworthy that she had even asked her son when her husband was returning. But it was too late to take it back.

"No. He didn't say. I mean, he didn't tell me where he was going."

"I hope he's back in time for Grandpa and Eva's."

Henry said nothing. He liked Eva, who—unless some massive transformation took place in the life and psyche of Jonathan's mother—was all the grandmother he was ever, properly, going to have.

Both of Jonathan's parents had spent decades buried in their unacknowledged addictions (Naomi was an alcoholic, Jonathan said; David had not spent a day without Valium since the 1970s) and in their indulgence of Jonathan's younger brother, a committed ne'er-do-well who had never finished college or held a job and who lived in his parents' basement, monopolizing their attention and financial resources. Jonathan's ambitions for himself had been baffling to them, clearly, and his wish to participate in the lives of other people, especially people in dire, challenging circumstances, plainly appalled them. They still lived in Roslyn, but they might as well have lived on the moon. Henry hadn't seen either of them since infancy.

Grace herself had spent very little time with Jonathan's family. There had been the formal introduction, an uncomfortable outing in the city with an awkward meal at a Chinese restaurant, followed by what felt like a forced march around Rockefeller Center to look at the Christmas tree, and only the most careful conversation. Neither parent had attended their wedding. (Only the brother had turned up, standing somewhere to the rear of the small group on the sloping back lawn of the lake house in Connecticut and leaving without actually taking leave sometime during the reception.) After that, she had seen the parents only a handful of times, including during a tense visit to Lenox Hill Hospital the day after Henry's birth, where they arrived—she had never forgotten this detail—bearing an old comforter, obviously handmade, but not within the current or even previous decade. It might have had some meaning to them, she supposed, but the obtuseness of it appalled her. No, she was not going to cover her adored and long-awaited infant with a worn, faintly malodorous blanket they might have found in a jumble sale or thrift store. With Jonathan's permission, she had left it in the garbage pail of her hospital room.

Not one of the three of them—father, mother, or younger brother—had ever shown any real curiosity about Grace herself (which, at the end of the day, wasn't really a problem) or about Henry when he'd come along. She now understood that Jonathan, who had been a very smart and self-motivated kid, had made himself into a person of his own design, and from a very early age, and this Grace found thoroughly heroic. It was more than she had done. Her own parents might not have been overly demonstrative, but they had always made her feel welcome and valued, and they had been utterly clear in communicating the notion that she needed to move in the world, be educated, live in curiosity about other people, and make her mark. Jonathan had had to figure those things out on his own: unguided, unsupported, even unobserved. She didn't feel sad for him because he didn't feel sad for himself, but she felt sad for Henry, who deserved at least one real grandmother.

"How's the homework?" she asked Henry.

"Not bad. I did some in study hall. I have a test, though."

"Want me to help?"

"Maybe later. I have to study first. Can we get Pig Heaven for dinner?"

Pig Heaven was their go-to takeout for nights on their own. Jonathan was of course not religious, but he didn't care for Chinese. They did not tell her father and Eva about Pig Heaven.

"Nope. I got lamb chops."

"Oh. Good."

She went to the kitchen to start dinner. He went into his bedroom, presumably to study. She banished the last of her hostility toward the two men in the lobby with half a glass of Chardonnay from the fridge and dug out the steamer basket for the cauliflower. Once the pot was on the stove and the lamb chops were seasoned and half a head of Boston lettuce was soaking in the salad spinner, she had recovered sufficiently to try Jonathan again, but again his cell went straight to voice mail. She left a brief message asking him to call, then phoned her father's number, which rang in that drawn-out, old-fashioned way you knew could lead only to the pre-digital species of answering machine, complete with blurry recorded message and extended beep.

But then Eva answered. "He-low?" she said, and you knew by the question in her voice that she truly did not know who it was. There was no caller ID in her father's home, no DVR, and no computer. Grace's father and stepmother had ceased to absorb new technology with the touch-tone phone and the videocassette (for which they were content not to expand their library of 1980s *Masterpiece Theatre* collections). They did have cell phones, which Grace and Eva's children had insisted upon, but each of the phones had a bit of paper taped to the back with instructions and important phone numbers. Grace knew not to call her father on the cell, and she had never received a call from it, either.

"Hello, Eva, this is Grace."

"Oh, Grace." She sounded not so much disappointed as confirmed in some earlier disappointment. "Your father is out."

"Are you well?" said Grace, continuing in their set script. Eva, who had brought all the formality of her parents' prewar life of wealth in Vienna to her own postwar life of wealth in New York, required very specific exchanges. She would—if she had ever desired a profession—have made an excellent drill sergeant.

"Yes, quite well. We are expecting you for dinner tomorrow, yes?"

"Yes, we are looking forward to it. I'm not sure whether Jonathan will be back in time."

This—this very tiny irritant—was all it took.

"What do you mean, that you are 'not sure'?"

"He's in Cleveland, at a medical conference."

"Yes?"

"I'm not sure what time his flight gets in."

This, to Eva, would be egregious enough. That she wasn't actually sure what *day* he would get in would be incomprehensible. Eva simply had no comprehension of a wife whose entire life was not fueled by the needs of her husband. The reality of Grace's family, with its burdens and schedules, its looming commitments (of course, Eva had been told all about the upcoming book, the tour, the media appearances, but did she really comprehend any of it?), not to mention the innate uncertainties of a doctor's life, which required the jettisoning of social obligations when actual people got suddenly, palpably, acutely sick, was so distasteful to Eva that she routinely blocked it out.

"I do not understand," Eva said. "Can you not find out? Is it too difficult to make a phone call?"

She was, thought Grace, the absolute antithesis of the classic immigrant mother. The classic immigrant mother of any ethnicity, whose pasta or goulash or roast could be made to stretch if you wanted to bring your friends home for dinner. Eva had always run a beautiful but profoundly unwelcoming home. Grace's own mother, her real mother, had not been any kind of a cook, but at least she had made you feel she was glad to see you when she ladled out her Dominican cook's very good soups. Eva, on the other hand, was a precise and excellent producer of meals, but good food without a welcome was not very hospitable either.

"I have been trying," Grace said lamely. "Why don't we say that it will be the three of us, and I'll of course let you know if I hear otherwise. It's better to have too much than too little, isn't it?"

She might as well have asked if it wasn't a good plan to store extra garbage in the refrigerator.

"This is a terrible thing, at Henry's school," Eva said suddenly, and the non sequitur caught Grace so much by surprise that she didn't immediately understand what her stepmother was saying.

"His school?" she faltered. She had been trimming the stalk of the cauliflower and now paused, her knife suspended above the cutting board.

"One of the parents, murdered. Your father rang this morning, from the office."

The notion that her father had learned of Malaga Alves's death before she had was in itself alarming. He wasn't exactly on the grapevine, personal or technological.

"Yes, I know. It's terrible."

"Did you know her?"

"Oh no. Well, yes. But just a bit. She seemed like a very nice person."

This emerged naturally, in classic speak-well-of-the-dead fashion. Though she hadn't, really, seemed particularly nice. But what did it matter now?

Grace placed the cauliflower head into the steamer basket and started warming butter for the roux. She had trained Henry to eat cauliflower by smothering it with a cheese sauce her old friend Vita had once shown her how to make. The cheese sauce, sadly, was now one of the few traces of Vita still in her life.

"Was it the husband?" said Eva, as if Grace could possibly know. "It's usually the husband."

"I don't have any idea," said Grace. "I'm sure the police are looking into it."

In fact, she thought grimly, *I* know *the police are looking into it*.

"What kind of man kills the mother of his child?" her stepmother said, and Grace, who was now grating cheddar over the cutting board, rolled her eyes. *I don't know*, she thought. *A bad one?*

"It's an awful thing," she said instead. "How is Daddy's hip? Is it still bothering him?"

Even this, she knew, trespassed on Eva's sense of propriety, the hips of her eighty-one-year-old husband being simply too intimate a topic for discussion with his only child. That he would certainly require one hip, if not both, to be replaced sooner or later—probably sooner—did not make the subject any more palatable.

"He is fine. He doesn't complain about it."

Grace, sensing the impasse, finished the call, promising to confirm Jonathan's attendance as soon as she heard from him. Then she put the lamb chops into the broiler and began stirring flour into the melted butter.

After dinner, when Henry had returned to his room to practice and Grace had finished clearing up, she went to her own room and removed her laptop from the leather satchel she kept it in. Their bedroom, by agreement, had always been a technology-free zone, apart from the Bose CD player on Jonathan's side of the bed. (He kept his hundreds of CDs in leather binders in his bedside cabinet, meticulously broken down by genre and then organized alphabetically by artist. Unlike most people who claimed to like "all kinds" of music but never listened to anything but rock or jazz or blues, Jonathan really did have musical tastes so bizarrely wide-ranging that he was as likely to bring home a collection of Aboriginal didgeridoo or Baroque chamber music as the most recent Alison Krauss.) Grace wasn't a Luddite. She fully managed her life and her husband's (at least the nonprofessional part) and her son's on an iPhone, and she had written her book on a laptop, but she didn't like to be assailed by information, at least not at home. In the wider world it was inescapable; products and ideas were pitched to her constantly, wherever she looked or listened, and even her beloved NPR had taken its finger out of the dam, letting torrents of corporate sponsorship swim through. She might not share her husband's appreciation of didgeridoo ("didgeri-don't," Henry—who agreed with her—had once called it), but at least it wasn't trying to sell her anything but itself.

Still, their bedroom, with its mossy green walls and red toile curtains and the Craftsman bed in which her parents had once slept (new mattress, of course!), was a haven for other forms of communication. She loved waking up here, especially before the day had properly started and it was still dark, to the rising curve of her husband's bony shoulder. She liked waking up at night when Jonathan came home, being pulled back from sleep and into the warmth of his body with that strange and malleable uncertainty about whether she was dreaming or awake: love in a liminal climate, powered by REM and lust and the grown-up privacy of the marital bed. When Henry was very small, he had slept here between them, first because she had placed him there, very, very carefully, to make sure, in her new-mother terror, that he stayed alive through the night, and later because he climbed in himself. Soon, though, Jonathan insisted he decamp to his own room down the hall, a room she had once stenciled with a gender-nonspecific moon-and-stars motif, now long since painted over. It was around that time that she made a conscious effort to change their own room around. Apart from the bed, which she had always loved, and the dressing table, which she did not, really, but kept because it brought her mother close to her, everything belonging to her parents' time had been altered, from the liberated parquet (kept pristine, at least, by the beige carpeting she had grown up with) to the glowing green of the walls. When the decorator Grace had hired showed real horror at the fabric she'd chosen for the curtains, Grace fired her and hired a seamstress without an opinion. Jonathan, for his part, said he didn't care so long as she was happy.

And she was happy. She was very happy, here, in this room, here in her life. Happy enough to presume to tell other people how to be happy in theirs. She had never been the richest or the prettiest. She was not the luckiest. She still thought, sometimes—not often, because even all these years later it retained a sharp punch of sadness—of the babies who had begun to be hers and somehow never arrived. She still sometimes reached for the phone to call Vita and then stopped herself, and then felt a kind of baffled but still very painful dismissal, because she had never understood why they were no longer friends. She still missed her mother. But most of the time she could not believe she was actually living this life, with this brilliant, compassionate man she continued to look at and think: *I'll have him*, as if she didn't already, and their beautiful, clever son, in this apartment where she was daughter, wife, and mother, all at once. The brutal truth was that she had been very fortunate, and Malaga Alves, who had returned to Grace now—on her parents' bed, in her marital chamber, with her son safely doing his homework down the hall—had been so very much the opposite.

She opened her laptop and began to find out what everyone else already seemed to know. Predictably, the *Times* website had nothing about the murder of a woman whose child happened to attend a highly regarded Manhattan private school, but both the *News* and the *Post* had small items, worded so similarly that they might have been written by the same person. In the *Post* version:

> Tony Upper East Side Rearden Academy—

Sic! thought Grace.

> is in shock over the death of fourth-grade mom. According to police, 10-year-old Miguel Alves returned home to find Malaga Alves, 35, dead in their blood-strewn apartment.

"Blood-strewn"? thought Grace. This was why she never read anything but the *Times*.

An infant girl, also in the apartment, was unharmed. Police have not been able to reach Alves' husband, Guillermo Alves, 42, a native of Colombia. Alves manages Amsterdam Printing at 110 Broadway, one of the oldest and most successful financial printing service providers in the Financial District. Rearden Academy is one of the city's premier college prep schools, routinely sending its graduates to Ivy League universities and Stanford and MIT universities. Tuition for Rearden Academy reportedly costs between $30,000 and $48,000 per year, depending on grade. Current Rearden students include the children of media titan Jonas Marshall Spenser and Aegis Hedge Fund founder Nathan Friedberg.

Persons with information related to this or any ongoing case are encouraged to call Crime Watch at 1-888-692-7233.

And that was all she wrote, Grace thought. Not much to go on. Surely not enough to brew a scandal. Still, she had been reading *New York* magazine long enough to know that they, at least, were unlikely to leave a Rearden parent's murder alone, especially one in a "blood-strewn" apartment. Even if it turned out—as, let's face it, it almost certainly would—that Colombia-born Guillermo Alves, the conveniently unreachable husband, had struck down his wife for any of the classic, time-honored reasons (jealousy, addiction, financial distress, adultery), the prospect of such a pulp-fiction plot line against a backdrop of Manhattan elitism would be hard to resist.

There wasn't much else, just a few pointless shout-outs on Urban Baby ("Anyone know anything about the mom at Rearden who got killed?"). A Google search on "Malaga Alves" produced reassuringly austere results; Malaga was a person, clearly, with what J. Colton the publicist would have called "a negligible online presence." (Grace herself had had "a negligible online presence" before

J. Colton had gotten her virtual hands on her. Now Grace had a website, a virgin Twitter account, and a Facebook page, all thankfully managed by a young woman in North Carolina, hired by the publisher.) Scanning the Google results page, watching the construct "Malaga+Alves" quickly break down to its parts (**Malaga** Spain, **Malaga** Rodrigues, Celeste **Alves**, Rentals **Malaga**/Jose **Alves** Agency Villas Self-Catering…), she was surprised to feel a kind of validation of her own distance from the search terms and the person they nominally represented. She did not know anyone named Malaga Rodrigues or Celeste Alves. She had never been to Malaga, Spain, and if she ever chose to go there, she would not be renting a self-catering villa.

Of course, the husband would be long gone by now. Back in Colombia, probably, having left his children behind like the prince he obviously was. Even if they found him, they probably wouldn't get him back, or if they did, it would take years. There wouldn't be anything like justice, and what would happen to the kids was hard even to think about. The baby girl might be all right, if she got adopted or even fostered with the right family, but the son, Miguel, would never recover from what he had seen and what had been done to him. He was lost—plainly, irredeemably lost. You didn't have to be a therapist to see that. You didn't even have to be a mother.

With this thought, she felt herself soften toward the police detectives. It must be frustrating to know that the person most likely to have murdered their victim was already out of reach and likely to remain so, and all they could do was circle around the remainder of her obliterated life, pointlessly massaging the periphery. So much water, but not a drop to drink! Thinking of this, Grace wished she had had something, anything, to tell them that might help. But she didn't.

Mostly, though, she wished Jonathan were here. Jonathan, so well versed in the nuances of death, would know what to say to her, how to assuage this inexplicable tinge of guilt she carried, ever since her conversation with Sylvia. (But why? What was she supposed to have done, inserted herself into a stranger's life and said, "Do you happen to be married to a man who might murder you? And if so, do you need my help to leave him?") She wished he would pick up his messages already. Or just call in. Or maybe not turn off quite so completely when he was away on these junkets. What was the point of so many channels of communication if you just couldn't get through?

She favored the phone. It was her preferred medium. But Jonathan had moved with the times, first to e-mail and then to texting. She might have more luck with one of those, she decided, navigating on her laptop to her e-mail account. E-mail they used mainly for the kind of low-stakes, practical communiqué that had no great impact on their inner life as a family but came in handy for a certain class of reminder ("Please try to get there before 7 tonight, you know how freaked Eva gets if we don't sit down on time...") or schedule readjustment ("I've got something going on with a patient. Can you take Henry to violin?"). The circumstances at hand were obviously in the e-mail ballpark. She typed in her husband's address and in the subject line a pithy "Wife Seeks Husband." Then she wrote:

> Honey, would you give me a call? Need to figure out when you're getting back so I can tell Big E if you're coming tomorrow night. Also, something's happened at Rearden that doesn't affect Henry but, if you can believe this, the police actually came around to talk to me about. So bizarre and pretty horrible. Hey, guess what, I did an interview with Today today! Love you, G.

And then she clicked Send.

And then she heard that sound, like a technological gulp, once and then again, and then again. It was a sound from the sound track of her life, or at least her married life, because when you were married to a doctor, at least the kind of doctor who had—always—sick patients in the hospital and parents of those sick patients who should never feel that they could not reach their sick child's doctor, a sound that had, in its time, interrupted dinners with Jonathan and concerts with Jonathan and walks and sleep with Jonathan and even lovemaking: *click/gulp, click/gulp, click/gulp*, and then silence. It meant: *Someone has just sent your husband an e-mail.*

She looked toward the sound and saw only Jonathan's familiar bedside table, with its white ceramic lamp (the twin of her own) and last week's *New Yorker*, a Bobby Short CD (*At Town Hall*, one of his favorites), and one of the many pairs of reading glasses she regularly supplied him with (the cheap ones from the drugstore, because he lost or destroyed them too regularly for expensive frames). But none of those items had made that noise, and she had heard that noise—she knew she had. She did not know enough to be afraid. Why be afraid of a familiar sound in a familiar place, even if hearing it made no sense?

Grace put aside the laptop. She eased off the bed and knelt beside it, ignoring the thrum that had gripped her, quite suddenly and with so much force that, had her brain succeeded in conjuring any thought at all, she would not have heard it for the noise. She opened the door of the bedside cabinet and saw only the familiar things: three bulging leather binders full of jazz and rock and vintage Brill Building pop and "didgeri-don't," plus a few takeout menus and a folded program from the last recital of Vitaly Rosenbaum's students. It had been a phantom, a mechanical phantom, signifying nothing except, perhaps, the fact that she missed her husband and—this was only just occurring to her—was not entirely, completely persuaded that she knew exactly where he was. And yet if that were true, if she really were convinced that she had imagined the sound, that clicking, gulping *Someone has just sent your husband an e-mail* sound, then why did she reach forward to grasp and then remove first one and than another of the binders, to look behind it and see what she was not prepared to see: the terribly familiar sight of Jonathan's BlackBerry, its "low battery" light blinking in mute distress and the green message indicator letting her know—as if she needed to be told—that someone had just sent her husband an e-mail.

CHAPTER NINE

Who Listens?

On the end of the world came, now with a rumbling baseline of low-grade fear. She had closed the cabinet door against that mystifying cell phone, turning the latch on it as if it might try to escape, then all through the terrible night that followed she sat on the bed, thinking around but not through the quagmire that was opening at her feet, its parts still blessedly separate, though in themselves they were bad enough: something about Jonathan, something else about a near stranger who had been murdered, and something involving the police. Henry went to bed around ten, first coming in for a hug, which she gave with a very false cheer, hoping he would not feel her shake. Hours later, Grace was still awake.

There were some avenues open to her, of course. She could call Robertson Sharp III (but whom Jonathan for years had called Robertson Sharp-the-Turd or sometimes just "the Turd"), and explain that Jonathan—"Such a space cadet sometimes!"—had left his phone at home, and was there anyone else from Memorial at the conference she could get in touch with? Or she could call the conference itself, if she could first figure out exactly what it was called and exactly where it was—"pediatric oncology in Cleveland" being fairly nonspecific. She could call Stu Rosenfeld, who was covering the practice for him, but that would be akin to sending out an e-mail blast that Jonathan Sachs's wife had no idea where he was and was freaking out.

She was not. Freaking. Out.

And yet.

She kept running the film back to Monday morning, their usual relay involving the coffee and the breakfast for Henry (the only one of them who ate breakfast) and the daily download, which—she barely recalled—featured, for her, patients straight through until four, and then Henry's violin lesson, and a dentist appointment for Jonathan, to finally get a permanent crown on the bottom tooth he had broken the year before, tripping and falling against a staircase at the hospital. And hadn't there been some quasi plan about dinner, with one of them picking something up on the way home? Cleveland, she thought now, going through it again and then again, had not figured into the plan for the day—unless, had he planned to leave later on? After dinner with the two of them? Perhaps, somewhere along the way, he had decided that this was a bad plan, that the rare enough dinner at home with them was not enough to offset a late flight before an early conference the following morning? Maybe he had decided this suddenly, checked the flight availability, and come home quickly to grab his stuff, opting to phone her later and update her on the change. And he had indeed called, on Monday afternoon, though she hadn't picked up the message until she checked her messages in Vitaly Rosenbaum's dim corridor during Henry's lesson, which was why she and Henry had ended up eating dinner at the Cuban restaurant on Broadway. The message itself had been so unremarkable: "*Heading to the airport for that conference. Can't remember the name of the hotel—it's in my bag. See you in a couple of days. I love you!*" She hadn't even kept it—what was there to keep? He had gone away for a couple of days. He often went to conferences, and they were often in Midwestern cities with important hospitals, like the Cleveland Clinic—that was Ohio—or the Mayo Clinic—that was... Minnesota? She didn't always keep them straight, but why should she? It's not as if New Yorkers had to go somewhere else for the best medical care. Besides, he would call her, or she would call him—whether you were in China or around the corner, you called the same phone number and the same person—your husband—answered the phone.

But then Jonathan had forgotten his phone.

Or no, he hadn't forgotten exactly. One thing she saw now, with a kind of brutal clarity, was that Jonathan's cell phone could not possibly have been forgotten in the place she had found it—wedged behind the leather binders in the bedside cabinet. One did not "forget" such a critical object as a cell phone in a place so inconvenient to access.

This was the oddity she kept coming back to.

Download of plans for the day: check.

Change of plans: also check.

Inadvertently left behind phone after hurried use to communicate change of plans: not a problem.

But placement of phone in the back of the bedside table, behind the leather binders?

None of it made sense. The fact was that Jonathan *liked* to check in. He told her once that the sound of her voice, even the professional version of her voice on the office line, made him feel safe and calm, and this had moved her. She knew—she had always known—that he had thought of her as his "real" family more or less since they'd met. She knew that she had brought him the very safety and sense of belonging that was so important for a child, but which he had never experienced in his family of origin. That he had come out the other end of such an unpromising beginning as a nuanced, loving, and eager person said everything she had ever needed to know about what he was made of.

But even as she thought this, she was remembering something else. Or someone else. A woman from years ago on her office couch—the same couch she still had, but in a different office, her first in Manhattan, over on York in the upper 80s. She had been a new therapist then, just done with her training, just out from under the overly claustrophobic wing of Mama Rose, and this woman, this patient... Grace couldn't remember her name now, but she remembered her throat, which had been sinewy and long, rather enviable, actually. The woman had come alone, but not to talk about herself. She wanted only to talk about her husband, a Polish attorney working as a paralegal she'd met first at her neighborhood gym and then at her favorite coffee shop, where the man had, over their brief courtship, spilled out the story of his terrible childhood, a catalog of deprivation and abandonment that would have stirred the staunchest misanthrope. To get from a practically illiterate family to university, then to emigrate alone and arrive penniless with a law degree that was useless in the United States, and thus to be stuck working for attorneys who were younger and less gifted than himself, living in an awful shared flat, practically a dormitory, in Queens, and threatened constantly with deportation—well, it was a terrible story. Until, that is, she had rescued him with love and marriage and the navigational tools to secure his legal credentials. That woman had said something once, when Grace had suggested, rather gently, that perhaps she did not really know this man as well as she thought. *Look at what he came from, and what he is,* the woman said, the muscles of her beautiful neck tightening in resentment. *That's all I need to know.*

He would never come to a session, she recalled. As a Pole, the woman explained, he simply did not believe in therapy. Then the woman stopped coming, too. Years later, Grace had seen her at Eli's on Third, at the cheese counter, and cautiously reintroduced herself. The woman was still living in the same small apartment but was now raising a daughter on her own. The Polish husband had left soon after the little girl's birth, imported and then married some woman from his pre-emigration life, and hired an associate at his new law firm to represent him in the divorce. And yes, he had managed to secure a settlement for his pain and suffering.

Grace sat very still.

A siren blared down Park Avenue. She pulled a blanket around her shoulders. She had not been able to open her laptop again. She imagined typing the words "pediatric," "Cleveland," "oncology," and "conference" but somehow she couldn't bring herself to do it. Besides, this was all going to untwist itself somehow. She'd gotten herself into a kind of eddy of anxiety, that's all it was. She'd seen it a hundred times in her own practice, and sure, sometimes it was something. Often it was something. But not always. It wasn't always something.

And in fact, Grace thought with what felt almost like relief, this had sort of happened once before, with no terrible aftereffects. Years ago, back in the early days of their marriage, she recalled—and indeed, the experience came flooding back to her, that same jolt of dispersing panic, so pointless!—there had been an incident a tiny bit like this, when she had gone a day or so without quite knowing where Jonathan was. He had been a resident at the time, and yes, of course residents, with their insane thirty-six-hour shifts, did disappear into the hospital for these total immersions, emerging at the other end exhausted and addled and typically uncommunicative. Those were also the days before ubiquitous cell phones, so when you went under you went under completely: no blips on the radar, no trail of crumbs into the woods. It was ironic, she thought, that it might have been better for everybody, back then, to be unable to make contact. She wouldn't ever want Henry walking around without a cell phone—without, if she were being honest (and if such a thing were possible!), an implanted GPS locator—but it hadn't felt this terrible fifteen years ago when Jonathan had disappeared for a couple of days, failing to return the messages she'd left for him at the hospital and later at his answering service. They were only a little bit married that year, and both working crazy hours, so it had taken some time to realize that she flat out didn't know where he was. She'd thought she knew his rotation schedule, and when he could be expected to stumble through the door of their unlovely apartment on 65th and collapse on the double bed in their sleeping alcove, but when he failed to materialize, she spent the better part of a day second-guessing herself and then another few hours leaving messages. Had he filled in for somebody else, piggybacking another shift onto the one he'd just completed? Maybe he'd been too tired to make it home and had crashed in one of the rooms the hospital set up following the Libby Zion fiasco, in which a teenager's death had been—rightly or wrongly—laid at the feet of a very sleep-deprived resident. Ironically, with fewer ways for them to contact each other, it had been much easier to persuade herself that everything was all right. It had been like a dull, insistent pulling sensation, redirecting her thoughts, whatever her thoughts back then had been. (What had she thought about in those days, before she'd had a child? Current events? What to cook for dinner?) That was unpleasant enough, but it wasn't like now. Now was a building, blaring, tunneling infiltration of something she declined to name. But it felt very, very bad.

How long had it lasted, that other time? A day and night, and then another, and most of a third until he suddenly came home, looking—of all things—rather chipper. She had been so glad to see him. Where had he been? she demanded. Had he taken another shift?

Yes.

Had he stayed in one of the residents' crash rooms?

Yes, he told her. He had.

Had he not received her messages?

Messages? He hadn't, it turned out. The call desk at the hospital was notorious for not following through. True, it was technically their job, but so far down the totem pole of critical communication in a large cancer hospital that a certain amount of failure was expected. And yes, earlier in the day he'd picked up the automatic page from his service with her number, but by then he knew he'd be home in a few hours, and he hadn't wanted to wake her.

But *why* hadn't he called her, and long before that? Why hadn't he let her know what had happened? Didn't he realize she'd be worried?

Why on earth would she have been worried? Jonathan had wanted to know. He wasn't the one with cancer. He wasn't one of the kids at the hospital getting pumped with poison while their weeping parents looked on.

Of course, that had felt horrible. And of course, she was ashamed of how she had let herself become so hugely, disproportionately distressed. So he hadn't called in every second, so what? He was busy. He had sick little kids in the hospital. His life was very full of very important things. She had chosen him for that, hadn't she? And by the way, what exactly had she been so afraid of? If something terrible had happened—if, for example, he had collapsed with some sudden-onset horror (heart attack! stroke! brain tumor!)—then somebody, one of Jonathan's colleagues, even one of those awfully busy operators at the call desk, would have made an effort to get in touch with her. They hadn't, ergo, nothing awful had happened to her husband, ergo, she was acting irrationally.

She wished she could fall back on the same logic just now.

Just now, she was so focused on the idea that it had happened before and signified nothing that she utterly failed to note the significance of it having happened before at all. Which, had a patient performed this sleight of hand in her presence, she would certainly have pointed out.

It had never occurred to Grace that Jonathan might leave her. Never. Not all those years ago, during her self-inflicted three-day (and -night) ordeal. Not now. In fact, not once since their first moment, with her own sigh of recognition, lust, and relief in the basement of the Harvard Medical School dormitory. A long-ago patient had once described her thoughts on first meeting her future husband as: "Oh good. Now I can stop dating." And that, too, had been a part of her own moment. *Finis!* she had thought at the time, though that small voice of practicality had nearly been drowned out by her instantaneous, accompanying hunger for him. All that speculation about which man she was supposed to love, marry, procreate with, and grow old alongside—she had not been immune to such things, of course. But as far as her own story went, her story with Jonathan, from the moment she first encountered him it was no longer a question of *which* man, only of whether she'd be allowed to be with *this* one for the rest of her life. Jonathan Gabriel Sachs: aged twenty-four years, dimpled, wiry, tousled, brilliant, adoring, and alive. And look at what he'd come from.

Her night passed that way, in some physical discomfort and far greater psychic agony, with perhaps a few spells of brief and unrefreshing sleep, each of them ending with a new twitch of reentry. At seven, she forced herself upright and got Henry ready for school, making his toast and her own coffee as if it were a normal morning. She was uncharacteristically impatient, waiting for him to finish collecting his things, which made no sense to her because she was already dreading the moment she had to watch him walk away up the Rearden steps and turn to these repetitive thoughts once again.

The differentness of the school could be gleaned the moment she and Henry turned the corner off Lexington, with the addition of a news van (NY1) and a few clear media types on the pavement beside it. Certainly, there were parents—lots of parents, or, more accurately, lots of mothers—because who would let the nanny bring the children to school on such a momentous occasion as this? The mothers wore yoga gear and sweats, and held dogs by leather leashes, and were locked everywhere in intense communication, all over the sidewalk and in the courtyard. There were so many of these women that the sight of them pulled Grace back from her private distress and reminded her what was happening in the real world—a dead mother, injured children, psychic overflow for their own kids and the school as a whole—and she felt, for a moment, almost a little better. This situation with her husband would work itself out, of course, but there would be no restoration for Malaga Alves and her son and daughter. She gave Henry's shoulders a discreet squeeze and sent him off, then allowed herself to be enveloped by Sally Morrison-Golden's group.

"Oh, my God," said Sally as Grace approached. "This is so awful."

She was holding an oversize cup from Starbucks, alternately shaking her head and blowing over the surface.

"Anyone met the husband?" said a woman Grace didn't know.

"I saw him once," said Linsey of the Birkin bags, who looked even younger and fresher today than the day she'd dispatched Grace from her son's birthday party with the helpful information that the doorman could hail her a cab. "I didn't realize he was a parent at first. I thought he, you know, worked for the school. I think I told him they were out of paper towels in the ladies' room."

Remarkably, this was said with no self-consciousness whatsoever. Grace, notwithstanding the fact that this missing Mr. Alves had apparently bludgeoned his wife to death, was offended on his behalf.

"Parents' Night?" someone asked.

"Yes. And then he came in the classroom and sat down and I thought: 'Oh! The janitor's kid is in Willie's class!'"

Evidently, this was still amusing to her, because she rolled her eyes.

"Y'know, I'm from the South. It's just how it is down there."

"It" meaning... what? Grace thought. She decided it really wasn't worth pursuing. Instead, she thought she might as well ask if anyone had any real information.

"Where are the kids?" she said, and they all turned to her.

"What kids?" said a preschooler's mom.

"Malaga Alves' kids. Miguel and the baby."

They looked at her blankly.

"No idea," somebody said.

"Foster care?" someone else said.

"Maybe they'll get sent back to Mexico," said a woman Grace didn't know, one of Sally's regular crowd.

"They're having a counselor come in this afternoon," Amanda said. "For the fourth grade. To talk to them about Miguel. I don't know, shouldn't they have asked us first?"

"They did ask," said the woman whose name Grace didn't know. "Didn't you get the e-mail? They said if anyone had an objection, they should call the headmaster's office."

"Oh." Amanda shrugged. "I hardly ever look at e-mail anymore. It's Facebook for everything."

"Did they bring in counselors for all the kids?" asked Linsey. "I don't think Redmond mentioned it."

Redmond, Linsey's older son, had become the seventh grade's reigning Internet tormentor and generally a vile young man. Which was hardly surprising.

"No," Amanda said somewhat importantly. "Only for the fourth grade. Only for the kids in Miguel's class. Like Daphne," she reaffirmed. "Daphne said they sat in a circle and talked about Miguel and what they could do to be especially nice to him when he comes back."

"If he comes back," said Sally, stating the obvious.

"God," said Linsey, who had fished a pair of sunglasses from her Birkin of the moment (a fuchsia ostrich) and was looking up toward the school steps. "Did you see those guys?"

Grace looked. Her two friends from yesterday, the Irish and Hispanic duo from the lobby, were talking to Helene Kantor, Robert Conover's second in command, just outside the main door. Neither of the men was taking notes, but they were doing a lot of nodding.

Mendoza, Grace said, though not aloud. Mendoza of the neck fat.

"You talked to them?" Grace asked instead.

"Yesterday morning," Sally said. "They called to ask about the benefit, and the committee and whatnot. Of course I would have called them, but they came to me first."

The friend whose name Grace didn't know said: "What did you tell them?"

"Well, obviously, that she came to a committee meeting at my house, and what happened at the benefit on Saturday."

What did happen? Grace thought, frowning.

"What do you mean, 'what happened'?" Amanda asked helpfully.

"Well, don't you think it matters that she had about ten men inhaling her at the Spensers'? I don't think that's insignificant. I'm not saying she did anything to invite it. This isn't 'Blame the Victim,'" Sally said defensively. "But if it helps them figure out who did this to her, isn't it important?"

"Who did it?" Linsey looked appalled. "What are you talking about? The husband did it! He's vanished, hasn't he?"

"Well," said the woman whose name Grace didn't know, "you know, it could be a drug thing. Maybe some drug cartel was after the husband and they came looking for him and found her. So he's in hiding somewhere. He's from Mexico! That's all drug violence down there."

Not Mexico, Grace thought grimly. *Colombia*. But if it came down to drug cartels, she wasn't sure any of them knew the difference.

She had had about enough, and she started to look around for an escape. The courtyard was covered by these knots of mothers, all—she supposed—exchanging similar shards of non-information. There was very little of the usual merriment going on—that was good. But at the same time, there was something definitely off-putting about the general mood. Note had been taken of the tragedy, concern had been expressed over the needs of their own children, and now, with those preliminaries behind them, Grace was detecting a whiff of actual excitement. The news van was outside on the street; it had to stay outside the school enclosure, but they—the mothers—were inside. As a group, of course, they were not unused to being insiders. They were accustomed to being ushered to their tables and having their phone calls taken. They were accustomed to getting their kids accepted by the city's best schools, and circumventing the waiting list by ordering through a personal shopper, and driving through the gate of the high-security development with just a friendly wave at the guard. But Grace supposed that very few of them had ever been on the business end of a criminal investigation, and now they were—close enough to the action for the frisson of attention, but not close enough to be, themselves, of interest to the police. It was a rare opportunity for them, a rare . . . perspective. They were making the most of their moment.

Then someone was saying her name.

Grace turned. Sylvia was at her elbow. Grace had not noticed her in the crowd.

"Did you see Robert? He was looking for you."

"Oh?" she said dully. "What for?"

But she realized that she knew what for. Robert, understandably, was reaching out to the mental health professionals in the parent community, for advice. She wished he'd done it before calling in the counselors and alarming the entire community with his cryptic e-mail.

"I don't know," Sylvia said. "*This*, I imagine."

"I imagine," she agreed. "Well, I can talk to the kids if he wants."

"He said he might open up the back alley tomorrow," Sylvia said.

The alley ran between the street and the playground area behind the school and was sometimes used during fire drills. Grace had never known it to be deputized as an alternate entrance. *Desperate times*, she thought.

"Oh, I'm sure things won't get any worse than this," she told Sylvia. "It'll calm down. It's not about the school."

"I hope you're right." Sylvia shrugged.

Grace left the scrum of mothers and went into the lobby, then upstairs to the administrative floor. The walls of the stairwell were covered in student artwork, framed class photographs, and posters from the musicals and plays dating back to Grace's own time at Rearden. Passing one, she glanced automatically at a preadolescent version of herself in costume for her seventh-grade production of *The Gondoliers* (she had been in the chorus), and she noted for perhaps the hundredth time how sharply the straight line of her middle-parted hair stood out, very white against her very dark braids. She could not remember the last time she had braided her hair. Or parted it.

His heavy oak office door was open a bit, but she knocked on it anyway. "Robert?"

"Oh—" He nearly leapt up from the desk. "Good. Oh, good, did Sylvia find you?"

"Downstairs."

"Oh." He looked a little confused nonetheless. "Why don't you shut the door."

She did, then sat in one of the chairs on the other side of the desk. Inevitably, she thought of being summoned to the principal's office. Though she never had been, either as a student or as a parent. She had always been dutiful and rule-abiding, and so had Henry.

After a moment in which he seemed, weirdly, to have forgotten what he wanted to see her about, she said, more to help him out than anything else: "This is a terrible thing."

"Awful." He sat, oddly not looking at her. "How are you?"

Grace frowned. "Oh, fine. I barely knew her, but you were right to try to get on top of this right away."

She did not mention the e-mail. If he wanted to know whether he should have handled things differently, he would ask her.

He didn't ask her. In fact, he didn't seem to be asking her anything.

Finally, she said: "Do you want me to talk to the kids? I don't normally work with children, but I'd be glad to help if you need more hands."

Robert looked at her directly for the first time. "Grace," he said, "you know, the police were here."

She sat up a little in her chair. "Well, I assumed. I assumed they came to tell you what happened." She said this very carefully. Very deliberately. But he still looked at her as if he were grasping for some basic meaning. *Is he losing it?* she thought. He was so altered from the easy, triumphant, slightly drunk Robert she had chatted with on Saturday night. How many days ago was that? She counted back. Not many. He looked traumatized. Well, she reminded herself, of course he did.

"We've had a number of conversations, actually."

"About her son?" Grace frowned. "Miguel?"

He nodded. A ray of morning sun happened to catch his hair in just the wrong way, making his scalp shine through. *Poor Robert,* she couldn't help thinking. *It's going to go fast. And you have such a pretty face.*

"They were very interested in Miguel's financial arrangement with the school," said Robert. "About his scholarship."

"Well, that's bizarre," she said, thinking: *And so is this conversation.* "I mean, why should they care about his scholarship?"

He pursed his lips, looking at her. He seemed genuinely at a loss.

"Grace," he finally managed, "I hope you understand that I need to cooperate fully with the police. I may not understand the methodology, but I'm not in control of this situation."

"Okay," she said, baffled. "I'm . . . I can't imagine how the school's system of awarding scholarships is relevant, but like you said, they're in charge."

"Miguel's scholarship was not a conventional arrangement for us. It wasn't set up through the usual channels."

Oh, my God, she thought wildly, abruptly locating her inner adolescent self: *Ask me if I care!* Then, because she had no rational response to this, she just put up her hands.

Now he was merely looking at her. He looked and looked, as if he, too, had lost the very slender chain of logic in this unutterably strange conversation. She had been in his office now for how many minutes? And she still had no idea why he'd wanted to see her. And the atmosphere was getting murkier by the second. Frankly, she preferred it downstairs, even among the other freaked-out moms.

"So . . . ," she said finally, "did you want me to talk to the students? I have a pretty full morning today, but I could come in the afternoon."

"Oh . . ." He sat up straight and attempted a very strained smile. "No. That's kind of you, Grace. But I think we have enough."

She shrugged again and thought: *Well, all right, then, I'll just . . .*

And she just went out. And wished she had spared herself the entire episode. Now she was far from sanguine about Robert and for the first time concerned with how he was holding up under the obvious pressure. Maybe he had wanted help for himself, it occurred to her, passing again the photo of herself as a braided gondolier. Maybe that was what he had found so obviously difficult to say. *I'm overwhelmed by what's happening. Can I talk to you?* All at once, she felt so concerned for him and so guilty that she stopped, her hand on the handrail, and looked back up the way she had come.

But she couldn't go back. More than anything, she just wanted to get away from here. And air. She wanted air.

She left by the front gate, turning east along the tree-lined street and then south on Third, heading, she supposed, to her office on 76th. But in fact her first patients weren't due for nearly an hour, and when she thought about going there and sitting alone in silence (or, worse, opening up her computer again), she understood that she was afraid. Her cell phone, which she had been checking every ten minutes or so, still showed nothing, or nothing that wasn't maddening. A CNN news alert about an earthquake in Pakistan, an offer from a store she had never heard of for a product she didn't want, an "update" from Rearden letting parents know that counselors would be available to meet with them in the K/pre-K dining room after three p.m., to "discuss any concerns about your children's well-being." *What narcissists we've all become!* she thought, mystified and enraged. *What terribly sensitive, terribly important people we are! I have a concern about my child's well-being? My concern is that there are people in the world who murder women and leave them in "blood-strewn" apartments for their children to find. I think this might be bad for the children. It might give them "issues." It might signal "dysfunction" in the family and be "traumatic."*

Also, I don't know where my husband is.

She reached her office about ten minutes before her patients were due and went about her customary routine: lights on, bathroom checked, Kleenex replenished, and a final look over her schedule for the day. There seemed to be a theme here, she thought, running her eye over the booking page of her office program. The couple about to arrive had separated the previous year after the husband's affair, then made a sober, iron-willed decision to attempt reconciliation, though Grace (while lauding their effort) did not believe the husband, a screenwriter, could actually stop pursuing other women. After them came the woman whose husband's "college experimentation" with men had returned to haunt them both and become the predominant theme in their sessions. Today she was coming alone, and while Grace generally did not agree to see partners individually, she was pretty sure that the joint sessions were now well and truly ended and that the wife would want to keep seeing her alone after they formally separated. And after that was a newer patient whose fiancé had been arrested for embezzlement at the company where they both worked and who was in a very fraught state.

Then she was supposed to go to her father's house, for dinner.

She didn't know where Jonathan was.

She opened her e-mail and typed in his address. It galled her that she was doing this, that she had to instruct him to get in touch with her. Yes, he could be absentminded. Over the years, he had slipped up on any number of appointments, dinner reservations, violin recitals, and certainly stupid things like Mother's Day and Valentine's Day, which were only manufactured holidays meant to sell chocolate and greeting cards. But always there had been a reason, and the kind of reason that made you ashamed for having demanded a reason—like, for example a little kid dying of cancer.

"Jonathan," she typed, "would you please get in touch with me RIGHT NOW. And I mean AS SOON AS YOU READ THIS. Henry's fine," she wrote, feeling guilty for the freak-out she would certainly be experiencing upon receipt of this particular communiqué. "Just call me ASAP."

And she sent it off into the ether of e-mail, to find him wherever he was, in whichever Midwestern city the pediatric oncology conference was actually taking place. But had it actually been a pediatric oncology conference? Maybe he'd only called it that because his own interest was pediatric oncology, but the conference itself was really pediatrics as a whole or oncology as a whole or even something merely adjacent to one of those. It might be...a conference on new antibody-based drugs or genetic technologies, or a meeting focused on palliative care or even alternative care. Well, probably not alternative care. She couldn't see Jonathan wanting to attend a conference on alternative care; like nearly every doctor he'd ever worked with, he was firmly trussed to the mast of Western medicine. Grace had only ever known one of his colleagues to show any interest in what the woman herself had apparently called "parallel healing strategies," and she had left New York long before, to practice somewhere—Grace seemed to recall—in the Southwest.

No, but the point was, this whole thing might be her own fault, the fault of her general distraction due to...well, a lot of things. Work as a whole, her son, the benefit, her book, for goodness' sake! She might easily have taken a few disconnected concepts like pediatric...oncological...flyover state, and somehow conjured the fully fledged notion of a pediatric oncology conference in Cleveland. *Typical me!* she thought almost jovially.

But it really wasn't. Typical her. And it never had been.

Her couple arrived. When Grace asked how their week had been, the husband began a vicious monologue about the producer who had bought his script the previous year but now seemed disinclined to make it into an actual film. His wife sat grim-faced, tautly wound, at the other end of the couch as he went on, gathering many of his other aggravations and resentments to himself in a building fulcrum: the producer's assistant, who was so passive-aggressive, who obviously did not understand that it was to your own benefit to be kind to people on the way up the ladder, and his own agent, who took four days to return a call, though he'd been seen at Michael's for lunch on the second day and was obviously not at death's door, unable to push the buttons on his phone.

Grace—listening, not listening, not really—head spinning a little, nodded whenever he paused for breath but couldn't bring herself to interrupt him, and she felt terrible about that. There had been a joke, passed among the students in her master's program, that she had not found very funny at the time, about two psychotherapists who rode the elevator together back and forth to their adjoining offices for years: up at the start of the day, down at the end of the day. One was dour, depressed, burdened by the burdens of his patients. The other was eternally upbeat. One day, after years of this disparity, the dour therapist said to his colleague: "I don't understand. Our patients have so many terrible things in their lives. How can you listen to them all day and still be so happy?"

The other man's answer: "Who listens?"

She had always listened.

But today, right now, she just couldn't listen. She couldn't *hear*.

The wife was shifting, growing palpably more resentful with each fresh character assassination from the other end of the couch. The actress who was supposed to be considering the part but was obviously too old. The young Tarantino freak in the screenwriting class he taught who had complained about him on Facebook, saying he wasn't qualified since he hadn't had a movie made. His wife's sister, who was insisting they all go out to fucking Wisconsin this year for Christmas, which was ridiculous because she didn't even like them and had always been a bitch to her older sister, his wife, so why she thought they would go spend a fortune on tickets and deal with the airport on the busiest travel day of the year just showed how deluded she was.

"Yes?" said Grace.

The wife exhaled, very carefully.

"This is all about Sarah's mother," the husband went on. "She called Sarah a few months ago and told her to bring Corinne back to Madison and live with her. You know, as if my family is any of her business."

"Steven," said his wife in a warning tone.

"But my wife politely declines. Because she is my *wife*, and Corinne is my *daughter*. And whatever issues we have, we're working on, no thanks to her mother. But now we're supposed to pretend that this episode never happened and just fly out to fucking nowhere for figgy pudding."

And she knew what she was supposed to say. She knew she was supposed to say *something*. But she didn't say anything.

"They're worried about me," said Sarah, his wife. "Just the way you'd be worried about Corinne if she was having trouble in her life. In her marriage."

"I moved back *in*," he said petulantly, as if this matter of geography swept all attendant issues aside.

"Yes, and they understand that. They know we're trying. They just wanted us all"—Grace, glancing at the husband, noted that he was as unpersuaded by this "all" as she herself was—"to feel supported at Christmas."

He glared at her. Then he said: "I'm Jewish, Sarah."

"We're all Jewish. That's not the point."

He exploded. This being another of his sand traps, one they had not previously trod upon in therapy, but so similar to the others (his career, his parents' interference, his now pubescent daughter's sudden lack of outright adoration for him) that Grace could, from the comfort of her armchair, plot the hills and valleys of the forty minutes remaining in their session. So he raged on, both women uncharacteristically silent. Grace looked past them both to the venetian blinds covering the window behind them and through those angled slats to the glass pane that was grimy with New York dust. Sometimes she gave the doorman, Arthur, some extra money to wash the outside of the pane, but it had been awhile. She could slip out now and do it herself, she thought, and neither of them would notice, and then at least she would have accomplished something today, and the sun would come in. If there was sun. She suddenly could not remember whether there was sun.

When it ended, she used what remained of her wherewithal to resist apologizing to them and saw them out with a request that they not discuss the Christmas travel issue before their next session, but that they each think carefully about what they wanted the holiday to represent for them and for their daughter. Then she used the five minutes before her next patient to check her phone and e-mail.

There was nothing. At least, there was nothing from Jonathan. A Sue Krause from NY1 had left a voice mail asking for a statement about "the situation" at Rearden and wondering whether she had any memories of Malaga Alves she would like to share with her seven million fellow New Yorkers. That this unpleasant request had materialized on her office phone was of course preferable to finding it on her cell phone, or in her personal e-mail, or God forbid her home phone, but it still galled her. No, not everyone was eternally eager to thrust himself before a television camera in order to toss some "Me too!" filament of non-information onto a genuine tragedy. Grace deleted the message, but even as she did so, the phone rang, emitting its silent "in session" blink. She didn't recognize the number, a New York cell, but she played the message as soon as it materialized.

"Dr. Reinhart Sachs, it's Roberta Siegel from Page Six."

Spoken as if she were supposed to know who that was. But in fact, Grace did at least know what Page Six was. Everyone knew what Page Six was, even those who—like herself—declined to indulge in the daily download of so-called boldface names. That Page Six was showing an interest in what was going on at Rearden boded very ill, for where Page Six went so went the nation. At least, the nation of those with too much time on their hands.

"I've been told you were a good friend of Malaga Alves, and I wonder if you have a few minutes to talk to me."

Grace closed her eyes. How she'd been upgraded from fellow committee member to "good friend" was a mystery, but not, she supposed, one worth solving. This message, too, she deleted, but not before wondering whether Sally Morrison-Golden, another "good friend," had also heard from Page Six. She hoped not.

Her next patient arrived and began, without much preamble, to cry. This was the woman who had canceled her appointment the previous week, the woman whose husband was now somewhere in Chelsea, address withheld, and reachable only at work (and there only by leaving a message and awaiting a callback). He was no longer interested in counseling, said the wife—wailed the wife—other than the legal kind. Her name was Lisa, and she was in her thirties, muscular, on the short side, and by her own definition "sort of a klutz"—something Grace herself could have confirmed, as there had been innumerable bangings against one particular corner of the coffee table. This week she had indeed been advised of the end of her marriage—in a kindly enough manner, she reported to Grace almost defensively—and given the name of an attorney her husband had hired, as well as a few names of divorce attorneys that attorney had recommended—for her. (Was that absurd politeness? Grace wondered. Or plain old shady?)

She cried for a long time, crumpling tissue after tissue, alternately covering and uncovering her face. Grace did not try to stop her. She imagined it must be hard to find time to cry like this, with a full-time job at one of the city's more beleaguered public agencies and those five-year-old girls, just barely in kindergarten. With the husband already moved out, Grace worried that she would no longer be able to afford her apartment or the private school she wanted to send the girls to next year. Or therapy, for that matter. Not that therapy would be an issue. Grace had been in this situation once or twice over the years and had always managed to carry her patient at least through the crisis.

The husband, it turned out—surprise!—had a boyfriend, and the boyfriend had a tricked-out duplex on a tree-lined street in Chelsea, where—surprise again!—the husband was now living. She had followed him there, the woman said, sobbing. "I had to. He wasn't answering the phone. And I left a message for him at his office and he didn't call me. And Sammy kept asking why Daddy wasn't walking them to school, and I finally thought, *I am* lying *to my* kids. *And I have no idea* why."

"That must have been very painful," said Grace.

"I mean," she said bitterly, "okay, I get it, he's out of the marriage. I get it. He's gay. But we still have these kids. What am I supposed to tell them? He went to the Korean grocer for cottage cheese and he hasn't come back? Oh, and by the way, Mommy's an imbecile because when this handsome man supposedly fell in love with her and wanted to marry her and have a family, she actually believed him?"

Grace sighed. They had been down this road before.

"I was always this totally pragmatic, totally rational person, you know? I mean—duh!—I wasn't skinny and blond. I'm not a babe. I'm not going to date the football captain. I know this! And it was okay, because the truth was I didn't really want the football captain. And I had all these nice boyfriends who appreciated that I didn't act like I wished I could do better. I could have had a great life with one of those guys, but suddenly this great-looking man comes along and it's like, 'You mean I could have him?' And like that, it's all gone. I guess he thought I'd be so, like, blinded and pathetic that I wouldn't notice he was full of shit when he said he wanted to get married and have kids."

"But, Lisa," Grace told her weeping client, "I think a lot of what Daniel told you was probably the truth. He really did want to be married and have a family. Maybe he even said to himself, 'I want that so much that I'm going to…to try to excise the other part of me that wants other things.' But he couldn't. Most of us can't do that. The pull toward what we really crave, it's just too strong."

"I don't give in to everything I want," Lisa said a little petulantly.

"You've never tried to not be attracted to men," she said. "You know, men used to enter the priesthood because they wanted to be protected from their own homosexuality. That's how terrified of it they were. To actually go out looking for a way to not be sexual for your entire life is a big gesture, obviously; you'd really have to hate or fear your sexual identity for that to seem like a good idea. And then there's the fact that Daniel obviously loved you—loves you—I think he wanted very badly to be a husband and a father. He tried to do something that would make that happen, and he failed—and that's his own issue, not yours. Your issue is that you had an opportunity to anticipate this, early on, and that opportunity passed you by. At some point, I do think it's going to help you to look at that, but not today. Today is about being sad, which you're absolutely entitled to be."

"You mean I should have known," she said bluntly.

Yes, Grace thought.

"No," she said. "I mean that in the context of your real love for him, and your trust in him, and the fact that you wanted the same things he was saying he wanted, your ability to see clearly what you might have seen in other circumstances was compromised. You're a human being. You're fallible, not criminal. The last thing you need to be doing right now is punishing yourself for not having seen this. It serves no purpose, and it takes a hell of a lot of your energy, and you need every bit of your energy right now to take care of yourself and the girls. Besides, I know that Daniel is beating himself up about his inability to be honest with you."

"Oh, goody," she said, reaching for another tissue.

They sat in silence for a moment. Grace felt her thoughts begin to detach, against her will. She wanted to stay with this, with someone else's problem, even though it was a very bad problem. Her own problem, which was probably going to turn out to be not really much of a problem, hurt too much to think about.

"Did you know?" said her patient.

Grace frowned. "Did I know what?"

"About Daniel. Could you tell?"

"No," she said. But this was not really true. Grace had suspected from the beginning and known shortly after. She had watched what felt like an epic war play out inside him, in which the part of him that truly wanted to be married to Lisa slowly, inexorably, succumbed to the cataclysmically greater force of his sexuality. In their eight months as her patients, she had never seen him touch her.

"He has a Rothko."

"Daniel?" said Grace, wondering if they were going to start talking about financial settlements.

"No. Barry. The guy on Thirty-Second Street."

She couldn't bring herself to say "boyfriend," Grace knew.

"Is that significant to you?"

"He has. A fucking. Rothko. Over the fireplace in his brownstone. Which I saw through the window while standing outside on the adorable tree-lined street in highly desirable Chelsea. I'm sharing a box with two little girls on York Avenue. I've produced his children so now he can be a father on the weekends like he always wanted, and spend the rest of the time being his 'authentic self.'"

"Authentic self" was a phrase Daniel had brought into therapy. It had attained "Rosebud"-like status, apparently, to Lisa.

"I'm certainly not going to tell you you're not entitled to your anger."

"Oh, good," Lisa said bitterly. Then she said: "You'd like to tell me something else, though, wouldn't you?"

"What is it you think I'd like to tell you?"

She followed Lisa's glance to—or was it her imagination—the galley of her book, there on the corner of her desk. She had not specifically informed any of her patients about the book (she thought it was improper, like a doctor pushing his own products at the front desk), but a few of them had seen or been told about the *Kirkus* review, and one, who worked for *Good Morning America*, had been privy to her competitive courtship by all three network morning programs.

"That I could have avoided all this. I could have listened more carefully."

"Is that what you think I believe?"

"Oh, don't give me that Freudian shit!" Lisa leaned forward. She had said it fiercely. She had suddenly, and without warning, turned a corner to some well-thought-out and very focused anger. The focus, Grace realized, *c'est moi*.

"I mean," she continued, now with discernible sarcasm, "if I'd wanted somebody to sit there and just toss it all back to me, I'd be in analysis. Obviously, you think I should have seen this, I colluded in this. I know you've been thinking from the beginning, you know, *How come she didn't know she was marrying a gay man?* I've been watching you for months, thinking that. So, okay, it's abundantly clear to me that you're not going to turn into some warm and fuzzy person who's going to comfort me, but I could do without the judgment, thanks."

Breathe, thought Grace. *And don't say anything. There's more to come.*

"I didn't want you. I wanted the other one we went to see, last January. This therapist near Lincoln Center. He was enormous. He had sideburns. He was like this big bear. I thought: *I feel safe here. I feel supported.* But Daniel wanted you. He thought you were tough. He thought we needed tough. But I've got plenty of tough already, thanks. I mean, do you ever show any *feeling*?"

Grace, aware of the extreme tension in her back, in her crossed legs, made herself wait another moment before she said, very carefully, very *deliberately*: "I don't believe my feeling is going to be helpful to you, Lisa. Therapeutically. I'm here to bring you my expertise and, if appropriate, my opinions. My job is to help you work through the issues that brought you here. It's going to be much less useful to you to have comfort from me than to learn how best to comfort yourself."

"Maybe." Lisa nodded. "Or maybe you're just a cold bitch."

She willed herself not to react. The moment stretched, in all its misery, as a car horn blared outside. Then Lisa leaned forward and plucked another tissue from the box.

"I'm sorry," she said, looking past Grace to the door. "That was uncalled for."

Grace nodded. "Therapy isn't a social occasion. I'll recover. But I'm curious as to why you wanted to continue seeing me. Especially since I seem to have been Daniel's choice, not yours. Maybe, in spite of what you perceive as my lack of warmth, you've come to believe that I can help you."

She shrugged miserably. She had started to cry again, a little.

"And I do think I can help you," Grace went on. "I see how strong you are. I've always seen that. Right now, you're angry at him and at yourself, and obviously at me, but I know that's nothing to the sadness you feel about losing the family you thought you had. And the truth is there's no way around these feelings of anger and sadness.

You've got to go through them to get to the other side of them, and I'd really like to help you do that, so you can have some peace for yourself and the girls. And peace with Daniel, because he's going to be in your life, regardless. So I may not have facial hair or a cuddly disposition, and believe me, you're not the first of my clients to point that out to me—"

Lisa emitted a moist little laugh.

"But if I didn't think I could help you, I'd have told you so already. And I would also have helped you find a more bearlike therapist, if that's what you really wanted."

She leaned her head back against the couch and closed her eyes. "No," she said, sounding exhausted. "I know you're right. But…it's just…sometimes I look at you and I think, *Well* she *never would have fallen for this*. I'm, like, personally a disaster and you're personally composed. And I know we're not supposed to talk about you, and I don't really want to talk about you, but sometimes I just see: *composed*, and I think: *cold bitch*. Which I'm not proud of. And…well, of course I checked you out, back in the spring when we started. Which I hope you won't be offended by, but you know, today we practically do a background check on a plumber, let alone someone you're going to tell all your secrets to."

"I'm not offended," Grace said. And she shouldn't have been surprised, either.

"So I know you've been married for ages and you have this book coming out about how not to marry a psycho or something. And here I sit, your, like, target moronic reader."

"Oh no," she said evenly. "My target reader isn't a moron. She's just someone who isn't through learning."

Lisa crumpled her current tissue and shoved it in her purse. Their time, they both knew, was nearly up. "I guess I better read it."

Grace did nothing to suggest that this was a good idea. "If you feel it might interest you, certainly," she said. She turned to her desk and began writing Lisa's invoice.

"It will help me next time," she heard Lisa say.

And despite herself, Grace smiled. *Good girl*, she thought. It boded well that even in the depths of her present misery, Lisa could conceptualize a next time. She was going to be all right, Grace thought. Even poorer than she was now, and more burdened, and possibly humiliated, and with her husband in an art-filled brownstone on (Grace knew perfectly well) one of the loveliest streets in the city, she still saw a glimpse of future.

Then again, thought Grace, *at least she knows where her husband is.*

CHAPTER TEN

HOSPITAL LAND

After the last couple left, she didn't know what to do with herself. She couldn't bear to stay in the office, listening to the phone not ring and dreading the ring that wasn't coming. But then again she couldn't stand the thought of going back to Rearden, retracing her steps from the morning no wiser and no less scared even than then. She didn't want to count the news vans or see the self-consciously frantic parents in the forecourt, and she didn't want to hear anything that Sally Morrison-Golden might say to her on any subject, but especially the subject of Malaga Alves. She had no idea what had happened to Malaga Alves, and with every passing moment she found herself caring less. Malaga, the poor woman—the dead woman—had nothing to do with her, but there was an asteroid on the horizon, and it got bigger, denser, and more terrible with every passing hour.

Where was Jonathan? Where was he, and why wasn't he letting her know that he was safe? And how dare he disappear so thoughtlessly? What was she supposed to be telling their son about where he was, had Jonathan thought of that? What was she supposed to tell her father? And fucking Eva, who needed to know how many plates to set at the table?

She could not remember ever having been so angry at him. Or so terrified.

Grace left her office at two and walked into a wall of bad weather, something neither the *New York Times* nor the earlier sky nor any of her arriving patients had given her any warning about. She pulled her coat around herself and found that she remained very cold and more than a little wet, and she leaned into the wind, feeling the strangely not unwelcome bite of it and the wetness of the rain on her face. Everyone's face was wet. *We could all be crying*, it occurred to her, and she reached up with one very suddenly freezing hand to brush her own cheek. She was not crying. She was just . . . not right at the moment. Which was not a crime, and frankly no one else's business but her own.

She went south, away from Henry's school and down Lexington, past magazine shops and Korean grocers and the kind of now rare luncheonettes she had always loved—dingy places with stools at the bar and great hamburgers and mints in a little bowl at the counter where you paid your bill. Everyone seemed to be struggling with the wind. Two older women came out of Neil's and yelped in surprise, then ducked back inside, frantically buttoning their coats. Neil's was a place she'd gone with Jonathan, many times, during his residency at Memorial. It was near enough for him to get to quickly, far enough from the hospital that he didn't have to run into colleagues, and she loved the Russian burger on their menu. There had been times, all those years when she was trying to get pregnant and was so finely attuned to any little tweak in her body and its wants, that she had literally run to Neil's for a hamburger, as if satisfying a sudden craving would actually make her pregnant or nurture a zygote into personhood. Well-done meat, just to be safe, and no cheese, because you couldn't really be sure about cheese, and why take a chance after so many disappointments, so many filaments of life fallen out of her and flushed away?

She hadn't thought about that for a long time; it seemed churlish to do so, after Henry was born. Then, she had been persuading herself that all those missing filaments, those stricken possibilities, had been something anticipatory, like a red carpet unfurled before the arrival of the real movie star. From the minute there was a Henry, it had always been about Henry. Wanting Henry. Waiting for Henry. Being ready for Henry.

She hadn't been to Neil's in years, with Jonathan or anyone else. Once she had ordered a delivery meal from here, but even though the luncheonette was only a couple of blocks from her office, and even though she had called at the very start of her hour-long break, the burger had arrived fifty minutes later and cold in the middle, so that had been the end.

She was on the corner of 69th and Lexington, waiting for the light when the phone, deep in her coat pocket, vibrated against her thigh. She clawed for it, lost it once to the depths of the pocket, then snatched it up to the daylight.

The number on the caller ID ran through her like a white-hot blade. She wanted to throw the phone down into the streaming street, but she couldn't, and she couldn't ignore the call, either. She answered with a damp finger.

"Hello, Maud."

"Grace!" said Maud. "Wait, J. Colton? Are you on?"

"Present!" the publicist said brightly. "I'm in L.A., but I'm present!"

"We wanted to call you together," said Maud. "Are you in your office?"

Grace steadied herself. She looked around for a canopy but there wasn't one, only a small overhang in front of the Chase Bank. Miserably, she backed up against the glass storefront. "No, on the street," she told them. She held the phone tightly to her ear.

"How's California?" Maud was saying.

"God. Glorious."

"And our movie star?"

"You're not paying me enough."

Maud laughed delightedly. To Grace, it sounded utterly wrong, it did not compute. Laughter on Lexington Avenue when it was pissing with rain and an awful thing was tugging at her—incessantly, interrupting every other thought.

"A certain lady thespian to be named later," said Maud, evidently to Grace. "Not, shall we say, known for her modesty."

"Okay," said Grace. She closed her eyes.

"But listen. I had a call about you. Are you ready?"

She looked bleakly across the street at a large man struggling with his umbrella. "Yes!" It came out sounding tragic, but they seemed not to notice.

"*The View*!"

This was followed by what sounded like silence. "The . . . few?" said Grace.

"*View.* Five women on a couch? You don't watch it? It's Whoopi Goldberg."

"Oh. Yes, I've heard of it. I'm doing that?"

"Knock wood!" Maud crowed.

"Great," Grace said, looking down. There was a line of damp across both leather boots. *Ruined*, she thought sourly. She could not understand why she had gone out in this. What was she thinking? When had it become so uncomfortable to think about anything?

"Can't tell you how hard it is to get a book on *The View*," J. Colton was saying. Grace imagined her by a pool at an L.A. hotel. But then she couldn't remember what J. Colton looked like. "I mean, we send them everything, of course. But do they read it? Who knows? So I get this call from Barbara Walters' producer, and she goes, 'Women need to read this book.' And I said, '*Exactly!*'"

"Exactly," Maud confirmed. "This is huge, Grace. Oh, and what about Miami?"

What about Miami? Grace thought, but the question was apparently not for her.

"Miami's a go," said California J. Colton.

"The Miami Book Fair wants you," said Maud, sounding merry. "How do you feel about Florida in general?"

Grace frowned. Her face was still wet, and her feet were very cold. The conversation contained so many unknowns. She wondered if they had segued into another dialect. She had no particular feelings about Florida in general. She didn't want to live there, she knew that, though at the present moment it was probably a far more pleasant place to be, weather-wise. Were they suggesting she move to Florida? "I don't know," was all she managed.

Because the Jewish Book Council, said Maud, had let them know that she, that Grace, that her book, *You Should Have Known*, was going to be their lead title for the winter. "You know what this means?" J. Colton said.

Grace told them no, she didn't know what it meant.

It meant more trips, to big Jewish centers full of readers, many of them in Florida.

She frowned. "But it's not really a Jewish book."

"No, but you're a Jewish author."

Not really, she nearly said. Her parents' home had been mainly absent of Jewish practices and utterly absent of Jewish belief. Her mother, as close to an anti-Semite as a Jewish person could get, would don the necessary accoutrements for her friends' children's bar mitzvahs and weddings but preferred to stoke her inner life with classical music and other beautiful things. Her father had the German Jew's general disdain for things of the shtetl but had taken, mysteriously enough, to his second wife's observance of Jewish ritual. Grace believed nothing and did even less.

"And they never do this kind of book," said Maud. "Novels and memoirs, and lots of nonfiction. But a book like *Should*—"

Should was Maud's personal abbreviation for *You Should Have Known*. Obviously the title was in need of a nickname, but Grace could not bring herself to call her book *Should*.

"I can't remember, ever. J. Colton? Have they ever taken a book like this?"

"They took *The Rules*, I think," said J. Colton.

Grace automatically rolled her eyes. She was glad they couldn't see her.

"They took Dr. Laura."

"Oh God," Grace said, mere aversion progressing to outright horror. "She's appalling."

"She's appalling and she has a gazillion listeners, Grace," said Maud, laughing. "We're trying to get you on her show."

Grace said nothing.

"And the tour," Maud went on. "We're working on early February. Give people a chance to hear about the book before we send you out. Did you know people need to hear the name of a new book three times before they buy it?"

Grace had not known. She had never thought about it.

"So, a story in a magazine, a prominent book review, then you're on a talk show and people go, 'Wait, I heard about that book!' Or they go to the bookstore and it's there on the front table, which is paid real estate, by the way. You know that, right?"

Assuming she was understanding what "paid real estate" meant in this context, no, Grace had not known that either. The things she had not known were piling up. The rain was bouncing off the pavement, falling down, jumping up. Farther down the street, a portly dachshund was refusing to walk. He cringed and shuddered on his stubby brown legs, and his owner looked down balefully at him. She began to wonder what it would take to make this conversation end.

"But we're doing a full month at Barnes and Noble. You know, I'm so glad we moved it up. Aren't you glad, Grace?"

She nodded dully. "Yes!" she managed.

You Should Have Known had first been scheduled for February 14, a gesture Grace had considered more than a little cynical, but Maud had moved it to early January in order not to compete with a relationship book by a sex columnist from another imprint within the same company. January books got a bad rap, she had explained to Grace (as if Grace had ever even noticed what time of year certain books were published), but this was actually a good thing. Because January was a slow time for books, review editors had fewer books to weed through, which meant there was a better chance of having reviews and features written. And besides, after the holidays people got in the mood for a little self-reflection, a little tough self-love.

Maud had said it, so it had to be true.

"It's much easier to get on the List in January than, say, in the fall."

"Like, remember...you know that memoir we did?" J. Colton was asking from poolside. "About the girl who was bit by the rabid dogs? That was a January book. It took only twenty thousand in sales to get on the List with that book."

Grace thought hard—girl, bit (bitten?), rabid dogs, the List—but of course it turned out that J. Colton wasn't speaking to her.

The two of them were talking about books again. These people talked constantly about books—books they wanted to read or wished they'd read, books they'd heard were wonderful, books she—Grace—should read, books she *must* read, books she couldn't possibly *not* have read. *You Should Have Read That!* They made Grace, who had always liked to read, feel entirely illiterate.

She thought: *I am standing under an overhang on Lexington Avenue, in a wool coat and wet boots, holding an open phone in a cold hand that is shaking. The phone is shaking, too. I am thirty-nine years old, married for eighteen years, the mother of a twelve-year-old son. I am a therapist in private practice. I am the author of a book. I am the lead author, for winter, of the Jewish Book Council in Florida. I will have to go to Florida. All of these things are true. I know them for sure.*

"Grace?" It was Maud. "Are you there?"

"Oh, I'm so sorry," she said. "It's all fantastic news."

She must have been persuasive, because they let her go.

Grace put her head down and walked out from underneath the overhang, south down the avenue, and then east to the familiar streets of her first years with Jonathan. She did not know where she was going until she passed the grubby postwar tower on First Avenue where she and Jonathan had once lived in a charmless one-bedroom at the end of a dingy beige corridor. The place seemed utterly unchanged, even to the artificial plant on the lobby coffee table and the Staten Island–fabulous light fixture hanging from the ceiling. She did not recognize the uniformed doorman but gave him an automatic half-smile anyway, a gesture toward her own history. Emerging from the front door and pausing beneath the awning were younger versions of herself and her husband: newly minted professionals with briefcases and yoga mats, dry-cleaning sacks slung over their shoulders and environmentally responsible canvas grocery bags dangling at the wrist, bound for D'Agostino's. She would hate to be living here now, she thought. She had hated it then, though she had made the best of it, painting the walls with colors from Martha Stewart's midcentury palette ("midcentury" was the best she could conjure from such irredeemably bland rooms) and refusing to supplement the few bits of actually good furniture they had with the abundantly available cheap stuff (which made for very sparse rooms). She was not all that distracted by décor back then. Neither of them was, since at the time they had really had only a few things on their minds: their careers, first and foremost, and making a baby. She stopped in the rain, took out her phone again, and looked at it balefully. Then she stuck it back in her pocket and went on.

Now that it was clear where she was going, Grace walked more quickly, heading south again, down York. She had entered Hospital Land—Jonathan's name for this neighborhood and now hers. It was not merely a part of the city in which hospitals—Cornell and Special Surgery and of course Memorial, the mother ship—were present, but an area that had gradually transmogrified into feudal lands encircling those hospitals, serving them, housing their workers, anticipating and fulfilling their needs.

Hospitals, of course, were not like other places to work—not remotely. Shops and restaurants emptied at night and were locked up. Offices wound down, diminishing and diminishing until the very last worker turned out the very last light. But the hospitals never emptied and they certainly never closed. They thrummed with the sheer imperative of what was going on inside, jittering on in perpetual crisis. They were worlds unto themselves, informed by the art, the science, and of course the commerce of illness. They were dramatic stages on which an incalculable number of great stories (mostly tragic) were playing on a perpetual loop: scenes of recognition and reversal, religious fervor, redemption and reconciliation, cataclysmic loss. In Hospital Land you lurched from event to event. In Hospital Land, the very stuff of human experience was perpetually cracked open and held to the light. The general urgency and sense of higher purpose, it permeated everything in the neighborhood.

Jonathan thrived in Hospital Land, just as he'd thrived in medical school, and before that in college. He was one of those people who somehow knew everybody's name and was pretty much current on the main events in their lives. Grace, who'd never shared this ability (or, to be honest, desired to have it), had observed him deep in conversation with absolutely everyone, with hospital administrators and doctors and nurses and orderlies and the guy who wheeled the soiled linens down to the immense laundry in the basement, and she knew he sometimes held up the line at the hospital cafeteria because he was chatting away with the hairnetted lunch ladies. He had the exact same kind of intensity with absolutely everyone, king or commoner in the land, an avid interest and a need for connection. When you placed him beside another human being, something just happened to him: He slowly, inexorably, turned the full beam of his glorious attention on that person, and that person responded—turning, turning, orienting to this marvelous new source of energy. It made Grace think of those time-lapse films, where the flower slowly twists its face to the sun and opens its petals. She had been watching this happen for almost twenty years, and it was still just a little bit enthralling.

Jonathan inhaled other people. He wanted to know who they were and what mattered to them and maybe also what wounds their lives and characters had formed around. Almost without exception, he could get people to talk about their dead fathers or drug-addicted sons, and she did admire that quality very much, though it had meant many episodes of waiting on the curb as her husband wrapped up his exchange with the taxi driver, or pointedly holding their coats beside him as he wrote down the title of a book or the name of a hotel on Lesbos from some waiter. He had always been like that, she supposed. He had been like that with her, from that first night in the tunnels. She thought he must have been born that way. One did not always expect the best from doctors, in terms of their characters. It was said, with some justification, Grace believed, that they were cold or self-aggrandizing or labored beneath a God complex. But imagine you had a child who was sick—very sick—and think how comforted you must be to find your very sick child in the care of someone who clearly reached beyond himself and his own needs, who was so respectful not just of your child, but of you, who thought deeply about the human experience your child's illness had created, even as he labored to relieve suffering.

Grace felt invisible now, walking east on 69th, letting the men and women in scrubs of various hues and patterns walk past her. She watched the usual smokers (even in the rain, even backed into the alcoves of a cancer hospital) and saw that they were the only ones not moving fast. She felt as if there were some kind of light around her that was glaring and noteworthy and made her seem suspect, as if she were doing something transgressive. She had never done anything suspect or transgressive. All she wanted, now, was to get away from here. She had nearly reached the corner. She might simply turn—north on York, away from Memorial's entrance—and no one would have the slightest idea that something had gone very, very wrong in her afternoon, if not her life. But instead, for some reason she did not anticipate, let alone examine, she spun abruptly, as in a square dance or a marching formation, in order to charge back up the street she had just walked down, and so she found herself hurtling into the unprepared people who had been behind her, who were very busy citizens of Hospital Land, a few of whom gave looks of some displeasure, and one of whom called her by name.

"Grace?" he said.

Grace looked up, into the rain and into the face of Stu Rosenfeld.

"I thought that was you," he said, affably enough. "You've changed your hair."

She had colored her hair, just a bit. She was starting to find gray streaks near her part. She was ashamed of how much this had upset her. Jonathan, actually, had not noticed, but—incredibly, surreally, given the circumstances—Stu Rosenfeld had.

"Hi, Stu," she said. "Lovely day."

He laughed. "I know. Tracy told me to bring an umbrella. Of course I forgot." Tracy was his wife, the one she had *not* had a quarrel with, she was nearly certain.

"How is Tracy?" said Grace, as if they were not standing on a street corner in the rain.

"Wonderful!" He grinned. "Second trimester! We're having a boy."

"Oh . . . ," she said, trying not to show her surprise. "That's fantastic news. I had no idea."

Of course she'd had no idea. One thing she had always remembered was Tracy Rosenfeld's jovial assertion that she and her husband had no intention of having children. "Some of us just don't want that," she had said, as if "that" were something society as a whole had long since decided was beyond the pale. And Grace, who had just suffered a miscarriage (her third? or fourth?), nearly cried, although just about everything at that time had nearly made her cry, and she probably would have been far *more* miserable if the rather unpleasant Mrs. Rosenfeld had blithely announced that she and her husband did, in fact, want "that."

Stu, who was very good-natured, clearly did not remember this long-ago pronouncement. He grinned delightedly and began (despite the rain and the strangeness of their meeting) to describe how oddly easy the whole thing had been. No nausea! No fatigue! Tracy, in fact, still doing her usual three miles in the morning, around the reservoir twice, despite her horrified OB and the case she was handling at work, which was a nightmare. How old was Tracy? Grace tried to remember.

"How old is Tracy?" Grace asked. It sounded rude when it came out. She hadn't intended it to be rude, but maybe she couldn't help herself.

"Forty-one," Stu said, affably enough.

Forty-one. Grace braced for, and felt, the wave of resentment. To change your mind at forty-one, get pregnant, and be so carefree, even reckless—how dare she jog, at forty-one, while pregnant?—it felt like a personal affront. But why? What on earth did it have to do with her?

"It's fabulous," she said instead. "What a wonderful thing."

"And I hear you're having a baby of your own."

She stared at him. She was so baffled, she hadn't the first idea how to react, let alone respond.

"Tracy told me she saw you wrote a book. In the *Daily Beast*, I think she said. 'Hotly anticipated books for the winter' or something. What kind of book is it? Is it a fiction novel?"

No, I'm Truman Capote. It's a nonfiction novel. She nearly said it out loud. But why take it out on him?

"Not at all." Grace smiled. "Nothing so clever. It's just a book about some things I've learned in my practice, that I think can help someone who's looking for a partner."

"Oh, like that *Rules* book? My sister read that a few years ago."

"Did it work?" Grace asked. She always wondered. She knew it *shouldn't* work. But did it work anyway?

"Nah. I mean, I don't think she took it too seriously. Don't call the guy back the first time? Break up with him if he doesn't get you a present on Valentine's Day? I said to her, most guys don't even know when Valentine's Day is. Our dad never got Mom a Valentine's Day present, and they've been married, like, thirty years."

Grace nodded. Standing still in the rain, she was now freezing.

"But seriously, that's so great you wrote a book. I'll get it when it's in the store. It'll be the first thing I've read that isn't in a medical journal since . . . I don't know, college?"

"Oh no," Grace said bravely, but she couldn't think badly of him, really. Stu was a smart, compassionate man, exactly the kind of doctor you'd want by your side if your child was sick. He and Jonathan had covered each other's practice for at least eight years, and Jonathan, at least, had never been critical of Stu's handling of anything, which was frankly remarkable given the complexity of the treatments involved and the personal relationships surrounding a child with cancer. Of many of his other colleagues, Jonathan had sometimes spoken less warmly. Ross Waycaster, his direct supervisor, was an emotionally remote, overly cautious, and uncreative doctor, so incapable of explaining to parents in clear, uncomplicated language what was happening to their child that Jonathan sometimes found them distraught in the hallways, weeping in thoroughly unnecessary frustration. The fellow resident who had moved to Santa Fe or Sedona—what was her name? Rona? Rena?—the one who was into "parallel healing strategies," she had been an airhead who probably never should have become a doctor in the first place. Why go to medical school if you're just going to wave a smudge stick around and chant druidic incantations? And the nurses who sometimes pretended not to hear him when he asked them perfectly nicely for something, because they were so wrapped up in their eternal power struggle with the doctors as a whole, and the press relations office, which never even acknowledged his profile in the Best Doctors issue of *New York* magazine, something that had clearly brought attention and goodwill to the hospital. And then there was Robertson Sharp-the-Turd—the Turd himself—a punishing, withholding man and a myopic, shortsighted, rule-obsessed administrator.

But not Stu Rosenfeld. He had a wide receding hairline and a broad nose, but a truly cherubic smile. She imagined his little boy: happy and likely very smart, with Tracy's fleshy cheeks and that smile from his dad, riding on Stu's not insubstantial shoulders. She was happy for him. For a tiny moment, she was happy in general. She was not outside in the rain, terrified of some unnamable thing tracing its fixed circle around her (biding its time, not drawing closer) and trying very hard not to hear the bad whisper that had somehow begun to accompany her. For this tiny moment there was almost no whisper, no circle, no bell jar slowly descending over her. She was just a woman standing on a sidewalk in the rain with her husband's closest colleague, chatting away as if she were not rigid with dread. Chatting—not that it mattered—about books, and a baby who was going to be named Seth Chin-Ho Rosenfeld, and Valentine's Day. Jonathan always brought her something on Valentine's Day. Flowers—not roses. She had never liked roses. She liked ranunculus. They were so dense but so delicate at the same time. She could look at them forever. Stu Rosenfeld was grinning because his wife was with child and all was well, and Grace was happy because she was so close to believing him. She wanted it very badly. She was nearly there.

And then Stu Rosenfeld said those words, and the bell jar came crashing down, making its airtight seal around the toxic air inside. Seven words: She counted them later. She took them apart again and again, and rearranged them, and tried to make them not cataclysmic, not life-altering, not life-ending. And failed. The words were:

"So. What's Jonathan up to these days?"

CHAPTER ELEVEN

EVERYTHING THAT RISES MUST CONVERGE

How she even got herself from there, that terrifying point on the sidewalk of East 69th and York, back up the long and wet and horrible East Side streets to Rearden, she was never entirely sure. What kept her legs moving? What prevented her from looking into shop windows and seeing the frozen woman who looked back? Her heavy brain ricocheted between racing and jolting to stillness, back and forth as each in its turn became intolerable. And there was shame, of course—for her, something unaccustomed. Grace had given up shame many years before, with the grown-up epiphany that she no longer needed everyone to like her, and moreover accepted that everyone probably wouldn't, whether she needed them to or not. After that liberating insight, and with only herself and her nearest family members authorized to approve or disapprove her actions, there was little chance that she would ever need to be ashamed of anything, and indeed she never was.

But the sight of him on that street corner. God, how he had stared at her, and she—she supposed—had stared back at him, both of them just dumbstruck by his simple, careless question. The expression on her face—in a blinding flash, Stu Rosenfeld must have known everything, or at least enough: that she, Grace Reinhart

Sachs, had somehow missed something essential, that an episode had taken place, unknown to her. And now, the problem of only a moment earlier—that she wasn't sure, wasn't at all sure, couldn't be completely sure where he was—had been abruptly displaced. But the new thing was so much worse.

She stepped back, away from him on the pavement. It felt like tearing Velcro from Velcro, pain and painful sound, and the tilt of the sidewalk seeming to change its mind about where it wanted to be.

"Grace?" she heard him say, but already his voice sounded as if it belonged to another dialect, just near enough to be decipherable, but only with effort. And she didn't have the strength to do that and also get away. And she had to get away from him.

"Grace?" he called after her as she took off. She ducked past him like a football player aiming for an elusive space between bodies. And she never looked at him as she passed. And she certainly never looked back.

69th and First.

71st and Second.

76th and Third. Somehow, she was covering ground, but not in any conscious way. Not like walking and thinking at the same time, noticing things along the way. This was like waking up in the night and taking note of the numbers on the clock before sinking back into fitful blackness, as the night passes in spasms, without rest. The wildness in her brain was unbearable, but whenever she tried to shut it off she merely lost time.

Then two more blocks had gone by.

Then a jolt. And a blast of pain.

Then two more blocks had gone by.

It felt like sickness. She had never felt this sick.

All she wanted was to find Henry, if that meant storming into his school and screaming his name down the corridors, blasting into his lab or homeroom and grabbing him by his thick dark hair, making a scene like the crazy person she had so unexpectedly become. *Where is my son?* she imagined herself screaming. And the weirdest thing of all was that, in her imagining, she didn't mind how they—the others—were staring at her. And then she would drag him away, down the hallway and out into the courtyard and back to their apartment.

But then what?

There was nothing after that; she simply could not progress a single step further. It was like rushing and rushing blindly until you found yourself at the foot of a cliff. And there you stopped: progress arrested, breath struck out of you, confronting the impossibility of a sheer face of rock.

At Rearden, moreover, the street was full of outsiders. There were more of those trucks with the broadcast logos and the satellite dishes affixed to their roofs—at least three more—and a density of unknown people filling the sidewalks: scavengers, of course, for scraps of poor Malaga Alves, but Malaga Alves had been far from her thoughts for hours now. And when one sleek young woman with a patently disingenuous smile had attempted to pull her aside with, "Hi, can I talk to you for just a sec?" Grace had nearly swatted the girl away. In another life, she would concern herself with the death of a woman she had spoken to exactly once. Today was about the chasm at hand. What was happening to her now—and no, she could no longer deny that something was happening—had nothing to do with anyone but herself, her husband, and her child.

She did not want to talk to the mothers, either, and as she stood among them in Rearden's inner courtyard (the school's archway having served as a kind of velvet rope, admitting only the true insiders), she found to her vague relief that an air of sullen solidarity had begun to set in. Now, in contrast with that morning's drop-off, there was little buzzing among the moms; they stood grimly, separately, together but alone, and beyond the most peripheral of nonverbal communication there was no interaction at all. It was almost, thought Grace, as if each of them had experienced some private, life-altering crisis since leaving this spot, only hours earlier, or perhaps the sober reality of the dead woman had asserted itself, overwhelming the perceived gradations of class and money that had seemed to keep Malaga Alves so far away from them. Or that the problem of her death would not, as they might first have assumed, be resolved so quickly—witness the fact that none of them knew anything now that they hadn't known at drop-off—and that they might be in for a bit of a long haul with this thing, and so, as a result, some attempt at decorum was really going to be called for.

Inside the courtyard, on the privileged side of the velvet rope, Grace saw that there were very few nannies in evidence. The concerned mothers of Rearden seemed to have decided, en masse, that some moments in a child's life, like Max's first school murder or Chloe's first media circus, were just too sensitive to leave to a surrogate. So the mothers themselves had dropped everything and were here for their children, waiting for the kids to be released by Robert Conover's grief counselors. They were indeed the parents they prided themselves on being, and this was an important moment in their children's lives, a moment to be, quite possibly, long remembered. Years from now, perhaps, their daughters or sons would recall the day a schoolmate's mother had died—no, been brutally murdered—and how confused and frightened they had been, confronting this first reality of inexplicable human cruelty, and how Mom herself had come to collect them at the end of the school day, and reassured them, and whisked them off for a special treat before heading home or to ballet or to the SSAT tutor. Quite uncharacteristically, no one seemed to be making eye contact.

The kids came, looking not very traumatized at all. A few seemed stunned to see their mothers. Henry lagged near the end of the crowd, his book bag slung across his body and his coat shoved through the straps, dragging a bit on the floor. She was so happy to see him that she didn't even tell him to pick it up. "Hi," she said.

He looked up at her from beneath his remarkable eyelashes. "You see the TV trucks outside?"

"Yes." She put her own coat back on.

"They say anything to you?"

"No. Well, they tried. It's ridiculous."

"Like, what are you supposed to know?"

Obviously, nothing, she thought. Maybe they had pegged her as someone who actually knew something.

"Is Dad back?" said Henry.

They were walking down the steps, into the courtyard. There were people there on the sidewalk, holding cameras. At least two were actively speaking to a camera, with the school as a background. Instinctively, she ducked her head.

"What?" Grace said.

"Is Dad back?"

She shook her head. "No." Then something occurred to her.

"Did he tell you he was coming back today?"

Henry seemed to consider. They passed through one of the two iron archways out onto the pavement and walked purposefully west to the avenue.

"Not really," he said. They were nearly at the corner.

Grace caught her breath. For one awful moment, she thought that she was going to cry. Right here, on the sidewalk.

"Henry," she said, "can you please tell me what 'Not really' means? I'm very confused."

"Oh..." He seemed uncertain. "No. I mean, he didn't say when he was coming back. He just said he was leaving."

"Leaving...what?" said Grace. The ground was doing that thing again. She couldn't stand straight.

He shrugged. He looked, for one nauseating moment, like any adolescent talking (or not talking) to any parent. That shrug. That universal *Leave me out of your shit, please* shrug. She had always made fun of it a little, because it had never happened to her. Please don't let it be happening to her, not today.

"I didn't ask. He just called to say he was going away."

She reached over and gripped his shoulder. Her hand felt like a claw, even to herself.

"Can you remember exactly what he said? And I mean, the exact words."

He looked at her directly, then he seemed to see something he didn't like and looked away.

"Henry, please."

"No, I know. I'm trying to remember. He said: 'I have to go away for a couple days.' He called me on my phone."

"When?" Her head spun. She held on to her own purse as if it might save her.

Again: that shrug. "He just said he was going away."

"Going . . . to Cleveland. For a medical conference."

"He didn't say where. I guess I should have asked him."

Was it the beginning of guilt? Was this the place where some lifelong psychic wound was going to open, one tiny preoccupation that would ultimately flower into: *I could have prevented my parents from . . .*

No. *No.* She felt insane.

"Henry, that's not your responsibility." She said it carefully, too carefully. The way a drunk person speaks when trying to convince someone he's not drunk. "I just wish he'd been clearer about his plans."

That came out beautifully! Grace thought, feeling a tiny bit smug. It sounded appropriately annoyed, but also sort of nonchalant. *You know your father!* "I mean, he told me about Cleveland, but then he forgot his phone at home, which is a huge drag. And you know who's definitely not going to be amused. So just be prepared to be extra charming tonight."

Henry nodded, but now he didn't seem able to look at her at all. He stood on the pavement, both thumbs hooked under the wide strap of his book bag, his gaze locked on some vague thing on the far side of Park Avenue. Grace considered for one brutal moment the possibility that Henry actually knew something critical about Jonathan, where he was or how long he was planning to remain there, something that she did not know herself, but the pain that came with this notion was so blinding that she couldn't think. In the end she said nothing. They started south along the avenue together, and he said nothing either.

Tonight, she was dreading. Her father, whose general remoteness could at least be a blessing at times (like right now), was sadly matched by his wife's relentless intrusiveness, and the pattern was that once Eva unearthed some discrepancy or squishiness of decorum, Grace's father felt compelled to request some sort of clarification, a sensation somewhat akin to a dentist prodding a soft spot in the enamel. Why on earth (Eva had asked, in one classic example) was Grace taking Henry to preschool in the West Village every day—on the *subway*—when there was an excellent preschool—the city's best!—on 70th and Park? Well, for one thing, she'd had to explain, because like virtually everyone else who'd applied to Episcopal, Henry had not been admitted. With anyone else, or at least anyone even remotely attuned to the absurd ways of New York preschools, this would have produced a simple shrug of the shoulders, but not with her stepmother, and not, as a result, with her father. *But why had Henry been turned down?* he had demanded in that particular case, and Eva, whose two supernatural children, weaned on opera and the essential understanding of their own superiority, had sallied forth through Ramaz and Yale and straight on to their respective promised lands (Jerusalem and Greenwich/Wall Street), had regarded Grace with an appalled glare, as if she had never heard of such a moronic thing.

Henry was actually very attached to Eva and his grandfather, though he seemed to grasp their limited range of motion. The undeniable pleasures of dinner at the Reinharts' (good food, very good chocolate, the praise and attention of two people who clearly appreciated him) came Superglued to formality and the need for superlative manners. To sit at the wide mahogany table in Eva's dining room or perch uncomfortably on one of Eva's long finely made couches required focus and effort—from Grace, let alone from her twelve-year-old son. But tonight, perhaps, all that discomfort, and the distraction that came with it, might be no bad thing.

There were holiday lights on the trees in the Park Avenue medians, blinking yellow and blue in the now clear evening. She and Henry shuffled, only a few feet apart but still not speaking. Once or twice something occurred to her, but even as she opened her mouth to say it, she knew either that it wouldn't help or that it wasn't true, and she said nothing. She had no great qualm about lying at this particular moment, which did sound bad, but if it helped maintain the fiction she had already told him, then she could live with it. Unfortunately, Grace was having trouble remembering exactly what fiction that was, and where, exactly, it departed from reality. Unfortunately also, she was hopelessly unclear on the reality itself. She knew nothing, and the murkiness of that opening rift, the constant shifting of its shape and dimensions, was like a howling voice at her ear.

She pulled her coat even tighter around herself. The wool of its collar scratched the back of her neck.

Henry walked with his shoulders a little hunched, as if he were not yet ready to be tall, his gaze fixed on the pavement except when they passed a man or a woman walking a dog. Henry desperately wanted a dog and had asked for one, unsuccessfully, for years. Dogs were foreign to Grace, who had never had a pet of any kind, and Jonathan, who as a child had owned a black Lab named Raven (really the pet of his indulged younger brother), had not been at all willing to bring one into their home. Raven, he had told her long ago, had disappeared when he was in ninth grade, on a day everyone else was out of the house, and the mystery of his departure (loose gate? dognapper?) had been a source of ongoing grief for everyone involved, even to the point of accusations: They blamed him, Jonathan had explained to her. They blamed him for the escape or loss or who knew what of a dog that wasn't even his. So typical of his terribly nonfunctional family, she understood. But still—what a horrible thing to have done to him.

Besides, Jonathan also had an allergy to dog dander.

Eva had had a dog when Grace's father had begun seeing her. Two dogs, actually: somewhat overfed dachshund brothers named Sacher and Sigi, whose primary interest in life was each other and who required coaxing to even acknowledge Henry. Now long gone, they had been replaced first by a Pomeranian (so inbred that his fur had fallen out in patches, and feebleminded to boot), who had died of some purebred Pomeranian ailment, and more recently by Karl, another dachshund whose personality was only slightly more welcoming. Grace's father seemed to hold the primary responsibility for walking Karl (it still amazed Grace to see her father walking a dog). Her father's lifelong habit of biweekly tennis had declined with the integrity of his knees and hips, and he needed the exercise.

She saw them ahead, man and dachshund, as she and Henry crossed Park at 73rd, and Henry ran down the street to greet his grandfather. He was, Grace saw to her mild shock, so tall beside him that for a moment she wondered whether her father was shrinking, and when they embraced, her father scarcely leaned over his grandson. Grace had a momentary image of the two of them continuing to grow in opposite directions, until one disappeared into the ground and the other soared out of sight into the clouds. It made her shudder.

"Hello, Karl," Henry was saying when she caught up to them. He had moved on to the dog and coaxed enough interest out of him to gain a faint wagging of the tail, for which Henry praised him rather too much. Frederich Reinhart handed over the leash and Henry began very conscientiously leading the dog to each and every tree along the pavement.

"Grace," her father said, giving her a brief hug. "My goodness he's getting tall."

"I know. Sometimes, I swear, I go in to wake him up in the morning and he's longer on the bed. Like Procrustes got hold of him."

"I certainly hope not," her father said. "Jonathan coming from the hospital?"

She had forgotten to call Eva, to say that he wasn't coming. She suddenly felt ill. "I'm not sure," she managed. "He may be."

Maybe neither of these statements was a lie, she told herself. He might come. By some miracle.

"Fine," he said. "It's cold, isn't it?"

Was it? Grace felt so hot. The back of her neck itched from the wool of her collar. She was noticing the perfect line of her father's gray-white hair, a precise half inch above the collar of his own heavy coat. Eva cut it herself, with a pair of long, sharp scissors. It was a skill of hers, carried over from her first marriage, when her late husband (in their shared abstemiousness—which was bizarre in view of their shared wealth) had devised strategies for not spending money. In fact, over the years Grace had more than once allowed Eva to cut Henry's hair. Eva seemed to notice first (and react most) whenever its length slipped the bounds of propriety, and it seemed to make her highly cheerful to snip away at her husband's only grandchild. She also happened to be very good with those scissors, making a busy, clinical sound as she moved around Henry's beautiful head, leaving little piles of his (also beautiful) hair on the tile floor of the master bath. It made Eva cheerful to point out disorder wherever she might find it, and then clean it up.

Eva had taken good care of her father, Grace thought, looking at that straight line of hair as she followed him into the lobby. Of course, she had thought this many times in the past; if only that were enough to make her love her stepmother. And she had thought *that* many times as well.

"Carlos," her father said to the elevator man as he pulled shut the gate, "you remember my daughter and grandson."

"Hello," Grace said, only a millisecond behind her son.

"Hello," said Carlos, eyes on the numbers overhead. It was the old kind of elevator, the kind requiring some skill to land just at the level of the floor. They all rode in the customary silence until the fourth floor, where the elevator man pulled open the grate again and wished them a pleasant evening. Henry reached down and detached the leash from Karl's collar, and Karl ambled freely to the front door, one of a pair on the same small landing. When her father obliged him by opening it, the smell of carrots reached them immediately.

"Hi, Nana," her son said, following Karl to the kitchen.

Her father removed his coat and then took Grace's and hung them both up. "Something to drink?" he asked her.

"No. Thanks. You go ahead."

As if he needed her permission.

The apartment had not changed even slightly since the first time she had come here, the year after her marriage to Jonathan, for a slightly terrifying dinner at which she was to meet Eva's children and their spouses. Rebecca, who was only a few years older than Grace and had recently given birth to her second son (tended by a nanny in one of the bedrooms), had traveled for the occasion from Greenwich, and Reuven—already considering immigrating to Israel—from 67th Street with his irritable wife, Felice. It was the evening all three of the "children" were to be told that their parents were going to be married—definitely. A date, indeed, had been set for merely two months hence, and Grace's father, astonishingly, had decided to take an unprecedented two months' holiday from his firm in order to go on a long honeymoon in Italy, France, and Germany.

It was hard to say which of the three of them—"the children"—was least elated by this news. She did know that she was glad for her father, glad that he had found a companion and that Eva's focus, from the outset, seemed to be the care and organization of Frederich Reinhart, who had not quite been managing this on his own since Grace's mother had died, and could clearly use the help. But Grace had not persuaded herself to love Eva and feared that she never would. She also knew right away that she would never love Eva's children.

That had been a Sabbath dinner, of course, and Eva's son and daughter had scarcely been able to contain their disapproval of Grace and Jonathan's imperviousness to Jewish ritual. It was a question not of belief (whether she and Jonathan believed, whether Eva's children believed, that was not the point), but of their insufficiently expressed Jewishness itself, which was obvious to one and all. That evening, she and Jonathan had approached the Shabbos table with de facto good manners and the usual intention to observe and mirror when it came to the unfamiliar, but those two had seen through the ruse immediately.

"You don't know the kiddush?" Reuven had asked Jonathan, with such palpable disdain that the mood at the table—tenuous already—had dropped like a stone.

"Afraid not," Jonathan said lightly. "Bad Jews. My parents even had a Christmas tree when I was growing up."

"A Christmas tree?" said Rebecca. Her husband, also an investment banker, actually curled his lip. Grace watched it happen and, like a coward, said nothing. And neither she nor her father, needless to say, offered the information that they, too, had celebrated Christmas—the marzipan and Handel and William Greenberg's version of Christmas—all through her childhood. And enjoyed it very much, too.

"Ah," said Eva, arriving in the hallway, both Henry and Karl trailing behind her. She kissed Grace politely enough, on both cheeks. "Henry tells me Jonathan isn't joining us."

Grace glanced at her son. He was bent over, patting an indifferent dachshund who completely ignored him. Eva, wearing the more polite of her disapproving expressions, had on one of her many, many cashmere twinsets. She possessed these in a wide spectrum of beige, veering on the pale end to nearly white and on the dark to nearly brown, but concentrated mainly on the shade of manila folder she had chosen tonight. They flattered her in two ways: first by just revealing her rather impressive collarbones, and second by giving the best possible presentation to her bosom, which appeared almost preternaturally youthful and rather voluptuous.

"What's that?" her father was saying. He had returned from the bar in the living room with his tumbler of Scotch.

"Jonathan is apparently not coming to dinner with us," his wife said crisply. "I thought it was arranged that you would phone me if that were the case."

This was true, Grace understood. Yes, she had said that. Yes, she was clearly remiss in not having done it. But really? This degree of disapproval?

"Oh, Eva," said Grace, throwing herself on the dubious mercy of the court, "I am so sorry. It just went right out of my head. And I was hoping to hear."

"Hoping to hear?" Her father looked nearly affronted. "I don't understand. Why should you be 'hoping to hear' from your husband?"

She gave them each a warning look that conveyed only a small fraction of her own disapproval, then asked Henry if he had any homework.

"Science," he said from the floor, where he was rubbing an ungrateful Karl behind the ears.

"Why don't you go to the den and do that, sweetie?"

Henry went. The dog stayed.

Perhaps she ought to make light of the whole thing. Perhaps a miracle might occur, and her father and Eva would simply, for once, let it go.

"I haven't heard from him." Grace gave a forced little laugh. "To tell you the truth, I've got no idea where he is. That's pretty bad, right?"

It was not to be, of course.

They looked at each other. Eva, with an expression so arctic that Grace practically shivered, turned on her heel and went back to the kitchen. This left her father, still holding his drink and looking nearly furious.

"I wonder how you managed that," he said shortly. "I know you are very consumed with the feelings of your patients, but it does strike me as strange that you never concern yourself with Eva's feelings."

He went and sat. She supposed she was meant to do the same, but for the present moment she was so fixated on this notion that she couldn't quite move.

Consumed with the feelings of your patients. No, that wasn't new. Grace's father had never been sympathetic to therapy in general and certainly had never been warmly approving of the profession as a profession for her. But what, pray tell, did any of that have to do with Eva?

"I'm so sorry," she said carefully. "I'll be completely honest, it just went right off my radar. And I was still hoping Jonathan would check in, so I could ask him about his plans."

"And did you not think to check in with *him*?" her father said, as if she were ten years old.

"Of course. But..."

But. *But my husband has arranged to be unreachable, hence I cannot reach him. And I am so terrified by that, and what it might mean, because obviously it does not mean nothing, that frankly I am having difficulty functioning at all, let alone concerning myself with whether your wife—who does not like me, let alone love me, and whom I will never, ever care for one tiny bit more than I must, because she is your wife—has set the appropriate number of plates at the table and whether she might actually find it necessary to remove one.*

"But?" her father said, declining to excuse her.

"I have no excuse. I know how important these dinners are to her."

And lo: It was worse. She might as well have said: *If it were up to me, we would be over at Shun Lee, munching spareribs and Cantonese lobster instead of trekking here one night a week to endure the formal hostility of Eva, who long ago decided that I am not as good as the fruit of her own loins and therefore not deserving of her highly prized sole and potato croquettes, let alone her general goodwill, and absolutely undeserving of... what do we call that thing a mature woman might have for the only child of her beloved spouse, a child who no longer has her own mother? Oh yes! Affection! Maternal affection! Or even, you know, a halfhearted facsimile of maternal affection, just for the sake of appearances and out of general respect for the aforementioned beloved spouse.*

Certainly not.

Then she tried, as she sometimes did in situations like this, to imagine a patient standing in for herself. *I miss my mother*, Grace-the-patient—a woman in her thirties or forties, married, with a child and a moderately successful career—would say to her, to Grace-the-therapist. *I love my father, naturally. And when he remarried after Mommy died I was happy for him, because I had worried about him on his own, you know? And I did really want to have a relationship with his wife. I wanted a mother again—I can admit that—though I knew, of course, she wasn't my mother. But she always made me feel like she was doing me a favor. Or my father a favor—probably more accurate. And all things being equal, she wished I weren't in the picture at all.*

And then Grace-the-patient would start to cry, because she knew that deep down there no longer was a picture for her to be in. That was the truth.

And Grace-the-therapist would look at this very heartbroken person on her couch and probably say how sad it was that her father had so emphatically declined his only child's affection. And they would both—Grace-the-therapist and Grace-the-patient—pause for a moment to really think about how sad that was. But in the end, both of them would reach the only conclusion possible: that this father was a grown-up and he had made a choice. He might change his mind, but not because his daughter persuaded him to.

And as for the wife.

She isn't my mother, thought Grace. *My mother's dead, and that's that. And now I have gravely offended her by not telling her that my husband isn't coming to dinner. "Guess who isn't coming to dinner?" I should have said*. And at this, inadvertently, she smiled.

"I don't see why this is funny," said her father, and Grace looked up at him.

"It's not funny," she said.

No, Grace thought, *we do not choose our families, and yes we must—we really must—cultivate the ones we actually have, because they are the ones we actually have*. And wasn't that precisely what she had been doing here, at least a few times a month, for *years*, ever since the day her father had taken Eva Scheinborn out for dinner at the Ginger Man following a performance of *Four Last Songs*? Yet at no point, ever, in all the years since, had she felt the slightest warmth from Eva or any real interest directed at her or at Jonathan. *And yet I keep coming back*, she thought: *ever dutiful and ever hopeful*.

Silly of me, really.

Then, with her father still glaring at her and Eva, presumably, now actually lifting and carrying the heavy, heavy extra plate and ponderous napkin and silverware and the unbearably weighty wineglass and water glass back to the kitchen, it occurred to her that she could walk out of here right now and not care at all.

Or, in the words of that ubiquitous kiss-off, from the probably enhanced lips of every current celebrity, actual or delusional: *I am so over this*.

But these words, she did not say. She said, instead:

Daddy, something's wrong. I'm really scared.

Or wait: Maybe she only meant to say those words. Maybe she was only about to say them, when the thrilling sound of her cell phone heralded the narrowest possibility of salvation from deep in her leather handbag; and forgetting everything—her father, her dignity—she ripped it off her shoulder and bent over it, tearing into the purse and pushing aside notebooks, wallet, pens, the iPod she hadn't actually listened to in months, her keys, the permission form for a class trip to Ellis Island she kept forgetting to return, and the business card of a violin dealer that Vitaly Rosenbaum had recommended for Henry's recently outgrown three-quarter-sized instrument—all to retrieve this slender ribbon of hope. She must have looked like an animal, burrowing frantically for food, or perhaps an action hero who has only seconds left to find and disarm the bomb, but she probably couldn't have stopped herself even if she'd wanted to. *Don't hang up!* she told it frantically. *Don't you dare hang up, Jonathan!*

Then her hand closed over it and she brought it up, like a pearl from the depths, and blinked at it, because the little screen showed not the stethoscope she had so irrationally expected to see (how could it? unless Jonathan had returned home, retrieved his still-sequestered cell phone from the cupboard by the bed, and used it to call her), or some unknown Midwestern number ("I'm such an idiot! I've lost my phone somewhere!"), but the non-word NYPDMENDOZAC, surely—of all the irritating and irrelevant things that might have appeared there—the most irritating and irrelevant of all.

And then it came to her that he was dead, and they had found him and were calling to tell her the worst news she would ever hear. But what a strange coincidence that it should be the same police officer, out of all the police officers it might have been, to make this call. Perhaps this was her personal police officer, the one called upon whether she jaywalked or had a passing acquaintance with a murder victim or had to be informed that her husband had suffered some terrifying mishap. How many of these officers were there, for how many New Yorkers? And how bizarre that she would need hers twice, in only a couple of days.

Well, I just won't answer, she thought. That should fix it.

But her father was looking at her, still. And he said: "Is it Jonathan?"

Grace held up the phone, as if it might change its mind and be Jonathan after all. It wasn't Jonathan.

"Dad?" she heard herself say. "I don't know if I really made this clear before, but I don't know where Jonathan is. I thought he was at a medical conference in the Midwest somewhere, but now I'm not sure."

"Have you tried calling him?" her father said, as if she were stupid.

In her hand, the phone stopped ringing. *So easy!* she thought. *Wish granted.*

"Yes. Of course I have."

"Well, what about the hospital? They must be able to reach him."

What's Jonathan up to these days?

Grace shuddered.

In her hand, the cell phone shuddered, too. It was ringing again. NYPDMENDOZAC really wanted to speak to her.

And then, in a location so deep inside her that she had not known of its existence, really, let alone its whereabouts, something heavy and metallic chose this moment to creak the tiniest bit open, with a grating of rust and the release of a new, terrible thought: that everything rising around her was about to converge.

"I need to take this," she said nominally to her father. "I really do."

In response, he left the room.

Then she did the strangest thing. She made herself walk, very deliberately, across to one of Eva's long, uncomfortable couches and place her disordered handbag very carefully on Eva's scarily expensive antique Kirman rug. And then, with the utmost specificity, and in such a severe and disciplined voice that she did not immediately recognize it as her own, she told herself the outright lie that everything would be all right.

CHAPTER TWELVE

Snap, Snap

This time, they wouldn't let her talk to them in the lobby, though they had called from the lobby, so they were right there when she came down in the elevator, and despite the fact that Eva's lobby (being far more grand than her own) had even more elaborate furniture at hand. No.

This time, there had been a "request" that they speak at what they called "the office," where they could have privacy.

Privacy for what? she asked them. And when they didn't answer right away, she said, "I don't understand. Are you arresting me?"

Mendoza, who had already started leading their little group outside, stopped. His neck, she noted—not without some misplaced satisfaction—overflowed the collar of his coat as he turned back to her.

"Why would I be arresting you?" he said.

Then, she was exhausted. Already, a part of her had handed herself over. She let them open the door of the sedan for her and slid onto the backseat beside O'Rourke. The one with the neck stubble. Like a criminal.

"I don't understand," she said again, but without much conviction. When neither of them reacted to this, she went further.

"I told you, I barely knew Mrs. Alves."

Mendoza, who was driving, said—not unkindly—"We can talk when we get there." Then—and this, under the circumstances, seemed the strangest thing of all—he turned on the radio. WQXR, the classical station. And no one said another word.

"There" was apparently the 23rd Precinct on 102nd Street. Only two miles from the neighborhood where she had grown up and was now raising her own child—a smaller distance than she was happy to walk almost anytime and less, in fact, than the distance she put in on the treadmill on the rare occasions she made it to her gym on 80th and Third—yet Grace had never set foot on 102nd Street in her life. Driving up Park, past Lenox Hill, where she and Henry had both been born, and the Brick Church, where two of her Rearden classmates had been married, and the 96th Street apartment building where her once friend Vita had grown up—a building perched literally on the edge of what Grace's parents had considered permissible Manhattan—she had watched each landmark pass into her wake.

The city of Grace's youth came to a screeching halt at 96th and Park (which helpfully crested after a long incline at just that point and then seemed to plunge downward into Spanish Harlem, just where the subway emerged from its subterranean travels). So strict was the rule laid down by her mother—also a native New Yorker—about going north of 96th that there might as well have been one of those doomsday highway signs advising "Abandon All Hope, Ye Who Enter Here." Grace and Vita never had, though they did enjoy, from time to time, the mild rebellion of trawling the length of 96th itself, from Fifth, where the brownstones were still anybody's idea of elegant, to the East River, where things verged on just as dangerous as Marjorie Reinhart had always feared.

Of course, as an adult she had been to Harlem many times. It wasn't such a big deal, not today. There had been her graduate school years at Columbia, for one thing (though Columbia and its environs had an Ivy League exemption from the above 96th Street rule), and her counseling internship at a women's shelter on 128th. And there was the awful play on 159th Street in which the mother of one of Henry's friends had portrayed a character so experimental that the role had been called simply "The Woman"—she had gone to that with Henry and Jonah, when Henry and Jonah were still friends. Jonathan also loved Sylvia's Restaurant with a passion she had never shared, and occasionally coerced her and Henry there for smothered pork chops and macaroni. And of course more than a few of the people they knew had opted for brownstones in this formerly beyond-the-pale neighborhood, where for the price of a postwar box on the Upper East Side you could buy three floors of prewar glory and a back garden, only a slightly scary ten-minute walk from the subway. These days, there was even a Brown Harris Stevens office here, she had read somewhere.

Still, she felt the old, instinctive tightening as the car began to descend.

Abandon all hope, ye who enter here.

The 23rd Precinct station house, it turned out, was in a building that looked like an imploded Rubik's Cube in generic beige. When they brought her inside, taking her swiftly down a side corridor to a little meeting room, Detective O'Rourke only increased the surrealism of the occasion by offering Grace a cappuccino. She very nearly smiled.

"No, thank you," she told them. *A shot of whiskey*, she almost said, but the truth was that she didn't want that, either.

O'Rourke went for coffee for himself. Mendoza asked if she needed to use the bathroom. She declined. Were they always this polite? But then she saw him looking at his watch—bored already?—and writing down the time.

"Do I need a lawyer?" she asked them.

They looked at each other.

"I wouldn't have thought so," said O'Rourke. They were both

writing now, one jotting long lines on a yellow legal pad, the other filling out a form. She watched, for a moment, the steam rise from their paper cups.

"Mrs. Sachs," Mendoza said quite suddenly, "are you comfortable?"

Was he crazy? No, she wasn't comfortable. She looked at him with a kind of dull disapproval and said: "Sure. But I'm confused."

"I understand," he said, nodding. And unless she was much mistaken, that nod—and the face that went along with it, a kind of bland and noncommittal face—and the tone of his voice, which was mild and vaguely musical, came right from the basic training manual for therapists everywhere. It made her enraged. And that only got worse when he said: "This must be very difficult for you."

"I don't even know what 'this' is," she said, looking first at one of them, then at the other. "What is 'this'? I told you, I didn't know Malaga Alves. I had no feelings about her one way or the other. I'm very sorry that she was..."

What? Grace thought frantically. How did you end a sentence so stupidly begun?

"She was... harmed. It's a terrible thing. But what am I doing here?"

They glanced at each other, and Grace, in that instant, saw the compressed and silent dialogue of two people who knew each other very well. They were disagreeing. Then one of them prevailed.

It was O'Rourke who leaned forward, elbows on the table, and said: "Mrs. Sachs, where is your husband?"

Grace caught her breath. She shook her head at them. They were like exotic creatures. They made no sense at all.

"I don't understand. I thought this was about what happened to Mrs. Alves."

"It is," Mendoza said severely. "It is very much about Mrs. Alves. So I'll ask you again: Where is your husband, Mrs. Sachs?"

"I don't think my husband ever met Mrs. Alves."

"Where is he? Is he in your apartment on Eighty-First?"

"What?" She stared at them. "No. Of course not!"

"Why 'of course not'?" said O'Rourke, with what sounded like sincere curiosity.

"Well, because..." Because if Jonathan were in the apartment, she wouldn't have spent the last twenty-four hours in a state of such sickening fear. She would know where he was. She might not understand, but she would know. But of course she couldn't say that. *That*—whatever was happening to Jonathan, to them as a couple—was none of their business. Instead she said: "Because...why would he be in our apartment? I told you, he's at a medical conference. And if he were here, in the city, he'd be at work. But he's not here."

They both frowned. O'Rourke pursed his lips and inclined his head forward a little bit. The skin of his bald head caught the overhead fluorescent light. "And work would be *where*?"

It was the way he said it, so carefully, so anxious not to blow a punch line. There was cruelty in it and pity at the same time. It was so radioactive, it made her flinch. They were both looking at her, waiting for her. They had both kept their jackets on, though it was—she now realized—kind of hot in this room. Purposely so? Or did the city overheat its buildings as a rule? But it was unquestionably hot. She had taken off her own coat and was holding it across her lap, bundled up. She was holding it tight, as if it might try to get away from her. She had been hot. She wouldn't have done it otherwise, since taking off your coat meant you were going to stay awhile, and she had no intention of staying a second longer than necessary to satisfy their "request." Weren't they hot? O'Rourke, the bald one, he looked hot. He had a fine sheen of perspiration on his brow, or bald head, or the place his hairline would have been if he'd had hair. The other one looked uncomfortable as well. Though perhaps their jackets made them look that way. Ill-fitting jackets, both. Both bulging at the armpit.

And then, without warning, she had an image of herself hanging over a cliff, held up by ropes, and there were many ropes—enough to feel secure. She had always had ropes, she knew that: stability, good health, money, education. She was smart enough to appreciate all that support. But the ropes—they were breaking. Snapping. One by one—she could hear them: little pops, little rips. But it was still all right. There were still so many ropes, holding her up. And she wasn't that heavy. She didn't need much.

"Memorial Sloan-Kettering," she said, trying to summon any authority she could access, if not for herself, then for the institution. Usually, even mention of the institution was enough. Though even as she did it, some part of her wondered: *Is this the last time?*

"He's a doctor there."

"Doctor of . . . ?"

"Medical doctor. Pediatric oncology. *Cancer*," she said, in case—if *only*—they were idiots. "In *children*."

Mendoza sat back in his chair. For a long moment, he let this weighty thing hang in the open. He seemed to be scanning her for some coded information. Then, apparently, he made up his mind.

There was a box on the table. A document box, nothing remarkable. It had been there when the three of them came in and sat down—perhaps that was why Grace had not paid much attention. Now, however, Mendoza reached across the table and dragged the box over to himself. He peeled off the top and dropped it on the seat beside him, then he reached inside and withdrew a file. It wasn't very thick. That was good, wasn't it? At least, in a medical file, thick was usually worse than thin. When he opened it, she was surprised to see the hospital's familiar logo, a deconstructed caduceus in which Asclepius's staff was an upward-pointing arrow and its entwining snakes transformed to postmodern crosses. She regarded this simple image with utter stupefaction.

"Mrs. Sachs," said O'Malley, "it's possible you don't know your husband no longer works at Memorial."

Snap.

For a moment, she wasn't sure what felt more shocking to her: what he said about Jonathan not working at the hospital or the fact that he had used the hospital's familiar abbreviation. "No," she said. "It's not possible. I mean, I don't know that."

He held up the paper and scrutinized it, leaving Grace to focus on that familiar logo through the sheet.

"According to Dr. Robertson Sharp—"

The Third, she added automatically. The *Turd.*

"Dr. Jonathan Sachs' employment was terminated on the first of March of this year."

Snap. *Snap.*

He looked over the page at her. "You were not aware of this?"

Say nothing, some frantic voice cautioned her. *Don't give them anything they can use to make it worse*. So she shook her head.

"Are you saying: No, you were not aware of this?"

For posterity, she thought. For the paper trail.

"I was not aware." She managed to get the words out.

"You were not aware that his termination followed two earlier disciplinary actions at the hospital?"

She shook her head and then remembered. "No."

"And that it resulted from a third violation of the hospital's code of conduct, requiring what the hospital's legal counsel described as a permanent separation from the institution?"

No. Snap *snap*.

So. What's Jonathan up to these days?

"I want to stop this," she told them. "Can we stop?"

"No, unfortunately we're not going to stop."

"And you're telling me I don't need a lawyer?"

"Mrs. Sachs," O'Rourke said angrily, "why would you need a lawyer? Are you hiding your husband? Because if you're hiding him, then yes, you're going to need a very good lawyer."

"But... No, I'm not!" Grace felt the heat in her face, in her throat.

Though she wasn't crying. And she wasn't going to. "I thought he was at a medical conference. He said he was going to a medical conference." Even to herself, she sounded pathetic. Grace-the-therapist wanted to scream at her. "In the Midwest."

"It's a big place. Where in the Midwest?" Mendoza said.

"I think... Ohio?"

"Ohio."

"Or... Illinois?"

O'Rourke snorted. "Or Indiana. Or Iowa. They all sound alike, don't they?"

To a New Yorker, yes, they did. Like Saul Steinberg's famous view of the world: Beyond the Hudson River, there was only "out there."

"I can't remember what he said. There was a medical conference. Pediatric oncology. He's..."

But then she shuddered. Because apparently he wasn't, anymore. *Jesus Christ, Jonathan.*

"And he's not in your apartment."

"No!" she yelled at them both. "I told you. He's not."

"Though his phone seems to be. According to Verizon."

"Oh. Well, yes. His phone is there."

O'Rourke sat forward. His beard seemed to have grown more, even over the past hour. *He must shave twice a day*, Grace thought dimly. Jonathan shaved in the morning, though sometimes he missed a day if he was rushing away to work.

"Your husband's phone is in your apartment, but your husband is not."

Grace nodded, since this, at least, was a non-event. Or ought to be. "Right."

"A detail you might have mentioned," O'Rourke said disapprovingly.

She shrugged. It almost felt a little good to see him so irritated. "You didn't ask where his phone was. You asked where he was. He forgot his phone at home—he left it. It's not the first time he's forgotten his phone. But so what? I found it last night, and that's why I don't know where he is. Because he forgot his phone and I can't call him."

Quite the speech, she thought in conclusion. Grace-the-therapist thought: *And this makes sense?*

"And that makes sense to you," Mendoza said.

She nearly laughed. No, of course it did not make sense. Sense was now rather hard to come by, in general.

"Look, this..." Whatever this was. "What you're telling me, about Jonathan, I'm not accusing you of making it up. And it's terrible, and obviously I've got a lot to absorb here, but I still don't see what it has to do with you. I mean, if it's true that he lost his job, and hasn't told me, then clearly—"

She paused, took a breath. It had been hard enough to get that much out.

"He and I are going to have a lot to talk about. And it's going to be pretty awful, but it's going to be private. So why are we talking about it at a police station?"

O'Rourke reached down the table and took the folder now. He looked through some pages, and then, with a little sigh, he closed it, drumming his fingers on the gray cover. "You know what confuses me," he said finally, "is why you haven't asked what he did, to get fired. Don't you want to know?"

Grace considered this. The real answer was: No, she did not. She really, really did not want to know. Of course she would have to know eventually. The two of them had never gotten along, obviously, her husband and his boss. You don't get along with someone and nickname him the Turd just for the hell of it. From what Jonathan had told her over the years, Robertson Sharp represented the worst of the old school in terms of patient care. Obsessed only with clinical results, he refrained from any but the most perfunctory contact with patients and their families. And with the rise of various social support systems within the hospital structure, he had withdrawn even more. The patient advocates and family consultants and supportive therapists in all their rainbow permutations could do the touchy-feely stuff; Dr. Sharp would examine and evaluate and order the tests and prescribe the drugs. It was how they had been trained, that generation, in the medical schools of the 1960s—you couldn't really fault them for that. And his personality...well, some people are just not that interested in being liked.

"Mrs. Sachs?"

She shrugged.

"We obtained the records yesterday from Memorial."

She sat up. "You obtained. His confidential records."

"Yes. By court order."

"His employment records?" she said in disbelief.

"Yes. His confidential employment records. As a result of a court order filed yesterday morning. I have them here. You truly don't know about any of this?"

She shook her head. She was trying—really trying—to breathe.

"All right. From 2007 through 2012, multiple citations for harassment involving staff. Two citations pertaining to cash gifts received from patients' families. Two citations for inappropriate contact with patients' families."

"Oh wait," said Grace. "Now we're...This is bullshit, obviously."

"In January of this year," O'Rourke went on, "a formal warning after a physical confrontation with a doctor on staff, resulting in injuries. The other doctor declined to press charges."

"Right." She actually laughed. Jonathan causing injuries. Had they *seen* Jonathan? It was hysterical. "Of course. *Injuries.*"

"Two broken fingers and a laceration requiring two stitches. For the other person involved."

Snap, snap, snap. She reached out and held on to the table. *Oh no*, she thought. *Someone has custom written a horror story for my life.* Like those people who take your family memories and turn them into a song for the golden anniversary celebration. But not like that at all. This horror story, for example, would somehow have to explain the tooth he had chipped when he fell in the stairwell.

"That's not how he broke his tooth," she said.

"I'm sorry?" It was Mendoza.

"That's not how he broke it. He fell in the stairwell. He tripped." *They're lucky he didn't sue the hospital!*

"The other doctor was treated in the emergency room at Memorial. The aftermath of the event was witnessed by a number of people, and the victim gave a statement for the disciplinary hearing."

The event. The victim. The disciplinary hearing. There seemed to be a lot of "*The*'s." Just as if this were really happening. But of course it was all, just, crazy.

"He fell in the stairwell. He had to get a false tooth. They couldn't save the tooth!"

Feel sorry for me, she thought wildly.

"It's still a different color, if you look closely."

"And finally, in February of this year, a full disciplinary hearing alleging inappropriate contact with another family member of a patient."

"Listen to me!" She could barely connect the shriek she was hearing with herself. "It's cancer! It's children, with cancer! He's a warm person. He's not some asshole who comes in and pronounces your child is going to die. He cares about people. I mean, maybe there are doctors who do everything by the rule book, and they just give you the worst news of your life and turn around and walk out the door, but Jonathan isn't like that. Of course... he might hug someone or touch someone, but it doesn't mean..." She stopped, trying to catch her breath. "It's a horrible thing to accuse someone of."

Mendoza was shaking his head, and the neck, the fat of the neck, pooled on one side and then the other. She hated his neck and she hated him.

"The patient's name—"

"It's *private!*" Grace yelled at them. "Don't tell me the patient's name. It's none of my business."

And I don't want to know, she thought, because she did know, she already did, and it was too wrong, and there was only this one rope left, this one tiny filament of silk holding her up over the edge of the cliff, and down there, so far down she could not see the bottom, was a place she had never been before, not even in the darkest days after her mother died, or when the children she longed for with her husband had declined to come, or else come and left too early. Even that had been bearable, but not this.

"Your husband's patient was Miguel Alves. Diagnosed with a Will's..." He squinted at the page. Then he looked up at his partner.

"Wilms'," his partner said, sounding very nearly bored.

"Wilms' tumor, September 2012. Miguel's mother...well, obviously, Malaga Alves."

Obviously. Everything that rises must converge.

"So you'll forgive me for asking, Mrs. Sachs, because I am going to be seriously pissed off at you if you keep telling me I'm wrong, I'm mistaken, your husband's at a fucking medical conference for fucking kids with cancer, he forgot his phone—whatever you think you're going to do next. I told you already: *Don't protect him*. It's not a—what do you shrinks like to call it?—a healthy decision. And I don't know how good you are at your job, but I am very good at mine, and wherever Jonathan is, I'm going to find him. So if you know something, this would be the time to tell me what it is."

But Grace said nothing, because her mouth was full of wind, because nothing was left to hold her up and she had fallen, was falling, was going to fall forever.

CHAPTER THIRTEEN

The Spaces in Between the Houses

Probably, there was more. There had to have been more, she was there another two hours. Or three. Or... well, it was late, anyway, when she left, walking out onto the East Harlem street at a time of night that would, on any other day of her life, have at least concerned her but today carried no impact of its own. Today... tonight... all she could feel was the sweet numbing cold of December and the dream of hypothermia. Not the most terrible way to die, it turned out. Jonathan had told her that, actually. He was a connoisseur of cold places, polar places. He had been reading a book about the Klondike the night they had met and had read many more since then. On the wall of his dormitory room upstairs, which she had visited later that very night, there was a postcard of the iconic image: the long line of Gold Rush pilgrims hiking slowly up the Golden Stairs of the Chilkoot Pass, single file, bent low in pursuit of their fortunes, walking straight into the storm and the freezing cold. The Jack London story her husband loved, about the man and the dog and the elusive fire on an arctic night—that had ended in hypothermia. If she stopped right here, on the pavement, she might end in hypothermia, too.

There had been no offer of a ride home, and she probably would not have accepted it if there had been. She could not wait to get away from them and from the grimy, horrible precinct house with its waiting area full of unhappy people: exhausted women and men, whole families, sometimes, like a hospital emergency room. (What were they doing here? she wondered, shooting past them and making for the front door like someone fleeing a smoke-filled house. What did the officers of the 23rd Precinct have to offer anyone at this time of night?) They barely looked at her as she fled, but still she could not shake the ugly, penetrating idea that they saw something in her—*on* her—that she did not quite see herself. The thought of it made her ill. When she got outside, she took off at a full run, west on 102nd toward Lexington, and then kept going. Nothing was open but a single bodega on the corner with Pampers and Mexican sodas in the window and a door plastered with lottery ads. Halfway up the block she ran out of breath, but only because she was sobbing.

When she got to the corner of Park Avenue, she understood that she was not going to have access to the ordinary things of her ordinary life. Park Avenue didn't mean here what it meant just six blocks away. When she came to the elevated subway tracks, they seemed to stretch on for eternity without an obvious place to ascend. There were no buses, of course. Park Avenue did not have a bus line. (Why, it occurred to her for the first time in a life lived on and off Park Avenue, should Park Avenue alone be exempt from a bus line?) In the end, she just turned south and walked briskly beside the tracks, while the cold wind ripped at her cheeks and a black devastation bayed at her heels.

Henry would still be at Dad and Eva's house, of course—they would hardly have taken him home, not that she'd had the wherewithal to make any arrangements for him. When the call came, she had told them all that a patient was in crisis and that she had to go to the hospital, an untruth that had come to her so quickly and so fully formed, and been communicated so naturally, that she had marveled at her own powers of deceit. How *long*, it occurred to her now, walking across 99th Street, the vision of Park and 96th, with its canopied apartment buildings, just tantalizingly in sight, *have I been such an accomplished liar?*

When she saw Jonathan again, she thought furiously, she would ask him to explain to her how this metamorphosis had taken place, how they had each become so seamlessly capable of quick-return falsehood. It was a skill she had always inwardly marveled at when she discovered it in one of her patients, the smooth transitions and fancy footwork with which someone took a nugget of non-negotiable fact, modified it on the spot, and handed it back, an altogether new and tangible animal. Thus does a quarrel with a colleague become a fall down the stairs. Thus does a pair of detectives waiting down in the lobby become a suicidal patient in need of her therapist.

But it wasn't the same, what she had done. For herself, it didn't matter what she told Eva or her father. She could have off-loaded her woes to relieve this horrible, private burden, but her instinct—and misleading them had been thoroughly instinctive—had been to keep the poison of it all to herself.

Then she thought: *But how do I know Jonathan isn't doing precisely that? How do I know there isn't... something... he has been protecting us from? Some threat, some information that has been making his life intolerable?* Hope leapt from this murky insight, blossoming out of insubstantial soil. It could be. It was possible. Something so dreadfully sad or frightening that he had protected them, herself and Henry, as she had protected Henry and her father. He was protecting them now, wherever he was, leading this awful thing away from the ones he loved.

Stop, she told herself. She was shocked to note that she had said it out loud.

As if in response, a car—old, dark, she was no good at cars—slowed down beside her. She raced across 98th. He had to wait at the light.

Grace sprinted up the hill, passing the opening through which the trains emerged from underground. As if by preordained arrangement, a cab materialized the instant she reached the corner of 96th and Park. She hurled herself inside.

"Eighty-First and Park, please."

The driver, if there was one, barely looked around. The video screen affixed to the divider chirped to life with some baffling story about weekend stoop sales in Park Slope, and she wasted a pointless minute trying to figure out how to mute it. When she failed, she nearly covered her ears in petulance.

Stoop sales. She wanted to kill everybody. She wanted to kill every single person who flew into her head.

They caught the red light at 86th, and Grace watched the driver tap his finger against the wheel. He still had not looked back or—it occurred to her—into the rearview mirror. He made her think of the spectral cabdriver in Elizabeth Bowen's "The Demon Lover," in which a terrified woman is spirited away through a "hinterland of deserted streets," and she duly noted that Park Avenue, the central thoroughfare of most of her life, now felt like something altogether new and worrisome, a road not traveled, a road of no return.

The light turned green.

She paid him in cash and stepped out at the corner, making her way down the silent street, walking the half block she had walked only twenty thousand times or so since arriving as a newborn. It was no different, she instructed herself, noting the now mature trees her mother had organized the block association to request from the city, and the spot by the fire hydrant where she had tripped as a six-year-old and broken her elbow in two places, and the cardiologist's office she had stood in front of, watching Henry wobble upright on his bicycle and pedal in triumph. Vita had once called 81st between Madison and Park an "under the radar" street, meaning that it boasted no building of particular prestige, no landmark like a church or hospital or private school. And although most side streets on the Upper East Side at least had a few town houses to entice a genuine tycoon or a nouveau climber, her street had none. Instead there were only four apartment buildings (all but one a comforting prewar of limestone, the last a postwar of unfortunate but at least unobtrusive white brick) and doctors' offices between them or lodged within their lobbies. Just a little backwater for families like the one she'd come from and the one she had.

And yes, she told her appalled self firmly: *The one I do have.*

The doorman met her at the door and let her in with his customary "Good evening." He walked her to the elevator, and she felt herself avert her gaze from the couch and armchair in the lobby. Already it was hard to imagine a time before the advent of O'Rourke and Mendoza, before she had known intimately the whiskered neck overflowing its collar or O'Rourke's spatter of reddish moles. Only yesterday, it occurred to her, or—given the fact that it was now past midnight—the day before yesterday, and now those two were so burned into her, she felt them superimpose on anything else she tried to think about. After a painful attempt or two, she stopped trying.

Rather pointlessly, the doorman held back the elevator door for her as she went inside and stood as it closed between them.

As soon as she got through her own apartment door, the weight of it all seemed to find her, and she stumbled her way across the foyer to a little slipper chair just inside, sinking onto it in a moment of overwhelming nausea. She put her head between her knees, as she sometimes instructed patients to do when they seemed on the point of losing control, but it just pounded and pounded and pounded, and the only thing that stopped her from vomiting was the absolute knowledge that there was nothing in her stomach to be vomited. She hadn't eaten since . . . she thought back now, nearly relieved to have some concrete problem to solve . . . since morning. That morning. No wonder she felt so ill. Perhaps, she thought, she should eat something now. And then—this felt entirely logical—she would be able to throw it up and feel better.

The apartment was dark. Grace got up and turned on a light, then, as if it were any other evening, home from a day of seeing patients or planning a benefit for her son's school, she walked through the dining room and into the kitchen, where she opened the refrigerator door and looked inside. There wasn't much. She hadn't shopped in... it was hard to remember. Wait: the lamb chops and the cauliflower. Those she had bought at Gristedes, before the men in the lobby. How long ago was that? And the usual half-full cartons of milk and juice and the generic condiments and an open box of English muffins and a takeout container of leftover empanadas from the Cuban restaurant where she and Henry had had dinner on Monday evening, the evening of the day her husband had departed. She didn't want to eat them. She hated them. Incensed, she pulled out the cabinet containing the kitchen trash bin and threw them away. And that was it except for the cheese.

There was always cheese, large blocks of it in shiny, greasy cellophane wrap, taking up a good half of one of the shelves. Jonathan had bought the cheese. It was the only thing he ever bought in the way of food, unless she made a point of asking or actually gave him a list. He bought it in great chunks and wheels, as if he were concerned about running out, but he didn't have much interest in moving beyond the generic Wisconsin and Vermont varieties. Once she had had the idea of giving him a "cheese of the month" subscription for Christmas, and each month exotic and artisanal offerings would arrive from their far-flung origins around the American culinary diaspora. He ate them dutifully and with appropriate recognition, but when they were gone he went straight back to the pale and undistinguished wedges of low-rent cheese. As a medical student, this was what he had lived on, installing it in his knee-high fridge alongside the common tools of the sleepless, like iced coffee, and the nutritionally deprived, like edamame (very exotic back then). *Medical students are very basic creatures*, he had told her around that time; they rushed so fast and worked so hard, there never was time to do more than fulfill the basic commands of *ingest protein*, *empty bladder*, and above all: *sleep*.

Grace had never much liked cheese, and cheddar in particular. But these circumstances were beyond special. *Now I am a basic creature*, she thought. *Ingest protein. Empty bladder. Save son. Save self.* She reached into the fridge and broke off a thumb-sized block of the stuff and force-fed it to herself. Immediately, she fought another wave of nausea.

Then she yanked out the sliding garbage pail again, grabbed the cheddar with both hands, and hurled it in.

A moment later, she was retching over the sink.

No protein, no crime, she thought, giving in. Still hanging over the sink, she laughed helplessly.

Somewhere in the dark, quiet apartment, a thing or a combination of things or even a network of things had eluded her. There was a system in place beyond her ken, and it had broken her life apart into pieces she was now supposed to be able to interpret for horrible men, drawing a chalkboard line from a disciplinary hearing to a murdered woman, as if she knew anything about either. These pieces had been marched before her over the past hours, in a baffling parade. An ATM card? A bank account she had never heard of—from Emigrant Bank? What was she supposed to be able to tell them? (Besides: Emigrant Bank? It sounded like something from another century. Where was it, on the Lower East Side?) And a pair of corduroy pants—they were very interested in corduroy pants. But Jonathan had lots of corduroy pants. He found them comfortable, and they looked good on him. Which pair did they mean? He had never worn corduroys until Grace first took him shopping years ago, back in Boston—did that make her responsible for this?

And exactly how was she supposed to explain anything to anyone when she couldn't even get her head out of the sink?

Up, Grace thought. She stood, gripping the granite edges of the under-mounted steel basin. That thing, those things, the network of elusive truths, she couldn't stand the thought of them any longer. If there had been any possibility of sleep, she might have waited for another day or another midnight, but there wasn't, and she couldn't do anything else until this was done.

She went first to Henry's room, since it seemed the least likely place and thus the first to dispatch.

On his walls, in his drawers, lining the shelves, and stuffed into the closet: There was nothing here that she hadn't placed herself or watched her son produce—drawings, clothing, an autograph book from camp, folders of violin music covered in Mr. Rosenbaum's terse commentary ("Forte! Forte!"). On his shelves were the books her son had read, the textbooks from last year, a curling photograph of his happy younger self with his friend Jonah, the one who no longer spoke to him (Grace, pleased to be able to strike out at somebody, took the opportunity to rip this into shreds), and a framed picture of Henry and Jonathan at sixth-grade graduation. She held it up and searched their faces: so similar and so similarly pleased, both a little sweaty (it was hot in the outdoor area behind the school that June day). But she had been there. She had taken the picture. This, too, was a known thing.

There was nothing in Henry's room.

There was no Henry in Henry's room. Henry was where she had left him, at her father and Eva's house, and there he would stay for the night—that much was obvious to her. That much would be obvious, at this point, even to her father and his wife, who by now must have understood that some massive thing was taking precedence over questions of table setting and general bad manners. Henry would need things, now. He would need a number of things, but some far easier to provide than others.

She turned on the light over his desk. *Lord of the Flies* lay facedown, open at a page near the end. She turned it over and read the passage that seemed to describe Piggy's death, but it was so obscure that she read through it a few times, trying to figure out how he had actually been killed, before remembering the irrelevance of the question. She set it back down. Henry would need the book for tomorrow, she thought, looking around. And his math folder. And his Latin textbook. She tried to remember if he had orchestra the next day. Then she tried to remember what the next day was.

She went to his closet and instructed herself to collect a long-sleeved shirt, a blue sweater, jeans, and from the drawers of his bureau new underwear and socks. These and the books and papers she shoved into an old Puma bag that was in his closet. It had once been Jonathan's gym bag, but she had bought him a new one, a nicer one, the year before—brown leather with a long strap—and he had given this one to Henry, who for some indeterminate adolescent reason had decided Puma was cooler than the ubiquitous Nike. Jonathan's bag, the brown leather one with the long strap. She caught her breath. She hadn't seen that bag in a while.

Take the packed gym bag to the front door and set it down, where it will not be forgotten by a traumatized brain at the start of a terrifying new day.

She moved on to the hallway, passing one of the oddball art school portraits she had collected, mainly at the Elephant's Trunk flea market in Connecticut. They were from the 1940s or '50s, of sour-looking models, captured by less than brilliant students. Together they formed a kind of gallery, of unlovely faces and rather judgmental observers:

You're wearing that?

It's not what I would do.

I hope you're not too proud of yourself.

The painting in the hallway was of a severe woman about her own age, with bobbed hair and a nose that looked unnaturally small for her face and an expression, Grace had always thought, of pervasive misanthropy. The picture hung, rather regally, over one of those stripped-down English or Irish tables, imported by the boatload, which she and Jonathan had bought from the Pier Show. Not a good decision, really, since it wasn't nearly as old as the dealer had promised and cost far too much for what it was; and because it had been so expensive, they'd pretty much felt obligated to hold on to it. In the table's single drawer: tape, batteries, gym brochures. Had he been thinking of changing gyms? No, the brochures were hers, she remembered now. From a year ago. Nothing.

She went through the hall closet, shoving her hands deep into each pocket and finding only crumpled tissues and a gum wrapper. Every coat had been purchased by her, and every one she recognized: Brooks Brothers, Towne Shoppe in Ridgefield, Henry's favored Old Navy parka with the fake fur trim, the red fox coat that had been her mother's, which she could not wear because she did not wear fur, but which she could not get rid of because it had been her mother's. Every boot and glove and umbrella could be vouched for, the scarves on the overhead shelf had all been bought by her, except for one Jonathan had brought home, once. A couple of years before.

She pulled it out. It was green wool, not at all objectionable. Handmade? Grace frowned at it. It had no tag. It had been very nicely done, with a kind of coarse, authentic texture. She might have bought it herself, in a shop, for her husband. But she hadn't. Immediately, she was furious with the thing, as if it had wormed its untrustworthy way into her home, for who knew what purpose. Holding it carefully between thumb and forefinger, she dropped it on the hallway floor and went on to the next room.

The living room couches and chairs had been purchased in a general overhaul a few years earlier (out with anything that felt too "starting out on a shoestring," in with one particular alcove from the fourth floor of ABC Carpet & Home). Jonathan had been there that day, and Henry with a book, reading his way through Narnia in one of the armchairs as his parents bought it out from beneath him. All very verifiable. The paintings here, two studies of the same young man—from, undoubtedly, the same art school class, but very different painters—also found at the Elephant's Trunk, had been framed in identical black wood, as if to underscore their differences. One version of the man was so stiffly delineated that he bordered on cubism, his classic white button-down shirt and khaki pants rigidly arranged in a posture (half-crossed legs, torso in a forward incline, elbow braced almost impossibly on thigh) that looked profoundly uncomfortable; the other rendered him so breathtakingly sensual that Grace assumed some highly mutual (though necessarily silent) flirtation had been ongoing throughout the class. Grace could only imagine the corridor of fate that had brought them, the mismatched pair they made, from separate but simultaneous creation to side-by-side display at the flea market on Route 7, to the Upper East Side.

She moved on. There was a linen closet in the hallway to the master bedroom: musty towels, stacks of sheets (the flat ones gratifyingly neat, the fitted ones teetering), soap and mouthwash and Jonathan's antidandruff shampoo, bought in bulk (by her) on the uppermost shelf. Nothing. Nothing. The sling from when Henry had sprained his wrist. Her own traumatic pharmacy of fertility drugs, which she had not looked at in years but was still somehow unwilling to throw away (she also had, elsewhere, the positive home pregnancy test that heralded the arrival of Henry; whenever she came upon it, she thought of the myth of Meleager, who was fated to live only as long as the log burning on the fire at the time of his birth, and which his mother consequently snatched out of the flames). But nothing else. Nothing of his, really—nothing dubious a man with limitless access to any drug under the sun might have spirited away to his own home. Of course not.

With a steadying breath, she went into the master bedroom and stood for a long moment, trying to decide how to begin. The room had only one closet, and its door was slightly ajar, a bit of plastic bag protruding into the gap from the dry-cleaning delivery she had hung up Monday evening. She went to it and opened it the rest of the way.

The closet was evenly divided, more or less, and fairly orderly, which was possible only because neither of them shopped recreationally, but only to replace clothing that was being discarded. Her side was hung with blouses and sweaters, the linen and wool skirts that had long signified "discriminating grown-up" to her and "unimpressed by trend." Good fabric. Good cut. Soft colors. Quiet jewelry, the older the better. Nothing flashy or showy or "look at me," because she had never wanted anyone to look at her for any other reason but to think: *Now there's a woman who has her shit together.* And she did! she told herself now, glaring at her classic clothes, drifting briefly, dangerously, close to tears. She *did!* But she wasn't here to look through her own things.

Jonathan, like Grace, had made most of the big decisions about clothing long ago. She might have seen him first in sweatpants and a far from pristine Hopkins T-shirt, but soon after that she had gleefully purged most of what he had (highly suspect items of clothing from college and even high school) and taken him shopping for corduroys and khakis and striped button-down shirts, all of which he continued to wear to this day. Like a lot of guys, he didn't really care what he wore. He was going to be a doctor, after all. Who even noticed what doctors wore under their white coats? Now the right half of their shared closet rod was hung with brown-striped shirts and blue-striped shirts and green-striped shirts, a few solid shirts in mild colors, a half dozen or so plain white.

The cleaner had returned six shirts encased in a single plastic bag: more stripes, including the deep red that was one of her favorites, and racy multicolored stripes of green and blue that she had noticed at the Gap one day and bought for him. But there was something else in there, something she had vaguely noticed three days earlier when she'd carried in the delivery, tired at the end of her long day of patients and the violin lesson and dinner at the Cuban restaurant with Henry. At the time, she had declined to investigate; if the dry cleaner had made a delivery mistake, it would have to—inconveniently—go back: another item for the endless to-do list. She looked more closely at it now. It was a shirt like the others, but not striped and not a solid color. Grace tore away the plastic and eased apart the hangers to isolate the offending item. *Wonderful*, she thought. The shirt was a garish hot-rust-and-orange pattern that looked like something from a mass-produced Navajo blanket, but with solid black lapels: completely hideous. It stood out from the rest of his clothes like something BeDazzled, a Vegas showgirl in a pastel Balanchine corps de ballet. She pulled back the collar to see if there was a name there, but the only name was "Sachs," just like Jonathan's real shirts. Grace plucked it off the rod and glared at it, then she unbuttoned it and spread it out, making a meal of its awfulness. What was she looking for? Lipstick on the collar? (She had never really understood why there should be lipstick on a collar. Who kissed a collar?) Of course there was nothing there. She smelled it, too, though it had obviously just come back from being cleaned. Most likely it belonged to somebody else—somebody with terrible taste!—and had migrated over to their weekly delivery of classic button-down shirts and very fine cashmere sweaters. But she was being merciless. The shirt couldn't be vouched for, so she threw it (not without satisfaction) on the floor.

It practically didn't count, since she'd been thinking about the unfamiliar object in the dry-cleaner bag from the start of this... this dig, of sorts. Not a dig like a treasure hunter's, or a speculator's, more like what an archaeologist did, armed with a theory to be proved or—she still faintly hoped—disproved. She had not forgotten the shirt, or rather, she had, but it had come back while she was deep in the hall closet. *Where have I felt this before?* she had thought, holding that rather nice and thoroughly unfamiliar green scarf.

A moment later, in the breast pocket of a heavy jacket he hardly ever wore, she found a condom.

Grace knew what it was even before her stunned fingers

emerged, holding it pinched like something that might get away, but she still gaped at it, ricocheting back and forth between sense and bafflement. A condom. A condom did not signify in the world she occupied. A condom—even back at the beginning, back when they were students, back before their marriage, when they knew it wasn't all right for them to have a baby yet, they had not used condoms. She had been on birth control pills for about a year, and then that horrible IUD she still blamed—irrationally, since she had seen the studies—for every month of failure that would follow and, more pointedly still, for every miscarriage. Never a condom. Never.

But somehow a condom had materialized in the breast pocket of this jacket, which—like nearly every item of clothing her husband wore—had been purchased by Grace herself, this one at Bloomingdale's, at one of their big sales. But the jacket was of an awkward weight: too hot for summer and sort of too hot for winter, too. She couldn't remember the last time she had seen Jonathan wear it or why she'd kept giving it a reprieve every time she went through the closets to send things away.

The condom wrapper was red. It had not been torn open. It was incomprehensible. It was just, completely, incomprehensible.

Holding it far away from herself, she dropped this, too, on the floor.

"Fuck," she pronounced over it.

It was now two o'clock in the morning.

What do I know? And what do I not know? Whatever she knew, could verify, could comprehend—that thing could remain in situ, at least for now. Anything that could not be witnessed or vouched for she would leave in the open, an isolated artifact to be returned to when her strength returned, when—if—she became clearheaded again. A mysterious scarf and a hideous shirt and a wrapped condom. Three things in all this searching—it wasn't much, really. It was within normal bounds, even. The scarf—he could have picked it up by accident somewhere, mistaking someone else's for his own.

He didn't pay that much attention to things like that. Lots of men didn't. He might have been cold one day and stopped into a store and bought it for himself. That was allowed. It wasn't a crime. It wasn't something he had to clear with her! And the ugly shirt—she had already persuaded herself that the dry cleaner was responsible for that one. The "Sachs," written in some kind of permanent marker on the tab, just above the breakdown of cotton and polyester (another indictment)...well, "Sachs" was not the rarest of names, not in New York. It might be as simple as that. An Upper East Side dry cleaner? Come on! How many Sachers and Seichers and Sakowitzes were there, just within the immediate neighborhood! How many other families called "Sachs," for that matter? Really, the only surprise was that it didn't happen more often.

But then, the thought of that condom punched through her little moment of reprieve.

She stood still to let the now familiar sensation have its way with her. It felt like screaming acid, poured directly over her skull, then flowing through her and out the tips of her fingers, the tips of her toes, pooling around her in a black, treacly mess. She was becoming used to it. She was becoming tactical in her response to it: *Don't fight, go loose, let it pass.* In only a few minutes, she could move again.

There might be other objects. They might be hiding. They might be pretending to be things they weren't. She pulled at the books on the bedroom bookshelves, which were tightly wedged and a little dusty, without much room behind them. They were mainly hers—mainly novels. There were some biographies, some books on politics. The political books they both read. They had shared a fascination with Watergate that expanded over the years into adjacent areas: Vietnam, Reagan, McCarthy, civil rights, Iran-Contra. It didn't seem to matter, now, which of them had brought which book into the apartment. One of the books wasn't a book at all, but a book safe, some remaindered tome that had been outfitted with a plastic insert. It had been given to her a couple of years earlier by a patient whose company bought unpopular books and adapted them for this purpose, on his last day of therapy. Grace had wondered aloud whether the books' authors ever spotted their works on a shelf, then were humiliated to find that their opus now hid bracelets and necklaces, and the patient had laughed: "Nobody ever got in touch to say so!" She had to admit the idea was very clever. "Thieves are not book-minded," her patient had told her, and she supposed that was true. She had never heard of a burglary in which someone took the time to pore over the Stephen Kings and John Grishams.

This one was a Jean Auel novel, one of those prehistoric sagas, not her kind of thing at all. As she took it down and opened it to its interior plastic chamber, she made herself think about what she had placed inside it that night, the night the man had given it to her, but already she knew that there was something wrong. The book was too light. It made no sound when she shook it, very gently. The book...well, it was an open book. What was supposed to be there could not much matter now, because nothing, when she finally got around to opening the cover, would be there at all. This was already, abundantly, clear.

Jonathan's good watch, the one she had given him when they were married, was supposed to be inside. It was a gold Patek Philippe, and he hardly ever wore it, but every so often there was an occasion, like her father's wedding to Eva, when she had made a point of asking, or one of Eva's grandchildren's bar mitzvahs, when the appearance of Jonathan's usual watch—whatever Timex or Swatch he was wearing to death at the time—would have caused more trouble than it was worth. And the cuff links her father had given Jonathan one year for his birthday—he had received them from Grace's mother, and now...well, it would be a nice thing to keep them in the family. And a few things belonging to Grace herself, that she had just never wanted to mix in with her mother's jewelry in the old mirrored vanity, like a Victorian cameo an old boyfriend had given her for a birthday (she had not loved the boyfriend, but she had loved the cameo), another necklace, also Victorian, she had bought on a trip to London with Vita the summer after their sophomore year, and a strand of gray pearls from 47th Street. Also—and this came to her with its own, dedicated physical stab—the classic Elsa Peretti cuff she had bought for herself the previous year, in a surge of self-satisfaction the week her book was sold. She had always wanted one. It was the first great thing she had ever bought for herself—not crazy extravagant, but certainly out of the ordinary. But she had worn it only a few times. It wasn't very comfortable, that was the truth. So it lived in the book safe.

Now the book safe was empty.

Grace sat on the edge of their bed, holding the thing, which was not the real thing it had been created to be—an actual work, whatever its literary merits—but only a stupid box with a dreamy, romantic cover and a hole in the middle. A zero at the heart of a thing is still a zero. She wanted, incredibly, to laugh.

Then she looked across the room with a kind of dread.

He wouldn't. He would never.

The vanity that had been her mother's. It was one of the very few objects belonging to her mother that remained in the apartment.

The "classic six" rooms of Grace's childhood had all been redecorated, her mother's chintz and beige redefined in pale blues and browns, the carpeting lifted to liberate long-obscured parquet. The walls of the kitchen were now filled with Henry's artwork and photos of the three of them, or Jonathan and herself at the lake, and the rest of the rooms mainly hosted the paintings from the flea market or from the Pier Show, except for two from the Clingancourt market in Paris, the year before Henry was born.

Henry slept in the room Grace had once slept in. It had been yellow with a green shag rug then; now it was blue, robin's-egg blue, with glossy white trim, and Henry, who was fastidious, kept it bizarrely pristine. The bulletin board that had once covered the entire wall above her bed had been a crazy mosaic of fan magazine photos, pictures of clothes she liked, snapshots of her friends (mainly Vita), certificates of merit from Rearden and the New York Turn Verein on 86th Street, where she took fitness and gymnastics classes. *My brain on cork*, she had thought of it, after the antidrug commercials of her youth. Henry had only one photograph over his bed, of himself and Jonathan on the dock at the lake, holding fishing poles. She had given them the fishing poles for Jonathan's birthday. It may have been the only time he and Henry had ever used them.

But the vanity, in the room she had finally forced herself to stop calling "my parents' room," was an island of stasis, inhabiting a magic circle of preserved time. It still wore its classic chintz apron and its ring of worn brass studs. There were mirrored drawers along the back of the table, meant for the armor of women—rings, earrings, bracelets, necklaces—but her mother had not always used them. When her husband, Grace's father, gave her something—an abstract pin, perhaps, of pearls and emeralds on an amoeba of gold, or a bracelet of rubies and diamonds—she liked to lay the object out on the vanity's cool glass tabletop. Perhaps it was a way of offsetting the fact that she never actually wore these objects (Grace had only ever seen her in pearl necklaces and simple gold earrings). Perhaps she preferred them as art objects, to be enjoyed by being put on display. Perhaps she had not wanted Grace's father to know how little they suited her taste. He had always seemed very sentimental about them, very intent that they be passed on to Grace, and promptly, as her mother would have wanted. Only a week after her mother's funeral, as she was packing to head back to Boston, Grace's father had come into her childhood bedroom (now Henry's bedroom) and deposited these former gifts, a ziplock bag of diamonds and rubies and emeralds and pearls, on her bed. "I can't look at them anymore," was what he'd said. It was the only thing he'd ever said about it.

Crossing the room to the vanity now, sitting before it on its low matching bench, Grace used the sleeve of her shirt to wipe the mirrored drawers of the table. Something held her back. She had continued to keep her mother's jewelry here, but never in plain sight, on the tabletop. Like her mother, she tended toward the understated end of the jewelry spectrum: a strand of pearls, a wedding ring. The big garish pieces, the pins with large misshapen stones and the chunky necklaces, remained in the vanity's mirrored drawers, where she seldom visited them. But Grace actually loved these objects. She knew what they had meant to her father, who gave them, and her mother, who received them—even if she never wore them, even if she so clearly viewed them as love letters, they were still just as potent as a stack of envelopes tied with a ribbon, kept in a special box. Jonathan, who was more comfortable articulating his feelings than her father had ever been, had not needed to use jewelry as a proxy for those feelings. In fact, he had given her only one piece of jewelry in all the years they'd been together: the simple diamond engagement ring he'd bought on Newbury Street. It was modest by anyone's standards, a single square-cut diamond, with the so-called Tiffany mount, on a platinum band, a ring so classic that it might have (but hadn't) been passed down to her. And that was that. He hadn't gotten the memo about presenting a gift on the birth of their child. (To be fair, Grace hadn't either. The first time she'd heard the truly tasteless term *push present* had been in the baby group she'd briefly joined with Henry.) But even if he had, it would far more likely have been a book or piece of art than an item of jewelry.

There was the issue of worth, of course. The objects in the mirrored vanity might have been unworn by mother and daughter alike, and valued sentimentally, but obviously they were worth money, too. At her behest, Jonathan had added them to their insurance policy, and she vaguely saw in them some future help with college tuition or down payments, but she never followed through on the idea of purchasing a safety-deposit box and putting them away. She preferred to keep them here, close to her—close to *them*. A shrine to the kind of long and good marriage she wanted for herself.

He would never, she thought again, as if that made it true. Then she opened up the drawers.

Gone, gone: the leopard-print bracelet of black and yellow diamonds, the diamond clip-ons that had pinched her earlobes at A Night for Rearden, and the sapphire necklace and the big chunky necklace of gold links, the pin of pink stone held by little gold hands. Drawer after drawer full of air. She struggled to remember the objects: red, gold, silver, and green. All those crazy things her father had brought home over the years, and that her mother had pointedly not worn, and that she herself had also not worn but had loved nonetheless.

She kept closing the drawers and then opening them again, as if admitting the possibility of a new reality each time, which was not logical. Doing the same thing over and over again and expecting different results? Grace nearly laughed. Wasn't that supposed to be the definition of insanity?

Which would at least explain a few things, she thought.

Those objects from the book that wasn't a book…well, she would survive. The Elsa Peretti cuff had hurt her wrist. The pearls…she loved them, but come on, pearls were pearls: They were hardly irreplaceable. Not that she would ever replace them now. They had been ruined now: one little lost battle in a vast conflagration, sweeping past. But the empty drawers, the air where her mother's things should have been—she could not get her brain to make sense of them.

She got to her feet so quickly that she was abruptly dizzy and had to put her hand down on the mirrored tabletop to steady herself. Then she went back out to the hallway and opened the door to the apartment's third and smallest bedroom, the room that had once been her father's classically masculine den, the only place in which her mother had permitted him to smoke his pipe and that still—in Grace's imagination, at least—possessed a certain lingering aura of pipe smoke. Once, she and Jonathan had hoped the room would belong to a second child, and it had never been actually rededicated. They had not had *a discussion*—she had never been able to initiate that, and Jonathan, in deference to her feelings, had never done it either—but gradually the room had taken on, soundlessly, an alternate designation, if not an actual name. It had turned into the place Jonathan went to read, or do his e-mail, or sometimes make phone calls to his patients' families if he hadn't had a chance to speak to them at the hospital. She had not technically decorated in here, but there were a few low shelves on the walls, lined with old issues of *JAMA* and *Pediatric Research*, and textbooks from Jonathan's medical school. A few years earlier, she'd moved in a big easy chair for him, with a matching ottoman and a desk she'd found in Hudson, New York (a town, Jonathan was fond of saying, that was "going up" and "going down" at the same time). He had a computer here, too, a big, boxy Dell she hadn't seen him use in a long time (he used his laptop, of course—his now very much absent laptop), and beside it a box of patient files—the kind of box with sturdy handles that you might use to bring home your possessions on your final day of work.

Nice catch there, Grace, she made free to tell herself.

She did not have it in her to look through that box. Or turn on (*try* to turn on) the computer. Or open the drawers of the desk. Or even enter the room itself. *This far but no farther*, she thought. So she stepped back into the hallway and closed the door in her own face.

Then she thought of the phone.

She went back into the bedroom and opened the bedside cupboard. It was still there, naturally, right where he had left it, behind the phone books. Of course it was dead as a stone now, its flicker of battery power from the last time thoroughly departed. She held it up anyway, trying to make herself focus on the buttons and remember how Jonathan usually held it and what he did with it. It was one of the less user-friendly types, more technical, vaguely space-age, and she, being still at least three generations behind in the rapidly mutating genus of the cell phone (and associated technologies), was not even sure how to get it turned back on. But she did understand that even trying meant crossing a line she hadn't yet crossed, not by walking through her own home, searching through the drawers and closets of her own possessions. For some reason she could not fully make herself understand, she wanted desperately not to cross that line, but she also knew that this might be her last chance to... well... if she wanted, to help him. And helping Jonathan had been her default instinct for many years. Helping him study for his medical boards. Helping him move out of his dorm. Helping him buy a decent suit, get new plates for his car, roast a chicken, splint a broken finger, feel good, choose a wedding ring, make his peace with the sad inadequacy of his family of origin, father a child, be happy. It's what you did when you chose a partner, hopefully for life. It was how you made a marriage.

It was not so easy to stop helping.

But then again, she reminded herself, they knew about the phone, the police did. They knew it was here, in the apartment; it was why they'd thought Jonathan himself might be here. Which meant that they would want to see it. They would ask her for it, and she would have to hand it over, because if she didn't, there would be... well, it was a crime of some kind not to, wasn't it? And when they asked for it and when she gave it to them, they would know—somehow they would be able to figure out—that she had done something to it, read something or changed it or eliminated it. And that would be a very, very bad thing for her, and also for Henry. She had to do everything right now, for Henry.

So she put it back in its strange place, thinking she would simply leave it where it was, for them to find when they came to look for it. And then, because this was the first time she had imagined them in her apartment, looking into drawers and closets and cupboards the same way she had just been looking, and because the minute she imagined this, she realized that such a scene was now an inevitibility, she opened the cupboard again and took out the phone and left it on top of the cupboard, in the open, where it didn't look as bad, as...*incriminating*, as it would if he had hidden it. She had told them the phone was here, in the apartment. She had not said that it was squirreled away. Why shouldn't she do that for him, anyway?

I know you want to protect him, one of them had said, though which one she couldn't remember now.

Grace lay back on the bed, on top of the covers, and closed her eyes. She was weary, hollow with weariness. She kept thinking about objects, the objects she had discovered—the scarf and the shirt and the condom—and how they explained nothing, how they were some sort of rune or hieroglyph she could not comprehend. That sparse little trail of things on the floor whose appearance could not be explained—the scarf and the shirt and the condom—it wasn't the right trail at all. The right trail, it came to her, was the one of objects that were no longer here.

That missing gym bag, the good leather one she had given Jonathan. It normally lived on the floor of the closet. It was not there now. Say he picked it up and moved around the room with it, placing things inside: What things would he take? Underwear. Shirts. Toiletries. Pants. The corduroy pants those detectives had seemed so fascinated by? How was she supposed to know which ones they meant? Jonathan had at least six pairs of corduroy pants. She should know, she had bought them all, and all of them were now absent from the shelf in the closet, above the closet rod. There were orphaned hangers and empty drawers and a newly vacated shelf in the bathroom where his toothbrush and his razor usually lived. No wonder it hadn't registered until now; it was *barely* registering even now. Everything looked every bit as it should for a man out of town for a couple of days—on a trip, for example, to a medical conference in Cleveland—due back before he ran out of clean underwear.

Not what is here and does not belong, she told herself, *but what is not here and does.* It sort of made her think of that poem by James Fenton, about war—some war, she could not remember which:

It is not the houses. It is the spaces in between the houses.
It is not the streets that exist. It is the streets that no longer exist.

Added and taken away, plus and minus: but without a prayer of canceling each other out. All of the new people in her life—police detectives and murder victims—not making up for the person unaccountably gone. *And not some other war but my own war*, she understood, squeezing shut her eyes. *My very own.*

CHAPTER FOURTEEN

Rushing to Its End

Somehow, she slept. By the next morning she had traveled from her own side of the bed to Jonathan's, as if over those ragged, uncompromising hours she had begun to doubt that he was gone and needed to be sure no one was there. No one was there—no head (dark curling hair, dark growing beard) making its customary dent in the soft pillow, no shoulder, rising and falling over the duvet, no presence at all. Grace woke in the same traumatized clothing she had put on twenty-four hours earlier, when she had been merely concerned, merely annoyed. How wonderful to feel merely those things now.

It was just after six and not yet very light. She dragged herself upright and did all of the necessary things, dressing herself, washing to the extent she could. The room looked disheveled, with the sheets and duvet half twisted off and her shoes on the floor. The strange shirt and the condom in red foil seemed to glow in some malevolent way from where they had been deposited in front of the closet, as if they had been outlined—like the way a dead body might be outlined—but in neon. She kicked them aside as she went to the closet, then threw down her own shed clothes on top of them, as if to hide them from herself. She put on a new sweater, a new skirt, both close in style to what she had worn the day before (because it hurt to think about clothes), and then she did a couple of things that also hurt to do, but which she had fallen asleep thinking about doing, and had woken up thinking about doing, and saw very clearly that she had to do.

So, with her laptop open on the bed before her, she canceled every one of her appointments that day, and every one of her appointments the next day, Saturday morning, which was as far as she felt able to look ahead. For explanation, she cited only a "family illness" and said she would be in touch to reschedule. Then, bracing herself against her own distaste, she called J. Colton's number and left a message saying that she would be unable to speak with the writer from *Cosmopolitan* this afternoon and to please not schedule anything for her for the next week because she was dealing with something in her family, and she would be back in touch as soon as she could be. "Thank you!" she told the dead silence of the tape recorder—though it wasn't, of course, a tape recorder. There no longer were any tape recorders.

When these two things had been accomplished, she felt as exhausted as if she had toiled, physically, for many hours.

With Henry's Puma bag she went down to the lobby and set out into the cold predawn of the morning, still exhausted but now also brutally wide awake—a very uncomfortable combination. There were eight blocks separating her apartment from her father and Eva's, and the frigid air she hauled into her lungs along the way felt awful but just possibly therapeutic, the way only a truly awful sensation could. The streets were mainly empty, though the pavement in front of the redoubtable E.A.T. was alive with delivery trucks and prep workers, and she looked longingly inside as she passed, as if the familiar pleasures of the city were already unavailable to her. Waiting for the light at 79th, she found herself staring at the nearly forgotten contours of Malaga Alves's face on the cover of a newspaper in a blue metal dispenser. The headline, whatever it was, could not be seen, and when the light changed, she walked on.

Upstairs, a terse and typically unwelcoming Eva led her to the kitchen, where she got the extra little blow of seeing Henry eating cereal out of one of her own mother's china bowls. That Eva had elected (for this occasion? Grace wondered; or—which was even worse—merely for every day?) to make use of her parents' wedding china, circa 1955, as a receptacle for Henry's cornflakes and skim milk was nothing less than a shot across the bows, and even in the present circumstances Grace had to fight herself not to rise to the challenge.

Eva had taken a shine to the china upon her marriage to Grace's father, but not so much of a shine that it was used for very fine occasions, like Passover or even Shabbos dinner. Instead, the classic Haviland Limoges Art Deco, with its delicate green edge, was trotted out for morning toast, and the Entenmann's Danish her father consumed before he went to sleep every night, and the canned soup Eva's grandchildren ate (which was particularly galling), and naturally the weekly visit of Grace's own family, at which—for years—it had tormented its rightful (in her opinion) owner. Needless to say, Eva was not hurting for dishes. She still had two enormous sets from her own first marriage, to the father of her son and daughter (an extremely wealthy banker, who had died of a ruptured appendix while on an island off the coast of Maine—a terrible story, really): one also Haviland (the less formal, actually) and one from Tiffany, used on the most special of special occasions. There was also, somewhere in her cupboards, a perfectly adequate white pottery set from Conran's, ostensibly for those everyday occasions when one would not think of using good china. And yet, in accordance with some vicious logic of her own, Eva seemed to make a point of setting out the possessions of her predecessor whenever Grace came to visit.

Of course she had wanted them. She had complained to Jonathan about the injustice of this, about how wrong it was to withhold from an only daughter (an only child!) such an important artifact, one that by tradition (Emily Post tradition, at any rate) ought to have come to her just as soon as her father and Eva joined households. And no, she was not being petty. And yes, her father had given her many things: the apartment, first and foremost, and her mother's jewelry (none of which—as of this morning—she still possessed). But that wasn't the point.

Henry looked up when she entered the kitchen. "I forgot my Latin book," he said after swallowing.

"I've got it." She put the Puma bag on the chair beside him. "And the math."

"Oh yeah. I forgot about math. And I need clothes."

"Well, what a coincidence!" She smiled at him. "I brought clothes. I'm sorry about last night."

Henry frowned. He had a crease between his dark brows when he did that. Jonathan had the same crease. "What about last night?"

She felt such gratitude for the natural narcissism of being twelve years old. Wasn't it a good thing, thinking so little behind and so little ahead and so little around that the most intense of cataclysms, the greatest ruptures in the fabric of the world, had so little immediate impact? She imagined that if the two of them were walking across limitless space, Henry would be all right as long as she could keep tossing bits of solid mass beneath his feet. How wonderful it must be not to realize that something had gone very, very wrong in the world. At least, for now.

"Did Nana let you stay up late?" she asked him.

"No. I got to watch TV with them, but only till the news."

Well, that's a plus, thought Grace.

"Karl slept on my bed with me."

"Oh, goody."

"Where's Dad?" said Henry, upending the equilibrium. It had been nice while it lasted.

"I wish I could answer that," she said honestly enough. "But I can't."

"Isn't he where he said he was going? To Iowa or wherever?"

"Ohio," she corrected, before remembering that she herself had most likely supplied the Ohio. She glanced behind her, but Eva had left them alone. "I don't know. I can't reach him."

"Why don't you just text him?" said Henry, employing the logic of the iPhone generation.

Grace looked around for coffee. The coffeemaker, mercifully, had a half-full carafe.

"I would, but unfortunately he left his cell phone at home."

She got up to pour herself a cup, using (with very mixed feelings) one of her mother's teacups.

"I'm scared," Henry said, behind her.

She went back to him, set her cup on the table, and hugged him. He let her gather him in, and she tried not to let him feel her own hurtling fear. She thought: *I'll take yours, too*. Grace let out a long, shuddering breath. She tried to think of something she could tell him, something that might be both helpful and true, but anything she thought of fell down in one of these attributes. True but not helpful, helpful but not true—seldom both. Actually, never both. Were they going to be okay? Would she be able to figure it out? And could she really take care of him? She wasn't at all sure she could take care of herself.

But even as she thought this, Grace understood that there was a slender, brittle layer of resistance she still seemed to be holding on to. It hadn't been there the day before, not on that street corner in Hospital Land with Stu Rosenfeld or in the small, overheated room in the 23rd Precinct house with O'Rourke and Mendoza. It certainly had not been there in the hours she had just spent, clawing through her own drawers and closets, raging and distraught at what she'd found and not found. But somehow, somewhere along the way, it had seen fit to materialize and now it was present: a certain edge of resolve, fragile enough, but tactile. It made her feel... not exactly strong. She was not strong, not at all. She was in no position to storm the barricades or face the mothers at Rearden. But she did feel, somehow, lighter now and sort of different. *Because*, she thought, squeezing the thin shoulders of her child, and pressing her cheek against his, and inhaling the vaguely, newly adolescent smell of his skin, *I have less to protect than I did before*. It made things easier somehow.

She managed to get them both out of the apartment without seeing Eva again, or her father, and they walked, mostly in silence, to Rearden. Henry seemed to have passed through whatever turbulence of need he'd experienced and now seemed as placidly contained as he did any other morning. When they turned down the street toward school, it took him only a moment longer than her to see that the media presence had intensified. Massively.

"Whoa," she heard him say.

Whoa is me, Grace thought.

No, she did not want to walk past the vans.

The courtyard gates were shut, which they never, ever were, and the streets were full of mothers: no nannies or babysitters again this morning. They lined the sidewalk in front of the gates, their backs to the school's marble edifice, their determinedly impassive faces turned toward the cameras. They were beautiful and fierce. They were a herd of some elegant mammal, ready for flight but actually hoping for a fight. Apparently, none of this was fun anymore.

"Look," Grace said, pointing. "You see where Mrs. Hartman is?"

Jennifer Hartman, the mother of Henry's once best friend, Jonah, was standing halfway down the block, at the entrance to the alley that ran behind the school, holding a semi-official-looking clipboard.

So Robert had indeed activated the secondary entrance.

"Come on," she told Henry, taking his elbow.

They arrived with two or three others, and everyone—bizarrely, given how unprecedented any of this was—seemed to know what to do. "Phillips," said the woman in front of Grace, peering over Jennifer Hartman's shoulder. "There. Rhianna Phillips, second grade."

"Great," Jennifer said, making a check next to the name. "Go on back. It's kind of ad hoc, as you can imagine."

"Logan Davidson?" said the mother in front of her, as if she weren't quite sure. "Kindergarten?"

"Okay," said Jennifer Hartman. "Go on in."

"Hi, Jennifer," Grace said. "I see you've been recruited."

Jennifer looked up, and for the briefest moment not one thing happened. And then came a draft of ice, so sudden and overpowering that it left her almost incapable of speech, her own inappropriate smile stuck (frozen) to her face. She looked automatically at Henry, but Henry was only looking up at Mrs. Hartman, the mother of his lost friend. She was a woman of middling height but extraordinary bearing, with high, sharp cheekbones and eyebrows many shades darker than her ash-blond hair. She had been in Henry's life since the boys began kindergarten together eight years earlier, when Grace's practice and Jennifer's own business (she did publicity for chefs and restaurants) had taken on the heft of real careers. Grace had always trusted her and liked her, at least until the Hartmans' marriage started to fray. She had tried to give Jennifer some distance, always offering to take Jonah for overnights or outings, but that had been around the time Jonah himself started to pull away.

Now Henry was standing a mere two feet away from her and looking into her stony face, and did he understand? Jennifer Hartman had taken him on dozens of trips to indoor playgrounds and to see countless animated films. She had gotten him through his first sleepovers, some requiring midnight calls home for reassurance. She had twice taken him to Cape Cod in August, herding him and Jonah through visits to the potato chip factory and the Plymouth Plantation. Once she had even brought him to the emergency room with a broken elbow after Henry had fallen off one of the stone perimeter walls in Central Park. And since the split—since Jennifer's divorce (which was understandable: she was a grown-up and unhappily married) and her son's denunciation of his once best friend (which was not understandable, but also not within either mother's power to prevent)—she and Grace had maintained formalized, civilized exchanges, the kind that might characterize relations between two countries that had once been allies and might someday be again. But this.

"Hi, Mrs. Hartman," said her beautiful son, her sweet, innocent, and good-hearted son.

She barely looked at him. "Go on in," she said stiffly. Then she looked down again.

Grace took him quickly, rushing them both away.

Down the alley, which smelled strongly of pigeon shit, she walked behind him, letting the sound of the tumult outside fade as they went. Before her, the kindergartner and her mother were stopped again, at the back door of the school, and again admitted, this time by Robert and his assistant, an intense young woman with John Lennon glasses and a French braid. "Welcome, welcome!" Grace heard him tell the kindergartner's mother. He shook her hand as if this were a normal day, perhaps a normal first day of the year, and the doorway were not the heavy iron always-shut back door but Rearden's grand front entry into its marble foyer, so impressive to prospective parents. The pair moved past him and up the dark fire escape stairwell. "Henry, hello," he said when he saw Henry. "Grace." He nodded.

She nodded back. If there was a script for this, neither of them seemed to know it. But though he said nothing, his foot had moved, barely perceptively, into her path. Grace stared at it, then at him.

"Can I go up to the classroom?" she asked, appalled.

He seemed to consider this, and she watched him, mystified. She could not seem to get her brain around it.

"I'm wondering...," he began.

"Mom?" Henry asked, turning. He was already halfway up the first flight.

"Wait, I'm coming," she told him.

"It's just," Robert said again, "I think, under the circumstances, Henry ought to go up alone."

"Mom, it's fine," Henry said. He seemed confused and irritated, in equal parts. "I'm fine."

"Robert," Grace said, "what the fuck are you doing?"

He took an extended, very careful breath. "I'm trying to get us through a crisis. I'm trying to get all of us through this." She felt as if she were gazing at him through some kind of film, like glass or Perspex smeared with grime. She could just barely make out the shape of him. "Grace . . . ," he said, and suddenly he was a different Robert. "Grace, I don't think you want to be here."

She looked down. He had taken hold of her. He had placed a hand on her arm, between wrist and elbow. It was not possessive, exactly. It was—it was trying to be—comforting.

And then she understood—finally, finally. Robert knew. Of course, he knew. He knew because they had told him, Mendoza and O'Rourke. He had known even before she—Grace—had known, about Jonathan and Malaga Alves. Jonathan, her husband, and Malaga Alves, the dead woman. He knew at least some of the things she knew herself. Perhaps less. Perhaps, it came to her very horribly, even more. How much more? She had given up counting the things she didn't know.

Grace made herself look him in the eye. "What did they tell you?" she asked him bluntly. Then she remembered Henry and glanced up at where he'd been standing, on the stairs, but he had already gone on. He had left her behind.

Robert shook his head. She wanted to hit him.

"I want you to know," he told her quietly, "that this is a safe place for Henry. If he needs to spend time in my office, he can come see me, anytime he likes. Recess and after school, for example. And if anyone says anything to him, he should come see me right away. The teachers will be looking out for him as well. I've spoken to everyone."

I've spoken to everyone. She stared at him.

"He's a Rearden student. I take that very seriously," Robert said, flagging a little, as if he knew he was losing her. "But…just not to make it worse. I've seen this kind of thing before. Not…of course not on this scale. But issues, within a school community. They can't be stopped once they've started. They need to…well, be given their heads, if you know what I mean."

She nearly laughed. She had precious little idea what he meant, except that it was very, very bad and it had somehow become about her.

"So I wouldn't hang around. And…if you want to come a little later for him this afternoon, miss the regular pickup crowd, he can wait in my office. It's no trouble."

Grace said nothing. She was torn between basic manners—she knew he was attempting to do something nice for her—and awful humiliation. Humiliation made people act in ways severely detrimental to themselves. She knew that; she had seen it so many times. She made herself breathe. There were other parents, she now saw, crowding behind her into the stairwell.

"Okay." She nodded. "That would be…it's a good idea."

"I'll go get him at the end of period eight and take him to the office. Why don't you give me a call when you're on your way? I'll be here until six, at least."

"Okay," she said again, but she still could not bring herself to actually thank him.

She turned and worked her way back through the mothers and the kids and through the doorway into the back alley, where there were more mothers and kids. Most parted amiably enough, and no one seemed to take special notice of her. But when one body seemed to freeze in place, forcing her to move to one side of her or the other, Grace looked up to find Amanda Emery, flanked by her twin daughters.

"Oh," said Grace. "Amanda. Hi."

Amanda merely stared at her.

"Hi, girls," Grace said, though she didn't really know the Emery girls. They were stocky, with round faces and what Grace assumed was their mother's natural hair color: light brown. Before her eyes, Amanda grabbed her daughters' shoulders, matching claws on either one. Grace nearly took a step back. She still said nothing at all, though one of the girls looked up resentfully and said: "Ow. Mom!" It was Celia. The one with the overbite.

Grace saw the backlog. It extended all the way down to the alley's corner and then went on out of sight. It filled her with the most intense dread.

"Bye," she told Amanda Emery, stupidly, as if they had just exchanged the most banal of social pleasantries. She had to turn sideways and squeeze, in places, and mainly she was ignored, but not always. There were other Amandas, some she knew, some she had never noticed before. But in her wake, as she moved, came little expulsions of sound and also something she didn't identify right away, that turned out to be the opposite of an expulsion of sound, but in its way was just as loud, and that was the silence that came after sound. And it was that silence that followed her, like a building wave.

When she squeezed past Jennifer Hartman and out onto the street, she found that the reporters now formed a rough semicircle around the entrance to the alleyway. She ducked her head and made for the edge of the building, but they seemed disinclined to let her go easily. They made a kind of herd, it seemed to her, with a herd understanding of whose job it was to shout and whose to listen, who got to push forward with microphones and who had to stay back, checking sound levels on their equipment or preparing to write things on the most ordinary of pads. But they communicated as one animal, and what the animal wanted from her was nothing she could part with, not without losing her senses: right here on the sidewalk, right now at eight twenty in the morning of such a very, very long and very terrible day ahead.

"Excuse me," she told them roughly, and, "Let me through." And to her own amazement, they did, because by some miracle they had not yet realized that she was any different from the next mother who emerged from the alley's entrance, whom they also crowded and shouted to.

Not much longer, she knew. Maybe not even one time more. But for now they seemed willing to let her go.

Then someone called: *Grace*.

Grace put her head down and started to walk, away from them and up the street.

"Grace, wait."

A small woman rushed up beside her and took her elbow. It was Sylvia, and she seemed determined to stay alongside.

"I have to—," she tried to say.

"Come on," said Sylvia. "There's a cab."

It had stopped for a light at the corner of Park, but with the peripheral vision that increased survival for New York cabbies from all four corners of the world, he saw the two women walking swiftly in his direction and immediately put on his right directional, to the predictable dismay of the cabdriver directly behind him. By the time Sylvia had the door open, the second driver had already honked twice.

"I can't," Grace said again once she had actually climbed inside. "I'm sorry."

"No, don't be," Sylvia said simply. Then she asked the driver to take them to Madison and 83rd. Grace, through the fog of her irritation and the vastness of her distress, tried to figure out what was at Madison and 83rd, but she could picture only the coffee shop on the corner. She couldn't remember its name, but it was the one Meryl Streep had watched her son from in *Kramer vs. Kramer*. At least, there used to be a framed photo of the scene, on the wall behind where the cashier sat. To her mild surprise, this was exactly where Sylvia asked the driver to stop.

Sylvia had refrained from speaking during the five minutes it had taken to drive, and Grace—who had brought her narrow reserves to bear on the challenge of not falling apart while riding in the backseat of a cab with a person she was not exactly on intimate terms with, to an uncertain destination, for an unknown purpose—had not said anything either. Now, watching Sylvia pay the driver, she wondered if she was supposed to know what was happening.

"Come on," Sylvia said. "I think coffee for us both. Unless you need a drink."

To her own surprise, Grace laughed out loud.

"Well, thank God for that," said Sylvia.

They took a booth near the back, just under the Heimlich maneuver poster, and Sylvia practically barked at the waiter—*"Coffee, please"*—who performed the classic New York grunt of understanding with great economy. Grace had nothing to say and nowhere to look. She was baffled by the mere fact of being here with Sylvia Steinmetz. Why her? Only because she had made the effort?

But then it occurred to her that this—that Sylvia Steinmetz—was now what passed for a friend in her life. It seemed impossible, but it wasn't. She could not comprehend how she had allowed this to happen.

Sylvia said something Grace did not quite make out, so she asked her to say it again.

"I said: I had no idea this was happening to you, until this morning. Sally e-mailed me this morning."

"Fuck Sally," said Grace. Then she laughed again, even less appropriately.

"Right. But irrelevant. Those reporters weren't there because Sally told them."

"But—" She stopped as the waiter brought two white mugs of black coffee, sloshing a little over the edge. "But I don't think they knew me. They didn't seem any more interested in me than in anyone else."

Sylvia nodded. "That won't last much longer. You have a few hours, I think. I wouldn't count on more."

And then Grace understood that she had been much too accustomed to thinking of her life in exactly the wrong way—in sort of a spatial way, which was no longer viable. It mattered very little, for example, that she had long seen herself as part of a little family, ringed in by parents and colleagues, then by acquaintances, and then by the city that had always been her home. Whether or not this topography was still accurate didn't matter at all, because the question wasn't relevant; what mattered now, as of this morning, was the temporal reality, not the topographical one. What mattered was the fact that her life, the one she had cherished, was rushing to its end. Rushing, rushing, as into a brick wall, and she knew there wasn't a thing she could do to stop it.

"I'm sorry," Sylvia said. "I went through this with a client once. We had a little more time."

Grace's head was still spinning. Ordinarily, she might have wanted first to satisfy her own curiosity. Sylvia represented workers who'd been unfairly terminated or who brought harassment suits of various hues. Which client? What had she done, or what had been done to her? Was she someone Grace might have read about—in the *Times* or *New York* magazine? She used to devour stories like this. They were so interesting. People were so interesting, the messes they made of their lives.

But she couldn't afford the distraction.

"What did you do?" she asked instead.

Sylvia frowned. "Well, we got her into a new home. We moved her bank accounts—they were joint accounts with her business partner, but he'd absconded with a lot. We also hired a crisis manager for her." She looked up at Grace. "But she had a public profile already. That was different."

Grace looked at her. She had never heard Sylvia speak about her work, at least beyond generalities. It was a different Sylvia, sitting across from her in the booth, stirring thin milk from a metal pitcher into her coffee till it threatened to overflow the rim.

"How did it turn out?" Grace asked.

"It was a long haul," said Sylvia shortly. "But it's better not to focus on that. It's better to think about what you can do now."

A shudder went through Grace. She felt the way she had for a brief time in college, when she'd let herself be persuaded to serve as coxswain for the women's crew. She'd been good at the actual manipulation of the shell, the management of the personalities, and even the strategizing of the race itself, but she couldn't bear the hour before the meet. An hour of purest fear, purest dread, an absolute conviction that she—and never the eight tall, powerful women facing her in the narrow shell—was about to ruin everything.

She bent forward over her coffee, and possibly it was the coffee, the heat of the coffee, that flew up into her eyes and cheeks and made her wonder if she was either about to cry or indeed already crying.

"Okay," she managed. Then she took a breath to steady herself and straightened up. Sylvia seemed to be waiting. "Just... first," she finally managed, "before I can do anything, I have to ask you. What do you know?"

Sylvia shook her head firmly. "I don't *know* anything at all. I want to be clear about that. I haven't accepted as fact anything I might have been told. My standard of proof is way too high for that."

"Okay," Grace said. Then, because it seemed appropriate, she said: "Thanks."

"But what I've been told was that Jonathan had some kind of involvement with Malaga, and that the police want to talk to him, but he's missing. And also that you know where he is and aren't telling them. Which I can't believe at all."

"Good," Grace said shortly, as if this were some kind of relief.

"Which part of it is *good*?" Sylvia asked, tearing a packet of Sweet'N Low and fluttering the contents into her cup.

"The part about not believing I know where he is and I'm hiding him. I'm not brave enough to do that. Or crazy enough. I don't know where he is. I just... This just..." But she gave up.

"Did he know her? Malaga?"

"Well... the little boy was a patient at Memorial. They told me that, and I guess I believe them. The rest of it is all..."

But she stopped herself. All what? A vicious lie? She knew it wasn't. She knew there was more, she was just letting it in as slowly as she possibly could. And she wasn't going to proclaim his innocence to anyone. Let him proclaim his own innocence. And let him show up to do it, thanks.

"Well," said Sylvia to her surprise, "that does make sense."

"Really."

"Yes. I'm going to tell you something that you may already know. But if you don't, I need you to pretend that you know it. I'm in a bit of a liminal place here."

Grace stared at her. "Am I supposed to understand what you mean?"

Sylvia sighed. "I guess not. I hoped you would, but I was afraid you wouldn't."

"You're acting very lawyerly," Grace snapped. It sounded unkind. Well, she was feeling distinctly unkind at the moment. Sylvia would just have to adapt.

Sylvia turned the white mug between her palms, rotating the handle between ten and two. "He hired me. Back in February."

"Hired *you*," Grace said in disbelief. It came out sounding like an insult. She was sorry for that.

"Yes. He called, made an appointment, came in, and signed a document hiring me formally to represent him."

"Jesus," Grace muttered. "In February."

"There was going to be a disciplinary hearing. He wanted advice." She took a sip of her coffee, winced in displeasure, and set it down. "You knew about the hearing?"

Grace shook her head.

Sylvia started to roll the mug between her palms again. "I never asked him, point-blank, whether you knew. All these months, whenever we ran into each other, or doing benefit stuff, I always wondered. But I couldn't say anything, not unless he brought you in himself, to my office. It was privileged. You understand."

She nodded. She did understand. She was bound to her own clients the same way. But then, she didn't know the people in their lives. She didn't walk to school with them or sit on committee meetings with them. It wasn't fair.

"And it's still privileged, technically," Sylvia went on. "I should not be having this conversation with you. The fact that he's a suspect now, or that we're friends, it's not relevant. And I can't take the slightest chance of being disbarred." She stopped. She seemed to be waiting for something from Grace, but Grace wasn't sure what it was.

"I can't be disbarred. I'm a single parent."

She waited again. Grace just looked at her.

"Grace, do you want me to continue?"

"Oh," she said, getting it. "Yes. I understand. I wouldn't do that to you."

Sylvia sighed. "All right. He only came once. He didn't like the advice I gave him, which was to apologize to hospital administration, and accept any arrangement they offered. Just to try to avert outright dismissal. That was not what he had in mind at all."

"What… did he have in mind?"

"He wanted to go after his bosses. He said one was a plagiarist, another was a pedophile. He wanted me to let them know he'd talk to the press if they went ahead with the hearing. He thought he was paying me for that, and I'd just do it. It's pretty common for clients to make that kind of assumption," she said, as if she were trying to be kind. "But even if he had some proof, even if it was relevant to his circumstances, somehow, which it obviously wasn't, I just don't have the stomach for that in my practice. I need to look at myself in the mirror when I brush my teeth, you know?"

Grace nodded, but she was losing the drift. Which one was the plagiarist? Was it Robertson Sharp-the-Turd? It was hard to believe that Jonathan, in all of his rants about Robertson Sharp-the-Turd, had never mentioned a crime as egregious, and easily proven, as plagiarism.

"I looked over the paperwork he brought me and I told him, There's too much here. They have more than enough to fire you. Go in and plead with them, say you'll take rehab—"

"Rehab!" Grace practically shouted. "For what?"

"Whatever they wanted," Sylvia said tightly. "However they wanted to package it in terms of a disability, that would have been ideal. And they were offering him something like that, but he wouldn't consider it. He told me..."

But she stopped herself. She took a deep breath, lifted her mug again, and then remembered and set it back down.

"Actually," she said, aiming for something sardonic, something less than horrific, "he told me to go fuck myself. But you know, he was under enormous pressure. I wished him good luck, and I meant it."

Grace squeezed her eyes shut. She had to stop herself from apologizing.

"I don't even know what happened with the hearing," Sylvia said.

She took a breath. "According to the police, they fired him," she said. It came out sounding miraculously like old news. "I didn't know anything about it till last night. All these months..." She took a breath. "I guess, when he told me he was at work, he wasn't." It sounded so utterly lame, she thought. It was perhaps the single lamest sentence she had ever uttered. "I don't know anything. I don't know how I'm supposed to do this."

"Well, let me help you," Sylvia said earnestly. "I can try, anyway. So listen to me, because I have two things to tell you. First of all, if you know where he is, tell them."

She shook her head vigorously. "I don't. I don't have any idea. I've already told them so."

Their waiter was back. Were they going to order anything? Sylvia asked for the check.

When he went away again, she said, "It's very important that you cooperate with them. The sooner they make it clear you're not involved, the better you'll be treated in the media."

"All right," Grace said, though she hated the thought of "cooperating" with Mendoza and O'Rourke.

"And the other thing, actually the most important thing you can do right now is get yourself and your kid out of the way." She leaned forward, moving aside her full coffee mug. "Jonathan, whatever his reasoning, did not stick around for this. So he gets to miss the circus, whenever it happens. Tonight. Or tomorrow at the latest. But you're here, and they have to point the camera somewhere. Take Henry and find somewhere to go. Somewhere out of New York."

"Why out of New York?" she said, horrified.

"Because right now it's a New York story. And as long as it's a New York story, news crews from outside the city aren't going to be as dedicated. And the New York outlets aren't going to field crews to... I don't know, Arizona or Georgia. Not for the wife. With him, it would be different, but right now you can't think about him."

Grace, who'd managed, more or less, to follow until this last part, asked her to explain what that meant.

"I mean, when they find him, and they're going to find him, it will be everywhere. Just... be somewhere else until it happens, and be somewhere else *when* it happens."

She paused. "I forget. Are your parents here?"

"My father," Grace said.

"Siblings?"

"No."

"Close friends?"

Vita, she thought immediately. But she had not spoken to Vita in such a long time. And there was no one else. How had she let this happen?

"Not really. It was always…"

Me and Jonathan, she was going to say. *Jonathan and me.* They had been together nearly twenty years. Who made it to twenty years anymore? Who had those long-and-great marriages that her parents' generation enjoyed, with multigenerational safaris to Africa and family compounds on a lakefront or a shore somewhere, and big raucous parties for the milestone anniversaries? *Only marriage therapists*, she thought ruefully.

"But…," she started to say. She was thinking: *my patients*. She could not walk away from her patients. That was not allowed. That was not ethical. Lisa and her missing gay husband and bewildered children, Sarah and her enraged, failed screenwriter who had deigned to move back in. She had responsibilities.

And her book. What about her book?

She could not bear to think about her book.

And then she felt as if she had taken hold of the very tight lid of a very old jar, very, very deep inside her, and let the tiniest breath of its contents escape through the tiniest of breaches, and even that was enough to bring her down. Acrid shame. The most powerful, the most poisonous, of human essences. It took only an instant to be absolutely everywhere.

"I'm sorry," Sylvia said, though if she felt real pity, she was kind enough not to show it. "Listen," she said with great care, "I know we don't think of ourselves as close friends, but I do want you to know you can call on me." She stopped. Then she frowned at Grace. "Should I say that again?"

Grace shook her head and said no, but the truth was that she had stopped listening again and really wasn't at all sure.

CHAPTER FIFTEEN

To Search For and to Seize

"They're upstairs," her doorman told her, unnecessarily. She had seen the cars and the two vans, one marked NYPD, one something else, she couldn't make it out, as soon as she'd rounded the corner from Madison, and for a long time she had stood there, alternately resigned to it and not, then trying to understand why she could not seem to stand up straight while she worked it out. (*Because of food*, she reminded herself. *Because you need to eat something soon—idiot—or just give up completely.*) And then she went on, little lamb that she was, down the lane to the slaughterhouse.

"Okay," she told him. Then, ridiculously, she said thank you.

"They had a warrant. We had to let them in."

"Sure," she said. His name was Frank. She had bought a baby gift for his newborn, back in the summer. Julianna, that was the baby's name. "How is Julianna?" she asked absurdly, and he smiled but said nothing. Instead, as if it were any other day, he walked alongside her to the elevator and waited until the door closed.

Inside, she leaned heavily against the elevator wall and closed her eyes. How far down would this go? she wondered. *If I get through today, if I get through tomorrow.* How long would it last? On which morning would she get to wake up back in her own life?

But even as she stood—leaned—thinking about that life, it was leaking away, disassembling itself, little bits of it detaching and flying off. So much lost, so quickly; she could barely track the slippage. Ever since Wednesday, and the news about Malaga. No, since Monday, the day of Jonathan's departure. The day Malaga had died. (She couldn't think about that yet. She was nowhere near ready for that.) But wait, of course it had begun far earlier—long, long before that. How long? How many years? How far back did it go?

But that was an equation for another day. The elevator stopped at her floor, and when the door slid open she saw the official notice, photocopied into a blur, fastened to the front door with a kind of tape that was bound to strip paint on removal, and realized to her own immense sadness that she didn't even care, because she didn't live here anymore.

How many times had she left home? Once to go to college. Again to set up a household with her husband. Each time had taken her further from the place of her childhood, where she had crawled, then walked, then run, and played hiding games with her friends, and learned how to cook, and how to make out, and how to get an A in virtually any course. But at the end of the day, and no matter where she might be living at the time, these particular rooms and hallways had always meant home, and Grace had always found them beautiful. She could not remember a time when she'd wanted more space or a better address or even a nicer view: This was her place, and it was more than good enough. They had been renting the unlovely postwar on First Avenue when her father met Eva, long ensconced in eight high-ceilinged rooms on 73rd that she had not the slightest wish to leave. The day he suggested transferring the title to Grace—rather nonchalantly, over lunch, she recalled—she had gone home and wept in relief. How else would she and Jonathan—without a Wall Street salary or hedge fund between them—ever have afforded to give Henry the New York childhood she had wanted for him? They'd have been in that white brick box, or one just like it, until Henry himself had left for college.

But now her home had an official NYPD notice affixed to the door, which itself was slightly ajar, and through the opening came the sound of talking and shoes on the parquet floor, and the flash of a white uniform, as if some very unpromising party were already in progress. For a moment, she actually fought the impulse to knock.

"You can't come in here," a woman said when she was barely inside.

"Oh no?" said Grace. She didn't have much fight in her. But she didn't really want to leave, either. Where was she supposed to go?

"Who are you?" the woman asked, rather obtusely, because wasn't it obvious?

"I live here," Grace told her.

"You have some ID?"

Grace found her driver's license, and the woman—the officer, she supposed—took it. She was heavyset and very pale. Her hair had been badly dyed a color that could not have flattered anyone, and Grace was not remotely sympathetic. "Wait here," the woman told her, and left her there on her own doorstep while she walked away down Grace's hallway and into the corridor leading to Grace's bedroom.

Two men in white jumpsuits came out of Henry's room and stepped around her as they passed into the dining room. They said nothing, neither to her nor to each other. She leaned forward a little, trying to see past them, and she did see the corner of a table—a portable table—that did not belong to her. But she didn't really want to move off the spot she'd been told to occupy. It had become a kind of challenge. And actually, the more she saw of what was happening here, the less she really wanted to know.

Mendoza arrived and handed her back her driver's license. "We're going to be awhile," he told her shortly.

Grace nodded. "Can I see the paperwork?"

"Yes, you can."

He sent the policewoman into the dining room, and she came back with a longer version of the document taped to her front door. "I'm going to read this," she said quite stupidly, but Mendoza, kindly, did not smile.

"Of course," he said. "Why don't you have a seat?"

And he gestured, bizarrely enough, in the direction of her own living room.

Grace walked down the corridor, holding her purse in one hand, the stapled-together papers in the other, and sat in one of the armchairs. It was not the same chair her father had always favored in this room, but it occupied the same position: between the two windows overlooking 81st Street, facing the hallway. He would sit here in an imposing but not very comfortable throne-like chair he had taken with him to Eva's, one long leg flung over the other, usually with a Scotch in one of the heavy crystal tumblers still kept in the bar in the corner (he was not sentimental about them, apparently, the way he was about the chair). From this seat he held forth, rising occasionally to make drinks for the others or another for himself. They had been—her father and mother—in the style of their era, very fine entertainers, with the routines and division of labor between them established and smoothly attuned. Everyone drank more then, and none of them had (or else all of them had) "a problem," and who was to say it wasn't better that way? There had even been silver boxes full of cigarettes on some of the side tables, boxes she had sometimes opened and inhaled deeply, imagining herself Dorothy Parker, smoking away while making a comment of great wit and insight. The boxes, naturally, were long gone, but the bar remained—it had been fashioned out of a piece of furniture, something English that had probably been built to hold sheets or folded clothes—and was actually still full of bottles from her parents' time: rye and crème de menthe and bitters, stuff nobody needed anymore. When she and Jonathan had had guests over for dinner, they served wine, or at the most a gin and tonic or a Scotch, which they went through at such a slow pace that the occasional holiday bottle from a patient's family kept them more than well enough supplied. Though, actually, it now occurred to her, she couldn't remember the last time they'd had guests over for dinner.

She turned to the search warrant in her hands and tried to make sense of it but quickly became entangled in the specific turgidity of legal documents. *The Criminal Court of the City of New York. The Hon. Joseph V. DeVincent. You are authorized and directed to search the following premises.*

And below that, her own address, the address of her entire life, from birth until today: *35 East 81st Street, Apartment 6B.*

And below that:

You are hereby authorized and directed to search for and to seize...

Here the type got smaller, as if they were going to attempt to cram too many things in. Which made no sense, because there was only one item listed:

Cellular phone of unknown make and model.

But she would have given them that, or at the very least told them where to find it! They only had to ask. She was the one who'd confirmed the phone was here!

And then she realized: That wasn't the point. The point was to find Jonathan or possibly even to connect him to Malaga—her life or her death. Anything they came across while looking for the phone that might help them do either one of those things would be fair game. She closed her eyes and listened. The older buildings didn't leak sound the way the newer ones did, but she had lived in this apartment too many years not to recognize where people were moving around. There was quiet talking in the dining room and rustling in the hall closet. She heard Henry's closet door shutting and the *thwap* of the Sub-Zero in the kitchen. How many in all?

She got up and walked back to the edge of the living room and peered down the corridor to her bedroom. The door, which she was certain had been left open this morning, was shut. They knew the phone was in there, Grace realized. They had looked in, seen it, and closed the door to prevent themselves from "finding it" too soon, so that they could keep looking for it everywhere else. For a moment, she felt so routed by anger that she couldn't move. When that passed, she went back and sat down again.

Two officers went past and turned down the foyer. One was carrying the desktop computer from Jonathan's room. The other had a box of files.

Well, she'd expected that.

And the drawers in that same room, full of old checkbooks? His date books? She knew he kept them somewhere. They would find those, she supposed, because unlike herself, they would have the wherewithal to look.

The first of the officers, the one who'd carried the computer, passed her again, returning to the same room. This time he brought out the box of files she hadn't looked through the night before.

The other officer came back again and turned into the corridor. This time she could hear Mendoza. He was speaking. He was standing at her bedroom door. Grace could hear the door opening. She wondered which of the two of them had opened it.

In her own dining room, a woman laughed.

Grace sat back, letting the deep couch catch her. She was imagining the two of them going in, looking around, perhaps "noticing," perhaps "not noticing," the cell phone she had placed on the bedside cupboard. How long would they be able to legitimately "not notice" it? And what else could they see while they were "looking"?

There were items of clothing on the floor. They shouldn't be on the floor, but Mendoza wasn't going to know that, was he? He wouldn't know that the ugly shirt marked "Sachs" was anything but an ugly shirt. Perhaps he would not even note that it was ugly. He wouldn't understand what a rip through her life that single condom had made. Mendoza wasn't going to care where a scarf had been purchased or what had happened to a strand of gray pearls. He wouldn't know about the pearls in the first place, or the sapphire necklace that had been her mother's, or the leather gym bag. But he might know about other things. He was looking for answers to questions she had never asked. Grace took a breath, forcing the air far down into her lungs, where it nearly hurt. For the first time in years, she wished she had a cigarette.

Mendoza walked down the corridor and turned toward the front door. He seemed to have forgotten her existence. Grace, in disbelief, saw that he was carrying a plastic bag containing Jonathan's hairbrush.

Unmistakably Jonathan's hairbrush: the expensive wooden kind from that fantastic, barely reconstructed pharmacy on Lexington and 81st, with the bristles from some animal, she couldn't remember what. It was supposed to last forever. The mere fact of it was like a syringe of purest adrenaline. No New Yorker who had lived through 9/11 and its aftermath could ignore a hairbrush in a plastic bag. It was one of those objects that had been ripped away from normalcy and thrust into a museum of the iconography of torment: the falling body, the airplane, the "Missing" poster, the tall building, the hairbrush in a plastic bag. It meant . . . well, it could mean a couple of things, but they were all terrible.

She had forgotten, for a brief moment, that it was already terrible.

"Hey," she shouted, surprising no one more than herself. "Wait a minute."

She was already up and across the room. She ran out into the foyer and stopped him. She was pointing at the hairbrush.

"Is he dead?" She had to choke it out.

Mendoza looked at her.

"Is. My husband. Dead," Grace said again.

He was frowning. He looked convincingly perplexed.

"Do *you* think he's dead?" he finally said.

"Don't give me that Freudian shit," she hissed at him.

It was exactly—but exactly—what her patient Lisa had said to her, only... when? The day before?

He seemed much calmer than her. She didn't even think she had upset him.

"Mrs. Sachs, I have no idea. Why do you ask me that?"

"Because!" she said, intensely frustrated. "Why are you taking his hairbrush?"

Mendoza looked down at the bag. He seemed to be thinking deeply about it. "We're taking a number of things that might help our investigation. Are you concerned with the legality of the search warrant? Because I can have someone explain it to you."

"No, no." She shook her head. "Just... explain to me why his hairbrush is relevant to this."

He seemed to consider this. Then he asked her to go sit down in the living room again. He would be with her in a couple of minutes. He would explain it all then.

And just like that, she did what he asked. She felt so docile, so pliable. If there had ever been fight in her, she couldn't remember when. She went back to the chair in the living room and crossed her legs, and folded her arms, and waited. He didn't make her wait very long.

"Mrs. Sachs," said Mendoza, when he came and sat beside her on her own couch, "I think you want to help us."

"Why on earth would you think that?" she snapped, but even as she said it, she knew that he was not completely wrong. Not anymore. Something had altered—some deep, rusted place inside her had been forced into a new position. When, exactly?

He shrugged. He was holding his head a little at an angle, the way he did. She had known him only a couple of days, but she already knew his angles. She knew the way his neck overflowed his collar. She did not know him well enough to suggest that he invest in larger collars, and she hoped she never would.

"I guess, because I think at this point you're more angry at him than you are at us. And just between us, you're right to be."

"Don't patronize me," she said tersely, but again, even before it came out, she knew he was only trying to be kind.

"I'm sorry. I didn't mean to do that. I've dealt with this kind of situation many times. Well, not precisely this. I've dealt with husbands who have kept their wives in the dark about a lot of things, and by the time I'm in the picture there's some fraud or a robbery, or maybe an assault. This is pretty extreme, the exact circumstances, but I've met a lot of very smart women who've had to go through some of what you're going through now. And I want to say I'm sorry it's happening. And sorry it's me making it happen."

And don't manipulate me, she wanted to add, because that was precisely what he was doing. But now there was no fight left at all.

"We need the hairbrush for DNA," Mendoza said. "We need DNA for…well, a couple of reasons."

Why didn't he just come out and say it? Did he think she was going to fall apart?

"You mean, for the crime scene," she finally informed him, but he didn't seem that impressed.

"Yes, but also for paternity. There's an issue with paternity. You probably know that Mrs. Alves was pregnant at the time of her death. That was in the *Post*, thanks very much. Pathology department is like a goddamn sieve. Doesn't matter how much we yell about it. I'm sorry you had to find out in a rag like the *Post*."

Grace could feel herself gaping. She could feel her own mouth open, but nothing came out, and nothing else went in, not even breath.

"Mrs. Sachs?" Mendoza said.

"Don't be ridiculous." Her head had come loose from her body and was galloping around the room. When it returned, if it ever returned, she would laugh and laugh and laugh. It was crazy, the idea of it, and not just inappropriate crazy, but logic crazy. And Mendoza could take his "Now we're friends" delusion and go fuck himself if he thought she was going to swallow this. How ridiculously stupid did they think she was?

Again, down the hall, in her own dining room, she heard the unmistakable sound of laughter. The woman from the door, she supposed. The man with the computer. How many people were in her house?

"Well, it's moot," he told her, "because we would have had to run a panel anyway. Mr. Alves . . . it's understandable he wants to take his wife back to Colombia as soon as possible. There's going to be a funeral there, and he wants to finish up his affairs. He doesn't want to return after that, apparently. And the body's been released, but he's refusing to take the baby, the little girl. You know what I mean."

Grace, who did not, who truly, truly did not know what he meant, found the wherewithal to shake her head.

"He's demanding a paternity test. He insists he isn't the father. And of course we can't force him to take her. But it has to be settled. His attorney is insisting. Social Services is insisting. We just need to fast-track this." He peered at her. He was beginning to see something, and she watched him doing it. That was how she came to see it herself.

Grace had started to cry. She didn't realize it until he handed her a handkerchief. An actual handkerchief. Not even a tissue. Then she felt her own face, which had lost all its surfaces.

"I'm sorry," Mendoza said. He was sort of patting her shoulder. "I'm so sorry. I just . . . I really thought you knew."

PART III

AFTER

CHAPTER SIXTEEN

THE FOUNDRESS OF THE FEAST

In 1936, when very few of his neighbors were going to work anywhere to do anything, Grace's maternal grandfather, Thomas Pierce, got up every morning at about five a.m. and took the Stamford train into New York. He had a job in advertising, which had not been the dream of his youth, but the firm was solvent and its president had given him to understand that his work was valued, and frankly, when you had to step over bodies to get out of Grand Central and there was a breadline across the avenue from the office and your wife, back in Connecticut, was greatly pregnant, you just counted yourself lucky and tried not to think about what could happen.

They already had a little boy, Arthur, and privately he hoped the new baby would be another boy, but Gracie was sure it was going to be a girl and wanted to call her Marjorie Wells. Wells had been her maiden name.

Typically, Thomas Pierce got home around six thirty, to the curious stone house (it had a round sort of turret with a design of faux timbers at the top) in the Turn of River neighborhood of Stamford, and he had a drink while his wife finished up with the baby and then made dinner for the two of them. Gracie, considering that she had grown up with servants and nobody'd ever shown her a thing, was fairly capable with a meal. She cooked out of something called *Mrs. Wilson's Cook Book*, which had just the kinds of dishes he had grown up with, but also a few pretty daring concoctions like "Chop Suey," an Oriental delicacy involving pork, cabbage, onions, and a thick brown sauce. Lately she had also discovered *The Settlement Cook Book*, and the arrival of Bundt cakes and "matzo pancakes" gave him a sort of thrilled but guilty feeling. He had never told his wife that his own mother was Jewish.

One night, he found himself leaving work alongside a new colleague, a man named George whom the firm had taken on to write radio scripts. George, it turned out, was living with his sister's family in Darien while he got settled, not the nicest of circumstances, apparently, and by the time their train reached Greenwich, Thomas Pierce had invited his colleague home for dinner. There wasn't an opportunity to let Gracie know about it. The phone at the station wasn't working, and by the time they drove to the drugstore there were already two people waiting for the single booth, so in the end he just drove them home, arriving as the sun set.

Obviously she was peeved, but she got drinks for them both and went off into the kitchen, presumably to work out what to do. It was not a Chop Suey night, more's the pity, but something far less stretchable—she had purchased, that morning, four and only four lamb chops from the butcher—and all Gracie could think to do was peel and boil more potatoes. Once the baby was down, she got herself a little sherry and went back in.

They weren't talking about work, at least. They were talking about George's sister, who'd married a pretty rough type and thought all college boys were pansies. Gracie, quite to herself, had already decided George was a pansy, but that was not the point.

"What a shame, for your sister," she said.

"Yeah. She's a smart girl. I couldn't think why she did it."

They had more to drink, and Gracie put the chops on to broil.

She set the table in the dining room for three. If she had known, if she'd had even a couple of hours, she'd have made a stew and there would be plenty for all three of them. There was a recipe she'd been meaning to try in *The Settlement Cook Book*, a Brunswick stew she could have made with chicken instead of beef. Making things for less was a bit of a specialty of hers. In four years of marriage, and four concurrent years of Depression, she had made it her business to leave over some of the housekeeping money—as much as four or five dollars a week. Whenever they needed something—something for the house or for the baby, even for Thomas—she said it would cost a little more than she actually thought it would and then kept the rest back. It was almost like having a job. The previous spring she'd even opened up an account at First Stamford—a joint account, of course, not that Thomas knew the first thing about it.

"I wish I could," their guest was saying when she returned with the chops. They were both polite—George, who was ravenous, seemed appreciative enough—though neither of them said a word about her own meal, which now consisted of mashed potatoes. Their guest did not pause in his speechifying to chew the food, and Gracie was forced to observe the mastication of her own much-looked-forward-to lamb chops in a little too much detail, but she focused on her mashed potatoes and tried to follow along.

There was an apartment in the city, in a place called Tudor City over on the East Side in the 40s, a good walk from the office. He'd been to see it and taken his "lady friend"—Gracie made herself not ask—and it was a sweet little place, and he didn't need to be told he could have it for a song, things being the way they were in the city now and half the building empty. But that was just it: He didn't have a song, just his salary and a house nobody wanted to buy, up in the northwestern part of Connecticut.

"What town?" Thomas asked. He was only being polite.

The closest was a place called Falls Village. Not too far from Canaan, George said. The house was on a lake and had been his mother's once, but now it was his. He hadn't been up there for a couple of years, but he'd put it on the market with a broker in Lakeville. Great timing, right? Nobody'd even been to see it.

What sort of house? Gracie wanted to know. She had to tell him there weren't more lamb chops but passed him the bowl of potatoes.

It was an old house, about 1880s, George thought. Then his own parents had put on a sort of ell about 1905, with a kitchen downstairs and a bedroom over that, so there were three bedrooms upstairs. It had been on a bunch of acres, about four, but he'd managed to sell off those lots, at least, just before the Crash, so the house had only about half an acre, but it ran down to the little lake. The lake was called Childe. That was his own family name: Childe.

"What are you trying to sell it for?" said Gracie. She had stopped eating.

When he told her, she got up from the table and went upstairs. She kept the checkbook in the top drawer of her bureau. It had a leather cover, which was stiff to open. She had never written a check before.

It was hard to say which of the two men was more stunned.

My wife, the foundress of the feast, Thomas Pierce would sometimes intone, years and years after the night in question, making a grand gesture with his arm. He was a man of property, a squire, and he liked to observe his domain. He liked to sit on the porch with his guests and look down the sloping lawn to the lake's lapping edge, and to watch the two children, Arthur and Marjorie, play on the little dock, pretending to fish. In the summers, he spent all of August there. It was the place he was happiest. After the war (he managed to return from the South Pacific; his colleague George Childe was not so fortunate), he told his wife that the sound of rain on the lake was what he had listened for when he tried to fall asleep, out in the open and far from home.

The stone house in Stamford, with the faux-timbered turret,

went to Arthur, who sold it and moved, of all places, to Houston. Grace Reinhart Sachs, his niece, never met him at all.

The lake house went to Marjorie, who would become Grace's mother, who would spend at least a week of every summer of her life there, except, ironically, for the year in which she gave birth to her daughter, and when she died it went to Grace. Grace loved it, too, like her mother, her grandfather, and her namesake—her thrifty and clever grandmother. But none of the others had ever needed it as much as she did now.

Where else could she have gone that very afternoon, fleeing her home on 81st Street with a duffel bag of her son's clothing, a suitcase of books and laptops, an already fraying garbage bag of her own underwear and sweaters and toiletries, and one very expensive violin? Already the front of the apartment building was lit up like a film premiere, with two news vans and a tangle of electrical wires and a waiting, chattering, bellowing firing squad. The wolf had found her door and was settling in to wait her out, but one of the doormen, in an act of unanticipated grace, had wordlessly taken her down into the basement, shouldered the duffel and hoisted the suitcase, and let her out into the alley that ran behind 35 East 81st Street. On Madison, he helped load up a cab and refused to accept a tip. On the other hand, he no longer seemed able to look her in the eye.

Only three hours after that, she and Henry were driving north on the Saw Mill in a rented car, the atmosphere without (frigid and overcast) perfectly matching the silent chill within. She could only tell him that Grandpa was fine, that Eva was fine, that something had happened, and yes, of course, she would explain about it and not lie (not lie *much*, she appended to herself), but not now, because now she had to concentrate on driving. And this was wholly true: The Saw Mill, twisty at the best of times, was slick to boot, and once or twice (and it wasn't her imagination) she saw the patches of black ice on the ground, and once or twice she even imagined the whirl of herself and her son and the car, spinning and splintering into oblivion. It made her grip the wheel tighter, until her back spiked with pain, and think—and she was thinking this for the first time, and it still felt so terrible and new—*I hate you for this*.

He was the love of her life, the companion, the partner, the spouse. He was every single thing she urged her male clients to be, and every single thing she had told the imaginary readers of her book they deserved, and now she would never not hate him, not one day for however long she lived. It felt as if she'd had to exchange every individual cell in her body that had chosen and adored and tended to Jonathan for a cell that rejected and despised him, running them through a monstrous dialysis machine that stripped and purified her, but the new and purified Grace didn't function the way a human body was supposed to function. It couldn't stand properly or speak or feel or care for Henry or drive at the right speed on a twisty road that might have ice, with her child in the car. It was so focused on where it was going that it had no idea what it was going to do when it got there.

At least she knew the way. She had been covering this same ground for so long that it felt almost mythic, first in her parents' faux-wood-paneled station wagon, crammed with a summer's worth of supplies for herself and her mother. (They collected her father off the Peekskill train every Friday night and drove him back each Sunday afternoon.) She and Vita had snuck up on their own, in high school, for various illicit activities (sometimes with boyfriends), and once, in college, they'd had their own raucously nostalgic weekend, pulling together their Rearden friends, home from college, to drink Rolling Rock and pore over their yearbooks. She came to write her senior thesis the spring after she met Jonathan, leaving him to his infectious diseases rotation and clinic hours at Brigham and Women's Hospital and then pining for him so much that she spent her time reading her mother's stash of yellowing old novels and barely managed a word on Skinner.

And then there was the wedding, right there on the sloping

lawn, only a few months after that. Maybe a little too soon, her mother would have said, but she was old-fashioned that way (in her mother's view, an engagement of Edith Wharton dimensions ought to be mandated for all couples), and besides, her mother was dead and therefore incapable of objection. And her father... well, it wasn't as if Grace were asking for a great production. They wanted to marry, not cohabit—it was important to them both. Or at least it was important to her, and Jonathan wanted whatever she wanted. They did not want a religious ceremony or a display of wealth. They were just two people lucky enough to have found each other, starting out in their professions, intent on the same kind of life: comfort and dignity and children of their own, and helping to eradicate human pain in at least a few of its myriad forms. They wanted enough money to be secure, a few nice things, perhaps, but nothing gaudy or undignified. They wanted contentment and of course a sense of accomplishment, the respect of their peers, the gratitude of their patients, obviously, and in return they wanted to feel that their own talents and hard work and altruism were being well spent in the service of others. It was not such an elaborate platform. It was not... she searched, now, driving the Saw Mill north into the early winter darkness... such hubris.

And as for his family, well, they talked about that at length. She had met with them for that strained and utterly unrewarding Chinese meal, and walk around Rockefeller Center. Jonathan had barely seen them himself since the day he left for Hopkins, and needless to say they had declined to support him financially or in any other way since college. His education had been underwritten by the trustees of the university, his own part-time employment, and also by an elderly woman in Baltimore who had taken an interest in him and had no children of her own. Jonathan had met her while delivering chairs for a party and ended up actually living in her guest room for his final year of college. He had deflected Grace's natural curiosity about his family by reminding her that these were the people who had declined to love him, who did not grasp his determination to become a doctor, who resisted any notion of responsibility to support his needs. But even so, this was a wedding, by any definition a new start, and worth confronting the obvious discomfort. They were duly invited, but they failed to respond, and it was only later, looking at the photographs when they came back from the developer, that she learned that one particular young man—tall and a little fleshy, with Jonathan's same curling dark hair but without his ready grin and general sense of ease—was actually Jonathan's younger brother, Mitchell. He had come, witnessed, and departed, all without ever speaking to her.

What a family, she'd thought.

How on earth could they have produced someone like Jonathan?

She'd worn an old dress found in a vintage clothing store off Harvard Square—Edwardian, the saleswoman thought—and some shoes from Peter Fox in the Village, and a necklace from her mother's mirrored vanity. And she'd had only Vita for a wedding party, because she wasn't about to start ranking her college friends: the three she'd roomed with in Kirkland House, the two she'd spent a summer with on the Vineyard, working as cater-waiters, the women from her Virginia Woolf seminar junior year, who'd become so close that they'd kept up with a monthly tea (and cannabis) party for the next eighteen months. Only Vita, whose prior claim trumped every relationship she'd started since leaving home for college.

Except, of course, for Jonathan.

Jonathan trumped Vita.

It had been an issue that same night, that very first night, at the medical school—more accurately, beneath the medical school—when Vita came in search of Grace, who had gone in search of a bathroom and found, instead, this disheveled, smiling, avid medical student with a laundry basket and a book about the Klondike.

Oh good. Now I can stop dating.

The two of them, Grace and Jonathan, had barely moved from that stretch of corridor, except for him to deposit his laundry and her to use the bathroom, which was handily right around yet another corner; but even so it was incredible how much ground they'd covered. In half an hour, or maybe even less, she knew not just his essential parameters—the settings of his upbringing, the shape of his family, the narrative of schools and scholarship—but the far more intimate geography of his world and the place in it he wanted to make for himself. And it had been so easy to get there: no tiptoeing around, no pretending not to be that interested. He had not been afraid to ask her outright who she was and what she wanted. And then, when she told him, he had not been afraid to let her know that it was what he wanted, too.

When Vita turned up about half an hour later, she was worried—obviously worried—but Grace had turned a beaming, rapturous face to her friend and said: "Vita! This is Jonathan Sachs." And had not said, and had not needed to say, not to her—not to her greatest friend, the one who had seen her through a small but necessary selection of lesser men: *Look who's here. This is the man.*

Behold the man.

Naturally, on being introduced to Jonathan Sachs—disheveled but adorable, smart as a whip, obviously ambitious, compassionate, already settled on pediatrics (the oncology part would come later)—Vita had given him only her best manners. Grace knew and understood these manners, the same ones Vita had once used on her most loathed teachers at Rearden, her barely tolerated father, and the parents of the boy she had been seeing since the previous winter—the one currently upstairs at the party, waiting for her to come back—who thought they were doing her a favor by not quite articulating their obvious anti-Semitism. Polite, polite, polite... *loathing*. It was worrying, but it would get better, Grace had thought. It had to and it would, because she was not going to give up her oldest friend, her closest friend, and she was also not going to give up this beautiful and kind and brilliant and fascinating man. She tried to make herself wait for this inevitable thing to happen, but it got harder and harder to wait, and she began to get a little irritated. And obviously, that first period when you fall in love—not that she was so practiced in such things as to have a *routine*—well, it's not a time that's known for socializing. She and Jonathan, who already had to contend with his class schedule and rotations and her course work, senior year being no walk in the park, had not done much to include Vita in their activities (their activities being generally of a more private nature and taking place in a more private setting), but on the few occasions they did manage to get together the evenings had been notable for the tension. Lots of tension. Though Jonathan tried—Grace could see how hard he was trying—to ask Vita about herself, and what she cared about, and what she wanted to do in her life, and though he looked at her with the focus and attention that was due only the close friend (and roommate) of the woman he had fallen in love with, Vita never let him in.

"Have you considered that she's envious?" Jonathan asked her once, that fall.

"Don't be silly," Grace had said. Vita had approved or disapproved of every single boy she had ever dated, back to seventh grade: Some she had endorsed with wild enthusiasm, and some she had felt were unworthy of Grace in some way (or every way). But the freeze-out, from that first night in the basement of the medical school dormitory to the day after the wedding less than a year later, when Vita took her leave and walked away into an altogether separate sunset—that was total. And, apparently, permanent.

The car was a Honda, or something that sounded like a Honda; Grace hadn't paid attention, she had merely pointed to the yellow laminated chart and thought: *Car*. She did not know much about cars and cared less. They had owned one for a while, a Saab Jonathan had bought, of all things, from the father of one of his patients, but the garage thing was so crazy expensive, and they really used it only in the summers. For the past couple of years, she had done a long lease from an agency on the West Side, but today the West Side was too far away, and for some reason she couldn't bear to go back there. She couldn't stand to go to anyone who knew her, even as a name on a rental agreement every July 1 through August 31.

She felt for the controls and pressed them randomly until the window went down, then gulped at the cold air.

It was fully dark by the time they reached Route 22, the road that began where 684 ended at Brewster. There were faster ways. Over the years, she had tried any number of routes, but in the end there was something calming about this one, and the progression of barely there towns that was so familiar: Wingdale, Oniontown, Dover Plains. After Amenia she crossed over into Connecticut. Henry, who had fallen asleep while trying to read, sat up and adjusted his seat belt.

"Are you hungry?" she asked him.

He said he wasn't, but she knew there'd be nothing when they got there, and she knew she wouldn't want to leave after that, so they stopped in Lakeville, at a pizza place, taking the only booth not occupied by Hotchkiss students. The pizza was shiny with grease, and the salad she ordered for herself came so saturated with dressing that it seemed to liquefy before her eyes. The two of them ate as if there were nothing to discuss. Before they drove away, they went into the general store and bought milk and apples. Walking around, she tried to find one other thing she could imagine eating, but there was nothing. Even the milk and apples were a stretch, thought Grace. She imagined herself telling Henry: *Now we will live on milk and apples.* He asked for a pint of Ben & Jerry's, Heath Bar Crunch, but they had only plain chocolate.

"How long are we staying?" Henry asked.

"How long is a piece of string?" This was how she tended to answer unanswerable questions.

There was a driveway, sloping steeply down from the road, but she knew better than to drive the car down in December. Ferrying the bags to the back porch, she felt the expected cold and wanted to get him inside quickly, but inside was exactly as cold. He turned on the overhead light and stood in the middle of the room, bewildered.

"I know," Grace said. "Let's get a fire going."

But there wasn't any wood; they had used up what they had at the beginning of September, when she'd closed the house down. And the blankets on the beds upstairs were for cool summer nights or rainstorms, not for the bone-hollowing cold that seemed to be entering through every conceivable crack in the structure. It wasn't winterized. That was something she'd been trying not to think about.

"Tomorrow," she told him, "we'll get a couple of heaters. And some firewood." She stopped. She had been about to say that this was like an adventure, like a brave experiment, but just in the past few hours Henry had stopped being a boy who might have believed that. He was now a boy who climbed without comment into the backseat of a rental car, which was full of their belongings, inelegantly packed, and lit out for some unexpected territory. He was a fugitive from other people's crimes. They both were, actually. "Henry?"

"Yeah?" He had not moved. He stood with his hands crushed into the pockets of his down jacket, blowing experimental steam in little puffs.

"I'm going to take care of this," she told him. She was surprised to hear herself sound so confident. She had not thought much beyond the getting away *from*, and not at all about the next morning or the following week. There were seven more days of Rearden classes before the holiday break. There were patients. There was a rental car she couldn't keep forever. There was a book supposedly about to be published. There was the very real possibility that her own name—God, her own *face*—was even at this moment on a local news broadcast or website, available to any colleague, any patient, any Rearden parent, anyone who had known her husband better than she had herself. But even those terrible things seemed, at this precise moment, far too abstract to waste her small reserves of sanity and will upon. Her world was now very tiny and very sparsely populated. It extended only a breath in any direction. "We're going to be all right," she told him, and then, in the frail hope that he, at least, believed it, she said the exact same thing again.

CHAPTER SEVENTEEN

Suspension of Disbelief

Afterward, what would astonish her was how easy it had been to disassemble her life. A life—she had to remind herself—of such continuity and such stability that not even her address, despite a few digressions, had changed since birth. The pediatric practice in which first she and then her son had been patients, the comforting promenade down Madison, in which only the names of the stores and the styles of the immensely expensive goods ever changed, the coffee shops, the bus stops, the nannies from every corner of the earth pushing their charges to the playground at 85th Street... all of it would float away over the next few days, lost in the critical pursuit of warmth and sustenance and in her own dogged suspension of disbelief.

The next day, she drove the car across the border to Pittsfield, where—with astonishingly little preamble—she purchased one of the rental agency's used vehicles, a perfectly unremarkable Honda. Then she and Henry went to an outlet mall near Great Barrington and purchased duvets, warm boots, and the kind of long underwear she assumed people who skied wore. At a Home Depot, she found a space heater the salesman swore up and down was safe and a caulk gun she wasn't sure she'd be able to figure out how to use and which she *was* sure wouldn't do much good in any case. Then they hit the supermarket. On the way back, she followed a sign up a long driveway to an A-frame on a wooded lot and arranged for a bemused man in a filthy parka to deliver a cord of cut firewood. She was used to buying wood in little bundles, wrapped in plastic, from Food Emporium and wasn't sure how much a cord actually was, but he promised to get it to her in the morning, so that was something. Henry, who wasn't acquisitive as a rule, made only one request all day (apart from the Heath Bar Crunch at the Price Chopper), and that—bizarrely—was an anthology of sportswriting he found in the supermarket. She bought it without a second thought.

Back at the house, they flung the duvets on the master bed and crawled beneath, Henry with the sports book he had already begun on the ride back, Grace with the legal pad on which she was attempting to reconstitute her client list, prioritizing those she was due to meet in the upcoming days. Everyone would have to be e-mailed, at the very least. Most, then, would have to be called. She wasn't going to think about that part now. The room, which was not the room in which she had slept during her childhood summers but the room she still thought of as her parents', took on an alien dullness in the watery winter light. The old knotty pine of the walls seemed drained, as if it lacked something available only in the warm weather and was merely on hold until it could be replenished. The old paintings—some from her grandparents' time, some from her own trips to the Elephant's Trunk on Route 7—had a sort of caul thrown over them, their colors dulled accordingly. It struck her now, looking around first idly and then with the recognition of yet another form of loss, that there was not one object that signified a real tie to a real idea of her own life. Not one. Instead, the catechism to which she had subjected every belonging in the New York apartment came flooding back to her, and she found herself interrogating the things she saw, demanding they account for themselves and justify their inclusion in what she now laughingly considered reality. The old photographs, her family's four generations of nominal possessions attested to, seemed meaningless; the ones of herself and Jonathan in particular were an assault. Childhood artworks (her own and Henry's), curious objects picked up in the woods or along the lakeshore, books she had brought from the city to read and, having read, left behind on the shelves, ripped-out articles from the *New Yorker*, past issues of the three or four scholarly journals she followed—what did any of it have to do with her now, here, huddled beneath a brand-new duvet in her parents' bed with her twelve-year-old son, for how long? Until the end of the night? Or the news cycle? Or the year?

Until the nuclear winter ended and somebody (who?) gave the all clear?

The weight of it all was imponderable, so she declined to ponder it, powering through the to-do list of massive life alterations as if they were another busy mom's hit list for a Monday morning and laboring over the message to her patients: "Because of significant and unforeseen events, it is necessary that I take a leave of absence from my practice. I cannot adequately convey to you my sincerest regret at having to suspend our work together, and I wish I could tell you how long I will need to be away. I am of course available to help you find interim care with another therapist, so if you need a reference or would like to discuss your options, please feel free to contact me by e-mail..."

Which was not, precisely, an empty offer, though she did not, precisely, have e-mail, at least at the moment. The summer before, she had paid a local company to set up a Wi-Fi system, and they had, and it had worked, albeit slowly, but neither she nor—more meaningfully—Henry had been able to make it work now. So she began—tentatively, by necessity, and with utter terror—to make her way to the David M. Hunt Library in the village, a Queen Anne pile so baldly impressive that it felt thoroughly suited to the heavy purpose at hand, and there, in half-hour increments on the sign-up sheet, she let down the guillotine between herself and all the men and women who had paid her for her good counsel. They would not want it now, she told herself, clicking Send again and again, severing whatever trust in her they might so unwisely have placed, negating any benefit she might once have brought them. (And every time she did it, every time she composed and delivered one of these identical messages—because she made herself do it fresh each time, because she declined to obliterate her entire career in a mass e-mail—it was like another blow upon the same bruise: the maximum suffering allotted.) And then she sat back, looking at the inert computer screen on its little ledge in the hushed, carpeted library, and noted how it had all been accomplished so quietly. Or not, precisely, quietly. It felt like a whisper made into the absolute stillness of a cave, which somehow comes back deafening and then disappears altogether. In reality, very little came back, and there was silence, at least from most of them. One woman, who had a habit of coming in only when she was acutely in crisis, e-mailed to ask for a reference. Lisa, the abandoned wife whose husband was now living with a Rothko and a man in Chelsea, sent a kind and beautifully written message to say that she hoped "everything" would work out for Grace. (Grace could not bear to think how much of "everything" Lisa knew by now.) And Steven, the perpetually enraged screenwriter, took a moment out of his busy life to write and call her "a sorry-ass cunt."

It nearly made her smile. It nearly did.

Oddly, the only person to actually protest her departure was not one of her patients, and not her son's headmaster (Robert had responded to her notice of withdrawal with a brief note saying that Henry would be welcome back at any time—Grace could only hope that was accurate), and not even her father (who was relieved to hear from her, but so full of appalled questions that she pretended to have lost the cell phone signal and hung up the phone). It was Vitaly Rosenbaum, who wanted her to know how greatly he was going to be inconvenienced by the sudden nonattendance of his student and how damaging any lacuna in Henry's musical education would certainly be. Grace read his e-mails with a kind of cherished nostalgia for the myopia of others. As a rule, the violin teacher was a stranger in the strange cosmology of e-mail. He had given in only when one of his students brought him an old desktop and set up a system for him, carefully explaining (and printing out) precise instructions for composing, sending, and receiving, and he used it only when deprived of more comfortable forms of communication. Still, he managed to convey (in no fewer than three terse and imprecisely worded messages) the fullness of his displeasure at Henry's absence and even made so bold as to suggest that Grace was being delinquent in her duties as a mother because of whatever selfish thing was keeping her son away.

Vitaly Rosenbaum, at least, was apparently not a consumer of news. Not a reader of the *New York Post*, or the *Times*, or *New York* magazine. Not a watcher of the six o'clock news. Not a follower of NY1.com. He was fastened so tightly into his own unhappy enclosure that he simply had no idea what Henry Sachs's absence might signify.

How she wished the world in general were like him.

Each time, as she finished her allotted minutes on the computer terminal and prepared, once again, to let go of some balloon—some person, some arrangement, some filament of normal—still bobbing tenuously overhead, she had to fight the roar of so much waiting information, so nearby, only a movement of the fingertips between herself and the gale force of it. A clicking sound—so soft, at that—holding apart the whispering of the country library in Connecticut and the deluge of what was happening a few hours south. Grace sat there in her swivel seat, hands poised over the keys, fighting herself to know and not know, inheriting the wind of her own hysteria. Each time it was an original contest: fought from the foundations and to the bitter end. Each time it was a victory for willed ignorance.

Then she would carefully log out and rise from the terminal and go find Henry, who had finished the sportswriting anthology and was now reading a biography of Lou Gehrig, and take him home to the cold, cold house on the frozen lake for another day of not knowing, and there she would light the fire (a task at which she had become necessarily adept) and tuck blankets around her son on the couch and turn on the light for him as he read and start to cook something hot for the two of them. And then, with the chilly air of the afternoon gradually replaced by the still more brutal air of the night, she would sometimes attempt, in the most careful and least inquisitive way possible, to assess her circumstances.

By default, she knew that Jonathan must still be—wherever he was—beyond the collective reach of Mendoza and O'Rourke and the NYPD and, for all she knew, the FBI or INTERPOL. He must be. If he were not, Mendoza would have called her cell. Mendoza actually *was* calling every few days, not just to find out whether she had heard from Jonathan but to ask how she and Henry were doing. (She took those calls because he had let her leave the city, or at least not made it difficult for her to leave. She owed him for that.) She never answered unless it was him or her father, but the cell had become an open tap, impossible to shut off. Her office line, listed on every Web directory of New York therapists (subspecialty: couples), forwarded to the cell, and it rang constantly until she silenced it, then it merely flashed and vibrated constantly. She wouldn't listen to the messages, not if she could see who was calling; if she couldn't see who they were beforehand, they might get in a greeting before she hit Delete. And then one afternoon the ancient wall phone in the kitchen started to ring, its antiquated blurt like something out of a midcentury television episode. It rang over and over again, beginning at about two in the afternoon a few days before Christmas and on into the evening. There was nothing like a caller ID, of course. Grace was pretty sure the cracked Bakelite phone could never be configured to reveal, in advance, a caller's identity, but it probably hadn't rung since the previous summer. She put her hand on it, still undecided.

When she lifted it, saying nothing, there was a pause, and then a tense female voice said: "Is that Grace?"

Grace set down the receiver, almost gently, as if she were trying not to alarm the woman on the other end. Then she reached down along the phone's vaguely dangerous-looking cord to its woefully outdated wall jack in the floorboard and maneuvered the plug free.

So at least one of them must know where she was, but nobody had actually turned up. That was good. That was the point of having left, wasn't it? To run farther away than they would be inclined to follow? And obviously they did not care enough to follow her to rural Connecticut. Only one state away, but she wasn't—which meant the *story* wasn't—important enough to come after her. It made her almost hopeful, the idea of that.

But then Grace remembered that somebody was actually dead and two children orphaned. She wasn't hopeful after that.

So easy to disassemble her entire life. Surely that, too, was a privilege she had not deserved, not when you thought about the "blood-strewn" apartment and what Miguel Alves had had to find in it. Grace knew (because she had spent a humiliating hour on the phone with a total stranger at Morgan Stanley) that most of the money she'd thought she possessed a few weeks earlier she still did possess, though a withdrawal of $20,000 from the cash reserves had been made on the afternoon of Monday, December 16, the day Malaga Alves had been killed.

That and a handful of jewels could get you most places, Grace thought bitterly.

Her own escape, and Henry's, to a house (albeit a freezing house) where they could stay as long as they liked—because it belonged to her—eating food and burning wood she could afford to purchase, was only the most recent in a long list of unearned advantages, from preferential admissions for legacy applicants to a (big) leg up on the

Manhattan real estate ladder. She did not feel, precisely...*guilty* about that. Not *guilty*. Actually, there had always been a sort of inverse pride in the fact that she didn't care much about money or crave extravagant things. But then again, she could afford not to care much about money. She knew that, too.

And now, stiff with cold on her parents' bed, in a house that four generations of her family had called home (at least for the warm summer months), with her son beside her (utterly absorbed in the life of Lou Gehrig), a refrigerator of food carelessly bought with a credit card, a new (if far from luxurious) car outside, thoughtlessly bought with the same credit card, she thought fiercely: *I have nothing to apologize for.*

That didn't last long, that defiance.

Sometimes, at night, after Henry had fallen asleep, she put on her parka and went outside with a packet of cigarettes she had found in one of the kitchen drawers. She had no idea whose they were or how they had come to be there, but she took them down the slope to the lakefront and lay down on the icy dock and lit one, and the pure bad pleasure of it came tearing back, wafting deep into the moist caverns of the lungs and shooting away through the bloodstream. She watched the white cloud rise up into the night, visible proof that, at least for this moment, she was still here, still sentient and more or less functional. This itself, it occurred to her, was the drug, just that bald proof of existence. It was intoxicating. It was a necessary, brutal, reassurance.

She had not smoked for eighteen years, since the night she met a future oncologist in the basement of the Harvard Medical School, and she could not recall the act of smoking as ever feeling so freighted with meaning. Now, inhaling and then watching the white smoke rise, she felt as if some great Pause button had been depressed when Jonathan stepped into her life, and only this instant had the finger come away and released her forward motion, and suddenly she was back at precisely that earlier moment, a college student again, with most of the big decisions and the big events still before her. Though this time she had been issued with a child and a nominal profession.

And a book about to be published. Or so it had been when she'd left the city. She saw all of their names, constantly, on her phone: Sarabeth and Maude and J. Colton the publicist. She had not returned even one of their calls. She had not even listened to the messages. Almost idly, she wondered what they must have considered was worth trying to say. The article in *Vogue* would never run. The *Today Show* must no longer wish to interview her, except perhaps in connection with the death of Malaga Alves. And the book itself... *Who* (and she made herself, deliberately, complete this thought) *would knowingly be counseled by an expert on marriage whose husband had become involved with another woman? Or had a child with that woman? Or, in fact, murdered that woman? Or had stolen, lied, abandoned his wife in a scorched earth of incalculable...*

Well, not pain, exactly. Whatever Grace was feeling right now, right at this moment, flat on her back, numb with cold, blowing smoke up into the brutal night, was not pain. But that did not mean the pain wasn't somewhere nearby. It was very close, very close. It was just on the other side of the wall, and nobody knew how long the wall was going to hold.

She took another lungful and breathed it out, watching it rise. She had once loved smoking, not that she had ever been in doubt of its lethal reach, not that she had wanted to die, ever. She wasn't ignorant and she wasn't a masochist. On the night of the medical school party, she had simply gone back to the apartment she and Vita shared near Central Square and finished off her final pack on the fire escape, thinking about Jonathan and what he meant to do with his life. She had never even told him she smoked. It had been, simply, not relevant to the only thing that really mattered to her after that night, because everything important had only begun that night. Did that make her a liar, too?

How many roads had there been, diverged in that endless dormitory basement, and why had it been such a simple matter to choose the one she had chosen, and did it make a difference whether that road was less traveled or more? Probably not, she thought now. Probably none of those points mattered now. What mattered was that she had made a mistake and somehow trundled along blindly for far too long, and now she was here on a winter night at the end of her own dock, terrorized, paralyzed, and behaving like a teenager, with her own newly fatherless almost-teenager huddled for warmth in an unheated house, ripped away from his own life and in great need of some serious guidance, not to mention a good deal of clarification.

I'll get right on that, Grace thought, exhaling.

The smoke went up to the hard sky, ink-dark, brilliant with stars. They and the moon made the only light except for a single lamp left on in her own living room, and the porch light, an old lantern with three bulbs, one functional. None of the other houses were occupied except for one, a stone cottage down at the lake's pointy end, which had a thin stream of smoke coming from the chimney. It was very quiet here. Very, very quiet. Except sometimes she could hear these sorts of wisps of music that seemed to come with the wind, from somewhere. It was unusual music. She thought there might be some kind of violin making it, but not the kind of violin Vitaly Rosenbaum would recognize, or at least credit. The sounds made her think of mountains in the South, people sitting on porches together, looking out into the trees. Some nights she had heard only the one instrument, and sometimes there were more: a second violin and maybe a guitar. Once she thought she heard human voices, human laughter, and when that happened she made herself concentrate on the sound of it, as if she could barely remember what the sound of that was like.

But mostly there was nothing to listen to except the crackling of her own fire or the sound of one of them turning a page.

And then it was nearly Christmas, a day that she had given no thought to at all, and she woke up on the morning of Christmas Eve in the classic state of an unprepared husband. For the first time, she left Henry alone in the house and drove north to Great Barrington to find something she could give him; but when she finally got to the shopping mall she saw that some of the stores were already closing, and she raced around, staring hopelessly at all the useless, illogical, irrelevant, and undesirable objects. Finally, in the bookstore, she found herself wandering the usual aisles, looking for something to interest him, but within the narrow confines of those subjects she herself sanctioned there wasn't anything—it was plain, now—that he truly cared about. There was nothing here for Henry, nothing he would do more than thank her for, as he had been raised to thank anyone who meant to do something polite. That wasn't going to be enough for him, she told herself. Not this year.

So she went to the sports section and forced herself to lift book after book. A history of the Yankees. All right. A book on the Negro League—at least it was history. And something about the NFL she chose because when she opened the book to a random page she read a fairly decent sentence. And another book, about basketball, she picked without opening at all, because she already felt awful about being such a snob. And then a DVD set of Ken Burns and Lynn Novick's *Baseball* series, which perhaps they could even watch together. She had everything wrapped right there at the counter.

The way back to the door took her past the books about marriage and family, and Grace felt herself slow her pace, and she made herself look. It was in an aisle like this one, a few years earlier, on the Upper West Side, that she had stopped to look at what was available to her patients and everyone else. Books about getting the man you wanted to want you back. Getting him to ask you out, commit to you, marry you. Accepting those impediments you yourself had created for the life you deserved. So much delusion. So much concession. Where was the cold clarity you might bring to, say, the search for a bra that really fit or the right breed of dog for your lifestyle? Wasn't finding a life partner at least as important as that? Didn't it deserve at least as much discernment and toughness? Why shouldn't a young woman read a sign for its actual meaning, not just its interpretive rainbow?

Over and over again, the readers of these books about getting and keeping had come into her practice and confessed their own failings, often amid the ruin of their lives. They thought they had failed to properly get or properly keep. A husband's flirtations with other women must be because of her weight gain. A man's coldness to his baby (and his in-laws and every one of his wife's friends and also, incidentally, his wife herself) was because she got off the fast track at work and was probably not going to make partner if they had a second child. The women were responsible for everything. They were guilty of crimes, real and illusory. They had not thought hard enough, tried hard enough, asked enough of themselves. It was as if the plane had fallen from the sky for the sole reason that they had stopped flapping their arms.

And the worst of it, she had thought, standing in the Relationships aisle of the Broadway Barnes & Noble, was that they actually *were* guilty, just not of any of those things, and they actually *had* failed, but not at what they thought. They hadn't *gotten* wrong and they hadn't *kept* wrong. They had chosen wrong. That was all of it. And where was the book that said that?

She had started tentatively enough, one afternoon when a client had failed to arrive and she found herself with an unanticipated hour alone. The couple who had just left were both enraged, and the whole room still thrummed with the stress of that and the uselessness of that. In the hour she suddenly possessed, she sat at her desk and wrote a kind of manifesto about the state of her profession, lamenting the fact that therapists seemed unwilling to state what was obvious to them, or ought to be obvious to them. How many times had they listened to a husband's or a wife's litany of latter-day complaints and thought: *But you already knew that.* You knew that when you met him or dated him. At least by the time you got engaged. You knew he was in debt: You're the one who paid off his Visa bill! You knew that when he went out at night he came back plastered. You knew he thought you weren't up to his level intellectually, because he went to Yale and you went to U Mass. And if you didn't know, you should have known, because it could not have been clearer, even back then at the very start.

For her patients, for any of their patients, it was almost certainly too late; the relationships on display in their consulting rooms could now only be accepted or unraveled. But for her readers—already, by the end of that first hour, she thought of them as her readers—there was time for a caution: You can know these things from the very beginning, if you're paying attention, if your eyes and your ears and your mind are open, as they should be open. You can know and then, critically, hold on to that knowledge, even if he loves you (or seems to), even if he chooses you (or seems to), even if he promises to make you happy (which no one, not one person on the planet, can possibly do).

And part of her, a big part of her, had obviously wanted to be the one who told them this.

Because I am such a competent and knowing person, she berated herself.

Like every one of her fellow authors, each so willing and ready to climb above the crowd of mere mortals and declaim their ideas to a grateful populace. *Hurrah for us! Hurrah for me*, thought Grace.

Well, that was over.

Driving home with a bag of marginally festive groceries and another of gifts for Henry, she gripped the wheel so hard that her back began to throb. The temperature had dropped yet again, and she made herself be vigilant against the lethal black ice. There was a patch of it just after the turn onto Childe Ridge, the road that connected most of the houses on the lakefront, and after navigating around it at a snail's pace, she looked up to see a man at a mailbox.

This was the stone cottage, most likely the only other lake house currently occupied, and even her wish to be entirely alone could not stand up to a practical imperative: To be on neighborly terms with the only other human in the vicinity, in the dead of winter, and deep in the countryside, was probably not a bad idea.

He held up his arm, and she carefully slowed and stopped.

"Hello!" he called. "I thought that was you."

Grace rolled down the passenger window. "Hi," she said. Her voice sounded unnaturally bright. "I'm Grace."

"Oh, I know," he said. He was wearing a down jacket, quite worn, spouting feathers in a few places. He looked about her own age, maybe a bit older, with very short gray hair. He was holding his mail: newspapers, flyers, actual letters. "Leo? Holland? We used to drive your mom crazy."

Grace laughed, surprising herself completely. "Oh, my God, you absolutely did. I'm so sorry."

And just like that, she was apologizing for her mother, decades after the fact. Marjorie Reinhart had never forgotten the summers when her own parents' little house was the only house on the lake. The boys from down at the other end, with their motorboat and water skis, had so unnerved and irritated her that she regularly dropped off notes pleading for quiet. In this very mailbox, Grace thought.

"Please," he said genially. "Water under the bridge. Water down the lake!"

"Okay." She nodded. "Are you living here full-time?"

"No, not really." He shifted the mail to his other arm and put his exposed hand into his coat pocket. "I'm on sabbatical. I was home, trying to finish a book, and they just kept calling me. Department meeting, thesis review. Even disciplinary stuff. So I thought I'd run away for the rest of my leave. You're not winterized, are you? Sorry, is that a personal question?"

He was smiling. He had a crooked smile.

"Not winterized. Are you?"

"More or less. It's never exactly warm, but I can take my down jacket off. But how are you getting along, then?"

"Oh"—she shrugged—"you know. Space heaters. Lots of blankets. We're all right."

Leo Holland frowned. "We?"

"My son. He's twelve. I should go, actually, I've left him alone there for the first time."

"Well, if he's there now, he's not alone," said Leo. "There's a car parked on the road. I just walked past."

Grace tried to breathe. She was calculating how many hours she had been away—not more than two. Or three. She was terrified.

One state away wasn't so far after all. Or maybe she wasn't—the story wasn't—so unimportant as she'd tried to believe.

"Do you need help?" Leo Holland asked. He suddenly looked very sober.

"No, I...just have to go."

"Of course. But come for dinner. Both of you. Maybe after New Year's?"

She might have nodded. She wasn't sure. She was driving down the road, through the thick woods, the iced-over lake just glittering through the trees on her right, passing the second house and the third, the fourth and fifth very close together. All she could think of was that Henry might be—*was*—alone with someone, anyone. A reporter. An infamy junkie—one of the legion of interested and highly informed bystanders, minted by *People* magazine and Court TV, who felt entitled to intrude on somebody else's nightmare. She thought, and tried not to think, and failed, and thought again, of somebody in the cold little house with her son, sitting on the sofa, asking questions about something that had nothing to do with them, upsetting Henry or perhaps—and then she realized how much of her outrage came from this bit of it—telling him things about his father that he was not (that she herself was not) ready to hear.

But most of all—and this was an idea that came so quickly, it had obviously been there all along—she was terrified that it was Jonathan. Surely it could not be Jonathan. He wouldn't come back. He wouldn't do that to them, or at least, she thought fiercely, be careless enough to do that to them.

The road bent to the right, and then, looking frantically ahead into the darkness, she was able to see the house and the car parked before it. Her surprise was nearly as strong as her relief. There, in the patch left vacant by her own departure only two (or at most three) hours earlier, sat a late-model German sedan of a make no sentient Jew should ever drive, but Eva—who controlled the car option—was not one to burden herself with excessive sentimentality. Grace's father, unexpectedly and against all logic, appeared to have arrived for Christmas.

CHAPTER EIGHTEEN

CHRISTMAS IN THE SHTETL

Inside, the two of them were sitting together on the lumpy green sofa near the fire, feet up on an old trunk, big mugs of tea steaming up into their faces. It was actually, she noted, not freezing in the house, and she wondered if there might be some basic thing that she had not understood about the boiler or the heat distribution system. But it was just the fire, after all. He had it going really well. He had always—strangely for a city man—been very good at making fires.

"Well, hello!" said her father heartily enough.

Henry, she saw, was holding an unfamiliar item: a portable DVD player, on which the two of them had been watching something she didn't immediately identify. For the briefest moment, she felt an intense wave of irritation.

"Dad," Grace heard herself say, "when did you get here?"

He looked at Henry. Henry, one eye already back on the little screen, gave a shrug. "Maybe an hour ago? I got the fire going."

"I see. And is this an early Christmas present?"

He looked over at the object in his grandson's hands. Then he frowned. "Well, no, no. It's mine, actually. I just thought Henry might like to use it while he's here." He turned back to her. "Is it all right?"

"Oh." Grace nodded. "Yes, of course. Thank you," she added

grudgingly. "Henry," she asked him, not very nicely (as if he had been the ungracious one), "did you say thank you?"

"He certainly did," her father said. "This child has excellent manners."

"It's *2001*," Henry added. "They just found the domino thing on the moon."

She frowned at him, momentarily distracted from her own irritability. "Domino?"

"Monolith," Frederich Reinhart corrected. He turned back to Grace. "I just grabbed what I had. One of the kids gave me this collection. Greatest science-fiction movies of all time."

One of the kids. One of Eva's kids, in other words.

You only have one kid, she nearly said.

"Like, ten of them," Henry chirped. He seemed delighted.

If there was anything—*one single thing*—she disliked more than sports-obsessed boys, it was science fiction–obsessed boys. Now her cultured, sensitive, violin-playing son was reading books about baseball and watching videos about spaceships. And he hadn't been near his violin since they'd arrived. And—what was even less comprehensible—she hadn't said word one to him about that.

"Well," Grace heard herself say, "that's very kind."

"Missed this one," her father said. He had hooked his arm around Henry's neck and pulled him closer. He was wearing one of his ribbed turtlenecks, soft and gray. Her mother had once bought them for him. Now Eva bought them. "Both of you," he added. "I wanted to come and make sure you were both all right."

Grace turned and went into the kitchen. Once she had recognized the car, once the awful, liquid fear had left her, she had taken her time gathering up everything from the trunk, because it was too cold outside to make an unnecessary trip. Now she started unloading, slapping each individual can onto the wooden countertop like an isolated element of percussion.

Missed you . . .

Sure!

Both of you . . .

Right!

The Berkshire Co-Op had been closed by the time she got to it, so it had all come from Price Chopper, and it did not a Martha Stewart feast suggest. There were two cans of cranberry jelly, the kind you squiggled out whole and cut with a knife. There was a can of fried onions, another of cream of mushroom soup. Obviously, she was going retro this Christmas. The entire holiday had been nearly an afterthought. She hoped her father wasn't expecting to be entertained.

"Grace?" she heard him. He had stopped in the doorway.

The turkey was at the bottom of the grocery bag, under the frozen string beans, and she was reaching in for it. It was only part of the turkey, actually. Just the breasts. And already roasted.

"What?" she said unkindly.

"I should have asked you first. I am sorry."

"Yes," Grace confirmed. "Someone up the road told me there was a car here. I was frightened. You should have called."

"Oh. Well, that part . . . I did call. I tried to call. There," he said, pointing to the kitchen phone. "I might have missed you."

She sighed. She hadn't the wherewithal to tell him about unplugging the phone. "No. I'm sorry. We've been living like recluses. Luddite recluses. But on purpose."

"So you don't know what's going on," he said, and not as a question. And there was just the tiniest edge of disapproval when he said it. Possibly he was thinking: *And hasn't that been a great part of the problem?* Or possibly she imagined that.

"In detail? No, I don't know. I've got the gist, though. I think it's better we're here."

He nodded. He looked haggard, she thought. The skin beneath his eyes was papery, and she could see, even across the room, the tracery of red blood vessels. Ten years older, just in a few weeks. *Thanks for that, too, Jonathan*, she thought.

"I'd like to help," said Frederich Reinhart. "I came to see if there was some way I could."

Grace shuddered. It was an unfamiliar place in which they found themselves. Two solitary travelers on a narrow mountain pass. The question was not which one of them would give way, but which one of them would accept the deference of the other. An absurd problem to have, Grace thought.

To cover her discomfort, she took the turkey to the refrigerator, but when she opened it she found that the shelves inside were crammed with orange-and-white bags. Before she could think, she was elated.

"I went to Zabar's," her father said unnecessarily. "I thought I'd bring a bit of home."

Grace nodded, still holding the fridge door open. She wasn't at all surprised to note that she was in real danger of crying. "Thank you," she told him.

"Henry likes the chopped liver," he said. "I brought extra to freeze. The strudel should freeze well, too."

"When did you become a domestic god?" Grace laughed, but he seemed to take the question seriously.

"Eva is very capable as a cook, and she does not see the point of places like Zabar's. I realized a good long while ago that if I wanted cucumber salad and lox to remain a part of my life, I was going to have to get them in myself. I remembered those cookies you used to like." He pointed. They had moist stripes of green and orange and white cake and were encased in chocolate. They had been her favorite treat, no contest. Now just looking at them made her a tiny bit happier. "I got a bit of everything, I think," her father added. "I even got matzo ball soup."

"We'll have a very Jewish Christmas Eve," Grace said, smiling.

"I suppose," he agreed, making room on one of the shelves for her supermarket turkey.

"Christmas in the shtetl."

"O little star of Bukowsko." Her father laughed. Bukowsko had been his grandfather's shtetl in Galicia.

"Ouch."

"My grandmother wouldn't mind. Her sister, she was the one who gave me pork to eat for the first time. An absolutely delicious sausage, I remember."

"And here we are," Grace said helpfully. "In hell."

"No. It only feels that way right now." He stepped back from the fridge and held open the door for her. "You'll come out of this, Grace. You're tough."

"Right."

"And Henry's tough. It's a huge blow, I'm not belittling it. But he's been a very loved child, one way or another, and he's smart. If we can all be honest with him, he'll be okay."

She was about to say something highly defensive (and probably unkind) when it occurred to her that she hadn't at all been honest with Henry. In the guise of "protection," she had told him very little of what had happened—what was happening—to his family. But every time she imagined that conversation, just now included, she fell completely apart. And "together" was the principle of her life right now. "Together" was the mantra.

"We will be honest," she told her father. "Just not right at this moment. There's too much I don't understand myself. I have to get us settled here. I have to make some parameters for us."

"Parameters are important," he agreed tentatively. "Stability, security for him, absolutely. I take it you're staying?"

She shrugged.

"What about your practice?"

"I've suspended it," she said. It felt unreal, saying it aloud. "I had to."

"And Henry's school?"

"There are schools in Connecticut."

"There's no Rearden in Connecticut."

"Absolutely right," she snapped. "Will Hotchkiss do?"

He closed the refrigerator and turned around. "You really are thinking ahead."

"Yes. I really am." Though she hadn't been, not till this moment. That Hotchkiss thing, it had come out of nowhere.

"Your friends?"

Grace went to the drawer, the same drawer where she kept her now half pack of cigarettes, and got a corkscrew. Then she went for one of the bottles of red wine on the top shelf.

What was she supposed to say? That not one friend or acquaintance from what she now laughingly thought of as her "past" had troubled themselves to come after her? She knew this was true. When she scrolled through the call list on her muted cell, she saw that they just weren't there. Amid the media gnats and the detectives and the relentless calls from Sarabeth and Maud, which she was also trying to ignore, they just weren't there.

The idea of it—the power of that—was just breathtaking.

"I seem to have misplaced them all," is what she finally told him.

He nodded sadly, and Grace, watching him, thought that her father must assume they had all deserted her in the scandal. But they hadn't been there in the first place, that was her point. That was what she knew now.

"Well, Vita called," he said a bit nonchalantly, as if what he was saying were not utterly stunning. "I told her you were up here. She's living in the Berkshires somewhere, I think she might have said where, but I'm not certain. Hasn't she been in touch?"

Grace, short of breath, turned her head to the old wall phone. How many times had it rung before she'd unplugged it? And when she'd picked up the receiver that one time. That woman's voice, the reporter's voice . . . had it actually been a reporter? Her hand shook a little as she dug the end of the corkscrew into the rubbery cork.

"Let me," said her father, and she handed it over. "You never heard from her?"

She shrugged. She still couldn't believe it.

"I said how good it was to hear her voice. I think she is very worried about you."

Well, she can join the club, Grace thought, eyeing the wine her father was pouring. But again, she remembered that there was no club. There weren't enough people worrying about her to form one. Besides, it was horrible of Vita to have gone away and left her, but even more horrible to come back now.

"Fine, fine," she said, taking the glass. It was a little bitter, but instantly effective.

"She's doing something for...well, she called it a rehabilitation center. I didn't ask for details. Isn't she a therapist, too?"

I wouldn't know, Grace thought, but she said: "She was training to be one. That was a long time ago. I really have no idea."

"Well, maybe you'll manage to reconnect. It happens that way sometimes. When your mother died, I heard from people I hadn't thought of in years. Lawrence Davidoff. Remember him?"

Grace nodded. She took another swallow of her wine and was rewarded with a sensation of fuzziness and warmth in the pit of her stomach.

"And Donald Newman. We were in Korea together. We'd lived five blocks apart for years, never ran into each other. He introduced me to Eva, you know."

She looked at him. "Really?"

"His wife was a real estate agent. Eva and Lester bought the apartment on Seventy-Third from her. So after Mom died he decided to fix us up."

Grace wanted to ask: *How long after?* It was a point of detail she had never been very clear on.

"I don't need any old friends fixing me up, thanks."

"I doubt that was on her mind. As I said, she seemed very concerned. And if you ever...became aware...of something like this, in her life, I'm sure you'd want to be in touch with her as well."

Grace, who wasn't sure at all, said nothing. She went to the cupboard and started taking down plates. She got the silverware and the napkins. Then she went back to the fridge and tried to figure out what was for dinner.

Her father really had brought a bit of everything. There were spreads and cheeses and plastic containers from up and down Zabar's long prepared-food display, a skinny baguette and a bag full of bagels and a loaf of sliced rye. Also, on the countertop next to the fridge, a stack of those gourmet chocolate bars they had piled up in the checkout lanes. "Wow," she said, unwrapping the two-inch-thick wedge of salmon, cut in thin, shimmery slices, folded between translucent sheets. "This is wonderful. I really appreciate this."

"Not at all," he said. He had put his hand on her shoulder and was standing behind her, looking into the fridge. "Is it enough?"

"To feed the entire population of the lake? Yes, I think so. Actually, it's just us at the moment. And someone in the stone house."

"Down at the end?"

"Yes."

He smiled. "The boys who water-skied? That house?"

"Yeah. One of them grew up to be a college professor. He said he was on sabbatical, writing a book."

"Are they winterized?" Her father frowned.

"No, I don't think so. He asked me the same thing. But it won't last forever. If I can get us through January, that'll be the worst of it, I'm sure. And if it gets too bad, I'll check us into a motel."

He did not seem mollified. He stood watching her put out the cheese on a board. She poured the soup into a stainless-steel pot and started to heat it up. "I'd really rather you weren't living like this," he said seriously, as if this were a radical notion.

No shit. She nearly laughed, but actually it was when she thought of her own home, her own life in the city, that she began to be frantic. This... there was stillness, and naturally isolation, and of course it was cold as hell, but it wasn't the screaming hell that came over her when she thought of back there. She couldn't go back there.

"And what are you going to do when the book comes out?" he asked her. "You'll have to come back then. Weren't you doing all those interviews? I know you mentioned one of the television shows."

She stopped what she was doing and looked at her father. "Daddy," she said, "that's all over. It's not happening."

He looked stricken. He stood straight, looking down at her from his full height, his face lined and slack. "They told you that?" he asked her.

"They don't need to. They don't need to explain to me that the only questions anyone's going to want to ask me will be about my own marriage, and I can't talk about that. Not with anyone, certainly not on television. I know I'm being laughed at—"

He tried to deny this, but she waved him off. It wasn't much of an attempt.

"I thought my book could help someone. I thought I had something to say to people, about how they went about choosing a life partner, but I don't. Obviously, I don't. I'm a marriage counselor whose husband had a mistress. He might have killed his mistress."

Her father's eyes widened a little. "Grace," he said carefully. "'Might have'?"

She shook her head. "I'm not trying to be difficult," she said deliberately. "I just... I need to stop at 'might have' for a moment. I'm not ready to go past it." She looked around the kitchen. The light was all gone now. It had become another winter night outside.

"He had a baby with her," she heard herself say. "Did you know?"

Her father looked down at the wooden floor. He didn't answer. From the next room came a thin rendition of *The Blue Danube* from the DVD player.

"I should have known something," said Frederich Reinhart. "He came to me for money."

She felt the now familiar ache of sudden bad news. Fresh, new, bad news.

"When?"

"Oh..." He thought. "May, perhaps? He said you were worried about paying for Rearden this year, you thought you might have to take Henry out."

"That's not true," she told him, amazed. "That was never an issue."

"So I understand. Now. But he told me you were terribly concerned about money and would never come to me. Of course I told him that neither of you should worry. I only have one grandchild and luckily I'm able to help with his education. But he asked me not to say anything to you about it, so I didn't."

She was holding on to the counter, trying to stop swaying. "Daddy, I'm sorry. I would never have asked. I didn't need to ask! We were fine!"

"I know. He was very persuasive. He reminded me that pediatric oncologists are not at the high end of the earning scale for doctors. He said he couldn't stand the idea that you and Henry might have to compromise because he hadn't been a good enough wage earner. That it wasn't fair to you."

Grace shook her head. "In May...he wasn't even working then. They told me—the police told me—there was a disciplinary hearing last February, I think. They fired him. I had no idea."

Her father was leaning forward on the kitchen table, arms braced, eyes closed. "I gave him a hundred thousand dollars," he told her. "I didn't want him to have to ask me again. I didn't want you to have to come to me. I thought it was for tuition."

"Well," she said darkly, "it might have been, but not Henry's. Jonathan was paying the fees for another child. I worked that out, finally."

"For...I don't understand. Wasn't it a very small baby?"

"The older child. He had been Jonathan's patient at Memorial. It's how they met. Then the boy became a Rearden student. The headmaster...I think he believed Jonathan and I were Miguel's benefactors. Maybe because this boy was a cancer survivor and

Jonathan had been his doctor. But I didn't know anything about the boy. I just assumed he was on scholarship." Grace sighed. "And I guess he was. But Jonathan paid for the scholarship. I mean, apparently, you paid for it. I'm so sorry."

Her father shook his head. When Grace looked over at him again, it took her a moment to understand that he was shaking. "Daddy?"

"No, it's okay."

"I'm sorry," she said again.

"No. Don't be. I'm just . . . I'm so angry at myself. I'm angry at him, but mostly at myself. How could I have let him do that to you?"

Only then did she understand how wounded by this he, too, had been, and maybe not only at this, or maybe the "this" had begun long ago, and she had not been a bystander to it. For years, she had allowed her father to see her only as a very specific construct: securely partnered, professionally successful, the provider of an excellent grandchild. She had been technically available to her father but never warm, not really. Perhaps, if she was honest about it, she had not even been very interested in him, and what he cared about, and what his life was like—now and in the past. She had been available for dinner and strictly controlled conversation on a weekly basis, but she did not feel close to him at all, and she did not believe he could possibly feel close to her. Then again, this was the first time it had ever occurred to her that her father might actually want to be close.

What if she had been wrong? What if he had wanted—or indeed *needed*—something from her, and she had declined to provide it, declined even to see it? As if she herself had not needed her father. As if she didn't still need her mother! As if you got points for doing it all alone, and someone was keeping score to make sure you never cheated. How arrogant to assume that she could make up her own rules and had all the time in the world to play by them.

"You didn't let him," she said. She put down her wineglass. "He did this all by himself."

"I thought I was helping you and Henry," her father said. "I thought, well, I know how private you are. You would never come to me for assistance. I don't know why. But I was actually grateful to him. I thanked him. For giving me the opportunity." He shook his head in private, bitter distaste. Then sighed. "Eva loves to give her children things," he said, as if it were something he needed to apologize for. "But you never wanted anything."

"Oh, I wanted lots of things," she corrected him. "But I had all of them. Or I thought I did. You know, wanting what you have is supposedly the secret of happiness." She smiled. "Somebody said that. I forget who." There was a sputtering sound from the stovetop. Grace took the wooden spoon from the drawer and gave the soup a stir.

"Having what you want?"

"No, wanting what you already have."

"Ah! So simple," her father said. He looked better now. It was a relief. So she put the spoon back down and hugged him.

A moment later, Henry appeared in the doorway, shaking his head. "This movie is so weird," he told them. "There's all these colors. And the astronaut just turned into a baby. I don't get what's happening."

"I never did either," his grandfather said. "Maybe Stanley Kubrick was counting on the whole audience being high on drugs. But your grandmother and I just had a martini before we saw it in the movie theater. I don't think that was enough."

She had the two of them set the table. It was the first time they'd used the dining room since arriving. It was the first time she and Henry had not eaten on the couch, off their laps, with a heavy flannel blanket across their shoulders. Actually, it was hardly any warmer now. But it felt warmer somehow.

They ate the soup and then salmon on bagels, because from the moment she saw the salmon and the bagels, she was struck with a convulsive longing for them. And she drank more wine, then started in on the dark chocolate, and it was all surprisingly not terrible. For a Christmas Eve in a freezing house, in flight from her life, and in the inescapable proximity of her father and her son, both of whom had been woefully harmed by Jonathan Sachs, the love of her life, it was surprisingly not terrible. And they talked about baseball, of all things, or at least Henry and her father did, and Grace was amazed to discover that her father had once regularly gone to games and had grown up supporting a team called the Montreal Expos and even knew how to keep score, which was something that sounded as if it ought to be completely straightforward but was in fact seriously complex, and which he promised to teach his grandson, perhaps as soon as tomorrow. And after Henry went up to bed, but before Grace got up to clear the table, they sat for a few moments in a not uncompanionable silence, until Frederich Reinhart asked whether she had any idea where Jonathan had gone or how he was managing to not be found by the police.

"God, no," she said, surprised. "I have no idea. If I knew, I would tell them."

"I have to say, I'm amazed he's managed it. I just think: Today, every time you make a move or spend a nickel, all kinds of people must see what you're doing. It's incredible no one has recognized him. He's been everywhere. His face has been everywhere, I mean."

Grace took a breath. She was trying not to process the meaning of this.

"He might have thought beforehand, about what he would do. I mean, how to disappear. He had some time."

Her father frowned. "Do you mean that he planned it? He planned what he was going to do to..." His voice trailed off. Perhaps he had forgotten the name. Perhaps he had simply been unable to say it.

It was another thing she had been incapable of considering. She shook her head. "I meant that he was losing control. It looks like things were falling apart for him long before the day he left. He could have thought about how to hide. Maybe he already had a place to go," she said carefully. It was something she had been thinking about. Except that when she said "place," what she really meant was "person." Maybe he had a person, or maybe he *was* a person. Maybe today, tonight, somewhere, her husband was hiding inside another person. Maybe "Jonathan Sachs" had been another person he had hidden inside. The idea of it brought such suffering that she had to close her eyes and let it pass.

"Jonathan is very smart, you know," Grace said finally. "That hasn't changed about him."

It was one of the very few things about him that had not changed.

"But so are you," her father insisted. "It's your job to be smart about other people. You wrote a book about it..." He stopped himself, though it hardly mattered now: *horse bolted, barn door closed.*

"Go on," she said tersely. "Don't worry, you're not telling me anything I don't know."

He shook his head. He was rolling the wineglass between his long hands, back and forth. His face was slack with grief, and his hair, she noticed, had slipped the bounds of its usual precise cut. Was Eva growing careless? Grace wondered, but even as the question, with all its attendant unkindness, occurred to her, she understood that it wasn't that. It was, instead, her own cataclysm, so intense and destroying that even Eva was having trouble maintaining the customary duties and rituals, which was nothing for her to be petty about. She also owed her stepmother an apology, and to her own surprise she felt genuinely sorry. In fact, she was sorry about Eva in general. How many times had she suggested to resentful patients that when good marriages ended, surviving partners often sought to be married again, sometimes very quickly. Happily married people liked being married: It was as simple as that. And her father had been happy with Grace's mother, and he wanted to be happy again, and he had met Eva and seen at least a prospect of happiness with her, and wasn't that preferable to living in mourning? Would she have wanted him to go on living in mourning? So why had she felt so harmed by it? *Therapist, heal thyself!* she thought miserably.

"I think," said Grace, "I just had an idea of what a good family, a strong family, looked like, from you and Mommy. And I tried to make my own family look like that. I did what Mommy did, and Jonathan seemed..." She was searching for what he had seemed like, but for the moment it evaded her. "And I thought that Henry was happy. I hope he was happy." It all seemed so brutally past tense now. "I just wanted to be like you. I wanted to be happy like you."

For a minute she thought that she had started to cry. She wouldn't put it past herself to start crying without even noticing—not now. It would take more than that to surprise her now. But in fact, the crying wasn't hers. It was Frederich Reinhart, attorney at law, who sat across from her at the pine table, weeping into his long hands. Her father: weeping. For the longest time, this simply did not compute. Then she reached across and took one of his thin wrists in her hand.

"Daddy?"

"No—" He shook his head. "Don't."

Don't? Grace wondered. Don't what?

He had to finish. It took a long while. And she couldn't do anything but wait for him.

Eventually he got up, went to the bathroom. Grace heard the toilet flush and the water run. When he returned, he had reassembled himself, more or less. He looked like his own father, a worn-out man Grace barely recalled, with rheumy eyes: an uncomfortable presence in the corner of the living room at her own birthday parties. Her father—like Grace, like Henry—had been an only child, and the relationship with his own father had not been particularly good. She knew almost nothing about her grandfather apart from a reverse trajectory of addresses (Lauderdale Lakes, Rye, Flushing, Eldridge Street, Montreal, Bukowsko) and a funeral she had furiously wanted not to attend, because it meant missing one of the grander bat mitzvahs in her Rearden class that year. Now she couldn't even remember whose bat mitzvah it was, but then they had seemed like such unequal claims on her attention.

"We weren't happy," her father said suddenly, with the kind of gulping, shallow breath that caught up with you after tears. "I wasn't. I know Marjorie wasn't. I tried to be. First I tried with her, and then I tried without her. I think I would have tried anything."

"But...," Grace heard herself say, "I never saw that. Never," she insisted, as if he were wrong about his own life and she, the child, had a better grasp of things. "What about..." She thought frantically, looking for evidence to prove his mistake, and found herself remembering the jewelry in her mother's mirrored vanity, this piece or that, laid out on the desktop. "What about all those beautiful things you gave her? Those pins and bracelets. It was so loving, the way you brought her jewelry all the time."

He shook his head quickly. "It wasn't. It wasn't about being loving. Not at all. I had a way of going off with people, and then I would decide that it wasn't the way I wanted to live, and I would come back and apologize, and bring her something." He stopped to make sure she was still with him, but she wasn't with him. She was flying wildly overhead, careening around the room.

"You bought jewelry? For that?" She was sort of amazed that she could respond to this at all; the fact that these particular words were the ones to emerge was barely relevant.

Her father shrugged. "She never wore any of it. It was like poison to her. She told me once, when I asked about it—we were getting dressed for something. There was a pin, something with an emerald; I thought it would look nice with what she was wearing. She said it would make her feel like she was wearing Hester Prynne's letter A."

Grace closed her eyes. She knew that pin. That pin had been taken away by Jonathan, to some unknown place. She hoped she would never see it again.

"I should have stopped." He shook his head briefly. "I should have stopped a number of things. It didn't make me feel any better, and it certainly didn't make her feel any better. How could it, looking at those things and knowing what they meant? I'm not even sure I remember my own motives clearly. It's possible there came a point when I no longer intended them as a kindness. Sometimes I came home and she'd have left something out on that dressing table. I felt as if she was saying, 'Remember this one? Or this one?' Why did she put herself through that? I understand why she'd want to put me through it, but herself?"

"You should have been in therapy," Grace said tersely. "Did that occur to you?"

"To be honest? No. For my generation it didn't seem like an option. If you were in a good place, or you could at least live together, you just stayed put. If not, you called it quits. There wasn't much of this trying to figure things out. I don't know why not. We had analysis if we wanted it, but it just seemed crazy to me. Hours and hours, and all that money, lying on a couch and trying to remember some key code from when I was in diapers that would explain everything. The fact was, I didn't much care about my neuroses. I just wanted to leave."

"Then why didn't you?" she demanded. She seemed to have located some speck of outrage after all.

He looked up and met her gaze, which must have shocked him, because he looked away quickly. "I asked for a divorce, but without at least a nominal consent I knew it wasn't worth separating that way."

"And she said no, I take it."

"She said absolutely not. I've never understood it. It made sense that she wouldn't advocate for my happiness, but what about her own? And I certainly didn't want to hurt her. Any more than I already had," he said. Grace found that she was holding on to the table, pinching the wood between her thumbs and forefingers.

"So we just went on. After you went off to Radcliffe I tried again, and I think she might have been considering it, but then she had her stroke."

They sat there for another few minutes. Grace, to her own surprise, discovered that she was still able to sip her wine, that the house hadn't fallen down. All systems continued nominally functional. *What next?* she thought.

"This makes me incredibly sad," she offered finally.

"Me too. For years I asked myself what I could have done better. Or at least differently. I would have liked to have more children, actually."

"Wow," said Grace, stunned. "Why?"

"I loved being a father. I loved watching you learn things. You were such a curious child. I don't mean academically—of course you were a fine student," he corrected himself. "But you just looked and looked at something, and I used to say to your mother, 'There's a lot going on in there. She looks at everything.'"

Looks at everything, Grace thought. *And sees nothing*.

"You could have started again when Mommy died," she said, still not very kindly. "You were only in your fifties. You could have had another family."

He shrugged. He seemed to be considering this for the first time. "I suppose so. But I met Eva and I felt this great comfort with her. And comfort was actually what I had been needing. It turned out to be a very basic need, not terribly complex after all. And then I had her kids and grandkids, and eventually I had Henry, and I've been very happy." He looked across at her frankly. "The thought that you based your ideal of marriage on what your mother and I had is terribly upsetting, Grace. I should have talked to you about this many years ago."

"I should have insisted on it," Grace answered. "It was my job as a teenager to pillory my parents, and I never did it. There's a reason rebellion happens when it does. I must have thought I was above all that." She swirled the last of her red wine around the base of her glass, following the sediment as it circled the stem. "Oh well, better late than never."

"Eva admires you," he told her. "She knows you resent her. It's been somewhat painful."

Grace nodded. She was not quite ready to embrace Eva as a compassionate, loving soul. But she could try. And then she heard herself ask outright for her mother's china, which amazed her. Now—with the myth of her parents' marriage in pieces around her—that she still harbored a desire for its symbols made no sense whatsoever. But the symbols were tactile: They took up space in the world. Now, more than she thought possible, she wanted to surround herself with symbols that took up space in the world.

"I would like to have it," she told her father plainly. "It means something to me."

"Her what?" he said, mystified.

"Mommy's china. The Haviland, from your wedding. It's hard for me to see it used so casually. I know it's silly . . . ," she said.

"The plates and cups?" he asked, still unclear.

"Yes. It's very old-fashioned, I know. But those things, from your wedding, I felt they should have come to me. I know how this sounds," she said, because she was hearing it out loud for the very first time, and she did, finally, know how it sounded, which wasn't very nice. "I'm not usually acquisitive, but she was my mother and I was her daughter. It felt wrong to me that they should have gone to your second wife and not to me. That's all," she said. She wasn't entirely sure what "That's all" meant.

"But of course you can have the dishes. Whatever you like. Eva is always telling me we should get rid of things, and she has other sets of dishes. I was a little sentimental about them, I suppose. And I thought it would be nice for you to come for dinner and use the same dishes we used when you were a little girl. But of course. Of course. I'll bring them up here."

"No, that's okay," Grace said, feeling idiotic. "But when this is over, if it's ever over, I want Henry to be able to feel connected to things that have nothing to do with his father. I want to have things from my past to give to Henry. I want to *have* a past to give to Henry. I don't need it to be perfect, just to be real."

And it occurred to her, as she heard these things spoken aloud, that she was a tiny bit closer to being almost ready for that herself.

CHAPTER NINETEEN

THE GREAT MISTAKE

As a product of private education from the first day of pre-kindergarten to the morning her crimson diploma was put into her hands, Grace was unprepared for the ease with which Henry came to be enrolled in the seventh grade of the Housatonic Valley Regional Middle School. There was no formal application required, let alone the terrifying Manhattan ritual of finding out how many openings the class was likely to have or whom she might know or have some vague connection to on the school's board of trustees or in the admissions office. And in fact, Grace's trepidatious call to the registrar a few days after the Christmas holiday yielded only a cheerful request for documents that seemed eminently reasonable and were no trouble at all: Henry's birth certificate, a utility bill for the lake house in his parent's or guardian's name, and a transcript from his prior school, which Robert Conover promptly e-mailed and which consisted of reassuringly unmitigated praise.

Still, she spent the first days of the new year nursing a private certainty that Henry was about to face a great ordeal, a rapid descent from the Parnassus of Manhattan education to some swamp of lowest-common-denominator institutions. Either the local school would lag so far behind Rearden—with addition and subtraction in seventh-grade math, for example, Dick and Jane in literature—or the other kids would be backwoods degenerates, glue-sniffing video game addicts who'd finger her son as an aesthete intellectual and loathe and shun him with the exquisite unity of seventh graders everywhere (except, that is, for places like Rearden, where school administrations claimed to be passionately vigilant against bullying of all kinds).

She kept these fears to herself, and it was a good thing she did, because Henry was eager to depart the isolation of their little home on the nearly abandoned lake and return to the world of twelve-year-olds. That first morning, she had driven him down the road in her own car, utterly ignorant of the fact that her son now attended public school and was entitled to pickup and delivery in a municipal school bus, and watched him walk inside. Then she went straight back home, climbed back under the covers, and fell apart.

Truly fell apart, in a way she had not really allowed herself to do since the first moment of the blinking light on her cell phone and the dismantling of her life and the escape to Connecticut and the practicalities of keeping them warm (enough) and fed and the distraction of Christmas and her father and the getting ready for Henry to go back to school. Through all of that she had remained her recognizable self: the small, capable person who kept things moving and seemed reasonable enough. Henry, whatever else had disappeared, still had his mother, that was obvious, who still took care of him and made sure there was breakfast and he had clean clothes when he got up in the morning. But Grace did not truly understand how much it had taken out of her just to appear functional until Henry began to leave the house and be, presumably, safe for a few hours at a time; and when she did understand it, that centrifugal force that had kept her upright began to slow, then creak to a halt. And then the surface of the earth just seemed to give way entirely.

In bed she lay mainly on her side, looking at nothing. She did this for hours, though it made her body actually ache, and she drifted into and out of wakefulness. Then, afraid that she would somehow miss the time when she had to go back and pick him up (because, again, she had not yet grasped that a school bus could bring Henry home), she forced herself upright long enough to set her alarm clock for two forty-five p.m. Then she went back to lying on her side, looking at nothing.

Days that way. It became like a job: Take him to school, go to bed, lie for hours, rise again, collect him from school. She was very diligent in carrying out her duties. She was very strict with her schedule. She felt nothing but the dull pinch of despair, and some dizziness, because she had to remember to eat, and sometimes she didn't remember very well. Occasionally she would think: *How long is this going to last?* But mainly she did not think. The emptiness in the place where her mind had once been was so vast. It was a big room with grimy windows and a dull, slippery floor. She lived there now, at least when he was out of the house. And when the alarm rang at two forty-five, Grace got up, changed her clothes, checked the refrigerator and made a shopping list, and went to pick up her son. It was all there was to her life. It was all she could tolerate. And it went on and on, the same every day. Or at least every school day.

Meanwhile, Henry's anticipated ordeal utterly failed to materialize. That first day, he had walked effortlessly into his new seventh-grade homeroom and been met by a cheerful lack of curiosity about what had brought him to deepest Connecticut in the middle of the school year. When he emerged at the end of the first day, it was with not one but two new friends, both of whom had been eager to know what he was "into" and both of whom were delighted to learn that he was "into" anime.

"Animation?" Grace had frowned. They were eating dinner at Smitty's, the pizza place in Lakeville.

"Anime. Japanese animation. You know, like *Spirited Away*."

"Oh," she had said. But she wasn't sure what he meant.

"Miyazaki?"

"I don't know that one."

"No, he's the filmmaker. He's like the Walt Disney of Japan, but much better than Disney. Anyway, Danny has a DVD of *Castle in the Sky*, and he invited me over on Saturday to watch. I can go, right?"

"Of course," she said, feigning delight, as if it wouldn't be an ordeal to let him out of her sight on a weekend. "Did you say... *Cabin in the Sky*?" She knew that one, but she couldn't imagine preteen boys being remotely interested in it, which was just as well.

"No, *Castle*. It's kind of based on Jonathan Swift and kind of on Hindu legend but also kind of set in Wales. There's a lot of 'kind of' in Miyazaki." Henry laughed at his own joke, if indeed it was a joke. Grace was already mystified. "But Danny has the Japanese version with English subtitles, which is always better."

"Oh. Good. Okay." She nodded. "So, anime. Since when? I mean, I haven't heard you mention it."

"Dad took me to *Howl's Moving Castle* last year," he said simply.

"Oh..." She nodded with great false cheer. "Fine." And they moved swiftly on.

The next morning, he went back to seventh grade and she went back to bed.

The other surprise about the school was how strong it seemed to be, academically. Social studies was doing a unit on Margaret Mead's work in Samoa, and history had begun an intensive period on the Civil War, with, it transpired, lots of primary sources. In English, the reading list for the rest of the year featured most of the usual suspects—*The Scarlet Letter*, *To Kill a Mockingbird*, *Of Mice and Men*—without any of the noncanon alternatives New York private schools had added over the past years to demonstrate their political correctness. And math was actually ahead of Rearden. She was not displeased to discover that Henry already had a French test to study for and a character study of Jem Finch due the following Friday.

And he wanted to try out for the baseball team.

What about violin? she asked him. It was the first time either of them had brought it up.

"Well, I'm supposed to choose between orchestra and band. Or chorus."

Grace sighed. A roomful of reluctant violinists scratching out the theme from *Forrest Gump* was a very great distance from the dusty parlor of Vitaly Rosenbaum, but for now…

"I think orchestra. All right?"

Henry nodded glumly. And that, at least, was that difficult conversation over and done.

She still took him in the morning and went to collect him in the afternoon, and oddly enough he never objected, though he certainly saw his classmates exploding from the yellow buses in the morning and clomping back onto them each afternoon. Maybe, Grace thought, he somehow understood how necessary the drives had become for her, that these two brief but highly ritualized journeys were providing a crucial structure to her own days of lying beneath the covers, staring into the void just beyond the wall of the bedroom.

Later, she would have to go back and check the calendar to grasp exactly how long this had gone on, but on some morning at the end of January, after Grace dropped Henry off at school, she found herself turning the car not south to the lake and the house and the bed and the alarm clock, but north into Falls Village and the library, where she sat and read, in one of the formal high-backed armchairs beneath the ornately framed nineteenth-century portraits and floral studies, the *Berkshire Record* newspaper, with its helpful accounts of local teams and editorials about the local zoning board. Then, a few days later, she went back and did it again.

Sometimes she saw Leo Holland at the library, and one morning early in February Grace went for coffee with him at Toymakers Café, a short walk down Main Street. Leo was not quite a stranger anymore; he had progressed from a barely remembered character from her childhood summers, distinguished mainly by his noise-producing antics and their effect on Grace's mother. He had come by the house twice since their meeting at the mailbox—once with a large plastic tub of what he called chicken stew (probably because he wasn't pretentious enough—or didn't want her to think he was pretentious enough—to call it "coq au vin," though it *was* coq au vin) and once with a loaf of homemade Anadama bread. Both items, he told her, had come from the dinners his "group" was holding in the house, every couple of weeks. "Group" was a term offered so nonchalantly that Grace didn't know what he meant by it. Study group? Therapy group? It might be a knitting group or an Amnesty International group for all the detail he offered, but she was curious enough, when he mentioned it over coffee that morning, to ask what kind of group he meant.

"Oh, the band," Leo said. "Well, we prefer 'group.' We're mainly just midlife string geeks. 'Band' seems a little teenagers-in-the-basement, you know? Though the other fiddler actually is a teenager. He's my friend Lyric's son. Lyric plays mandolin."

"Lyric," Grace repeated. "That's a great name for a musician."

"Hippie parents," Leo said. "But it suits her. She teaches mandolin at Bard. I'm at Bard. I told you that, I think."

"Actually, no." She was stirring sugar into her cappuccino. "You said you were on sabbatical. You didn't say where you taught."

"Oh. Bard. Great place to teach, not such a great place to be on sabbatical." He laughed. The little café had a big wooden farm table in one corner, at which some mom-committee (Grace could not help thinking of her own former mom-committee at a similar wooden farm table) was conferring over yellow legal pads. Elsewhere, a stack of motorcycle picture books was actually topped with a signed photo of Liza Minnelli that had to be twenty years old.

"I'm less than an hour away here, but it's far enough to get them to stop calling. Otherwise I wouldn't be getting any work done. And the group, I mean, we've been playing together for more than five years, and they were not pleased about having to drive all this way, but after they came out the first time, they kind of loved it. They loved being alone at the lake. Almost alone," he corrected. "Now we kind of make an evening of it. Or even an overnight if Rory doesn't have school in the morning. Rory's our other fiddle player. And we make these big meals."

"Of which I am the grateful beneficiary," she said kindly.

"Yes. Well, good."

"Oh," Grace said, realizing. "That's where the music is coming from. You can't always tell what direction. Sometimes it sounds like it's coming through the woods. That's a band? I mean, a group?"

"We have an extremely modest following around Annandale-on-Hudson," Leo said with amiable sarcasm. "You know, significant others, co-workers. Students hoping for a good grade on the final. We have a name: Windhouse. It's a ruin in the Shetland Islands. Very haunted, according to Colum—he's another group member—he grew up in Scotland, used to go hiking in the Shetlands. Everyone asks," he said a little lamely, because she hadn't asked. But she would have.

"Well, you sound great. What little I've heard."

He seemed to have decided to stop talking about himself. For a moment, they sat rather awkwardly, contemplating their coffees. Across the room, the women—now Grace recognized one of them from Henry's school—began to wind up their meeting. When the door opened, two enormous men came in and the cook, a woman with long gray braids wound around her head, came rushing to the counter and leaned over to embrace them.

"You said you were writing a book?" Grace asked.

"Yeah. Hoping to finish by June. I have to teach summer session this year."

"What's the book about?"

"Asher Levy," said Leo. "Have you heard of him?"

She started to shake her head. Then she said: "Wait, is he the same as Asser Levy?"

"Yes!" Leo looked delighted, as if she had specifically indulged him by knowing even this much. "Asher, sometimes known as Asser. I forgot you're a New York Jew. Of course you know Asser Levy."

"But I don't," she protested. "Just the name. There's a school in the East Village named after him, I think."

"And a park in Brooklyn. And a recreational center. And a street! The first Jewish landowner in New York and quite possibly the first Jew in America. That's something I'm trying to settle one way or the other."

"I had no idea..." She laughed. "The first Jewish landowner in New York? You think he could ever have imagined the Harmonie Club or Temple Emanu-El?"

"What, you mean Our Lady of Emanu-El?" said Leo. "That's what my father always called it. He belonged for a while. Then he became a Quaker when he met my mother. He used to say half his bar mitzvah class became Quakers or Buddhists. He said he'd rather meditate on a bench in a meetinghouse than sitting on the floor, so he became a Quaker. Also they had better bumper stickers."

"I remember him!" Grace said, because she did, or thought she did. "He had this big droopy sweater, right? Sort of light green?"

"Ah..." Leo nodded. "The bane of my mother's existence. For years she'd hide it, hoping he'd forget about it and find something else to wear that didn't come down to his knees. But he had like a sense about it. He always went right to the cupboard or the shelf or wherever she put it. But you know, after my mom died he just threw it out. I saw it in the garbage one day. I didn't even ask him why."

Grace nodded. She was thinking about her father and the jewelry, the ziplock bag of jewelry, so toxic that he couldn't look at it anymore.

"My mother died, too," she said. She wasn't sure that it followed, really. Leo nodded.

"I'm sorry."

"I'm sorry, too. About yours."

"Thanks."

They sat in silence for another minute. But it was actually less uncomfortable than it might have been.

"Never gets old, does it?" Leo said. "The death of your mother."

"Nope. Never does."

He took a sip of his coffee, then wiped his mouth, unthinkingly, on the back of his hand. "My mother died up here at the lake, actually. She stayed a few days after my father and brother left, to close up the house. This was eleven years ago. We're not sure what happened—probably carbon monoxide poisoning, but the autopsy was inconclusive. My dad replaced the heater anyway. It made him feel better."

"That's terrible," Grace said. She could not remember what Leo's mother looked like.

"What about yours?"

She told him about returning to Cambridge after the spring break of her junior year, and how the phone was ringing and ringing in her dormitory room as she fumbled with her key in the hallway, and how she knew—even in that prehistory before cell phones—that this call was going to mean something large and something bad. And it did: Her mother had had a stroke back in New York, no more than an hour after Grace had left for the train station. Grace had turned around and gone back, and over the next few weeks, in which her mother had never regained consciousness, and the possible futures had been of steadily diminishing returns, she had stayed and fluttered around both her parents in the hospital, until she knew she had to either withdraw for the term or go back. So she went back, and—incredibly, horribly, surreally—the exact same thing had happened. The ringing phone through the thick oak door in Kirkland House, the scramble for the key, the something large and something bad news. She had gone back to New York again, this time for the rest of the term, and was only able to make up her course work over the summer.

That fall, she had moved off campus to live with Vita, and then, almost immediately, she had met Jonathan. It would have been a nice time to still have a mother, she thought now. How would Marjorie Wells Pierce Reinhart—who had met and fallen in love with her own husband over the course of a single blind date in 1961, and whose marriage had not been happy—have responded when her only child phoned, elated, soaring, to describe the young man, ambitious, compassionate, tender, a little disheveled, and thoroughly in love with her?

She would have said: *Be careful. Slow down.*

She would have said: *Grace, please. I'm delighted, but be smart.*

Be *smarter*, in other words.

"I'm sorry I didn't get to know her as an adult," Leo said suddenly. "I mean: me as an adult. I know she didn't like me very much when I was a teenager."

"Oh . . . ," Grace heard herself say, "it wasn't you. She wasn't a very happy person, I don't think."

It was the first time she had said anything remotely like this. *Ever.* She listened to the silence those words left behind and was amazed at herself. She felt terrible. She felt she had let something terrible out into the world. Her mother had been *unhappy*. She had just *said so*. What a horrible thing to have done.

"Sometimes things happen so . . . untidily," said Leo, "that we have to make up a narrative. I think it happens with death a lot, actually."

"What?" said Grace.

"The narrative. You came back to school. The phone rang. You came back to school again. The phone rang again. The way you tell the story, you've almost made yourself responsible for her death."

"You think I'm being narcissistic?" Grace asked. She was trying to decide whether or not to be offended.

"Oh no, I don't mean that. Well, there is narcissism in all of us, of course. I mean, we are the protagonists of our own lives, so naturally it feels like we're at the wheel. But we're not at the wheel. That just happens to be where the window is located."

She laughed. Then, when she realized that she was actually laughing about this, she laughed again.

"Sorry," Leo said. "Chronic failing of professorial types. *Always. Be. Professing.* To misquote Mamet."

"That's okay," said Grace. "I never thought of it. And I'm supposed to be a therapist."

He looked at her. "What do you mean, supposed to be?"

But she didn't answer him, because she didn't know. Weeks had passed since Grace had even thought of a patient. It had been even longer since she'd last felt she was in a position to instruct another human being on how to better live his or her life.

"My profession," she said instead. "I'd rather not discuss it."

"That's fine," he said carefully.

"I appear to be on sabbatical, too," she said.

"Okay. Not that we're discussing it."

"No," Grace said, and they left it at that and went on to other things. Leo's father had not remarried, but he had a lady friend named, of all things, Prudie. Leo's brother, Peter, was an attorney in Oakland. Leo had a daughter.

"Well, sort of," he clarified unsuccessfully.

"You sort of have a daughter."

"I was involved with a woman who had a daughter already. Ramona. The daughter, not the woman. We decided to have the best of all possible breakups, and that meant Ramona stayed in my life, which was a big relief to me, because I adore her."

"The best of all possible breakups..." Grace said it wonderingly. "That sounds nice. Voltairean!"

He shrugged. "It's an ideal, of course. But I can't think of a better reason for trying. When you have kids. Even a sort-of kid." He looked over at her. She could tell he was wondering if he should ask.

She was here on the lake, in other words. Her son was here. She had to look down at her own left hand to check whether she was still wearing her wedding ring. She appeared to be still wearing her wedding ring. All these weeks, this had failed to make an impact on her.

"So... do you see her often?"

"About one weekend a month. Her mother lives in Boston, so it's tricky but doable. Then she comes up for a few weeks in the summer, but that's getting complicated, too. Because of *boys*," he said sarcastically.

Grace smiled.

"Yes, I said *boys!* Apparently, this matters to a fourteen-year-old girl. The lack of *boys* on a beautiful little lake in the country. I have tried to tell her that boys are not worth anything, but she is determined to go to summer camp with the disgusting creatures anyway, and I'm supposed to be content with picking her up in Vermont and taking her to Cape Cod for a week."

Grace laughed and drank the last bit of her coffee. "And so you shall be, if you know what's good for you," she instructed him. "The fourteen-year-old girl is a very tricky bit of ectoplasm. Be happy she wants to see you at all."

"I'm happy," he grumbled. "Don't I look happy?"

He asked them over again, for dinner, and again Grace demurred, but perhaps not as energetically as the last time and the time before. She attributed this, afterward, to Henry, and the notion that Henry would probably not dislike Leo, and that Leo might not be a problematic person for Henry to know, seeing that they all three lived on the same lake in the middle of the woods. And he—Leo—had said that it would be a nice thing if Henry could bring his fiddle (he called it a fiddle, not a violin) when they came, because he—Leo—would love to hear Henry play, or would Henry like to bring his fiddle (violin) over sometime at the weekend to sit in with the band? And Grace had very nearly said that Henry didn't really "sit in," that wasn't really the way he'd been taught to play, and actually just imagining a student of Vitaly Rosenbaum "sitting in" with other musicians (though the grim Hungarian might not even have deigned to consider Leo and the others in Windhouse musicians at all) was pretty hard to do. But she didn't. On the other hand, she didn't accept the invitation, either. Instead, she found herself inquiring—with an irreverence in her voice that was supposed to make him forget all about having asked—what the difference was, anyway, between a violin and a fiddle, and he told her, simply: Attitude.

"Attitude," she repeated, very skeptical. "Really."

"Simple as that," he said, looking pleased with himself.

"But... attitude toward what?"

"Oh, I could tell you, but then I couldn't be responsible for what happened next. Shall we leave it for a few weeks?"

Yes, she told him, nodding soberly. A few weeks.

Then they got up and left the café together, Leo waving back at the woman behind the counter, and Grace, who at the very least had been able to spend the past hour not thinking about what was going to happen next, went back to her car and got inside and drove north.

Her brief conversation with Vita had taken place a few days earlier, on the phone at the lake house, which Grace had plugged back in for the occasion. Vita's office number had taken all of thirty seconds at a keyboard in the David M. Hunt Library to procure, but the courage to use it had been far harder to come by. The talk had been... well, a little formal under the circumstances, but when the invitation came—to meet in Vita's office in Pittsfield, of all places, she had said yes right away.

It was not what she had wanted, exactly.

Well, she did not know what she wanted.

Grace leaned forward, reflexively searching for black ice on Route 7, especially when it curved. The road was familiar by now.

She had assigned Great Barrington the newly vacant role of "metropolis" in her life and had gotten into the habit of coming here for anything Canaan or Lakeville couldn't handle, which was most things. (Her attachment to the Berkshire Co-Op alone was now so potentially dangerous that it made her former penchant for Eli's on the Upper East Side seem benign—and very economical—in comparison.) She had also managed to lose time in a couple of the better restaurants, the butcher shop, and a shop that sold only antique china, including a complete set of the Haviland now officially promised to her.

It was a pretty town; she had always thought that. It had one of those utterly American Main Streets, but the town itself bent like a hairpin through a couple of areas that—if they were not actual "downtowns"—at least felt like places you might want to park your car and walk around. There were plenty of her own memories here: the long-gone general store where her mother liked the service and the shoes, the Bookloft on Stockbridge Road, where she had spent dusty afternoons ferreting out early psychology tomes, and a massive antiques store where she and Jonathan had bought the landscape of men haying that now hung in their dining room on 81st Street.

Or was it still *their* painting? In *their* dining room? Like everything else in that site-specific museum of the installation previously known as her marriage, she wasn't sure she ever wanted to see it again.

It was steely gray overhead by the time she cleared Lenox and headed northwest to the address Vita had given her. The road left the affluent Berkshire world of Tanglewood and Edith Wharton behind and succumbed to scattered farms and the industrial edges of Pittsfield (home—who could forget?—of a Superfund cleanup site) and the extreme northern boundary of Grace's own childhood territories, if only because she had been taken to the Colonial Theatre here once or twice as a child, and at least once a summer, on stormy days, to the Berkshire Museum. Quite possibly Vita had come with her on one of those expeditions while staying with Grace at the lake house, and how strange it was to think that a place she herself had once introduced her friend to was now the place Vita worked and had made a life. Pittsfield was one of those old towns you drove through to get to somewhere else, or because that's where the train or the bus actually let you off. It was a place in headlong decline: full of formerly grand homes, now in slightly scary neighborhoods, and formerly sylvan parks you might want to think twice about entering at night.

The Porter Center was located in some former Stanley Electric Manufacturing Company buildings, distinctively redbrick, forming a kind of campus, but the sign at the entry (and the guard who emerged as she slowed to read it) directed Grace to a converted residential house in classic white and green, with its own, smaller, ADMINISTRATION sign. She parked her car and took another moment to steady herself. Vita, according to the tagline on her e-mail, was the executive director of this place, which seemed to exist not only here on its own postindustrial campus, but in a kind of root system of programs all over the county, as far north as Williamstown and as far south as Great Barrington. According to the website Grace had pored over in the library, it did everything: drug treatment intervention, programs for teen mothers, individual therapy, anxiety and depression groups, and court-mandated courses for substance abusers and sex offenders. *One-stop shopping for mental health*, she thought, taking in the long brick buildings from her own front seat. Years earlier, at the time of her wedding, when she and Vita had both been about to enter graduate school (Vita for social work, Grace in psychology, but with the common goal of becoming therapists specializing in individual therapy), this was not the outcome she had envisioned for her friend.

And I was so gifted at envisioning outcomes, too, she thought grimly.

She zipped her parka and picked up her bag. After a moment, she locked the car door.

Inside, in the reconstructed front parlor, it was warm—very warm. A woman her own age with scalp shining through her severely thinning hair invited Grace to sit on the prim sofa, decorated with white lace circles, and Grace did, taking in the reading material on offer (*Psychology Today*, *Highlights*) and the picture book of historical Pittsfield. She picked this up and turned the pages: tinted postcards of the Stanley Electric plants, avenues of elegant Victorian homes, some of which she had probably passed on the drive, families at leisure on the grass, and baseball—lots of baseball. Pittsfield had always been a big baseball town, apparently. She would have to remember to say so to Henry.

"Gracie," said Vita's voice. It was unmistakably Vita's voice—a little clipped, as if she always had a half breath less than she required to complete her thought—and she turned, already smiling to herself if not to anyone else.

"Hello," said Grace. She stood and the two women looked at each other.

Vita had always been taller, as Grace had always been thinner, and both things were still true, but Vita had changed dramatically in almost every other way. The brown hair that had once been imprisoned in a pageboy (Vita's mother's idea of a universally flattering hairstyle) was now long—very long—and almost entirely gray, and worn loose, or more accurately not "worn" at all. It flowed and coiled at will, over Vita's chest and down her back, and was so extraordinarily unexpected that it took Grace another moment to gather in the rest. She had on jeans and work boots, a long-sleeved black shirt—very casual—and, of all things, an Hermès scarf knotted around her neck. Grace found herself staring at that.

"Oh," Vita said. "I know. In your honor. Do you recognize it?"

She nodded, still speechless. "We went to buy it together, didn't we?"

"We did." She smiled. "My mother's fiftieth birthday. You made me pick this one over the naval battle. Of course you were right." She turned to the woman at the reception desk, who was following this conversation with keen attention. "Laura? This is my friend Grace. We grew up together."

"Hello," said Grace.

"Hi," said Laura.

"We picked this scarf out for my mother's birthday," Vita said. "My mother loved it. I never went wrong following Grace's advice."

Perhaps not sartorially, thought Grace.

"Would you like to come on back?" Vita said. She turned and walked ahead. Grace followed to the back of the house and up a flight of narrow stairs into what must have been a bedroom.

"I have to warn you," she said as she held back the door for Grace to enter, "because I want you to be ready. I'm going to hug you. Okay?"

Grace burst out laughing, which was better than the alternative.

"Well, all right, then," Grace finally managed to say. And then they hugged. And when they did, she very nearly lost it again. It was a long hug, with nothing tentative about it, except for only the first little bit of it, and only on her own part.

The office wasn't large. It had a window overlooking one of the long brick buildings and its parking lot, but there was a tree in what would once have been the house's backyard that obscured part of it. She could imagine a child living here, with movie star photos tacked to the wall and curtains with rickrack. On one of the shelves behind Vita's chair, among the textbooks and journals and stacks of legal pads, were framed photographs of children.

"Want tea?" said Vita. She went out to fetch it and came back a few minutes later with mugs.

"Still with the Constant Comment, I see," said Grace.

"It is indeed a constant in my life. I had a serious dalliance with green tea, but I came back. You know, there was a rumor a few years ago that they were phasing it out. I was all over the Internet, chasing it down. I even wrote to Bigelow and they swore up and down it wasn't true, but just to be safe I bought around a hundred boxes."

"You can't trust those corporate tea folks," Grace said, inhaling. In a whiff, the smell of their apartment in Cambridge had overwhelmed her.

"No indeed. What kind of company makes money off a product called Sleepytime? There's obviously something underhanded going on. Remember that time your mother's favorite perfume got discontinued? And your dad tried to hire someone to re-create it? I never got over that. Today you'd just go on eBay and stock up, but back then—what was it, sometime in the eighties? When it was off the shelf you had to take matters into your own hands. It was very touching, wasn't it?"

Grace nodded. Touching like a piece of jewelry every time you had an affair with another woman. Which was also touching, on its own idiosyncratic terms. She had not thought about the perfume in a very long time. For months that year, there had been rows of little amber testers from the expert's laboratory: "Marjorie I," "Marjorie II," "Marjorie III," etc. After her mother's death, before pouring them down the drain, she had smelled each of them, and they were universally terrible. But yes, very touching.

"I heard about your father," Grace said. "I'm so sorry. I should have gotten in touch."

"No, no. You get a pass. We both get a pass. But thank you. I really miss him. Actually, I miss him a lot more than I thought I would. We sort of became very close at the end. I know..." She smiled. "Nobody was more surprised than I was. Well, my mom was more surprised. She kept saying, 'What do you talk about in that room?'"

"What room?" Grace said.

"He was pretty much bedridden for the last six months. He had hospice care at home. We'd just hang out and talk. You know they moved up here? Well, to Amherst. My mother's still in Amherst. She's doing great."

"Oh, please give her my love."

"She's having such an interesting life. She joined a drumming circle. She's become a Zen Buddhist."

Grace laughed. "Gotta love Amherst."

"They sold their apartment for an insane fortune. At the top of the market, too. And that was my mom. She just said, 'Jerry, look at these prices. We're selling right now.' For that ordinary little apartment!"

"On Fifth Avenue," Grace reminded her.

"Well, yes. But nothing special. And *off* Fifth."

"But with a view of the park!"

"Okay." She nodded. "You know, I haven't talked Manhattan real estate in ages. It's not much of a topic up here. I kind of miss it."

Grace kind of did, too. Lately she had been testing, with a very long stick, the notion of selling her home and, as a consequence, never living in it again. But whenever she did, it hurt too much to go on. "How long have you been here?" she asked Vita.

"In Pittsfield? Since 2000, but I was in Northampton before that. I ran an eating disorder clinic at Cooley Dickinson Hospital. Then there was an opening here at Porter to run the entire program, which was a huge challenge. You can imagine how much less community support there is for mental health services here than in Northampton. The Pioneer Valley's like a fairyland for mental health. But I love it here. I had to convince the rest of my family, but it's worked out well."

The word hit Grace squarely. It had seemed incomprehensible (but of course utterly obvious) that Vita had a family she knew nothing of. Grace also had a family of her own! Well, once, she had.

"I want to hear all about your family," said Grace, bravely, like a grown-up.

"Oh, you'll meet them. Of course! One of the reasons I wanted to see you was to make sure we got you over for dinner while you're here."

"I think 'while I'm here' is going to be quite awhile, actually."

"Good. Your father wasn't sure. I know there's been a lot of uncertainty," Vita said plainly, but with an encouraging—vaguely therapeutic, Grace couldn't help thinking—nod. They had arrived at the crux of the matter: A life crisis of fairly stupendous proportions had dragged one partner in a ruined friendship into the close presence of the other partner, and the other partner (who had presumably not suffered a life crisis of fairly stupendous proportions) was standing by to pass some commentary of "I told you so" or "This is what happens when you forgo the wisdom of my counsel" or similar content. Which Vita was being either too polite or too secure to say aloud. But she must be thinking it. Wouldn't Grace have been thinking it?

Considering this now, she thought: *Possibly not*.

She took a breath. "Yes. A lot of uncertainty. I have a lot to sort out. I have a son. He's here with me. He's wonderful."

"So I understand." Vita smiled. "His grandfather certainly thinks so."

"He's going to the local middle school. Do you know the seventh-grade math class at the Housatonic Valley Regional School is actually *ahead* of Rearden's seventh-grade math class? I never realized what a snob I was."

Vita laughed. "I've been happily surprised, myself. One of my kids, we had to find a private school, but not because we felt she was being held back. She had some other issues, and we just needed something small. A few more eyes on her, you know? But I'm sure Rearden has set your son—"

"Henry," said Grace.

"Henry. Has set Henry up to do very well, wherever he goes. I thought, when I got to Tufts, this is how I know I've been well educated, because I was just able to jump in and start learning. You get the tools at a place like Rearden. What's it like being a parent there?" she asked with real curiosity.

Grace, in spite of herself, started grinning. "The most bizarre thing ever. Do you remember Sylvia Steinmetz?"

Vita nodded.

"She's the only one from our time who has a kid in my son's grade. It's been like having one other sane person in the room. Everyone else—oh, my God, they have so much money. And you've never seen such entitled people. You just can't imagine."

"Oh, I can." Vita sighed. "I still get the *New York Times*. Well, I'm not sorry to miss that. But I have to confess, I did get a pang when I realized my kids weren't going to Rearden. It was so wonderful, all that utopian stuff when we were kids. About the children of the workers. Remember?"

Grace, smiling, sang:

Here may each eager worker find
A workshop for a thoughtful mind!

She did remember.

And then she remembered how Jonathan had taken that, too, away. He had killed another Rearden parent. Henry was never going to go back to Rearden, it was brutally obvious, and Grace was never going to go back either. It had been one of the smaller losses by comparison, but it was mighty on its own.

She asked about Vita's kids, who were Mona, a junior in a private school in Great Barrington, who lived to swim, and Evan, who was fourteen and obsessed with robotics, and Louise, who was so cuddly from birth that her family nickname was "the Barnacle" and who was just now, at six, starting to show some interest in the outside world, especially if it was in the form of a horse. Vita was married to an attorney who specialized in environmental litigation. Of which, even after the Superfund cleanup, there was still plenty in Pittsfield.

"You're going to meet them," said Vita. "You're going to be sick of all of us."

"Aren't you mad at me?" Grace heard herself say out of the silence. It was an uncomfortable silence, true, but no more uncomfortable than any number of the silences that had come before. "I mean, sorry to state the obvious. I was mad. Are we no longer mad?"

Vita sighed. She was sitting on the other side of her desk, an oversize and unlovely piece of furniture, weighted down with stacks of folders in various hues. "I can't really answer that," she said finally. "I don't feel mad anymore. Or, if I am, I'm mad at myself. Actually I'm *really* mad at myself. I think I gave up way too easily. I let him run me out of town. I let you down, I think."

"You . . . ," Grace said, mystified. "What?"

"I let your husband, who upset me and worried me in a very profound way, from the moment I met him, separate me from my very close, very beloved friend, and I didn't put up nearly enough of a fight, or—as far as I can remember—ever let you know exactly how grave my concerns about him were. And for that I have not been able to forgive myself. And I would like to apologize for that, to you. Okay?"

Grace stared at her.

"I don't expect you to just snap your fingers and forgive me, don't worry. It's been kind of a big issue for me. Thank God I live in western Mass, where the hills are alive with therapists! I can't tell you how often I've been encouraged to contact you and articulate some of this. Obviously I didn't do it. Well, they say we make the worst patients."

She laughed briefly. Then she tried it again.

"It was much more than my just not liking him. That guy you dated freshman year, I thought he was a total loser, and I didn't have any problem telling you that."

"Nope," Grace confirmed, with a sigh.

"And I could see why you were drawn to Jonathan. He was magnetic, it was obvious. He was adorable, and so smart. But when he looked at me, and I mean even back on that first night, remember? When I came downstairs to look for you, and there you two were in the hallway? When he looked at me, it was like he was saying: *You watch yourself. This is mine.*"

Dumbstruck, Grace could only nod.

"So I felt, right from the beginning, that it was going to be a very, very delicate thing. *Clearly* adversarial. And first I just tried to make myself go back to the beginning with him. You know, start over and try to like him, or at least be neutral about it. But that didn't help. And then I tried to just wait and see if you started to feel any of the things I was feeling, just on your own. But that didn't happen either. And then I got kind of frantic about where you two were going. And I tried to talk to you about it."

"No, you didn't," Grace interrupted her, but even as she said this, she did remember one particular night the following spring, when they had gone out for Scorpion Bowls, of all things, because it was Vita's birthday and they'd never been, and it felt like something they at least ought to do once while they were living in Cambridge. That night—it was hard to get a grip on the details. It was hard to remember much at all, except, not surprisingly, the combined wallop of gin, rum, and vodka.

"Yes, I did," Vita said, not unkindly. "I'm not saying I tried *well*. But I did try. Maybe it's not the kind of thing you want to attempt in a state of inebriation, but without the inebriation I might not have tried at all. I asked you to tell me what it was you loved about him, and then I asked you to tell me, for every one of those things, how you knew they were true. And you said, more or less, because they just were. And I asked you why you thought he was so estranged from his family. Why he seemed to have no other friends. I asked you if you were worried about how quickly he'd kind of become the most important person in your life. I asked you if the reason he seemed so perfect for you was that you had made it really clear to him what perfect for you meant, and he gave you back exactly what you wanted, and I remember—"

"Wait," said Grace, "how is that wrong? To find someone who gives you what you need from him? Isn't that what we were looking for? Someone to do that?"

"Yes," Vita said, staring unhappily into her now empty mug. "That's what you said back then. That's just what you said. But in his case it wasn't that simple. There was nothing simple about him. Or maybe it just seems that clear in hindsight. I kept asking myself: *Why don't I like him?* She *likes him! She's smarter than I am.*"

"Vita, that's not true," Grace said, as if the point mattered at all.

"Well, I thought of you as smarter. I certainly felt pretty stupid at the time. I couldn't be clear with myself about what I thought was wrong, for one thing. Back then I couldn't. Jonathan looked great. He was at Harvard Medical School, for Christ's sake. He was going to be a pediatrician. He never drank or smoked, unlike us, if you'll recall."

"Oh, I recall."

"And he was all about you. I mean, from the word *Go*. All Gracie, all the time. So I had to start asking myself: *Is this about jealousy? Am I jealous of this?* I did have a boyfriend at the time, remember? He was there that night, too."

"Joe," Grace said simply. "Of course I remember."

"Well, it wasn't that. Then I even did the whole *Children's Hour* bit on myself. I started thinking: *Is there something I need to look at here?* But it wasn't that, either."

"Oh, Vita," Grace said. She couldn't help smiling at this.

"Sure. Just... I was frantic to understand how upset I was. I even went to the counseling center at Tufts, but they just said: 'Of course it hurts when your friend has less time for you.' But I knew that wasn't it. It was Jonathan. He made my heart pound, and not in a good way. And I just couldn't put my finger on it. I couldn't then," she added darkly. "I think I could now."

Now it was Grace's heart that was pounding. Now they were at the door, she thought. They were at the door, which was still closed, but it was opening, too, and behind the door was a word she had so far kept penned to a place beyond her own awareness. She wasn't ready for this. She didn't want this. She reached frantically for a way to make this not happen. She was not remotely ready for the fact of that word.

"Well," she said, inappropriately lighthearted, "hindsight is twenty-twenty. Live and learn."

"You know," Vita said carefully, "I'm sure this has been true of your patients every bit as much as mine, but sometimes when people come in they are so completely enmeshed in the 'Great Mistake' they feel they've made, that's led to whatever crisis they're in. That's how I always think of it: the 'Great Mistake.' Usually it's that first drink, or that first drug experience. Sometimes it's a relationship. Or the Great Mistake is listening to someone's bad advice. And whatever happens later, it all goes back to that moment or that decision, and they'd have been fine if only that one time they hadn't screwed up. And I always sit there thinking: *You know, that's how it always works in a story or a film, but real lives aren't like that.* It doesn't always come down to those two roads in a yellow wood, you know? And a lot of the time, no matter what you did back there at the crossroads, you'd have ended up wherever you are now. I'm not saying it wasn't a mistake, just that it's more complicated than that. You don't have to be angry with yourself for a decision that brought some wonderful things into your life. Your son, for example."

But Grace didn't grab the bait. Yes, her son was wonderful. No, she did not regret one single decision she had ever made, whatever attendant mass destruction it had caused, that had helped bring Henry into the world and her own life. But she was distracted by what Vita had just said, because what Vita had just said was very much not the same as her own therapeutic outlook, at least in her long-ago life as a therapist. Because she actually did see human lives as a series of all-important decisions, some of which might magnanimously extend you a second chance, but many of which emphatically would not. Those patients who had come to her already clutching their Great Mistake, more often than not they knew precisely what they had done. Sometimes they were a tiny bit off—sometimes the patient was already speeding down the wrong road in that selfsame yellow wood when they arrived at what they had decided was their Great Mistake—but in general, yes, her work as a therapist had often meant going back to some moment of perceived error, and it was a terribly important part of her work to show them just where that junction was. Because only by doing that and taking ownership of that did you get to move forward.

Was it blame? Well, *blame*, that was a little strong. Blame might be counterproductive. But the stringing together of one decision and the next and the one after that into a clear narrative, a story line for a life as it was being lived, did she believe in that?

Oh yes. Oh, absolutely.

It was why she had so often wished she could tell her patients, and tell them—if possible—before they found it necessary to *become* her patients, *Don't make the Great Mistake in the first place.*

Like I did, she thought now.

"Maybe I need a therapist," she said as if Vita had been following all of this.

"Maybe you do," said Vita mildly. "I certainly know some fantastic ones around here."

"I've never done it," Grace confessed. "They made us do some in graduate school, of course. But otherwise, I've never done it." She considered this for a minute. "Is that strange?"

"Strange?" Vita pursed her lips. "No stranger than a dentist who doesn't floss. I'm only slightly amazed."

"I gather you've been in therapy."

"Oh, a ton, yeah. Some are greater than others, but it's never not been helpful. Louise wouldn't even be alive if Pete and I hadn't found a really good couples therapist at one point. I'm so grateful for that." She looked squarely across the desk. "Gracie?"

Grace looked at her. Vita had called her Gracie. No one else ever had. When Vita had left her life, the nickname had left it, too, and that was sad. Grace's mother had once told her that her own mother, for whom Grace had been named, was also nicknamed Gracie.

"I made a Great Mistake," she said sadly. "I have no business telling anybody else what to do with their life. I can't imagine how I ever had the arrogance."

"Oh, that's ridiculous," Vita said. "People may need kindness from their therapists and they may need to learn how to be kinder to themselves, but they also need clarity. You are extraordinarily gifted at that. You're a great therapist."

Grace looked up at her sharply. "You can't possibly know that," she said. "By the time I was in grad school we weren't speaking to each other. How can you know what kind of a therapist I was?"

Vita swiveled in her heavy chair. As Grace watched, she reached out and put her hand on an object that was instantly familiar, just so unexpected that she could not understand why it was here, in this room. Or why she had not noticed it until now.

"This," said Vita, tossing the bound galley on the desktop, "is a very, very fine piece of work."

Jesus, Grace thought. She might have said it aloud. The galley was far from pristine; clearly, it had been read, possibly more than once. It was the first time she had ever seen a galley of her own book that had already been read, its pages turned, some corners bent down. How often had she imagined, as most authors must imagine, watching a stranger—on a subway, say—reading a book she had written. She had imagined her colleagues reading her book, wishing they'd thought of some of her ideas. She had imagined her teachers reading, learning something from her, the former student. Mama Rose, especially. She thought of Mama Rose in her bower, seated on one of her big kilim floor pillows, holding open the galley in her lap, nodding along and feeling persuaded by Grace, formerly her pupil, now like an equal, almost a teacher! That had not happened. None of it was going to happen now. "I don't understand. How do you have that?" she asked Vita.

"I do some reviewing for the *Daily Hampshire Gazette*, if they have a psychology book. This one, though, I'll be completely honest, I asked for. I was curious. But it blew me away, Gracie. And if you're asking do I agree with every single thing you wrote? No, of course not, any more than you'd agree with everything in a book I wrote. But what comes through is your care for your patients, and how smart you are about the ways we do ourselves in. This is so valuable."

She shook her head. "No, it isn't. It's just me telling people they screwed up. It's just me being a bitch."

Vita threw her head back and laughed, and her hair—that long, graying hair—moved over her black shirt in a kind of ripple of silver. She laughed for what seemed a very long time, certainly longer than the occasion warranted.

"This is funny?" Grace said at last.

"Yes, very funny. I was just thinking that, to women like us, it's more of an insult to be called nice than to be called a bitch."

"Women like us?"

"Tough, bitchy, Jewish, feminist, New York women. Like us. Yes?"

"Oh, well..." Grace smiled. "If you put it like *that*."

"And the truth is, the world is full of therapists who'll sit you down, take your money, massage your self-esteem, and send you on your way, without ever helping you understand how you helped create the circumstances that brought you here."

Grace nodded. That much was certainly true.

"They're like, 'Let's figure out who to blame, then we can blame them, then we're done.' Do we need more of these therapists? We do not. Do they help anyone? Well, sometimes. Anything is going to help some patients sometimes. But as someone who works with patients who are grappling with horrendously powerful addictions, let me tell you that giving them kindness alone is like giving them an overcooked noodle and sending them off to slay a dragon."

She leaned back in her swivel chair and braced her legs against the wall. There was a big dark mark there already.

"To tell you the truth, I think the kindness part is the easy part. Most people are basically kind already, so most therapists are basically kind, right off the bat. But there's so much more to being really able to help your patients. Maybe you—I mean you, Gracie—work best at the other end of the spectrum. *Super*. So maybe you get to cultivate a little more kindness, over your entire career, say. Then you can do that. But you have a lot to offer. When you're ready, I mean."

"What?" Grace frowned.

"When you're ready to start again. I can help you, if you want. I mean, I can introduce you to some people. I work with some group practices in Great Barrington, for example."

There was something about this that Grace was not fully processing. After a bit, she gave up and said, again: "What?"

Vita sat up straight in her chair. "I'd like to help. Is that all right?"

"Help me join a group practice in Great Barrington?" she said, mystified. Until that moment, she had not realized how completely she had detached from the idea of herself as a therapist. She had placed it on an ice floe and watched it float away, not even waving.

Which only meant that she herself was now stranded on some arctic edge, perhaps already beginning that long, drifting decline that had so fascinated Jonathan. In that story, the one he had loved, about the man and the dog and the lost fire, the man makes only a single panicked bolt for survival before giving up, letting the sweet numb cold pull him out of life, but the dog trots onward, thoughtlessly in search of another man and another fire. He isn't tortured about it. He's just programmed to live. That was Jonathan, she supposed. If one scenario didn't work out, you just trotted along through the snow to the next.

Grace looked over at Vita. She could not remember what the question had been or whether Vita had answered it. "I don't know," she managed. "I'm figuring things out."

Vita smiled. "No sweat. Open offer. I just... I hated to think you might be in need of an old friend, and not realize you had one just over the state line. It has to be gruesome, what you're dealing with, Grace."

After another moment she added, a little awkwardly, "I think I told you, I still get the *New York Times*."

Grace looked at her. She was looking for disapproval, for outright schadenfreude, even. But in Vita's face she saw only that much maligned human frailty known as kindness.

She couldn't think what to say to it.

How about: *Thank you*?

"Thank you," said Grace.

"No, no, don't thank me. I'm just so fucking grateful to be in the same room with you, I want to do whatever I can to keep you here. Metaphorically, of course. You probably have to be somewhere else."

Grace nodded. She did indeed have to be somewhere else. She had to go pick up Henry at the Housatonic Valley Regional School and take him for greasy pizza in Lakeville. She got to her feet, and almost immediately she felt horribly awkward. "Well, this was really nice."

"Oh, shut up," said Vita, coming around the desk. "Do I need to warn you this time? Or can I just go ahead and hug you?"

"No," Grace said. She wanted to laugh. "I still need a warning."

CHAPTER TWENTY

A Couple of Missing Fingers

Robertson Sharp III preferred not to meet in his office, for reasons Grace had no real wish to probe, but when he arrived—late—for their appointment, he had barely settled himself into the booth before he unburdened himself about the breadth of his conflict.

"I want you to know," he said gruffly, "that it is not the wish of the board that we speak to each other." Then, as if this were all that needed to be said, he picked up the menu and started examining it.

The menu was vast. The place he had chosen was the Silver Star on 65th and Second, a coffee shop so eternal that she had once broken up with a boyfriend in one of the booths on the other side of the room. There was a long countertop where you could get a serious, if stodgily old-fashioned, drink (like a highball or a gimlet) and, just inside the door, a standing glass case full of revolving cakes and colossal éclairs and napoleons.

Grace said nothing in response; she didn't think it was necessary, and also she didn't want to be antagonistic if she didn't have to be. He was doing her a favor, even if his board hadn't objected. That he was seeing her at all—the wife of a former employee, a terminated employee!—she supposed she appreciated. Though she also wanted to kick him under the table.

Sharp was a big man, long-legged, well enough dressed in a blue bow tie and a shirt of narrow brown and white stripes, over which he wore his very clean, very pressed white coat. His name—his real name, not the one Jonathan had given him—was embroidered on the breast pocket, out of which peeked two pens and a cell phone. Then, amiably enough, as if his previous comment belonged to an entirely different encounter, he said: "What are you going to have?"

"Oh, maybe a tuna fish sandwich. You?"

"That sounds good." He slapped the heavy laminated menu shut and dropped it on the table.

Then they looked at each other.

Robertson Sharp, known for years within her own household as "the Turd," Jonathan's attending physician for the first four of his years at Memorial and later the chief of pediatrics, seemed to have momentarily forgotten why he was here. Then he seemed to remember again.

"I was asked not to meet with you."

"Yes," Grace said mildly. "You mentioned that."

"But I thought if you were motivated to reach out to me personally, you certainly have a right to whatever insight I can offer. Obviously, this has been a horrendous experience for you. And..." He seemed to search his own database for any available information but came up with nothing. "Your family."

"Thank you," Grace said. "It has been, but we're doing all right."

This seemed more true than not, at least as far as her "family" was concerned. Henry, bizarrely enough, now officially loved his school and had made a little cell of friends, all of whom had a passionate grasp of Japanese anime and the film school oeuvre of Tim Burton. He had contacted, on his own, the local baseball league and was now eagerly awaiting his opportunity to try out for something called the Lakeville Lions, and he even seemed to have adjusted to the cold, though he had made a request, this morning as they'd driven into the city, for a few more of his warmer clothes from home. It had taken longer to get into Manhattan than she'd planned, however, and she'd had to drop Henry at her father and Eva's and come right here.

A waiter appeared, a thick Greek man who could not possibly have emitted less warmth. Grace, in addition to her sandwich, asked for tea, and that arrived a moment later, the bag still wrapped in its paper envelope at the edge of the saucer.

Even in those few minutes she had decided that Dr. Sharp might be very mildly autistic. Brilliant, no doubt, but with marked social deficiencies. He did not meet her gaze except when thoroughly necessary, and then only to emphasize a point of his own, not to better take in anything she might be saying. To be fair, she wasn't saying much. She didn't have to. Sharp, as Jonathan himself had always insisted, had a great love for the contents of his own mind and the voice that shared those contents with the world. He began, without the slightest sensitivity, to discuss what he had long considered "the problem" of Jonathan Sachs, MD, and as she listened to him—tried very hard to listen to him—it was all she could do not to leap to Jonathan's defense.

There is no Jonathan left to defend was what she told herself. This did not make her feel any better.

"I didn't want to hire him. You can imagine the caliber of applicants we see."

"Of course," Grace said.

"I wanted to overrule the chief resident. The chief resident wanted him. The guy was just swept away."

Grace frowned. "Okay," she finally said.

"And I got that. I really did. You met Sachs, you just thought: *Wow, this guy's got a personality and a half.* And let me tell you something. You can't be any kind of doctor and not have the most profound respect for the power of placebo. Lots of things can be the placebo. Personality can be the placebo. I was trained by a surgeon. This was in Austin, where I was a resident. He specialized in a very, very difficult operation, on a kind of tumor that lodges in the aorta. You know the aorta?"

Then he looked at her, more or less for the first time since he'd sat down. This point, evidently, was important enough for that.

"Yes, sure."

"Right. So people are coming to Austin, Texas, from all over the world to have this particular surgeon operate on them, and they're right to do it, because he's one of the best surgeons on the planet for this particular operation. And here's my point. This surgeon is missing two fingers on his left hand. Crushed by a stone when he was a kid. Climbing accident."

"Okay," Grace said. She was trying to follow, trying to connect what he was saying to what she imagined they were here to discuss, but also wondering if she could stop him now. She didn't really care about a surgeon in Austin, Texas.

"Now. How many people you think ever looked at their surgeon's hand and thought: *You know what? I think I prefer the hand that's going inside my heart to remove a tumor to have all its fingers* and went and got another surgeon?"

Grace waited. Then she realized he was actually waiting for her.

"I don't know. None?" She sighed.

"Not one. Not one patient, or family member. He had that personality. He had so much personality it was like a drug of its own. Placebo! You see my point? I never had that."

No shit, thought Grace.

"Not that that means anything about whether the science is there, the diagnostic insights. Those were the only things we thought about a generation ago. But your husband happens to come along at a very particular time. The patients have been trying to say something to us about it for years and years, and now, for the first time, we're trying to listen to them. I mean"— he laughed, mainly to himself—"we're *trying* to listen. We're trying to think *patient* care, not just disease care, if that makes sense to you."

Did it? Grace wondered. But he wasn't looking at her, so she didn't have to say.

"In the eighties, early nineties, we're doing all this navel-gazing about what makes a good doctor and a great hospital. You know, the patient or the patient's family member shouldn't have to go running down the hallway after the doctor to ask him what he's talking about, or what it means for the patient. And for pediatrics it's like that times a thousand. They don't have just themselves to worry about, they're worried about how the child's going to react to what the doctor's saying, or his body language. And we heard it forever from parents, and we were trying to think about it in a new way. And then here's Jonathan Sachs from Harvard."

He was looking, of course, not at her as he said this, but across the room at the waiter, who was approaching with identical platters. He never took his eyes off the waiter and leaned back as the plate approached. Grace said thank you.

"So I let the chief resident talk me into it. And big surprise, Sachs is hugely popular with the patients. They love him. We get these devoted letters. 'He was the only doctor who took the time to really connect with our child and us.' 'The others didn't even know our names after four months in the ward.' One guy told how Sachs bought his son a stuffed animal on his birthday. So okay, I'm fine with being wrong. I don't need to be the authority on every single thing. There's more to being a great doctor than just knowing what to do," he said. He was chewing his dill pickle with less than dainty bites. "When you have a sick child it's very comforting to feel there's a strong personality in charge. I've known a number of very brilliant diagnosticians, very, very adept at formulating a treatment plan. They didn't communicate very well, not with the parents and especially not with the children." He looked actually thoughtful when he said this, and Grace marveled at his imperviousness to his own deficiencies. That in itself was something of a survival strategy, she thought. "You give a parent of a sick child a choice between the doctor who maybe won't look at them and the one who sits them down and says, 'Mr. and Mrs. Jones, I am here to make your child's life better.' What do you think they're going to pick? You've got kids, right?"

Now he was looking at her. Now she was the one who would have loved to look away.

"Yes. We have a son. Henry."

"Right." He plunged on, one hand holding his sandwich aloft, just to the left of his mouth. "So, say Henry's in the hospital. He's got... let's say, a tumor. Brain tumor, let's say."

Grace, feeling weak, just stared at him.

"What kind of doctor would you want? You want a doctor who connects, right?"

She would have said: *The one who will heal him, fuck the personality*. But she was quaking just from the briefest idea of Henry with a brain tumor on a ward in Memorial, and livid that Sharp—Sharp-the-Turd indeed—had so wantonly put her through it.

"Well...," she said, playing for time.

"But the truth is, if you're thinking in terms of the overall performance of the hospital team, which is a sum of everyone bringing their individual talents together to serve the patient, then we're better off if we have a Sachs as well as somebody like a Stu Rosenfeld or Ross Waycaster. He came in the same year. Stu did, too. He was Jonathan's supervisor."

"I remember," Grace said, trying to breathe through it. She took an experimental bite of her sandwich. It was heavy on the mayonnaise, but she'd expected that. "So you're saying Jonathan had some sort of... deficiency. Like being short some fingers. But he had such a big personality people overlooked it?"

"He had a big deficiency," Sharp said, sounding affronted. "Much bigger than a couple of missing fingers. I'm not telling you anything you don't know. This is *your* field now. Yes?"

No, Grace thought. But she nodded anyway. "How did you make up your mind about him?"

"Oh..." He shrugged, as if this were the least important part. "By the end of the second or third year, I'm hearing stuff. Not from the patients, or the family members. They're crazy about him, like I said. But I'm not the only one who's on edge around this guy. The nurses don't like him. A couple came to me right before he started his residency, but it wasn't anything you could base an action on. I didn't think I could even put it in the file. I just wrote myself an e-mail about it and hoped I'd never have to come back to it."

"What—," she said sharply, and then stopped until he had to look at her. "What was the complaint?"

"Oh, nothing earth-shattering. He was arrogant, blah blah. This is not the first time I've heard that about a doctor, from a nurse."

Grace surprised herself by laughing. "No, I suppose not."

"Flirtatious with some of the women. They didn't like it. Well, I think some of them didn't like it, and maybe some of them did."

Even at this, she noted, he didn't bother looking at her.

"But nothing concrete to my way of thinking, so I just let it go. And look, I've got other big personalities on my service. You know, shrinking violets don't become oncologists, at least not here. We have whole generations who never got the God complex memo, they're just grandfathered in, all over the hospital. The field!" he insisted, as if she'd challenged him.

But then, without being able to help herself, she did just that.

"I don't think Jonathan had a God complex. Is that what you're saying?"

"No, no..." He shook his head. "Well, I might have thought so at the beginning, but I watched him for a long time. Mainly because I had to, because he was a hot spot—he was someone my attention kept being drawn to. And I started to realize, here was a guy who didn't just *behave* differently to different people, he *was* a different person depending who he was with. Stu Rosenfeld never had a bad word to say. He covered your husband's patients for years."

"They covered each other," Grace corrected.

"No. Somebody else covered Rosenfeld. Different people—Sachs got out of it somehow. He wasn't covering anyone, not for years, but I never heard about it from Rosenfeld. He had a massive blind spot about your husband, like a lot of the others. I'm telling you, I got to be fascinated with the guy. I almost got to like him."

It wasn't mutual, Grace thought. She picked up one of the potato chips on her plate, looked at it, and put it back down.

"But you know what made me finally make up my mind was that story in *New York* magazine, for the Best Doctors. You know what he said?"

Of course Grace knew what he'd said. She'd read the short piece many times. But that didn't seem relevant.

"He said it was a privilege to be allowed into someone's life at the worst moment, when they wish they could tell everybody to go away. But they can't do that, because these are people who might be able to save their child's life. And how he's honored and humbled. And I read that and I said: *Hah!* That was it. Except he wasn't humbled, I knew that much. He was something, but he wasn't humbled."

Grace just looked at him. "I don't know what you mean," she finally said.

"I mean, he fed off that situation, of being at the center of intense emotions. He got a big charge from it. Even if he couldn't help the patient. Even if he couldn't *save* the patient, you know what I'm saying? He didn't care about that part. It was all the emotion coming at him. I think emotion fascinated him. Well," he said with real nonchalance, "you're the shrink. You know all about it."

She was finding it hard to concentrate. She made herself look hard at Robertson Sharp III. She found herself looking at the space between his eyebrows, which was sort of an eyebrow of its own. It was not a thing of beauty, but it was very interesting to look at.

"I don't know why people think you can't have a psychopath in a hospital setting. Why should we be immune? Doctors are such saints?" He laughed. "I don't think so." He wasn't looking at her. It wasn't an important point in the way that the aorta had been an important point, she supposed. And he was hardly the type to notice that she was having some difficulty. For one thing, she could not breathe properly. The word, so blithely spoken, had pierced her like a spike. And then he used it again. "A psychopath is a person. A physician is a person. Presto!" Sharp said. He was trying to signal the waiter. He wanted something, apparently.

"We're supposedly healers. That's supposed to make us great humanitarians—just one assumption on top of another, and it all adds up to complete bullshit. Anybody's spent time in a hospital you know it's full of the biggest sons of bitches you'll ever meet in your life!" He laughed a little. Apparently this nugget of wisdom never got old. "Maybe they happen to be very adept at making a sick body better, but they're still sons of bitches. I once had a colleague—I won't say who. He's not at Memorial now. Actually, he might not be a physician anymore, which isn't a bad thing, probably. We were in a meeting once with the director of volunteers in pediatrics, long meeting about setting policy for the playrooms and entertainers. Afterwards I said something to him about what a long meeting it was. You know what he says? 'Oh, I love do-gooders because they always do me so much good.' That's all he says."

For the first time since she'd sat down, it occurred to Grace that she could actually go. Anytime she wanted, she could leave.

"I think... Jonathan cared about his patients," she said carefully, though why she bothered she didn't have the faintest idea.

"Well, maybe yes, maybe no. Maybe we don't get to understand what 'cared about' means to somebody like Sachs." He took another monster bite of his sandwich and chewed like a ruminant. "I'll tell you one thing. He didn't care about his colleagues, by any definition. He moved them around like chess pieces. He liked a lot of drama. If he got bored, he'd tell somebody about something another person had said, or who was getting it on with somebody else. Whether any of it was true, who knows? He couldn't be part of any team, anything with a common object. Especially if there was somebody involved who he didn't like, and he didn't like a lot of people. He put energy into his patient care, because he got something from that. He put a lot of energy into the family members. A lot. And some of the people he worked with, if they made his life easier. But he never paid much attention to other people if he couldn't use them, even if it was someone he saw every day. No return on the investment. So there were a lot of folks he didn't really notice, but they still noticed him. They found him very interesting, watching him operate. And you know, it takes a lot of effort to hold up the mask he had." He seemed to consider. "Mask would not be the scientific term, I guess."

It wasn't. But she got the idea.

"And those people saw a lot. All the nasty bits. The comments he made, the way he just froze you out. If he was supposed to be in a meeting and he didn't think he should have to be there, he seemed to find a way to disrupt it somehow, so it would all end up taking even more time, which never made any sense to me. And all those co-workers he was ignoring, if they hadn't felt so dissed by him, they might not have been paying such close attention. I think that's what did him in, actually."

Sharp paused to dig his fork into the now soggy paper cup of coleslaw. It dripped as it rose to his mouth.

"It was an attending in radiology who came to me about it the first time. I had Sachs come in for a meeting. He was extraordinarily good-natured the whole time. He said he was going through a difficult period at home, and it wasn't something he'd like to see get around the hospital. He told me he and the woman had already decided to stop seeing each other." He had set down his fork. His fingers, all ten of them, were on the tabletop. Grace saw that they were moving, as if he were playing, silently and only in his mind, a fairly complicated piano piece. "But then it happened again, with somebody on the nursing staff. I said, 'Look, trust me, I have no interest in intruding into your life. This is none of my business. But you've got to keep it out of the hospital.' I mean, you can't object to that, right? And he always apologized and gave me some reason why it had happened and he was taking care of it. Once I had to call him in and he claimed he was being stalked by somebody. He wanted my advice on how to handle it. We spent the whole meeting going over hospital protocol and whether he ought to be making a formal complaint, after which he tells me what a great role model I am and if he's ever a chief he hopes he can provide the kind of leadership I do, blah blah. Utter crap, but then again, when he said it something in me sort of sat still and listened. So again, he took care of it, or at least I didn't hear anything else about it. But then he had something with Rena Chang. Dr. Chang. And I had to pay attention to that, because her supervisor came to me about it. But then she left. I never had to meet with him about that one. She went somewhere in the Southwest. Santa Fe, maybe?"

Sedona, thought Grace, shuddering.

"I heard she had a baby," said Robertson Sharp III.

"Excuse me," Grace said politely. If she hadn't heard her own voice, she might not have noticed that she'd spoken. Then she was on her feet, staggering across the room. Then she was in the bathroom, on the toilet, with her head between her knees.

Oh God, she thought. *Oh God, oh God, oh God.* Why had she asked for this? Why, why, had she wanted to know? Her mouth was full of the awful taste of tuna. Her head was pounding and pounding.

Rena Chang. She of the smudge stick. She of the "parallel healing strategies." Jonathan had laughed about her. They both had laughed about her. How long ago had that been? She tried to concentrate. She tried. But it wouldn't come. Before Henry? No, it had to be after. Had Henry been a baby? Had he been in school? She couldn't even get her mind around why this should matter. She had no idea how long it took her to get out of the bathroom.

When she got back, the waiter had removed both their plates. Grace slid back into the booth and sipped her now chilly tea. His phone was now on the tabletop. He had perhaps done a bit of business while he was waiting.

"Dr. Sharp," said Grace, "I know Jonathan had a disciplinary hearing in 2013. I'd like to know more about that."

"He had a few disciplinary hearings," Sharp said a little gruffly. It was rather late in the day for him to start getting gruff with her, thought Grace. "One for accepting a monetary gift from a patient's father. Allegedly accepting," he modified. "The father declined to speak to the hospital attorney. It had to be dropped. Then we had another one about the incident with Waycaster. In the stairwell."

Where he had tripped, in other words. He had tripped in the stairwell, chipping his tooth, which had had to be repaired and was still, wherever it was at this very moment, a slightly different color from the teeth on either side. She assumed. Except that he had not tripped, she knew that now.

"Waycaster," she said.

"Ross Waycaster. He was Sachs' supervisor at the beginning. I thought they got on okay. I never heard anything from either one of them about a conflict. But he confronted Sachs directly, about the situation with the Alves mother. It turned into a real scene. Four or five people saw it, and Waycaster had to have stitches afterwards. Even then I had to insist he file a complaint. There was a hearing about that, I can assure you. And then a separate one about the relationship itself."

And here, finally, he stopped. He looked up at her, as if he were truly noticing her for the first time.

"I assume you know about that relationship."

"I do," Grace said solemnly, but she was marveling at him. That he had even asked! After the bludgeoning death of the woman in question, the disappearance of the man in question, and the assigned moniker (courtesy of the *New York Post*) that had emerged from the tabloid foam in the wake of that disappearance, it would be stretching credulity indeed to imagine she did not. The moniker was "Murder Doc," and it had finally wormed its way through to Grace's awareness the previous week, via an AP story in the *Berkshire Record* (which was printed right next to an innocent local feature on lowering your heating bill). It was in this story that she also read, for the first time, that she—Dr. Grace Sachs, *sic*—had been eliminated as a suspect in the murder of Malaga Alves. It ought to have given her some comfort, but the concurrent revelation that she had once been under suspicion—no matter how briefly—quashed her relief. "The police haven't shared many details with me," she told him.

He shrugged. He had no knowledge of what the police had or hadn't done.

"So if there's anything you'd like to share with me, I'd be glad to hear it," she said, spelling it out for him.

Sharp pursed his lips. It made little difference to him, obviously.

"The patient was an eight-year-old boy with Wilms' tumor. Dr. Sachs was the primary doctor. The mother was here every day. One of the nursing staff came to me. She had concerns."

After a moment, Grace prodded him. "Concerns."

"They weren't discreet. They were not even trying. The RNs were extremely upset about it. Particularly after the warning he'd got. So I called him in again. I said this is going to stop or I'm going to file a complaint, and it's going to a full disciplinary hearing. This is back last fall sometime. Fall of 2012. Maybe . . . November? And he promised it was already over. He said—I think he said he was going through a difficult time. He was dealing with some things in therapy, and acting out. *Acting out*," Sharp said with distaste. "I wonder where he pulled that out."

Grace, for her part, did not wonder.

"But whatever he said he was going to do, it didn't happen. The next thing I was aware of, he and Waycaster got into it in the stairwell. But there were witnesses. As I said," he assured her.

"Yes," Grace said mildly. "You did."

"And injuries. There were injuries."

She nodded. She didn't think it was worth reassuring him anymore.

"So. Two separate incidents. Two separate hearings. But it was the latter one that was grounds for termination. And even then, I want you to know, I offered him an option. I said, 'Look, you could go into a treatment program. Residential program. You couldn't get away with outpatient for a situation like this.' I thought I might be able to persuade the committee to accept a medical leave. I know we could have found a way it wouldn't read as termination. Not that I thought he was somehow going to get cured," Sharp said. "I mean, they say it's not curable, don't they? Don't *you*?" he corrected himself. He was deferring to her professionally, she supposed.

"You did your job," she said. It was as far as she was willing to go.

"As I said, it wasn't a question of his skill as a physician. He was a talented guy. He had all the nuts and bolts to be a great doctor. He made his own position here impossible."

And then she felt her cell phone vibrate inside her jacket pocket. It was her father, or at least his home phone. "Hello?" Grace said, grateful for the interruption.

"Mom?"

"Hi, honey."

"Can we go to a movie? We can go at three thirty. The one I want's playing on Seventy-Second and Third."

"Oh. Okay. Grandpa's taking you?"

"Grandpa and Nana. Is it okay?"

"Of course," she said. "What time's it out?"

It was out at six. They were going to stay at her father's tonight. It was the first time they had been back to the city since that day in December.

When she set it back down, she noticed Sharp actually looking at her. Maybe it had taken her own distraction to make him notice her presence.

"Your daughter?"

"My son. Henry."

Who doesn't have a brain tumor, she nearly added.

"He's going to the movies with his grandparents."

"Jonathan didn't talk about his parents," Sharp said. His gaze had wandered off again. "I didn't find out till last year he grew up a town away from me on Long Island. He was from Roslyn. I grew up in Old Westbury," he said with meaning, though whatever he meant by it was entirely wasted on Grace. To a Manhattanite, Long Island existed as a single entity of Long Island–ness: Gradations of any kind were simply not processed.

"You know," Sharp said, "that Best Doctors thing, they usually come through the hospital. They ask the press office to suggest a few people. They poll the physicians all over the city, of course, but they always work through the press office. Not this time. First time the hospital heard anything about it was when the copy arrived in the office. They were furious, I can tell you. I get a call asking, Did I know about this? Of course I didn't know. Why would *New York* magazine call Jonathan Sachs one of the best doctors? I mean, usually there's some national or international achievement, yeah? So I'm baffled like everybody else. And then one of the attendings comes in and shuts the door, and she tells me there's a connection. Somebody at the magazine is the aunt of a girl whose doctor is Jonathan Sachs. And she tells me for a long time she's been struggling, whether or not to say something. But she thinks now somebody should know about it, and the relationship is over the line, she says."

"Wait," Grace said. "I don't—"

"The *relationship*," Sharp said testily. "Between Sachs and the family members of the patient. Specifically the aunt. Yes?"

Grace looked down into her teacup and her head swam with

nausea. That she had asked for this meeting, that she had called this upon herself, amazed her. What on earth was the point of it? Had Jonathan scuttled forever Robertson Sharp-the-Turd's cherished dream of being one of *New York* magazine's Best Doctors? Was she supposed to apologize because his subordinate—her own husband—had cheated him by fucking the editor?

She took her wallet from her purse and set it on the table. She didn't think there was anything else.

"No, no," said Sharp. "Happy to." He looked around for the waiter. "I hope this has been helpful," he said formally.

Afterward, on the sidewalk in front of the Silver Star, she let him shake her hand.

"I'll have to testify, of course," he announced. "If they find him. If they get him back. It's the right thing to do."

"All right," Grace said.

"What part of our internal case against him becomes part of the state case, that's up to the attorneys. I don't really understand it." He shrugged.

I don't care, Grace thought, and she was amazed to discover, for that moment, at least, that she really didn't. They walked off in opposite directions: Sharp heading north, back to the hospital. Grace, at first, had no idea where she was going. Not to her own apartment, which she couldn't face. Not anywhere in particular, because there was nowhere in particular she wanted to go. But as she came closer and closer to the street where her car was parked, she found herself looking at her watch. Henry's movie started at three thirty, ended at six. That was a lot of time on a Saturday, with little traffic in the city and a car waiting. It was enough time to go nearly anywhere, even a place that made no sense. So, without giving herself enough of an opportunity to really examine the idea, let alone to change her mind, that's where she decided to go.

CHAPTER TWENTY-ONE

THE CABOOSE

Only once, in all the years of their marriage, had he taken her "home," and then it had been essentially a drive-by. They had been coming back from the Hamptons one autumn weekend, Grace pregnant, Jonathan in flight from his punishing schedule as a resident, and they were relaxed, full of sleep and clam chowder and the salty wind from the beach at Amagansett; he had not wanted to stop, but she had made him. She had been curious, always, though reluctant to dredge up the unhappiness that seemed to accompany any memory of his father, mother, or brother. She wanted to see the house where he had been raised and from which he had escaped: to Hopkins and Harvard and Grace herself, and into the new family they were making. "Come on," she had pleaded. "Just show it to me."

So they had left the LIE and gone off into the narrower streets of the older part of the town, where the houses came from that post-war surge of the 1950s and '60s and were compact, not like the newer exploded palaces of wings and levels. It was the prettiest part of the fall and the leaves still crowded the maple trees everywhere, and she remembered thinking, as he made his way through the obviously familiar intersections, that it wasn't as horrible as she'd imagined. She'd imagined a barren neighborhood of neglected, unsightly homes, each housing a lonely child or a punishing parent, or indeed both. She'd imagined an intense air of hopelessness, out of which her adored husband had had to catapult himself, purely alone and unsupported. Instead, she'd found herself in a pleasant neighborhood of tidy smaller houses, with beds of mums in front and jungle gyms visible behind.

But of course, none of that mattered, and terrible childhoods could take place on lovely streets and in well-kept homes. Obviously, for Jonathan, at least one had, and that afternoon he had not wanted to be told how unexpectedly pretty everything was or how well somebody seemed to have maintained the front lawn of the house on Crabtree Lane, where a station wagon was parked in the carport. He did not want to step out and see if his mother or father (or the brother, Mitchell, who lived in the basement) might be home, or show Grace the room where he had endured each awful day of the first eighteen years of his life, until he could get on the train to college and medicine and her. He drove slowly around the corner and slowly down the street in front of the house he'd grown up in, declining even to stop the car, refusing to say much of anything about it. And all the rest of the way home he was silent and grim, the freedom and peace of their Hamptons weekend utterly undermined. That was what his family had done to him. That was how they still destroyed his happiness, his sense of peace within himself. She would never suggest such a detour again.

Surprisingly, though, with only that single viewing, she found it terribly simple to find the right exit now, and the first intersection and the second, until the street sign for Crabtree itself was plainly visible overhead. It was only four thirty, and the afternoon light was already going, and it only just now occurred to her that turning up like this was in its way a hostile act, though she did not think she felt any hostility to her husband's family, or if she did, she no longer knew how much of that hostility she could trust to be real, or even appropriate. She didn't know anything. She didn't know anything anymore about the man she had fallen in love with and lived with for eighteen years and made a child with. Except that he did not exist.

At the curb, she pulled over and looked at the house, letting the engine idle. It was white with black shutters and a red door, and a narrow walkway curving past the carport, where this time two cars were parked. The lights were already on inside, and even from this far away she could feel a sense of warmth from the colors inside: green curtains and rust-colored furniture. A body moved past the kitchen window, indistinguishable, and from the single dormer window protruding from the roof there came the blue flash of a television. It was a very small house in which to raise two boys, she was thinking. That little upstairs bedroom might have been Jonathan's. Or it might have been Mitchell's. Perhaps it was Mitchell's still, she thought, not without resentment, though why she'd resent a man in his thirties still living at home she couldn't imagine.

Then a hand knocked the glass near her ear, and Grace jumped.

Her foot went to the gas even as her hand went to the window switch. It was an instant confrontation between politeness and flight.

Then she noticed that the knock had been attached to a woman much older than her and wearing a massive down coat, clutched at the throat. "Hello?" this person said. And Grace moved the window switch and the window rolled down.

"Can I help you?" the woman said.

"Oh, no, thank you. I just..."

But she could not think what she had just.

"I just was driving..."

The woman looked at her intently. She seemed to be struggling with something.

"Why don't you people go away?" She sounded not precisely

angry, but exasperated. "Really, what is there to see here? It's ridiculous. I don't know what you get out of it."

Grace frowned at her. She was still parsing this.

"Don't you have anything better to do? Do you want them to feel worse than they do already? I'm writing down your license plate."

"No *don't*," Grace said, horrified. "I'll leave. I'm sorry. I'm going."

"Carol?" another voice said. A man had come out of Jonathan's house. He was tall—much taller than Jonathan. She recognized him instantly.

"I'm taking her license," said the woman in the down coat.

But he was already coming closer.

"I'm leaving!" said Grace. "Would you just...please move your hand, okay? I need to close the window."

"Grace?" the man said. "It's Grace, isn't it?"

"It's who?" said the woman named Carol.

"I'm sorry!" said Grace.

"No, don't leave!" It was Mitchell, Jonathan's brother. She had not seen him for years. She had not seen him since her own wedding day, or more accurately after her wedding day, in the photographs. Now he was standing beside her and talking to her as if they actually knew each other.

"It's all right," he told the other woman. "I know her. It's okay."

"It's certainly not okay!" the woman objected. She seemed to be taking the intrusion more personally than Mitchell. "First all those newspeople, and now the peepers. They think you're keeping him in the basement? These people haven't done anything wrong," she said unkindly, directing this last statement to Grace.

"You're right," said Mitchell. "But this is different. It's all right. She's invited."

I am not, Grace thought. She glared at him, but he was still comforting the neighbor. "No, I was just...I was out here anyway and I thought I'd come by, but I wasn't going to bother you."

"Please," he said warmly. "Please come. It would mean a lot to

Mom." He waited another moment. Then he said with an air of finality: "Please."

She gave in. She turned off the engine and tried to steady herself. Then she opened the door, forcing both of them to step back. "My name is Grace," she told the woman in the down coat. "I'm sorry I upset you."

Carol favored her with one final look of bitter disapproval and turned away. Grace watched her retreat to her own small brick house opposite the Sachses'.

"Sorry about that," said Mitchell. "It was very difficult here, at least until the middle of January. Lots of news vans, and cars just parked at the foot of the driveway. There hasn't been much since then, but sometimes people slow down in front of the house. Mom and Dad were in such bad shape about everything, they couldn't have a real conversation with the neighbors about what was happening. Not that they'd have chosen that one to unburden themselves to, just between us."

Just between us? She had never exchanged a single word with him, ever, in all the years they had been nominally related. But what he had said also made perfect sense. So she said: "Yes. Of course."

"It's a close street. I think a lot of these people just feel so bad about everything, but they can't bring it up as long as my parents don't, so it just comes out in this kind of little skirmish. Carol is trying to be helpful. Look, please come inside."

"I didn't want to bother you," said Grace. "Actually, I don't know what I did want. But not to bother you."

"You're not bothering us. Look, it's too cold to stand here."

"All right," she said, giving in. Forgetting that she was on a residential street in Long Island, she locked her car door. Then she followed him up the walk.

"Mom?" Mitchell called, holding the door back for Grace.

Jonathan's mother was standing in the doorway to the kitchen. She was a tiny woman—Jonathan had inherited his slightness, his narrowness, from her—with a thin face and indigo circles beneath her dark eyes. She looked far older than the last time Grace had seen her, in the hospital when Henry was born. She also looked far older than the age Grace knew she was—sixty-one. She looked terrified, though whether to see anyone or Grace in particular, Grace couldn't have said.

"Look who I found," said Mitchell. She hoped he knew what he was doing.

"Well," said a voice from across the room. Jonathan's father, David, was standing at the foot of the stairs. "Hello!" And then, when she couldn't respond even to that, he said: "Grace?"

"Yes." She nodded, just to confirm. "I apologize for the intrusion. I was nearby." And she stopped herself there. As if it were possible they didn't already know she was lying.

"Is Henry with you?" said Jonathan's mother. Her name was Naomi, but Grace had never had the opportunity (or, to be honest, the inclination) to be on a first-name basis with her. There was a thread of pain in her voice that was visceral, but then she recovered. Who they were, any of them, Grace didn't know, only that they had had a hand in making Jonathan. They were not good people, obviously. Or perhaps no longer so obviously.

She shook her head. "He's in the city with his . . . with my father. We're not . . . we've been living somewhere else." She wondered if any of them were following this. She was barely following it herself. "I wasn't nearby," she heard herself say aloud. "To be honest, I don't know why I came."

"Well, maybe we can enlighten you!" said David, the father. And without warning he took three great steps across the floor from the foot of the stairs and embraced her, enclosing her shoulders with one long arm and her lower back with the other and pressing his rough cheek against her ear. She was so stunned that she could not even step back or aside. Unlike Vita, he had not issued a warning.

"Dad . . ." Mitchell laughed. "Don't smother her."

"I'm not," said his father into Grace's ear. "I'm making up for lost time. This is my grandson's mother."

"Your grandson you've never seen since the day he was born," Naomi said with palpable bitterness.

"Not for lack of trying," said David, finally releasing her and stepping back. "The point is, Grace," he said, addressing her directly, "whyever you came, I'm very, very glad to see you. And when Naomi recovers she'll be able to show you how glad she is also. But until that happens, you might need to give her a little space."

"More space?" Jonathan's mother said. "More than the last eighteen years? More than my grandson's entire life?"

He shrugged. "Like I said, she might need a little time to recover. Let's have some coffee. Come on into the kitchen." He beckoned. "Naomi, we've got Entenmann's, don't we?"

"Are we on Long Island?" Mitchell said, grinning. "This is how you know you're on Long Island, somebody offers you coffee and Entenmann's. Come on, Grace. Coffee okay?"

"Okay," said Grace. "Thank you."

In the kitchen, an unreconstructed 1970s Harvest Gold décor with a plain, Formica-topped table, he pulled out a chair for her and went to make coffee. His parents followed, and David sat across the table while Naomi, still brimming with potent silence, opened the refrigerator and extracted milk and the blue-and-white box. The room was very clean—extraordinarily clean, Grace thought—but it was also obviously a kitchen that saw real use. The shelf over the stove held spices in little glass jars, each with a label and a handwritten date. The pots hanging from a pothook on one of the decorative beams were heavy stainless steel and dull with use. Grace looked up at her mother-in-law as the box landed on the table. Naomi gave back nothing. Jonathan had always said how cold she was. A terrible mother. Obviously he had been telling the truth about that, at least. He hadn't mentioned anything about her cooking, though.

Mitchell took a knife and cut into the coffee cake. It was an almond ring, dribbled with white frosting. He passed her a piece without asking, and without answering she took it.

"This must have been terrible for you," said David, accepting his own piece. "We've thought of you, many, many times. I want you to know that. And we did try to call, a couple of times, but no one answered the phone in New York. We imagined you'd gone away, very sensibly."

She nodded. It felt so unutterably strange to be talking to them at all, let alone about this. About their own son and what he'd done! And what that had done to her, and Henry. And still, they seemed so . . . unresponsible. For any of it. Could they possibly ignore, even now, how they had to have caused this, some part of this, by their neglect of Jonathan, their own unexamined addictions (Naomi's alcoholism, David's prescription drug abuse), their blatant preference for Mitchell, who had never finished college or had more than a temporary, entry-level job and was still, at his age, living right here at home? Was some acknowledgment of *that* going to be part of this kaffeeklatsch, this family reunion in suburbia? Looking at the three of them, she caught for a brief moment the wake of Jonathan's own resentment and sadness about where he had come from, here at the table with a family that ought to have acted more like a family but hadn't. How harmed he had been by these people. And that had *not* been his fault.

"I took Henry to Connecticut," she told them after a minute. "We have a house there. It's a summer house."

"Where the wedding was," Mitchell said brightly. He was pouring coffee into brown mugs for them.

"Yes. You were there, of course."

"Of course. I was still trying, back then."

"Trying?" Grace said. "Trying what?"

"To have a relationship with my brother," he said. He was still smiling. Smiling seemed to be his default expression. "I am the official optimist of this family," he said, as if to confirm that. "I can't help it. I don't know any better. I saw he was marrying a smart girl. I saw she was a nice person. She was interested in psychology. She was going to be a psychologist. I was thrilled."

Thrilled, Grace thought, testing the concept.

"I thought: *Grace will encourage him to reconnect with Mom and Dad.* Of course, he asked us not to come to the wedding."

"You were invited," she said, surprised. She had addressed the invitation herself.

"Yes, I know, but he called and asked us not to come. But me, official optimist, I went anyway. I felt badly about leaving in the middle. I hope you know that."

Naturally she did not know that. How could she be expected to know how he felt? She murmured something noncommittal and took a sip of her coffee. It had a hazelnut flavor and made her feel a little sick.

"He told me to leave, you know."

Grace put the mug down. "Who did? Jonathan did?"

Mitchell nodded. "Sure. Right after the ceremony. He came up to me and said: '*Super. You made your point. Now go.*' The last thing I wanted was to make anyone uncomfortable. So I slipped out." He was throwing sugar into his own coffee and stirring. "I thought the ceremony was beautiful, by the way. The way your friend talked about your mother. I cried a little. And I barely knew you and I never met your mother. What your friend said, you felt how much love there was, not just between you and your mom, but you and your friend."

"Vita," Grace said. She had not thought about Vita's tribute to her mother in many years. It had been, in its aftermath, the great pain of one loss magnified by the great pain of the other. "Yes, what she said was beautiful."

"So you've been living up there? With Henry? What is he doing about school?"

"He's in the local middle school," she told them. "Actually, that part of things has gone really well. I think he might actually be happier in his new school. He's made some good friends. He's in the school orchestra."

"He plays an instrument?" Naomi said. It was the first thing she had said since they'd sat down.

"Violin. He studied it in the city, before we left. Pretty seriously," she added unnecessarily.

"Aha!" David said. "Another Sachs fiddler. My grandfather played klezmer music in Kraków. My uncle still plays. He's in his nineties."

"No, no..." Grace shook her head. "It's classical. His teacher is very strict. He only takes students he thinks..." But then she heard herself and stopped. "Well, I hope he keeps playing. He is talented. Actually," she told them, "there's a neighbor of ours in Connecticut who's offered to teach him fiddle music. Sort of Scottish music. Like bluegrass."

"Second cousin of klezmer!" David said delightedly. "My point exactly. Is Henry going to have a bar mitzvah?"

She looked at him. How was it possible that they were talking about this? *This?* As if their son, whom they had not seen in decades, had not killed a woman and run away, leaving all of them behind to have this excruciating encounter.

"No. Not at the moment. To tell the truth, it's never really been on my radar. And especially not now."

"Dad..." Mitchell shook his head. "Come on. She's going to take time out from Armageddon to plan a bar mitzvah? Grace, it's good that you took Henry away to Connecticut. It's good you took yourself. But what about your business?"

"My practice is suspended for the moment. Maybe... it's possible I'll start a new practice. I've been thinking about it. But as for New York, no, that's finished."

"And you're living in the summer house."

"Yes. And yes, it's very cold. If you were going to ask," she said, looking at them. Maybe they weren't going to ask.

"Not insulated?" Naomi asked. "Is that safe for Henry?"

"We wear a lot of clothing. And sleep under a lot of blankets." She sighed. "My son wants a dog. He says the Eskimos stay warm by sleeping with a dog."

"Well, why not?" David said. "Can't he have a dog?"

She nearly said: *Jonathan's allergic*. That was the reason. But then she remembered the other reason: the childhood dog named Raven who had escaped from this very house, somehow, and disappeared, and how these very parents had blamed Jonathan for somehow having made that happen, though the dog had been Mitchell's, not even his. It had ruined dogs for Jonathan. It had been an awful thing for them to have done. One awful thing among who knew how many?

"You had a dog," she informed them, as if that were all that needed to be said. "Jonathan told me what happened to your dog."

All three of them looked at her. Jonathan's mother turned to Jonathan's father. "What did she say?" Naomi asked.

"Wait," Mitchell said. He had extended his arm, the way you do in a car sometimes, involuntarily, when you hit the brakes suddenly and want to stop someone from hurtling forward. "Wait a minute. Let me ask."

"We never had a dog," his mother insisted. "He told you we had a dog? And something happened to the dog?"

"You don't know that," David said. He looked at Grace. "We never had a dog. We would have liked it, but the boys were allergic."

So that was true, she thought with a strange wave of relief. He had always said he was allergic.

"And he said what?" Naomi demanded. "About this imaginary dog."

"That..." She tried to remember the details. Details seemed very important now. "There was a dog, called Raven. It was Mitchell's dog. And one day when he was home alone with the dog, the dog disappeared. Got out the gate or something, and nobody ever saw it again. And you blamed him, because he was the one who was here." She searched for anything she had left out, but there was nothing more. "That's it."

After a long and deeply uncomfortable moment, Naomi spoke. "That's not it," she said in a cracked voice. "Not by a long shot."

"Honey," David said. "Don't be angry. Obviously, that's what Grace was told."

"Please," she said. Her heart was pounding. It was pounding so hard, she could hear it. She didn't understand what was happening, but she was terrified of it. "Please tell me."

"Not a dog," said Naomi, who at some point in the last instant had begun to cry, and whose eyes, with their heavy dark circles, were now filled with tears. "Not a dog. A brother. He never had a dog, but he had a brother. I suppose he never mentioned that he had a brother."

"Of course. Mitchell!" Grace said. She couldn't hold on to any of this.

"Not Mitchell," Naomi said angrily.

"Not me," said Mitchell, almost at the same instant. He wasn't smiling now, Grace noted. Even his self-confessed optimism couldn't handle this. "Another brother. Aaron. He was four."

She shook her head. She didn't know why.

"He really never told you about it?" David said.

She thought: *I can leave right now. If I leave right now, I don't have to know this. But if I stay, I will have to. And then I will know it forever. Whatever it is, I will have to know it forever.*

But it wasn't a decision, really. She was in the grip of it, of them. Of whatever the truth actually was, she would tell herself later. By then, of course, she was an altogether different person.

On a Saturday morning in the winter of the year when Jonathan was fifteen and Mitchell thirteen, the four-year-old Aaron Reuben

Sachs—called "Boo" by his mother and "the Caboose" by his father, and nothing at all by his brothers (who were, after all, much older and involved in their own active lives)—came down with a bad cold and was running a temperature. It happened to be the day on which the daughter of David and Naomi's oldest friends was to be bat mitzvahed, and all five members of the Sachs family were expected at the synagogue and at the reception to follow. But Jonathan refused to go. He had no love for David and Naomi's friends, or for their daughter, who was two grades behind him in school and not remotely attractive, and he intended to stay home and do whatever it was that he did in his room, with his door locked. There had been a fight about it the day before, and the fight had ended with David's insistence that however Jonathan might feel about it, he would attend the bat mitzvah along with the rest of his family. The next morning, though, it was as if none of that had happened. Jonathan stayed in his room, insisting he wasn't going anywhere.

But Aaron had a fever. That's what changed everything around. And Naomi saw, in this confluence of events—both bad, neither of which could really be controlled—another possibility. One that would, yes, save face for herself, but also (and she told herself that it *might* work out this way) give Jonathan a chance to really spend a bit of time with his brother. Maybe it wasn't too late for him to find a connection, some bond that might outlast the experience of growing up with the same parents in the same house, albeit at different times. She had always hoped for that, though Jonathan had never shown much of what you might call a brotherly feeling, even to Mitchell, who was only two years younger. The arrival of Aaron, though surprising to all of them, had pushed her eldest son even further away from the rest of them.

And that was what she told herself when she dressed for the synagogue and checked her little boy's temperature one final time (101 degrees) and tucked him into his bed with a cassette of *Fable Forest* playing beside him.

When she phoned home from the reception a few hours later, Jonathan said everything was fine.

"He said Aaron wanted to play outside," Mitchell said. "He told us that for a while, and then I think he figured out that that wasn't working. It wasn't considered a nice thing you were doing for your little brother, letting him play outside when he wanted to, when your brother's four years old and running a fever and you're supposed to be taking care of him. You don't get sympathy for that. You get disapproval. So then he told people he had no idea Aaron was outside. He thought Aaron was in his room the whole time. He told the doctor he'd checked on him a few times, but he never said that to us. He knew Mom and Dad wouldn't have believed that, so he didn't bother."

"Wait," Grace said. She actually had her hands up, to stop them. "Wait, do you mean he... You mean that Jonathan was responsible for something happening to Aaron?"

"He was." David nodded sadly. "I fought against that, not nearly as long as Naomi did. She wanted terribly not to believe it was true."

Naomi was looking at something past Grace's shoulder. Her face was so full of pain, it looked swollen.

Mitchell sighed. "He was definitely outside. Definitely. I don't think we know how long, or whether he wanted to be there or he was told to go. It's very hard to imagine the chain of events. And of course, the human brain is very good at making up stories to feel better about something when it gets unbearable. So I've always had this little story about Aaron feeling better and wanting to play outside, because he had this swing set out back that he loved. With a ladder and a rope. And he just lets himself outside and goes and has a great time out there on the swing, and when he comes back in he doesn't have any chance at all to feel sick. He just goes back in his bed and drifts off and that's where he is when we all get back from the party."

"But then it was one hundred and five degrees. We took him right away," Naomi said tonelessly. "To the emergency room. But they couldn't do anything. It was too late to do anything for him."

"And also that wasn't how it happened," Mitchell said. "I just wanted that to be the story, but it wasn't how it really happened. And the police knew it, too. They took him through it again and again. I mean, Jonathan. He kept changing what he said. He knew where Aaron was. He didn't know. He might have known. He thought he knew, but he was wrong. No affect. No distress at all. But also there was no real action on his part. There was nothing they could say he'd *done*. And you know, I think they were trying to think of our family as a whole, and how we were going to survive this, and that holding Jonathan responsible from a legal perspective would make it all so much worse. I think they believed he was going to suffer enough, out of his own guilt, and putting him through an indictment and a trial wouldn't help him and it wouldn't help us. But they were wrong about him suffering. He couldn't suffer. He didn't know how."

Grace was trying to breathe, but everything seemed to be moving. The table was moving, and the chair. The kitchen was swirling in one great Harvest Gold blur, as if it had become detached. But . . . and this came to her as she watched it, spinning and blurring around her: That wasn't right. It wasn't the kitchen, it was her. She—Grace—had come unstuck from her own life at last, irreversibly unstuck. No more explanation. No more mitigation. No more attempting, just, to understand him, what had happened to him. There was simply nothing to go back to after this, after Aaron Sachs, the Caboose, who never made it to five. There was nothing to misunderstand: It was flatly obvious, and it was brutal, and it had nothing—not one thing—to do with her. This was Jonathan at fifteen: who had not wanted to go to the bat mitzvah or have a brother.

"He never said he was sorry," David told her. "Never. Not once. Even if it had happened exactly the way he said, he could still have said he was sorry. But he didn't."

"Well, he wasn't sorry," said Naomi. She wiped at her face with the back of her hand. "Why should he say so? He never said a word about it again. He just lived here until the first chance he could go away, and then he never came back. He never called us, or talked to us about anything personal when we called him. He let us pay his tuition—that felt like an accomplishment that he let us pay his tuition. Then he started living with this woman, much older than him, and she paid his tuition. She bought him a car."

"BMW," said David, shaking his head. "That killed me. No Jew should ever drive a BMW. I always said that."

"It doesn't matter what kind of car," said Naomi.

He looked as if he were about to respond, but thought better of it and let it go.

"You know," Mitchell said, "when Jonathan went to medical school, I thought: *Well, okay, this is how he's going to express his feelings for what happened to Aaron*. I thought, *a little more time, at some point maybe he'll give us another chance.* Me in particular," he said, smiling again. "'Cause I'd really looked up to him when we were both kids. So I held on a little while longer. I was the last one to give up. Dad gave up a long time ago, maybe a year or two after Aaron died. Mom went on for years."

He looked across the table at his mother. She turned her head away.

"Then he became a pediatrician. I thought, *All this time, he's been consumed by guilt about it. That's why he can't look at us or be with us, it's just too painful for him. But he can go off and save other children from dying and save other brothers and parents from losing a little boy.* And I sort of really respected that, even if he was still out of our lives, and you and Henry were still out of our lives. But actually I don't think that's true anymore. I don't understand him. I don't think I ever understood him."

"No," Grace said. She was stunned to hear herself offer an opinion. Then she decided that she must be speaking as a professional.

"No, you couldn't have. There's a very different brain involved here. You're not responsible for what this is," she said, turning to Naomi. "You couldn't have fixed it. Nobody understands how it comes into being." What was truly amazing, she was thinking at the same time, even as she spoke so soothingly, so professorially, to Naomi, was not that he had emerged from some awful, inadequate family to become a healer of children, a professional, a citizen of the world. What was amazing was that he had held it together as long as he had. It must have been difficult. It must have been exhausting. But he must have gotten something out of it. She didn't want to think about what he'd gotten out of it. "You know, the experts who study it don't understand it," she finished, running out of steam.

Naomi, to her surprise, was nodding. "I know. I know that. I just can't always hold on to it. I keep circling back to it must have been something I did, it must have been our life here, or what kind of mother I was. But I was a good mother. I was. I tried to be," she said, and again her voice cracked open and she cried. Mitchell put his arm around her shoulder, but he didn't interrupt. Finally, she stopped herself. "Thank you for saying it, though."

"My wife says the only thing you can do if a person like my brother comes into your life is just get out of the way," Mitchell told Grace. "She's done a lot of research into it. Of course, it's not her field."

"Your wife?" Grace asked. "You're married?"

"I know!" David laughed. "It only took them twelve years. You think it was long enough for the two of them to make up their minds?"

"But... I thought..." She went over, once again, what she'd thought, what she'd believed. Who was it who'd told her that Mitchell, the immature and indulged younger brother, still lived in the basement of his parents' house and relied on them entirely? "Where do you live?" she asked him.

Mitchell looked quizzically at her. "Not far. We've been over in

Great Neck, but we're about to move to a house in Hempstead. My wife is a physical therapist at St. Francis Hospital, that's very close to here. You should meet her, Grace. I think the two of you would like each other. She's an only child, too." He smiled.

Grace nodded. She was numb. "What do you... I'm sorry, Mitchell, but I don't know what you do for a living."

He looked amused. "That's all right. I'm the principal of an elementary school in Hempstead. I was in secondary education for most of my career, but last year I moved over to elementary. I'm very happy with the change. I do love being around kids. I think that's something I got from what happened to us, if that makes sense. I didn't notice Aaron very much when he was alive—it upset me terribly after he died. But afterwards I was very drawn to children, and how they learn." He reached over and took Naomi's mug and his own. "Would you like another cup?" he said, rising.

She thanked him but shook her head.

"Grace?" she heard Naomi say. "We would like, very much, to know our grandson. Do you think, now, that that would be possible?" She spoke very slowly, very deliberately. She did not want to do this wrong or be misunderstood.

"Of course," Grace said. "Of course. I'll... we'll set something up. I'll bring him out. Or... we can meet in New York sometime. I'm so sorry. I feel so terrible not to have known any of this. I never knew."

David was shaking his head. "You don't need to say that. He didn't want us in your life and Henry's life. It was difficult to accept that, especially when Henry was born. I didn't want to come in to the hospital the way we did, but it was something Naomi just had to do. I think it was the last time she thought Jonathan might turn into somebody else. You know, because now he had a baby of his own. She thought there was just a little chance he might let us back in."

Grace closed her eyes. She was imagining herself in those same unbearable circumstances. She would have clung to the same slender possibility.

"I made him take me," Naomi said. She was smiling, or attempting to smile, for the first time since Grace's arrival. "I forced him. I said: 'This is our grandchild, we're going to see him, and that's that.' And I wanted to give him the quilt, remember? The quilt we brought Henry?"

Grace, with a sick feeling, nodded. "Was that something you made?"

"Oh no. My mother made it for me. I used it for all of the boys. Jonathan, too, of course. I wanted Henry to have that from us, even if it was the only thing I got to give him. Do you still have it?" she asked with excruciating eagerness.

"I'm not sure," Grace managed to say. "I have to be honest, I haven't seen it in a very long time."

Naomi's face fell, but she recovered. "Well, it doesn't matter now. Seeing Henry is much more important than keeping an old quilt. I'm making another one now, anyway."

And then, from a corner of the kitchen, there came a small, almost electronic bleep. Grace looked around. Plugged into an outlet was a white plastic monitor, the kind she had used when Henry was a baby.

"Speaking of the devil," Naomi said, and her voice was suddenly bright. She leapt to her feet.

"I'll go," said Mitchell.

"No, I will." Then she stopped herself. "You'd better explain this to Grace," she said. And then she leaned down and kissed the cheek of her daughter-in-law, who was too stunned to speak. They all watched Naomi leave the room. She went back to the hallway and started to climb the stairs.

"Grace?" said Mitchell.

"So, I take it you and your wife have a baby? Congratulations."

"Thank you. Actually, we are having a baby. Laurie is due in June.

But we do have a baby. At the moment we all have a baby, bizarre as that may seem. And maybe, now that you understand about what happened in our family, it will be easier for you to understand why we've done what we've done. What we're doing."

"Oy!" David said. He got stiffly to his feet. "I can't stand it! It's like the Gettysburg Address."

"Dad, I just want Grace to understand that for us, it was different than it might have been for another family, where they hadn't lost a child."

"Would you like any more coffee cake?" said David. Grace, who'd managed only a polite half of the cake she already had, shook her head.

"We were—we *are*—very devastated by what Jonathan did. Allegedly did. What we believe he did. And of course we were also aware that the woman who died had two children. And we assumed, I guess most people assumed, that the woman's husband was going to take his children back to Colombia. It never occurred to us to involve ourselves in anything to do with this, more than we had to be involved, talking to the police about Jonathan and promising to contact them if he contacted us, which I told them straight out was the last thing he was going to do. But then one of them called just before New Year's to check in with us, and he said the little boy had gone back to Colombia with his father but the father declined to take the baby girl."

"Not his daughter," David said. He had slapped the Entenmann's box back into the fridge and removed a bottle of formula, already made up. This he began to shake vigorously. Then he took it to the tap, turned on the hot water, and started to run it back and forth underneath the stream.

"They said she was going into foster care, in Manhattan, but first they had to contact any blood relatives and eliminate them as caregivers. And we talked about it."

"Not for long!" David said with a little laugh.

"No, not for long."

"Oh, my God," Grace said.

"I know. I'm sorry. I'm sure this is a horrible thing for you to have to deal with."

No more horrible than finding out your husband murdered his mistress or caused the death of his younger brother, she thought. That hardly helped.

"But... none of this is her fault. That's what we kept coming back to. She's a beautiful little girl who had an incredibly unlucky start. She's going to have a lot to contend with when she gets older. I'm sure there's a lot of unhappiness in store for Abigail. And she happens to be my niece."

"My granddaughter," David corrected good-naturedly.

"Can I have a glass of water?" Grace said. She held out her hands for it. Both hands. David opened up a cabinet to find a glass. He turned off the hot water, turned on the cold water, and held his palm underneath it, waiting for it to cool. No one said another word until she had gulped it down.

Then Grace said: "Abigail?"

"After Aaron. Actually, Laurie and I chose the name Abigail. We're keeping Elena as the middle name."

"I love the name Abigail," said David. He had returned the bottle to the hot water. "King David's wife in the Bible. Not that anyone asked me," he went on.

"But..." Grace kept trying to form the question. "You're going to... or... you and your wife?"

It took him a moment, but he figured out what she was asking.

"Laurie and I are in the process of adopting her. Right now the arrangement is a little more ad hoc, because we haven't moved into the new house yet, and Laurie's had a rough first trimester, so Abigail's spending a lot of quality time with Grandma and Grandpa. Not that they're complaining."

"We love her," David said plainly.

Grace, who was still trying to control herself, gave him her best therapeutic nod. "Of course. This is your grandchild."

"My grandchild. The daughter of my son. Who I also loved, by the way. Hard as that might be to believe."

"No, it isn't." She shook her head. "I loved him, too." *Or at least*, it occurred to her, *I loved the person I thought he was*. That was a small but critical discrepancy.

Now Naomi could be heard descending the carpeted stairs in the hallway. Grace's chest grew tighter with every step. She knew that she was never going to be ready for this. For the first time since coming through the door, she thought seriously about bolting, but the idea of herself as a grown woman shamed by a baby girl made her feel horrible. She grabbed the seat of her chair and turned her grim and ready face to the kitchen doorway.

The woman who appeared, holding the child, was a transformation. Her dark hair swung loose around her face, and her way of moving was quicker and more supple, in spite of the fact that she carried the baby—Elena—Abigail—in the time-honored way of mothers, straddled across her hip. Even Naomi Sachs's skin seemed a different color: bright and hale. She had become a woman who looked capable of happiness.

She said: "You told her, I hope?"

Grace got to her feet. No one had asked her to do this. No one would ever ask, and that was perfectly understandable. But she reached out for the little girl. She hadn't planned to. She wasn't sure she wanted to. But she did it anyway.

"Can I?" she asked Naomi.

Naomi didn't answer, but then she lifted the baby off her hip and held her up, and Grace reached out and took her. Elena was no longer the dusky infant who had so discomfited the women at a benefit committee meeting by nursing at Malaga Alves's breast—*both* breasts. Now she was a sturdy baby with a halo of thin brown hair and a pair of bottomless dimples, muscular little legs, and an enthusiastic interest in Grace's ear. She was also a once and always child of tragedy, whose father had killed her mother, whose other father had rejected her, and whose brother had disappeared from her life, forever. And she was only six months old. She still, Grace saw, had the long, beautiful eyelashes she remembered from the time they'd met before.

Like Henry's eyelashes: also beautiful, also long.

"I'd better go," said Grace.

Naomi stayed inside with the baby. David and Mitchell walked her back to the car, and both insisted on hugging her again.

"You're not getting rid of us," David said. "Now you're going to be stuck with all of us. And Henry is, too."

"Dad..." Mitchell laughed. "Grace, don't listen to him. We're going to wait to hear from you. And if we don't hear from you, we're going to stalk you mercilessly. No, that's not funny. I didn't mean that."

"I thought it was funny," David said.

She reassured them both and got in the car and turned it on. It felt as if she had not sat here for many hours. It occurred to her that she had no idea what time it was.

When she got back on the LIE, she took out her phone and called her father's cell. He picked up at once, sounding anxious.

"Are you all right?" he asked. "Did you get my message?"

"No, I'm sorry. Are you having dinner?"

"We are. Well, some of us are. We're at Pig Heaven."

Grace couldn't help laughing. "How did you persuade Eva to go to Pig Heaven?"

"Henry told her that 'Pig' was just a metaphor. He used the word 'metaphor.'"

"Impressive," said Grace.

"And when we got here and she saw the menu, I ordered her a mai tai. Now she's fine. And your son is eating something called suckling pig. And he is indeed in Pig Heaven."

"Can I talk to him?" said Grace. She asked her father to bring home an order of the duck salad.

Henry came on sounding delighted, as only a twelve-year-old reunited with his favorite restaurant can be. "Where are you?" Henry asked.

"We're getting a dog," said Grace.

CHAPTER TWENTY-TWO

The First Thing They'll Say About Me When I Leave the Room

Henry wanted a smart dog. He wanted a border collie, the smartest dog of all according to his eager research, but there were no border collies in the animal shelters of western Connecticut. In fact, there weren't many dogs who weren't pit bulls or pit bull mixes. The dog they ended up choosing turned out to be a hound of some description, from the municipal pound in Danbury, the only non–pit bull in residence on the day she and Henry drove down Route 7, ready (in Grace's case, ready as she would ever be) to become dog owners. As luck would have it, he was a bright and affectionate one-year-old of medium size, with black and brown spots and a curious mirror image of curlicue patches on his hindquarters, like a doggie Rorschach test. On the ride home, he deposited himself directly in Henry's lap, gave a great sigh that seemed to involve every bit of his body, and went to sleep. Henry, now that the dog's hoped-for brilliance was apparently confirmed, decided that he would be called "Sherlock."

"Are you sure?" Grace said from the front seat. "That's a pretty big burden for a little dog."

"He can handle it," Henry said. "This dog is a genius."

He was also a southerner, it seemed. The shelter worker, reviewing Sherlock's papers, had explained that high-kill shelters in the South, when they got overcrowded, sometimes shipped adoptable dogs and cats to shelters in the Northeast. Sherlock, specifically, hailed from Tennessee. Perhaps he would bark with a twang.

"Can we stop at the pet food place?"

"We got dog food already."

"No, I know, but I want a special bowl. And Sherlock should have a special collar. Danny's dog, Gerhard, has a special collar that says 'Gerhard.'"

Gerhard was a show-dog schnauzer who got carted off to dog shows all year long. Danny's parents (his mother, whose name was Matilda, had insisted that both Grace and Henry call her "Til," because "that's my call name") had actually turned out to be awfully welcoming and generally a riot. One night, after arriving to collect Henry, Grace had accepted an impromptu invitation to dinner and enjoyed a hilarious download about the dog show circuit, with special reference to backstage coiffure and primping. Grace, to her own surprise, had found herself laughing like an idiot throughout the meal.

Still, she told Henry now, they would not be keeping up with Gerhard and his family.

"What does that mean?" said her son, genuinely mystified.

She told him what it meant.

It was all sort of miraculous, Grace thought, looking back at him in the rearview, noting the long lock of hair falling forward over her son's face. When he was a baby, the pediatrician had told her kids really did grow overnight. You could go in the next morning and the legs would be longer, the head larger; it really did happen that way. And over the years, she had often had cause to remember this. The day in second grade when he had suddenly leapt away from babyhood with utter finality: done! The summer two years earlier, when she drove into Great Barrington to find him some sneakers, and bought sneakers that were even a little roomy on his feet, and then barely a week later, he was complaining that his toes were sore from hitting the tips of the shoes. When they went back to the store, they ended up buying two sizes larger. Now it had happened again, not so much in his length or breadth or head circumference. He had shed, while she had been looking the other way, while she had been distracted by the unfolding disaster of their family, a large part of his little-kid-ness. Now, in its place, there was the vaguest trace of teen. Her son was in the antechamber to the land of teen, where boys with long forelocks and less than exemplary personal hygiene waited to discover that girls were different, and why that might actually matter. And he looked good. He looked... was it possible? Very good, not broken or depressed. In fact, he looked for all the world like a normal boy, a boy with friends at school and a science quiz on Monday morning and an obligation to play in the middle school orchestra and a brand-new spot (as outfielder) on the Lakeville Lions (a team sponsored by none other than Smitty's Pizza in Lakeville, the site of that first greasy meal on the night she now thought of as their escape). Not, in other words, like a boy whose father was known to millions of people, albeit in another state, as "Murder Doc." Or even (she tested the notion) like a kid whose parents had just enjoyed a garden-variety split and whose mother had taken him away one afternoon to an altogether different life: different house, school, friends. *And dog,* Grace thought. Was it possible that he was... actually... really okay?

"Maybe we should have gotten that crate they were talking about," she told him. It had just occurred to her that Sherlock-the-dog, the first canine to enter the lake house for at least thirty years, might at some point decide to shit on the premises.

"No. I want him to sleep on my bed," Henry said from the backseat. "And if he goes, I'll clean it up. He's my dog. I'm responsible."

Grace caught her breath. She had never heard him say those exact words—*I'm responsible*—and they sounded sort of incredible in his voice. His new voice—a little bit softer, a little bit deeper, no longer the voice of Henry-the-boy. That was another thing that had happened while she had been looking the other way, she realized, dizzy with regret.

Because she was the one who was, or who ought to have been, responsible. It had occurred to her for the first time only a few weeks earlier, as she had lifted the edge of her vast rage and vast sorrow and vast, vast, ultimately limitless pain because Jonathan was not there (that her family with Jonathan—her life, what she had with some defensible reason regarded as her life—was just *not there* any longer), and she had seen, lurking beneath that great encompassing tent of awfulness, a resolute finger pointing back in her own direction. All this—it need not have happened, or at least it need not have happened as it had. The fullness of it: Malaga Alves murdered, her children orphaned, the utter shame of her own public pillory, and the scuttling of her professional accomplishments and ambitions. And more, going down the list, so much more: the rifts between herself and Vita, between Henry and his grandparents, between the blasé idea of herself and the blunt, hard reality. Jonathan had done it, but she had let him. And even after all these weeks of days lost to bedridden sorrow, and trawling the Internet reports of her own supposed cognizance of the crime (at best) and complicity in the crime (at worst), and hours out on the dock, blowing smoke to the stars as if the explanation were up there—even now, she still had no idea how it had happened.

She gripped the steering wheel, attempting to regain control of herself, attempting to hide her sudden decompression from Henry.

So she had chosen to believe in the presented reality, the unexamined reality, of her life with Jonathan. Why be ashamed of that? Sitting in her office, day after day, as the parade of awful choices sat howling on her oatmeal-colored couch, the injured parties and devastated partners—who would not have been grateful for what she went home to at night? Jonathan had openly adored and valued her, encouraged her, supported her, given her unceasing affection, given her Henry. He had been—God, the cliché of it—her best friend. Actually, she thought with a new wave of sadness, what he had been was her only friend. He had made sure of that, by parting her from Vita, by encouraging her disapproval of anyone else who came along. No one was worthy of Grace—that was the message. No one deserved her except himself.

She would have spotted that in someone else, she told herself. She *had* spotted it, countless times, in the men on her office couch. They were husbands and boyfriends who delicately or brutally severed the ties between their partners and parents, siblings, friends, even children, so that the women might never make it back across the wasteland. So that they might be too demoralized to even try. They were just like border collies, who cut their chosen lamb from the herd and kept it away from the others. Border collies were such clever dogs.

"I think he's hungry," Henry said. Sherlock had wobbled to his feet, stretched, and now had his nose up to the window, smudging the glass.

"We'll be home soon."

When they got there they took him in through the front door and walked him around on the leash. Once, at the living room sofa, he looked as if he might be considering lifting his leg, so Henry dragged him away, explaining things as if the dog could understand: "No, no, Sherlock, you're going to go outside. We have a whole backyard for you."

Grace opened the porch door and they went down the steps to the lakefront, where she watched Henry fasten on the special collar, then tighten it until it fit.

"Ready for this?" she asked.

He nodded, but he didn't look ready. Earlier in the week, a man from the Invisible Fence company had come and buried the perimeter wire, using a special tool to burrow into the hard soil. He left behind little white flags along the boundary line, descending from both sides of the house down to the water. There was a lot of room to run around in. Once this part of it was done, the dog would be fine.

"I don't want to," Henry said, stating the obvious. The dog was straining at the leash, obviously dying to explore.

"I know," Grace said. "But he has to. He has to know what happens if he tries to go past the line. One shock, and then that's it. If he's as smart as we think he is, anyway."

"But I don't want him to get hurt."

"He'll get a lot more hurt if he runs out into the road and gets hit by a car, Henry."

Her son shrugged, miserable.

"Remember what the guy said?"

"Will you do it with me?"

"Of course."

They brought the dog up close to the perimeter. A few feet from one of the white flats, she could hear the high-pitched warning from the collar. Sherlock cocked his head but seemed otherwise nonplussed.

"No!" Grace said sharply to the dog. "No! No! No!"

Henry, rather halfheartedly, pulled back on the leash. "No, Sherlock. Don't go there."

Sherlock looked mildly at them both and then took another step toward the line.

"Sorry, sweetie," said Grace. "There's no other way."

He nodded. He let the dog pull him forward. He was very brave, thought Grace. With another step, they heard the warning tone again. And then, two steps after that, Sherlock yelped and jumped back. The cry was sharp and, even to Grace, baldly heartrending. Clearly, he had really been hurt.

"I'm sorry," Henry told him, dropping to his knees. "I'm really sorry, boy. It won't happen again."

Hopefully, thought Grace. *If you're as smart as all that.*

"Let's see what happens," she told Henry. "Try to take him up to the line again."

He did, but this time Sherlock wasn't having any. Even before the warning tone, he hung back. He looked terrified.

"Good dog!" said Grace.

"Good boy!" said Henry.

They took him around the rest of the boundary, letting him hear the warning in a few more places, petting and praising him when he leapt back. Down at the lakefront, he waded into the cold water until it covered his feet and then stared out over the surface. Then he looked up at the afternoon sky and gave a great hound howl that must have traveled for miles into the woods on all sides. "Oh wow," said Henry.

"Well," Grace said, laughing, "I think he's home."

Henry unhooked Sherlock's leash from his collar and stepped back cautiously. Nothing happened. He didn't bolt for freedom but remained where he was, paws covered by the inky water, staring raptly across to the other side. They returned to the back porch steps to watch him and sat there for a few minutes, Grace with her arm across her son's shoulders.

"He's a nice dog," Grace told him.

Henry nodded.

"I'm sorry it took so long. I think I'm going to like having a dog."

He didn't say anything right away. He shrugged. He seemed to have gone into himself somehow.

"What?" said Grace.

"I want to talk about it," Henry said. "I mean, are we ever going to?"

She took a careful breath. "Of course," she told him.

"But when? I don't like this. I hate not talking about it. I don't want you to be upset."

"It's not your job to protect me, Henry. And now's good. Now's fine, if you want to. Do you want to talk about it now?"

He gave a little laugh, but the laugh sounded anything but mirthful. "Now looks good. I can have my girl check on it and get back to your girl, but as far as I know, now is good."

She turned to him. Over the past week, the cold had ebbed just a little, and they had downgraded from parkas to lesser layers. Henry's dark hair coiled out of his dark hoodie. Over the hoodie he wore a heavy denim jacket from one of the closets upstairs. It had once belonged to Jonathan.

"I knew about it," Henry said.

"About...?"

"Daddy. I saw him with Miguel's mother. Once. In September. Or October. I know I should have told you. If I'd told you, maybe it wouldn't have happened." It came out all in a rush, and then he wasn't looking at her.

Careful, she thought right away. *Be very, very careful now. This is going to matter a lot.*

"What an awful thing for you." She willed her voice to be steady. "I'm so sorry you had to see that. But no, it was not your job to tell me about it."

"They weren't doing anything," he barreled on. "I mean, they weren't... I didn't see something, you know, like kissing or anything. But, I don't know. I just knew, when I saw them. They were outside on the steps. There were people around. But I saw them, and I knew. It was, like, I could just tell. But when he saw me, he just, you know, was totally normal. He kind of moved away from where he'd been standing with her, and he didn't introduce me to her or anything. And I didn't say anything."

Grace shook her head. "Henry, that's something no son should have to see."

"He was just, like, normal Dad all the way home! Like, 'How was school?' 'Did Jonah talk to you today?' But he knew I saw it."

Henry stopped. He seemed to be making up his mind about something.

"There was another time."

"With..." Grace looked at him in confusion. "Mrs.... Miguel's mother?"

"No, it was a long time ago. It was someone else."

Grace forced herself not to react. This was not about her, not any longer. "Do you want to talk about that?" she asked him. "You don't have to, of course."

"No, I know. I was with Jonah over near his house. We were on the sidewalk waiting for his mom because she'd gone into a store and we were on the sidewalk. And I saw Daddy. It was close to the hospital."

Grace nodded. The Hartmans had lived in the East 60s, a few blocks from Memorial, until the boys were in sixth grade, after which Jennifer and Gary had split up and Jennifer moved with Jonah and his sister to the West Side. That was when the friendship had taken such a turn. Before that, though, Henry had spent years in Jonah's neighborhood—Memorial's neighborhood.

"So I saw him coming up the street to where we were waiting. He was walking alongside the playground. You know that playground at Sixty-Seventh Street where we used to go?"

Grace nodded.

"He was with somebody. Another doctor. And they were just... I mean, again, nothing. Like, he wasn't doing anything, so I didn't realize it right away. They were just walking together and talking. She was a doctor, too. She had the same scrubs. He didn't see me right away. And when he crossed the street he still didn't see me. He was going right by me with the... her. So I said: 'Daddy!' And he, like, jumped, and he looked at me and went, you know, 'Hey, buddy!' and, 'Hey, Jonah!' and he hugged me and just started chatting away about something, I don't remember. But I turned around because the doctor he was walking with just kept walking. She didn't stop, and he never looked at her. I just thought that was so strange. It was . . . I don't know how to describe what it was, but like with Miguel's mother, I just knew. Well," he corrected himself, "I didn't *know*. I mean, I didn't know, like, exactly what I was seeing, only that I was seeing something that was . . . it was not right. Do you know what I mean?"

Grace nodded sadly.

"Maybe I should have told you that time, too."

"No, sweetie."

"But you might have gotten divorced."

"There was no right thing and no wrong thing. It's not your responsibility."

"Well, okay," Henry said sadly. "But then whose responsibility is it?"

The dog, having tired of the freezing water, was walking languidly up the slope back to the house.

"The grown-ups'," Grace told him. "Daddy and me. I think there was a lot going on with Daddy, for a long time. But . . ." Grace steadied herself. She hated that she had to say this, but she had to say it. "Whatever he did, and why he did it, I hope you know he always loved you. I don't think it had anything to do with you. Me, probably, but not you."

"But *you* didn't do anything wrong," Henry said, and Grace, with another clench of anguish, saw that he was crying now. Possibly he had already been crying for a while.

She reached over for him, and he let her draw him close to her. He was a little boy still, she thought, though she hated that it had taken this terrible thing to return the little-boy him to her. She held him anyway, smelling his hair, which was dirty.

"Maybe right and wrong isn't the best way to think about it. Maybe it's more complicated than that." She took a breath. "I'm sure I wasn't perfect. And I might not have known what was going on with Daddy, but I think I should have known. That's my part of being responsible."

The dog, Sherlock, had arrived at the foot of the porch steps and looked up at them plaintively. But Grace didn't let Henry go.

"I've spent a lot of nights going over this," she told him. "Nights and days," she amended, remembering the long hours while Henry was away at school, coiled painfully beneath the duvet of her bed upstairs. "I could spend years thinking about Daddy, and what might have happened to him. And Mrs. Alves. And poor Miguel. That poor kid. But I think...I'm not going to. I have other things I need to do. And I don't want my life to be about this one thing. And I really, really don't want your life to be about this one thing. You deserve a lot better than that, Henry."

Henry pulled back. The cold air invaded the place where his body had been. Seeing his opportunity, the dog came up the steps, climbing delicately. He went to Henry, who rubbed his ears.

"They call him 'Murder Doc,'" her son informed her. "Danny and I Googled it at his house."

She nodded, heartbroken. "Okay."

"There are pictures of you, too. From your book. There's a lot of stuff about you." He looked over at her. "Did you know?"

She knew. Grace nodded. She had known for a couple of weeks. One morning, she had dropped him off at school as usual and gone to the library as usual and sat before the computer as usual. But this time, not as usual, she had suddenly been ready. And then she had looked at herself, through the warped veil of a global community of total strangers. It was a torrent. It was endless. The articles themselves were bad enough, but the comments following them were grotesque. She was an ice queen who had stood by as her husband used, abused, abandoned, and finally slaughtered a woman who'd loved him. She was a hypocrite who had the gall to pass judgment on others, to offer "guidance" to others about relationships, to *write a book*—the greatest hostility was for having *written a book*—conveying her so-called wisdom. Her author photo was everywhere. And there were quotes from her book—plain inversions of what she had meant to convey.

It had been exactly as terrible as she had feared. But at least it had not been more terrible.

"How long is it going to be like this?" Henry asked her.

How long is a piece of string?

"We're going to be all right. That's the main thing."

"Okay," said Henry. He sounded brave, but not at all convinced.

"I had a patient once," she said, "who had a really terrible thing happen to her..."

"What was it?" Henry wanted to know, not unreasonably.

"Well, she had a son who was very ill. He had schizophrenia. Do you know what that is?"

Sherlock chose this moment to attempt to climb the topmost step, directly into Henry's lap. Henry laughed and pulled him up the rest of the way.

"Um...he was insane?"

"Yes. Well, 'insane' is a legal term. He was very sick. He had a severe mental illness."

"That was the terrible thing?"

"It was *a* terrible thing, but not the terrible thing she meant. What actually happened was that he died because of his illness. He was only nineteen or twenty."

"I didn't know you could die from being insane."

Grace sighed. She hadn't meant to share the details, but she supposed it was unavoidable.

"Actually, his illness caused him to commit suicide. That's what happened. And his mother, my patient, as you can imagine, was so sad. And she had to find a way to get some peace after this terrible thing. And one day she said to me, 'For the rest of my life, it's the first thing they'll say about me when I leave the room.' And I remember thinking: *Yes, that's true, it will be.* But we can't really do anything about what they say when we leave the room. We'll never be able to control that. And we shouldn't try. Our job is just to...well, be in the room while we're there, and try not to think too much about where we're not. Whatever room we happen to be in, just, be there," she finished lamely.

He didn't seem to take this in, entirely, but why should he? It was so abstract. Perhaps, to a twelve-year-old boy, it was also a little feminine, a little middle-aged-mom. And the truth was that Grace herself had very little idea of how to simply be where she was, while she was there. Until recently, she'd thought far too much about what she had thought and said and done, and not much at all about how she...just...was. And it didn't help that she had thought and said and done some pretty awful things. But at this particular moment she was sitting on a back porch, looking at a lake she had looked at for her entire life, with Henry beside her, both of them stroking a not very clean hound from Tennessee. That was not awful. So she was not awful, at least, not right this minute. And Henry...did he seem not awful, too? He did. Under the gruesome, appalling circumstances, yes, he really did. So it would be the first thing people said about them when they left the room—forever, for as long as they both lived—and that was grim indeed, no doubt about it. But on the other hand, neither of them would ever be able to change that, and it was kind of a relief to realize there was no point in trying.

Henry put his face up against the dog's face. Sherlock licked Henry's mouth extravagantly. Grace tried not to react.

"Is Daddy insane?" Henry asked suddenly.

"No. Not that way, at least. He won't hurt himself, Henry. I'm sure of that."

It was cold again, and the light was gone entirely. Grace moved closer to him on the step, and closer to the dog. The dog was warm.

Then Henry said: "Where do you think he is?"

Grace shook her head. "I don't know. I don't have any idea. Sometimes I hope they'll find him, because I'm so angry at him, I want him to be punished. And sometimes I hope they won't, because as long as they haven't caught him, I won't have to really face whether he did it or not." Then she realized that she had said this aloud, to her own son. And she was horrified.

"Do you think he did it?" Henry asked.

Grace closed her eyes. She waited as long as she could, which was not very long. Because he had asked, and she had to answer.

CHAPTER TWENTY-THREE

The End of the World

Vita came down to Great Barrington every Tuesday for a staff meeting at one of Porter's satellite clinics, and if there wasn't a crisis to keep her there, she and Grace had lunch somewhere in town. Knowing Vita again was like being readmitted to great chunks of her own life, memories she had allowed to atrophy or just put away because, without her friend, they were inexpressibly sad to think about. Now, at odd moments, she found these things restored to her—appearing, apropos of nothing, while she drove up and down Route 7 or waited for Henry outside the gym where his baseball team did their winter training. She remembered books they had read, clothing they had shopped for and shared or occasionally fought over. She remembered Vita's mother and her aunt, who was an eccentric—probably, she now understood, a tiny bit bipolar—who sometimes babysat for them at Vita's house, sneaking them each a Sugar Daddy after Vita's parents left for the evening. All of these things, and so many others, so inconsequential in themselves, but together a Victorian crazy quilt of her own life. She loved that. She was so grateful for that.

After lunch they went to Guido's together, for Vita to stock up on things that were not findable in Pittsfield ("a gourmet wasteland," she called it), and it was there that Grace discovered Guido's chicken Marbella, the paragon of its culinary species. Grace had made chicken Marbella any number of times in her own kitchen, and she'd always thought it came out fantastically well, but Guido's was better. Really massively better. Soon she and Henry were eating Guido's chicken Marbella most Tuesday nights, and Grace had yet to truly figure out why this version of the dish tasted so much better than her own, which annoyed her, but not so much that she declined to eat more of it. Tuesday had become Grace's favorite day of the week.

One Friday night in late February, Grace finally brought Henry to the stone house to meet the group, Windhouse. By then she and Leo had been getting together every couple of days, and not always with the excuse of having run into each other at the library. Leo was reporting good progress on his Asher Levy book and feeling optimistic about finishing the first draft before his sabbatical ended in June, though he had not been able to show that Levy (and his boatload of refugees from Recife) were the actual first Jews in America. A merchant in Boston appeared to have arrived in 1649, five years earlier. "A bitter, bitter pill," said Leo. But he laughed when he said it.

Grace had intended to cook something for the Windhouse dinner, but on the day in question she met with a rental agent in Great Barrington to look at office space. There was a newly vacant suite of rooms in a barn, converted for professional use and full of attorneys, consultants, and therapists of all stripes. The rooms overlooked a winter field (the farmer grew hay and corn, according to the rental agent) and were warm and sunny, even at this uncongenial time of year. She tried to picture her oatmeal couch here, the desk and swivel chair from her New York office, the leather Kleenex box holder, the kilim rug, but the truth was that she didn't want any of those things in this pretty place. New couch. New Kleenex box holder. The white ceramic mug Henry had made at camp, the one she kept her pens in—she would keep that. She loved that. Finally, she would be able to get rid of that Eliot Porter. It was about time.

She went back to the agent's office with him, and after that there wasn't time to go home and cook, so she ended up buying a big pan of chicken Marbella from Guido's, on her way to pick Henry up at his orchestra rehearsal. Henry looked a little tired and he had forgotten they weren't going home, but he perked up when he smelled the chicken Marbella on the front passenger seat. "Will there be other kids?" he asked, sounding dubious.

"I don't think so." She thought of Leo's stepdaughter. He hadn't mentioned her when they'd met earlier in the week. "He has a stepdaughter, though. Around your age. A little older."

"Great," he said with heavy sarcasm. To a twelve-year-old boy, the only thing worse than an evening of grown-ups was an evening with grown-ups and a slightly older girl. "I don't have to play violin with them, do I?"

"No, no," she said. This wasn't part of the plan. But now that he mentioned it, hadn't Leo once said something about Henry "sitting in"? He made her agree to leave his violin in the car.

At the stone house, she wedged into the only remaining space at the end of the steep driveway, parking behind a Subaru with a BARD COLLEGE QUIDDITCH bumper sticker and another that read: OLD BANJO PLAYERS DON'T DIE . . . THEY JUST STOP FRETTING.

"Can I bring a book?" said Henry.

She hesitated. "All right. But look, give it a chance first, okay?"

"Fine." He climbed out. She picked up the tray of chicken and got out, too. He followed her to the back door.

They were playing inside, loud enough that no one came to the door when she knocked. She knocked again. Then, with a shrug, she turned the doorknob and went in, carrying the tray. Behind her, Henry shut the door.

"Oh, hey!" Leo said. The music stopped. He bounded into the

kitchen. "Grace! Great!" He leaned forward and gave her a kiss, very chaste but very warm. "And you," he said, addressing Henry, "are Henry, the new fiddler we've been expecting."

"Um . . . no," Henry said. "I mean, I play the violin. I don't play the fiddle."

"Details," Leo announced. "Come in, we've got a fire. You want something to drink?"

Henry asked for soda. It was a calculated move, since they didn't drink soda at home.

"Oh, sorry. Not big on soda here. You like cranberry juice?"

"No, that's okay."

Grace accepted a glass of wine and sipped it nervously. She hadn't realized she was nervous until the wine actually came into her hand, but then it occurred to her that three of Leo's best friends were waiting in the next room. And then it occurred to her that she sort of cared what they thought of her.

She had been inside the house only once, many years before, when a summer storm knocked out the power around the lake for two or three days and the families had convened in unprecedented (and unrepeated) neighborliness on the stone house lakefront to grill up whatever remained in people's fridges. She had no specific memories of Leo from that day, but she did remember the house itself, or at least its single most impressive feature: the fireplace's massive mantel of river stones that seemed to take up an entire wall. Seeing it now as she entered the room, she knew that her memory had not exaggerated its size or general impact: It reached up to the ceiling and out beyond the edges of the fireplace itself, as if the stoneworker had simply been carried away by the beauty of the available rocks, which were variously brown, gray, and faintly pink. Wedged between them horizontally, almost as an afterthought, a long split log served as a mantelpiece. Alongside, as they entered, Grace saw Henry's eyes go right to the fireplace and travel up and down, taking it all in exactly as she had when she was his age, more or less. *I know*, she told him silently. *I felt the same way.*

There was a fire in the fireplace entirely equal to its grandeur. It popped and licked and threw warmth out into the room, which was perhaps why the musicians—there were three of them seated on the couch and armchairs—had drawn themselves away from it. One of them, a heavyset man with a fading hairline, stood up as they came in.

"This is Colum," said Leo.

The one who grew up in Scotland, she remembered, shaking his hand.

"Hi. I'm Grace. This is Henry."

"Hi," said Henry. He shook Colum's hand as well.

The others waved from the opposite couch. The woman named Lyric (hippie parents) had long black hair, gently graying in a way that black hair in Manhattan simply never did, a long nose with a markedly rounded bridge, and a lap full of sheet music ("Please, don't get up," said Grace, meaning it). The teenager beside her, her son, got to his feet, holding his fiddle. He was called Rory.

"I'm sorry to interrupt," said Grace.

"You didn't," Colum said, and Grace heard, even in those two words, his still-resonant Scottish accent. "You brought dinner. That's quite a different thing."

"Chicken," said Leo. "I put it in the oven."

"I'm really hungry," Rory said. He looked a little like his mother, with her same strong nose—a nose that might truly be called aquiline—and very dark hair, but he was a bit rounder, a bit softer. Dad, whoever he was, must be an endomorph.

His mother laughed. "You're always hungry." To Grace she said: "Feeding Rory is a full-time occupation."

Rory, sitting down again, put up his fiddle and began to trace a faint tune, not loud enough to interrupt. His hand seemed to move in its own world, as if it belonged to another body altogether. Henry, Grace noticed, was watching it closely.

"I'm so glad to see where the music's been coming from," she said. "I sit out on my dock sometimes and listen."

"An audience!" Leo smiled. "At last!"

"Oh, wait now, you said you had groupies. You said 'a modest following.'"

"Modest is right," Colum said. He had picked up the guitar that had been leaning against the armchair. "We're up to . . . well, I'd say a good two figures."

"That's . . ." Henry was frowning. "Isn't that like ten people?"

"Precisely." And he sat, taking the guitar across his lap.

"Well, that isn't much."

"No," agreed Leo. "But now that you and your mother are here, things are really looking up. Luckily we're not in it for the screaming mobs."

"Luckily," Lyric said with a small laugh.

"We're in it for . . . the love of the art form."

"I thought we were in it to meet girls," said Rory.

Henry, Grace couldn't help noticing again, seemed slightly captivated by him.

"The kind of girls you want to meet, my love," said his mother, "are not coming out to hear string bands."

"Wait," Henry said, "are you, like, a string quartet?"

"String *band*," Leo said. "Technically any group composed entirely of string instruments is a string band. I guess that makes a string quartet a string band, too."

"Yeah, right," Rory said with exquisite teenage disdain.

"But mainly it refers to bluegrass, Irish, and Scottish music. Sometimes it gets called roots music. Do you know any roots music, Henry?"

Henry shook his head. Grace, imagining Vitaly Rosenbaum's thoughts on roots music, nearly laughed out loud.

"Not a big thing in New York," Grace said. She had taken an empty seat next to the fire and crossed her legs at an angle away from the heat.

"Oh, you'd be surprised," said Colum. "There's a major scene in the city now. Mainly Brooklyn, but we're making headway in Manhattan. Paddy Reilly's on Twenty-Ninth has a lot. And the Brass Monkey. I go there if I'm in the city on Sunday nights. Anyone can go and play."

"Really," Grace said. "I had no idea. Just not on my radar, I guess."

Leo, who was on his way back to the kitchen, said: "Very Zeitgeist, obviously."

"Well, that would explain my ignorance. I'm far from the Zeitgeist."

"What's that?" Henry asked, and Rory, rather charmingly, tried to explain it to him.

Grace went into the kitchen and helped Leo set out the food. There was, as well as the chicken Marbella, a big salad, a pan of baked acorn squash, each half containing a little pool of melted butter, and two loaves of Leo's Anadama bread.

"He's great," said Leo.

"Oh. Thank you. Yes, he is."

"I think he's interested. What do you think?"

"I think you'd do anything for another fiddler."

He put down the knife he'd been wielding on his loaves and grinned at her.

"You know," he said, "I might. But even if I don't get him to come over to the dark side, he's still great."

"Yes," Grace agreed. "He still is."

The food was ready, so the others came in and loaded up their plates, then everyone returned to the fire, sitting back down carefully alongside the instruments. Henry tipped over his acorn squash, not difficult to do, and spilled melted butter over his plate. Grace went for a paper towel.

"It's so good," Colum said when she returned. "Did you make this?"

"No. Guido's in Great Barrington made it. I make this dish, too, but there's something in Guido's I don't put in mine. It's so much better. I wish I knew what it was. Some herb, I guess."

"Oregano?" Leo guessed.

"No. There's oregano in mine."

"It's the rice vinegar," said Lyric. "There's a little rice vinegar in here. I can taste it."

Grace, with a forkful of it even then on its way to her mouth, stopped and looked at it.

"Really?"

"Taste it," Lyric said.

Grace did. And as she did, she thought of sushi rice, Napa cabbage, Japanese pickles—the things she associated with rice vinegar. As soon as she put the fork in her mouth, there it was: rice vinegar—right there, floating everywhere. "Oh, my God," she said, "you're absolutely right."

It had made her almost absurdly happy. She looked around at them all, delighted.

"You work in Great Barrington?" Colum asked.

"I'm a psychotherapist. I'm moving my practice to Great Barrington."

"Are you at Porter?" Lyric asked. "I have a colleague whose daughter was in the eating disorder clinic at Porter. They saved her life."

"No, I have a private practice," said Grace. "But a friend of mine from New York runs Porter. I mean, a friend I grew up with, in New York. She lives in Pittsfield now. Vita Klein."

"Oh, I know who Vita Klein is," Leo said. "She came to talk at Bard a few years ago. Adolescents and social media. She was fantastic."

Grace nodded, aware of her own displaced pride. It felt good to be so proud of Vita.

"Why were you at a talk on adolescents and social media?" Rory asked, highly skeptical.

Leo shrugged. He was buttering a piece of his own bread. "Hey, I have a teenager. I have a teenager who'd just informed me that if I wanted to communicate with her, the fastest way to do it was to post on her wall. As in: in full view of her three hundred and forty-two so-called friends. That actually sounds intimate now. Ramona was up to seven hundred something the last time I looked."

"And Vita was helpful?" Grace asked.

"Yes, very much so. She told us not to think of it as a replacement for relationships, even if that's how the kids think of it. That's why they're kids and we're grown-ups. It's not a pronouncement on the real relationships, especially the parent-child relationships, even if they don't know any better. I was very encouraged. Also very relieved that I wouldn't have to join Facebook myself. I am extremely Facebook-resistant."

"Windhouse is on Facebook," Rory pointed out.

"Sure. And it's very useful that way."

"To communicate with your ten fans, you mean," Henry said slyly.

"*Twelve* fans, Henry," Leo said. "Why do you think we're feeding you and your mom right now? Obviously to buy your allegiance."

Henry, who was not immediately sure if he was joking, looked a little alarmed for a moment. But then he smiled.

"Well, I'd want to hear the music first," he pointed out.

Afterward, they played. They played tunes Colum had grown up with in Scotland and tunes they'd written themselves. Rory, it appeared, was the chief source of their original music. His bow hand, loose in the wrist in a way Vitaly Rosenbaum would have found intolerable, bobbed and danced over the strings, and Henry—Grace could not help noticing—seldom took his eyes off it. The sounds of the two violins (*fiddles*, she corrected herself) had a way of moving alongside each other, then suddenly drawing apart and crisscrossing back and forth (there was probably a musical term for this), and the mandolin and guitar made a kind of steady enclosure for them. The songs had names like "Innishmore" and "Loch Ossian" and "Leixlip"—which sounded like "leaks leap" and had to be explained to the guests (it was a town in Ireland that meant "salmon leap"). Grace sat, sipping her wine, feeling strange and warm and increasingly happy as the time went by. She thought she recognized some of the music, a few strains that had made it across the lake as she lay, flat on her back on the freezing dock, looking up at the winter night; but the truth was that they all sort of flowed together, not unpleasantly. Henry remained quiet for an impressive amount of time. He never asked for his book.

Around eight, they stopped for coffee and a cake Colum had brought, and while he was in the kitchen Rory suddenly turned on the couch and held out his instrument to Henry. Henry looked alarmed. "Want a go?" the teenager said.

Henry, to Grace's great surprise, did not say no right away. What he did say was: "I don't know how to play that."

"Oh. Leo said you played."

"Yeah, but I play violin. Classical. Well, in New York I played classical. Now I'm just doing orchestra at school." He hesitated. "I was pretty good, but, you know, not, like, going to conservatory. Most of the people my teacher taught were at least in conservatory, or they were professionals."

Rory shrugged. "Okay. But have a go."

Henry turned to look at Grace.

"Why not?" she said. "If Rory's willing."

"Sure," said Rory. "I love my fiddle, but it's not like it's a Stradivarius."

Henry took it. He held it up for a moment as if he had never seen a violin before, as if, for example, he had not very recently spent an hour after school in intensive rehearsal for the orchestra's winter term concert. Then he flipped the chin rest up to his neck and held it up in the posture he'd been taught.

"Well, that looks uncomfortable," said Rory. "You can hold it however you want."

Henry let his left hand wilt a bit, so the scroll descended. Grace imagined Vitaly Rosenbaum barking like a dog. Henry might be imagining something similar.

"Now shake out your bow hand. Shake it out," said Rory, and Henry did. "In bluegrass, nobody cares how you hold your bow, either. You can hold it in a fist if you want."

"But please don't," Leo said from his chair. He, too, was watching closely. "It'll kill your back."

"The point is, be comfortable." He put his bow into Henry's shaken hand. "Now: Give us a tune."

For a minute, Grace imagined that he was going to play "You Raise Me Up," the unfortunate centerpiece of the Housatonic Valley Regional Middle School orchestra's fast-approaching concert. But to her surprise, Henry (after the briefest of scales, just to feel the instrument) began to play Bach's Violin Sonata no. 1 in G Minor, the Siciliana movement. It was the last piece he had worked on in New York, before things fell apart. Grace had not heard it in months. He had not, to her knowledge, played it since New York, and although it was not as assured as it had been back then, it didn't sound bad. Really, not bad at all. And frankly, it thrilled her to hear it again.

"So pretty," Lyric said when he stopped after a minute or two.

"I haven't practiced much. I mean, apart from orchestra." Henry had carefully lowered the violin and was now holding it out to Rory.

"Can you do any jigs or airs?" he said.

Henry laughed. "I don't even know what that means."

"I wish we had another fiddle," said Rory. "It's easy to learn it when you play it together. I mean, if you can already play, it's the best way to learn."

"My violin's here," said Henry. "It's in the car."

Leo looked at Grace.

"Big concert coming up."

"I'll go out with you," said Leo.

There was a light wind coming off the lake when they stepped outside, but it wasn't actually cold. The worst of the winter had passed a week or two earlier, and something in the ground underfoot had seemed to break open as it began to release its frost. She had never spent a mud season at the lake house and wasn't sure how fast it would come on. In her imagination, the earth of Leo's yard already seemed to suck at her feet.

The minute the aluminum door slammed behind him, she knew something was different, and she knew what that something was. The idea of it was so remarkable that she forgot to be upset. When she remembered again, she realized there wasn't anything to be upset about. And that made her smile.

"What?" said Leo. The light in the car had come on when Grace opened the passenger door.

"I thought I might give you a kiss," she told him.

"Oh." He nodded, as if she had proposed a financially incomprehensible conservancy arrangement for the lake. Then he said: "Oh! Right!" And he kissed her without waiting another second. He had been waiting longer than she had. It was her first first kiss in nearly nineteen years.

"Wait," she told him as soon as she could manage it. "I don't want them to know."

"Oh, they know," Leo said. He looked down at her. "My crowd knows. I've never invited anyone over on a practice night. You should have heard them before you got here. They were thoroughly juvenile." He laughed. "Grace," he said, belaboring the obvious, "I really really like you."

"Really really?" she asked.

"I never told you, once I saw you on the dock in your blue bikini."

"Not recently," she clarified.

"No. When I was thirteen. That sort of thing stays with a guy."

"Well..." Grace laughed. "I don't know where that blue bikini is anymore."

"That's all right. I'll use my imagination."

She laughed. She reached in and picked up Henry's violin case.

"Would it be all right if I ran home for a bit?" Grace said, handing the instrument to Leo. "I want to look in on the dog, and feed him. He's been alone most of the day. I'll come right back."

Of course, he said. "But take your time. We're breaking in a new fiddler. When you come back he's going to be playing 'The Devil Went Down to Georgia.'"

"I guess...that's a good thing?" said Grace, and Leo, in response, kissed her on the forehead. This didn't explain the reference, not that she minded.

She climbed into the driver's seat and turned right out of the driveway and drove down the road, past the still, dark houses, rolling down the window to breathe in the wet air. Grace was not going to think very hard about what had just happened, not tonight, at least. That she had arrived at his house as a neighbor and left—for the moment—as a person he "really really" liked meant that some Rubicon had clearly been reached, if not crossed. But it had been so...well, "gentle" was the word that came to her first. She thought—yet again—of the night she had met Jonathan and how that instantaneous and mutual *I'll have that one* had seemed like proof of the rightness of it all. It wasn't, obviously. Maybe this was better: not quite so strict, not nearly so unyielding. Not so much *right* as *good*. Good would be very good indeed.

There were circulars sticking out of the mailbox, so she stopped and extracted a great wedge of papers, catalogs, and random correspondence and brought it all in. Sherlock barked from the yard and met her on the back porch with two muddy paws to the front of her legs (his exuberance was the only stain on his otherwise perfect manners). Grace fed him and went back inside, brushing the dirt from her jeans, then she turned on the lights and carried the great stack of mail over to the recycling bin, where she started to go through it. With luck there would be an estimate in here somewhere, from the contractor who'd come last week to talk about winterizing the house and possibly regrading the driveway. (One of the hardest things about winter had been parking up at the roadside and slipping treacherously downhill to her own front door.) She was dreading it, but she wanted it to be there, too.

It wasn't there, but something else was: a nuclear white envelope, perfectly ordinary, with an utterly unoriginal flowing American flag stamp and an address (*her* address, *her Connecticut* address) written in the classically bad doctor's handwriting of her husband, Jonathan Sachs. Grace, staring at it, forgot to breathe, and that went on for some time. Then, as if the part of her brain that required breath had seized control of the entire machine, she remembered again in a violent wave, and stepped smartly over to the kitchen sink, and efficiently vomited her dinner of chicken Marbella, with its oregano, bay leaf, and rice vinegar, into the basin.

Not the right time, she thought vaguely, as if there would ever be a right time for this, but it wasn't now. It wasn't right now. Right now, or mere minutes before right now, she had been, actually, happy, and proud (*so* proud) of Henry, and also happy that there was a Leo in the world who really (really really) liked her. She was happy that she might find work in which she might actually help somebody else, and happy that her dear friend had come back to her, or was coming back, and that her son was going to know all of his grandparents, and that her house might not have to be as freezing cold next winter as it was in the winter now ending. This was not *great* happiness, of course. She might not be in line for *great* happiness yet, perhaps ever—not after everything that had happened—but she wasn't asking for it, either. It was only modest happiness, but modest happiness was so much more than she had thought she would ever see again.

I don't have to open it, she thought. Then, to make sure the idea had gotten through, she said it aloud to herself: "I don't have to open it."

Inside were two sheets of unlined paper, covered with his writing, folded in precise thirds. She opened them up and looked at them from a distance, the words stubbornly refusing to translate into meaning, like hieroglyphics before the Rosetta stone. How comforting that was, Grace thought. She wanted it to stay like that. She could live with the writing if it stayed like that. But then, before her traitorous eyes, the words clarified and sharpened. *All right*, thought Grace. *Then if I have to, I will.*

Grace.

Writing this letter is the hardest thing I've ever done, but every day that has gone by without my at least trying to speak to you has hurt me, you can't imagine how much. Of course this has been devastating for you. I won't presume to know how much. But I know how strong you are and I know you can get through this.

I think what it all comes down to is that I failed to appreciate you and the family we were. Are—we are. Whatever happens now, that we are a family is something that can't be changed. Or at least, that's what I tell myself in the worst moments.

I made a terrible, terrible mistake. I can't believe I did it. It was like an illness came over me, and I just lost control. I let myself be persuaded that a person desperately needed me, because her child was very ill and I could help him recover—and I let that be enough of a reason to lose my own strength of character. I responded to her—I didn't initiate it. I know that doesn't make a difference in the long run, but it's important to me that you understand it. I felt very sorry for her, and I guess my wanting to help overwhelmed me. When she told me she was pregnant I thought—if I just kept her happy and took care of things I could keep her away from you and Henry and we could go on, even though I was just ripped apart by the stress of it. I don't know how I kept everything together. Then after everything, instead of being grateful for all the efforts I'd made for both her and her son, who is healthy now, thanks to me, she told me she was pregnant again. She wanted to destroy us as a family, and I just couldn't let her do that. I was just desperate to protect you. There was not a single moment that you and Henry were not my first priority. I hope you can believe that.

What happened in December, I can't write about it, except to say that it was the worst thing that has ever happened to me. It was a horrible, horrible thing, and I am distraught every time I think about it. I can't put it on paper, I just can't, but one day if I am far more lucky than I deserve, I want more than anything to talk to you about it, if you can bear to listen. You are the best listener I've ever met. There have been so many times I've thought: I am so lucky to be listened to like this, and loved like this. I think about it now and the suffering is so terrible.

Do you remember the night we first met? What a question. What I mean is: Do you remember the book I was reading and the place I said I wanted to go? I used to joke about going there in the dead of winter, and you said it was the last place in the world anyone in their right mind would want to go, the end of the world. That's where I am now, and it feels just like that, just as bleak as you predicted. But it's also safe for me, I think. At least for now. I won't stay here much longer, though. I know I can't—no place is as safe as I need it to be. But before I leave I wanted to give you the chance to do something I know I don't deserve. I don't think you will come—you should know that. But if I'm wrong, Grace, I'd be so happy. If you or both of you came here, and we got the chance to start over someplace, just thinking about it makes me cry. I think it can be done. I've been going over it. I think it can be managed. I have a country in mind that I'm pretty sure we can get to, and where we'd be all right, and I'd be able to work there, and it's a decent place for Henry. Obviously I can't write down any of the details.

I don't know why I think for a moment that you'd leave your own life for that, but I love you enough to ask you to. If you don't come, at least you'll know that, and that makes it worth asking. If you would just come and let me talk to you. And then, if you won't, or can't stay with me, I would understand. But I could at least say good-bye to you and Henry and you'd both know I didn't abandon you without a fight.

You shouldn't fly here. I know you know that. There are places a few hours away, where you can rent a car. Please be very sure that no one follows you. I've been renting a house near the town. Well, walking distance. I don't have a car. Luckily I like to walk, as you know. Most afternoons I walk along the river—yes, even at this time of year. It may be dark, but it's milder than you'd imagine. There is a ship there that is now a museum. It has the same name as the book I was reading that night I saw you and fell in love with you instantly. I'll look for you. Please do this for me. And if you won't, or can't, please know that I have never loved anyone else, and won't ever love anyone else, and I'll be okay.

It wasn't signed. As if it had to be signed.

She didn't realize how tightly she was gripping the paper until it tore, and then she gasped and actually dropped it on the floor. She didn't want to pick it up, because it was poison, but after a minute or two she couldn't stand the idea that it was down there on the floor, either. So she reached down and picked it up and set it on the wooden tabletop, as if it were the inanimate object it was pretending to be.

And then, because she did not know what else to do, she read the letter again.

Now she thought of him walking over snow, head down, parka drawn up around his face. He had his hands deep in his pockets.

He wore unfamiliar clothes. Probably his hair had grown, and his beard. He was making his way along an iced-over river, past a ship that was now a museum called Klondike. He was peering out from within the fake fur circle of his hood, looking for a small woman who seemed very out of place and very cold, who acted as if she might also be looking for somebody. What would it feel like when those two people actually recognized each other? Would it feel like that time in the dormitory basement, where she had met another man carrying a basket of laundry with the copy of a book about the Klondike balanced on top, who had been at that moment walking toward her just as she was walking toward him, as if they were looking for each other. Would there be that relieved *Oh good. Now I can stop dating* that her long-ago patient had once described? Would there be the comfort of recognition, the passion, the deep love no real person could ever just walk away from, just like that, not after so many years? And what would happen after that? Would they go back to a hotel room where their son—the son they had made together—was waiting for them? Would they go farther on, to a country he had been thinking about, that he was pretty sure they could get to and where he was pretty sure they would be safe?

Grace closed her eyes. All right. She had had to do that. She had had to follow it that far.

Now, though, her head was going somewhere else, and because she had no strength left to fight with herself, she went there, too, and the place it took her to was back again to the basement of the medical school dormitory at Harvard. She remembered the messy room upstairs where he had made love to her for the first time (*medical students are very basic creatures*), and then, methodically, all of the rooms in which he had made love to her ever since. But there were too many of them and they were too disparate: Maine and London and Los Angeles and the apartment near Memorial and the apartment she had grown up in on 81st Street. And here, right upstairs in this very house, where it was unimaginably cold in the winter, as she now knew. And Paris. There were three trips to Paris over the years, but different hotels. How was she supposed to count them?

She thought of pregnancy and then Henry's birth, and the nights getting up with him because he didn't sleep well for the longest time, and how Jonathan would take the baby and say, "Go back to sleep, it's fine." And the playground on First Avenue where she had sat with Henry in the stroller on summer afternoons, waiting for Jonathan to sneak away from the hospital and sit with them for half an hour, the same playground where her son had later played with Jonah, who would one day stop speaking to him, the same playground where Henry had once stopped his father on the pavement as an unknown woman continued silently on. She thought of interviews with kindergarten evaluators all over Manhattan (because she was afraid Rearden wouldn't take Henry—stupidly afraid), in which Jonathan had spoken so warmly about the kind of education he hoped his son would have, charming them one after another. Henry got in almost everywhere. And dinners at Eva's house on his best behavior, and countless dinners at their own dining table, and kitchen table, and the table at which she was sitting right now, right at this moment. Oh yes, and the one time he had come to her office with Russian burgers from Neil's, but they had not eaten them, or not right away. First, they had made love on her office couch. She had forgotten that time.

She thought of every single room in their apartment on 81st Street—her apartment, in which she had been a child first, and then a wife and mother, and then, briefly, an abandoned, terrified shell of a person waiting for annihilation. The parquet wood in the hallway, the dining room shutters, always kept closed by Grace's mother and always kept open by her. And Henry's room that was once her room. And Jonathan's office that had once been her father's den. And the kitchen that was once her mother's and then became hers, and the bathtub and the bed and the bottles of Marjorie I and Marjorie II and Marjorie III, poured down the drain. And the jewels, one for every infidelity of an unfaithful husband who still loved his wife but could not be happy with her.

She would never live there again. This was the moment it finally broke through to her. That apartment, that home, was gone. Like her marriage. Like her husband, who was now thousands of miles away in a cold place, asking for her forgiveness.

Wait. But he wasn't asking for that. She was sure before she took up the letter again, but she looked anyway, to be almost clinically thorough. This felt important—an important point. Jonathan, in the lines he had written himself, spoke of wanting to protect her and having lost control. He spoke of his own suffering. He said she would get through it. But he did not speak of forgiveness. Perhaps he knew there was too much he would need to be forgiven for, too much to be contained in even a letter like this. Or perhaps he did not think he needed to be forgiven at all.

So she went back again, further this time and broader. She thought beyond the boundaries of just her own story with Jonathan, to the story before and the story beside that story, and slowly it began to change and to look very different from what it had looked like before, only a few minutes ago. This time Grace saw the little brother who was sick and had to stay home from the bat mitzvah. She saw the father and mother he had walked away from, and the brother he had casually called a ne'er-do-well, an indulged boy-man who had never worked, who lived in his parents' basement. She saw the woman in Baltimore with whom Jonathan had mysteriously lived while in college. The time he had disappeared for three days when he was a resident. And the money he had taken from her father, to buy tuition for a boy at their own son's school. And the doctor he had hit: Ross Waycaster. And the lawyer he had consulted about the termination of his employment and told to go fuck herself. And the patients he had *not* just admitted to the hospital this afternoon. And the funeral in Brooklyn he had *not* just attended for an eight-year-old boy who had *not* just died of cancer. And the *New York* magazine editor who was also the aunt of Jonathan's patient. And the medical conference in Cleveland, or Cincinnati, somewhere in the Midwest, that wasn't in any of those places because it wasn't anywhere at all. And Rena Chang, who might live in Sedona now and might have a baby who might be her husband's child. Grace would never know the baby. She did not want to know it. But then she thought of the other baby, the one who would grow up on Long Island: That baby she would have to know for the rest of her life.

And Grace thought of Malaga Alves, who was dead.

She got to her feet and went to the back door and stepped out onto the porch, breathing deeply. Sherlock was on the dock, standing at attention, alert to some animal in the woods. He wagged vaguely when he heard the door, but he declined to be distracted. She went down the steps and out to him and stood there too for a few minutes, wondering what it was he saw or smelled. There might be something in the woods; it was a little early, but possible, she supposed. By summer the woods were full of animals, and the houses were full of people. The lake itself was stirring, she decided; everything down there would come back up, and the birds would come back—they always came back in the spring. She reached down to stroke the dog's head.

A long way off, she heard a strain of fiddle, coming over the water in stops and starts, the wind blowing it toward her from Leo's house. Now, because she knew what it was and where it was coming from, the sound seemed far clearer than it had her first weeks here, when she'd sat on the dock wondering what kind of music she was hearing and who was making it. Now, though, there was a tentativeness to the playing. It wasn't confident or fast, the way it had always been in the past. It wasn't very sure of itself. But it was pretty. She closed her eyes. This was Henry, she realized. Not Rory or Leo. Henry was playing the violin. Henry, she corrected herself, was playing the fiddle.

I loved my marriage, she suddenly thought. She did not know why it seemed so important to admit this. But she had, and she did, and now that was over, too.

Then she went inside to find the business card Detective Mendoza had given her, a very long time ago.

CHAPTER TWENTY-FOUR

SOMEBODY ELSE ENTIRELY

About fucking time," said Sarabeth. She had picked her up off hold after a scant five seconds. "Do you know how many messages I left for you?"

"I'm sorry," Grace said. "Sorry," she was well aware, wouldn't be cutting it. But it was what she had.

"No, seriously. I left, I don't know, twenty messages, Grace. I hope you know I was trying to support you."

She nodded, as if Sarabeth could see her.

"I ran away," she said simply. "I was trying to get lost."

"And I completely understand that," Sarabeth said. With that, her tone had shifted. "I have just been incredibly worried about you. Business aside. As a *friend*."

"Well..." Grace sighed. "I thank you for that. And I apologize. I am so extremely sorry for leaving you in the lurch, and I promise you, it will not happen again."

But then, why would it? Grace asked herself. After today, after this phone call, they would never have anything to talk about again. And Sarabeth was hardly going to stay on as her *friend*.

"Hang on," said Sarabeth. Grace heard her say, to someone else, "*Tell him I'll call him back...*

"So listen," she went on, "can you come in and talk to us? I think the best thing is for all of us to sit down together and figure it out."

Grace frowned at the wooden tabletop. She was at her own kitchen table on 81st Street. The surface hadn't been cleaned for a long time and was visibly grimy.

"I'd rather not, to tell you the truth. Whatever they have to say, and I know they have a lot, and they're absolutely justified, can't you just pass it along to me? Financially, I'm totally prepared to reimburse them. I haven't looked at the contract lately, but I'm aware of my obligation, and I intend to meet it."

There was a long moment of rare Sarabeth silence. Then she said: "Well, this is what happens when people don't answer twenty messages. They fill in their own side of the conversation that isn't happening, and it's never the right conversation. For example, I can assure you that Maud has no interest in being reimbursed. They pulled it for January, of course. But they still want to publish your book."

Grace heard the rain. She looked up, across the kitchen to the window. Rain was drumming on the air-conditioning unit, and it was suddenly dark outside. She had no idea what Sarabeth was talking about.

"Look, the last thing I want to do is be crude about this. But. You've gone from being the unknown first-time author of a fascinating, intelligent book to a very different kind of author, of a book that a lot of people are going to be interested in. That is a very major transition, to be handled with dignity and great care. I can assure you that your publisher has absolutely no desire to exploit you, Grace."

Grace couldn't help it. She laughed.

"Right," she said. "I believe that."

"Yes. Right. I've known Maud for ten years. I've done at least twenty books with her. She is scary smart, and she is very good at her job, but if she weren't a decent human being, I would never have given her your book in the first place. Now that this has happened, I'm happier than ever that your book ended up with her. In fact, if you came to me today with that book, she's the first person I'd want it to go to."

Grace still said nothing. But now she was at least thinking about it.

"Where are you?" Sarabeth said. "Do you realize I have no idea where you're calling from? Where have you been for the last three months?"

"I took my son to Connecticut. We have a house there. A summer house, we've never lived there in the winter. But it's been good, actually. We're going to stay. I'm in New York now, though. I'm packing up the apartment."

"What about your practice?" Sarabeth said.

"I'm opening a practice in Great Barrington. Massachusetts," she clarified.

"Wait, you're in the city right now?" said Sarabeth. "Can you come into the office?"

"No," said Grace. "I'm just packing. I sold my apartment, and I have movers coming in three days. I can't do anything. Besides, I need to think about this. I honestly... I thought we were done with the book. I kind of put it out of my mind."

"Oh, we are so not done." Sarabeth laughed. "In fact, I'm sure Maud's going to want you to write a new foreword. And there may be other things in the book you want to look at again. I think there's an even more nuanced and resonant book here, actually. An important book with the potential to reach a lot of people. Look, I hate that this happened to you, Grace, I really do. But I know at least one good thing that can come out of it. When can you come in and talk?"

She named a day the following week, then thought again and suggested two weeks after that. She would be back in the city that day, for the closing. Then she said she was sorry another time, and Sarabeth said it was all right another time, and they hung up.

It was raining even harder now, and the apartment was chilly. March was a grim month anywhere, but even in the city, where most seasons were beautiful to her, February and March had always been a bit of an exception. Even if she loved New York City far too much to leave it forever, she could stand to miss this time of year.

It was her second day here, packing full-time. Packing and sorting and throwing many things away. She had dreaded it, naturally, yet it had amazed her how quickly the sheer weight of logistical detail had silenced the blare of her great sadness. There were thousands of objects, every single one of which was stuck to a history, banal or profound, desperately happy or desperately sad. But every single one of them also had to be dispatched before Moishe's Movers arrived on Thursday. She was almost forty years old and finally leaving home.

Luckily, she had strategized all the way down to the city and for a few weeks beforehand. There were things to go to Connecticut—lots of them. Almost everything that was Henry's, except for some clothes he had already outgrown. Most but not all of her own clothes, because now she mainly wore jeans to work, something she could not have done in the city but that her Great Barrington patients (three, so far) did not seem to mind at all. Her books. Some furniture and paintings that she loved too much to leave behind and things from the kitchen she'd been sorely missing.

That was the easy part.

There were so many things she would not be taking with her. They heaped themselves up together in an imaginary room, vast and crammed. Everything of Jonathan's, for instance: objects belonging to Jonathan, objects loved by Jonathan. Also things of the marriage, not his in particular or hers, but tainted by association: coffee mugs, telephones, an umbrella stand. They were all going, too. She never wanted to see them again.

Actually, that part also turned out to be surprisingly easy.

The Birkin bag, the object of beauty, the single item of obvious status she had ever desired for herself, and which had been kept so carefully in her closet and so rarely worn—Jonathan had given it to her, and there was no pleasure in it anymore. Still, it was going to hurt, letting it go. Tenderly she placed it into its soft orange bag and carried it to Encore on Madison, where she had resigned herself to accepting a fraction of its value. But they declined to take it from her.

"It's a copy," said the Frenchwoman who guarded the case of Vuitton and Chloé and Hermès. She made a smacking sound with her mouth, as if it offended her to have to touch it. "Good-quality copy, but a copy nevertheless."

No, no, Grace had started to say. About this, she was sure. She was absolutely sure. She stood there in the second-floor room, jammed with clothing, jammed with women. She was remembering the birthday, the big orange box, how the two of them had laughed about Jonathan's great faux pas at Hermès, just walking in and expecting to leave with a Birkin bag. It was a funny story, a self-effacing story, a story that had made her love him for his sweet naïveté, his willingness to persevere even in the face of supercilious salespeople who were clearly laughing at him. But that was a made-up story, too. She left with the Birkin, and then she left the Birkin, still in its soft orange sack, in the garbage can on the corner of 81st and Madison.

In the end, that hadn't hurt, either.

What hurt enough to make up for what didn't hurt were the photographs—albums of them and walls full of framed portraits and candid shots: her husband, her son, herself, separately and together. Jonathan could not be removed from those, and she couldn't throw them away—they were her history, and Henry's—but she couldn't stand the idea of living in the same house with them. They were going to Eva's place on Long Island, of all places. Her father, in an act of considerable kindness, was coming to collect them specifically, tomorrow, and take them away to a place where she would not have to share space with them, but where they could be kept until Henry—or perhaps just possibly she—was ready.

He was also bringing her mother's china, all twenty settings of the Haviland Limoges Art Deco, packed by Eva herself. That would go to Connecticut, too, and somehow room would be found for it in the rustic little house. Amid the general devastation, she was a tiny bit elated. She had tried—and, she feared, completely failed—to convey to Eva how much she appreciated the gifts, but Eva proved to be as uncomfortable with the subject as she was herself. "Don't be silly," she told Grace. "If I'd had any idea you wanted it. You never said. I have more than enough dishes, Grace, you know."

Everyone left it there.

She was pulling sheets from the dryer, folding them as best she could, when the house phone rang and the doorman said a detective was downstairs in the lobby, and for a moment she tried to pretend that she didn't know what this meant. The sheet in her hands was warm. It was a good sheet and had not been inexpensive. It was . . . eggshell. Or ecru. Once, it might have been called beige, but sheets, she had noticed, were no longer called beige. There was nothing wrong with the sheet, except that she had slept on it, and made love on it, with Jonathan. She would not be starting her new life with marital sheets.

He arrived a few minutes later, and she met him at the front door. She was holding the other sheet, the fitted one. She had never known the right way to fold a fitted sheet and was doing a bad job of it. O'Rourke came off the elevator already looking distracted.

"Hello," Grace said. "Where's your better half?"

He glanced behind him. The elevator man was only just closing the gate.

"Sorry to interrupt," he said instead. "Doing your laundry?"

"Packing. I'm donating the sheets. Just wanted to wash them first."

"I see," he said, looking past her through the open door. "Wow. You're really leaving."

"I really am," she said, growing impatient. It was taking a lot out of her to keep bracing herself.

"Can I come in for a minute?"

"Can you just tell me, please?" she said. "I assume you're here to tell me something."

O'Rourke nodded grimly. "I'm here to tell you that we've located your husband. My partner has gone to see about his extradition. Would you like to sit down?" he asked her, as if it weren't her house.

Grace pushed back the door. She looked at her hand as she did it. The hand did not seem connected to her, but she tried to act as if it were.

"It's a shock," said O'Rourke, as if she didn't already know that. "We should sit down."

They went back to the kitchen. She put the sheet, badly folded, in the donation box. Then, obediently, she sat opposite him at the grimy kitchen table.

"Where you moving to?" O'Rourke asked.

"Connecticut."

"Oh. Nice. Mystic. I've been there."

"No, the other end. The northwest. Where we've been living since December." She stopped. Of course he knew where she'd been since December. "Where is he? Where's Jonathan? Is he in Canada?"

"No. Brazil."

She looked at him. But it didn't make what he'd said make any more sense. Brazil did not make sense.

"I don't understand. That letter."

"Oh, the letter was from him. And it was mailed from Minot, North Dakota. But we're sure he didn't mail it. Probably he paid someone. Or just found someone willing to do it. He was good at getting people to do what he wanted, as you know."

"But..." She was shaking her head. Her fingers were spread out flat on the sticky tabletop. "Why would he do that? Why bother to say he was anywhere?"

"Well," O'Rourke said mildly, "you know, Minot's less than an hour's drive from the border. And I mean, you got a thousand miles of unprotected border up there, and an Indian reservation. Chippewa. Can't be too hard to get someone to guide you across. It's exactly where you'd go if you were trying to leave the country without anybody knowing about it. It's where I'd go," he said, as if this conferred authority.

"Obviously, he didn't, though. *Brazil*," she marveled. She was holding up the idea of him, one final time: walking alongside the frozen river in the city of Whitehorse, Yukon, Canada, past a restored arctic riverboat called *Klondike* that was now a museum, waiting for her to materialize. She realized that she had dressed him specifically for this fiction, to her own taste, in a thick flannel shirt and a woolen hat pulled down over his now long hair, and set him off on the trail, head down, hands in pockets, longing for her and looking for her. She couldn't get over it.

"Why did he write me that letter?"

"Maybe just to fuck with you a little bit more," O'Rourke said simply. "Some people, they just never want to lose an opportunity to fuck with you, just for the sake of it. That's their thing, that's what gets them going. I used to try to figure it out. Like: really, what's in it for them? Now I just think...*forget it*. I'm never going to understand it. I just clean up after them." He shrugged luxuriantly, as if he had all the time in the world to ponder this and life's other mysteries. "But what am I telling you for? You're the shrink."

Right, thought Grace.

"You wrote the book about it. Right?"

No, she thought. *That was somebody else entirely.*

"Plus he got to fuck with us, too. That's a lot of birds for one stone. We sent people out to Minot, and Whitehorse, too. We got the Mounties involved. They watched all the trails up there, and around the boat he described, and they looked at every rental since December, but there just wasn't anything to find. Then we got a call through INTERPOL. It's him in Brazil, no question. Mendoza went down a couple days ago to file a formal extradition request. It might not be quick, but they'll send him back at the end of the day. Usually they only give us trouble if it's a Brazilian national. We do have a treaty."

He stopped.

"How you doing?"

"Just..." But she couldn't finish. She shook her head.

"We wanted you to hear it from us. I'd say you've got one or two days before someone gets hold of it. Of course it could happen sooner. We just wanted to tell you ourselves. We appreciate that you tried to help us."

She nodded. "He probably thought Rio's such a big city, he could get lost."

"No," said O'Rourke. "Not Rio. He was in some place I never heard of, way up the Amazon, called Manaus. I might not be pronouncing it right. It's Spanish, I guess."

Or Portuguese, Grace thought, but she didn't say that.

"Right in the middle of the rain forest. You can't drive there. You got to fly in or take a ship. We think he was on a ship, but we're not sure yet. Eventually we'll put it all together. And how he got out of the States, obviously we'd like to know that. But right now we're thinking ship. It's a big port. Mendoza got there on Saturday. He called me this morning. He said there's an opera house. Big pink opera house in the middle of the town, they shipped over from England in pieces like a hundred years ago. The guy's beside himself." He gave a small, vastly inappropriate laugh. "Mendoza loves the opera. It's his big thing. Took me with him once, down to Lincoln Center when his wife wasn't feeling well. Four of the most painful hours of my life."

To her own amazement, Grace laughed, too.

"What was the opera?"

"God, I don't remember. There was a horse on the stage. It didn't help. But I have to say, you don't expect an opera house in the middle of the Amazon."

She sat back in her chair. Her head was so full. She thought almost longingly of the laundry and the packing, the comforting boxes waiting to be filled and sent away. She wished he would go.

"*Fitzcarraldo*," Grace said. "It's a movie about building an opera house in the Amazon jungle. I've heard this story before."

"*Fitz*...?"

She spelled it for him, and he got out his pad and wrote it down. "I'll tell him. He'll want to see it." He looked around the kitchen. "Looks like you've got a system."

"Oh. Yes. Some boxes are going to Connecticut, but a lot of it's going to Housing Works. I'm getting rid of pretty much everything. You have what you need, I assume?"

O'Rourke looked at her.

"Jonathan's things? If there's anything else you want, speak now."

"No, we're good. Of course, if anything turns up you think we should see..."

She nodded, but she had done enough. From now on, they were on their own.

"Well," he said. He got to his feet. "I'll go, then."

She got up, too, relieved.

"Where's your boy?" he said conversationally, walking back to the front door.

"With his grandparents. It's his spring break from school."

"Ah. I met your father. We talked to him back in December."

"No," said Grace. "His other grandparents. He's out on Long Island with Jonathan's parents."

O'Rourke stopped and turned to her. "That's...well, I'm surprised. When we talked to them, they said they never saw either of you."

"We had dinner in New York last month. That seemed to go pretty well, so they invited him to stay for a couple of days. Henry wanted to go."

He nodded. His neck, as always, was so erratically shaved that it looked patchy.

"That's good. They're good people. They went through a lot."

We all went through a lot, she thought automatically. But what was the point of saying it?

She opened the door for him. He rang for the elevator.

Grace stood awkwardly in the half-opened door. It was a curious moment, for which she was unsure of the protocol. She had stood in this precise place on her own threshold ever since she could stand at all, waiting for the elevator to take her visitors away: play-dates, babysitters, party guests. Long ago she had seen off her own boyfriends here, leaning into the vestibule to make out as long as possible before the elevator arrived. Ordinarily, you waited for your guest to be taken away and made small talk, but this was not ordinary, and she had no small talk to make with Detective O'Rourke. On the other hand, she couldn't just close the door, either.

"Listen," he said suddenly, "I'm going to kick myself tomorrow if I don't say anything."

She gripped the door frame, physically bracing herself. Like quicksilver, every possible permutation of "anything" raced through her, and none of it was welcome. Whatever he might kick himself tomorrow for not saying—be it accusation or thank-you or some sage wisdom about her circumstances—she didn't want to hear it. But she didn't want him coming back to say it, either.

"I know this family in Brownsville. Brooklyn?" He looked at her.

Grace frowned at him. "Okay."

"Actually, I arrested one of the sons last year. But we realized he really was a good kid, just picked the wrong friends. And we misplaced the paperwork. Hey," he said with a little laugh, "it happens."

More lost than before, she just waited.

"Anyway, they've been in a shelter out there, but they got an apartment a few weeks ago. City apartment. You know, subsidized. Which is great. But they don't have anything. They're sleeping on the floor. I got to know the family, like I said. It's a good family."

Faintly, Grace could hear the elevator setting off from the lobby.

"I mean, you're giving it all to Housing Works, and that's great. I just thought, you know, if you wanted..."

"*Oh.*" At last, it got through. "Oh, right. Of course. Happy to. Whatever they want to take, it's fine. There are beds, sheets, and towels. There are pots and pans."

His face relaxed into an almost childlike happiness. He was transformed. He looked suddenly like a young man: young Officer O'Rourke. Just like that.

"It would be such a great thing for them. You can't imagine."

They quickly arranged for him to come back the day after next, with the father and two of the sons and a borrowed truck.

"They're a good family," O'Rourke said again. "Believe me, I've seen a lot of crappy families. This is a good family."

"I'm sure," said Grace. She no longer had any idea what a good family was, but she supposed he might. "You don't misplace the paperwork for just anyone."

"No." He looked a little sheepish. "Hey. I wanted to tell you. We knew you didn't know anything. After that first conversation, we were pretty sure. We felt bad for what we put you through. We knew you weren't a bad person."

Grace felt the heat flood into her cheeks. She nodded, but she didn't look at him. "Just... picked the wrong friends, right?"

"Picked the wrong guy. It happens all the time."

Don't I know it, Grace thought. The elevator was close now.

Behind him, the gate creaked open and O'Rourke stepped back with a wave. Grace waited at the half-opened door until he was gone, but she didn't go back inside right away. Instead she stood there, listening for the utterly familiar sequence of groans and clicks as the elevator made its descent, until at last she heard the far below scrape of the gate, releasing him to the lobby, and the rainy and dark midafternoon, and the street where she used to live.

ACKNOWLEDGMENTS

Thank you to Phil Oraby and Ann Korelitz for their insights into matters therapeutical, and in particular into that sadly ubiquitous creature: homo sociopathicus. Their expertise, so generously shared, was invaluable. Thanks to Nina Korelitz Matza for her acute observations about New York private schools. I am grateful to Tim Muldoon for helping me with the modus operandi of New York detectives. Thank you, James Fenton, for allowing me to use your beautiful poem, "A German Requiem." Deborah Michel, as always, is the best reader imaginable. I can't adequately thank Suzanne Gluck, Deb Futter, Dianne Choie, Sonya Cheuse, Elizabeth Sheinkman, and Sarah Savitt for their belief in this novel.

More general appreciation goes to my family and friends, the shipboard community of Semester at Sea's Spring 2012 voyage (on which much of this novel was written); and to Karen Kroner, Paul Weitz, Kerry Kohansky Roberts, Anna DeRoy, and Tina Fey, for reminding me that creative work is a conversation, even when you do it alone.